Breach
of
Trust

Also by Preston A. Pairo III

Winner's Cut
Razor Moon
Midnight Razz

The Ocean City/Dallas Henry Mysteries
The Captain Drowns
Beach Money
One Dead Judge

Breach of Trust

Preston A. Pairo III

St. Martin's Press
New York

A Note to Readers
The author welcomes your written comments, and may be contacted . . .
by mail:
c/o Pairo & Pairo, 9050-A Frederick Road, Ellicott City, MD 21042;
or via Internet e-mail addressed to:
nkwd88a@prodigy.com

BREACH OF TRUST. Copyright © 1995 by Preston A. Pairo III. All rights reserved. Printed in the United States of America. No part of this book may be used or reproduced in any manner whatsoever without written permission except in the case of brief quotations embodied in critical articles or reviews. For information, address St. Martin's Press, 175 Fifth Avenue, New York, N.Y. 10010.

Design by Basha Zapatka

Library of Congress Cataloging-in-Publication Data

Pairo, Preston.
    Breach of trust / Preston Pairo.
      p.   cm.
    "A Thomas Dunne book."
    ISBN 0-312-13034-1
    I. Title
    PS3563.A3129B74   1995
    813'.54—dc20   95-14712
                                                      CIP

First Edition: August 1995
10 9 8 7 6 5 4 3 2 1

Acknowledgments

With thanks, to all the attorneys I hung around with at the Court Square Building when I was a kid, some of whom I still have the pleasure of associating with today and some of whom are, regrettably, no longer here:

My grandfather, Preston Pairo, Sr.; father, Preston Pairo, Jr.; and uncle, Richard Pairo; and Edwin Shapiro; the Honorable Leonard Jacobson; Melvyn Weinstock; John Spector; Walter Seif; Ed Murphy; and William Wilson.

Breach
of
Trust

◆ 1 ◆

"Good morning, Mrs. Rosenthal." Harry Walsh rested his hip against the polished molding that framed the witness stand. His Hugo Boss suit was flashier than his taste normally ran, but Alena, with whom he was in love, insisted it was him.

Alena—an interior designer who earned considerably more at her job than Harry did at his—termed the suit "jury" blue: his color. It projected competence and matched his eyes, although not nearly with the same elan.

One day, Harry hoped to convince Alena to marry him; in the meantime, there was Mrs. Rosenthal, with whom he was about to engage in a far different, though still intimate, relationship.

"Mrs. Rosenthal, this case is bound to cause you to hear some testimony which will be rather graphic. *Very* graphic, even. Ex-*plic*it." Harry punched his delivery. "And before you're seated on this jury, it's important for you to *assure* this court that you will *not* be so offended by explicit language that it will taint your view of my client, Miss Jennifer Mulcaney." Harry gestured to the attractive young woman seated at the defense table in the purposefully nondescript suit.

"You *must*, Mrs. Rosenthal, be able to sift through all the sullied language and see the facts. To consider my client's innocence on the basis *of* those facts and *not* the sordid descriptions the State will use to describe what, in its slanted opinion, amounts to criminal activity." The way Harry said *criminal activity* made the idea sound interesting.

In the early stage of *voir dire*—the pre-trial examination of prospective jurors—Harry exhibited an undeniable image of Vindicator of the Wrongfully Accused. Twenty-five years ago, on vacation from sixth grade, Harry had spent the summer watching his father try cases; then and since, he'd observed juries were swayed by an attorney who took confident strides without stepping into the fatal jaws of arrogance.

Over one thousand cases into a successful—though some would criticize, underachieving—career, Harry still thought about his father every time he walked into a courthouse. He even carried his briefcase the way he remembered his father doing it: in a secure fist, as though packing a heavy satchel of weapons.

"You will hear testimony, Mrs. Rosenthal, that Miss Mulcaney was dancing in a rather provocative manner at a private party in the suburban home of Sam Giardino. To wit: she was not wearing any clothes and she was casting herself about in a rather libidinous manner. You will hear from undercover Officer Renngert a rather outlandish lie—"

"Objection." Assistant State's Attorney Tierny Wells slapped down her pen, making rare interruption of an opening statement. Tierny was unhappy; capital murder cases were being assigned back in the office and she was dealing with *this*.

Judge Lionna Barry sustained the objection, ruling, as was her method, with quiet decorum.

Harry Walsh maintained eye contact with sixty-two-year-old Irene Rosenthal. He leaned closer. The timbre of his voice indicated he was offering a secret though his words carried across the entire courtroom. "There will be accusations of wild *and* unadulterated fornication and sexual relations. There will be mention made of sexual intercourse performed and/or attempted . . . and other testimony regarding the use of devices commonly referred to in the *sexual* trade as French ticklers."

A few suppressed laughs sounded from the panel of forty-five potential jurors.

Harry concentrated on Mrs. Rosenthal and her sparkling eyes. "There will be talk of viewing videotapes that would not be of the Good Housekeeping Seal of Approval nature. *Movies* where the primary activity was maneuvers designed to bring about a sexual climax." Harry stood tall—all six feet, 195 athletic pounds of him. "Now, Mrs. Rosenthal, with full knowledge and warnings of the nature of this trial, how do you feel about hearing such wild and erotic testimony should you be placed on this jury?"

Irene Rosenthal smiled. "I look forward to it."

The entire jury panel erupted with laughter.

Judge Lionna Barry tapped a light gavel to bring order.

Back at the trial table, Harry Walsh picked up a legal pad on which he cross-rated each prospective juror. Beside Irene Rosenthal's name, he scribbled, not surprisingly, *YES*.

In hasty pursuit of opposing counsel, Assistant State's Attorney Tierny Wells descended the front steps of the County Court Building at a hazardous pace. She caught up with Harry Walsh on the sunny front street. "Let's get rid of this case, Harry."

"You didn't enjoy your morning," he observed pleasantly. "I can tell by the way you smirked at my voir dire."

"It's cute how you're trying to get the jury laughing about this case before the first witness is sworn."

"It's a laughable case."

"So let's work it out and get on with our lives."

Rather than comment about that, Harry said, "Sung."

"What?"

"Your perfume . . . Sung."

Startled, Tierny sniffed her wrist. "I guess it is. I don't remember what I put on. I'm not good in the morning."

"I recognize it from samples—what do you call them?—those little cardboard inserts in women's magazines."

"I don't know what you call them." She almost laughed. "You read women's magazines. *Vogue? Glamour?*"

"*Bazaar, Elle, Allure, Mirabella* . . . You think that's funny?"

Tierny wasn't sure how to respond to such an unusual admission; she didn't know any men who read the same magazines she did.

"The woman I'm seeing is very much a follower of trends. Very much the reader."

"Oh."

For simplicity's sake, Harry omitted from his explanation that *he* was a keen admirer—well beyond prurient intent—of how women

◆ 3 ◆

dressed. He and Alena enjoyed an ongoing dialogue as to how clothes revealed character. Attire even rated its own category in Harry's juror-selection grid, and contributed to his evaluation of witnesses and other lawyers.

Tierny Wells, for example, was a contrast of images, unsure how to portray herself. Her suits were tailored conservatively to her slender frame, yet her skirt was slit and she wore heels—not flats—that accentuated her calves. She favored expensive perfume, but little make-up. Her straight dark hair was trimmed simple and short, yet she had a habit of raking her hand through it in a motion that suggested recovery from pleasant sex. Whether she was attractive and trying not to be, or plain and trying to be attractive, Harry couldn't decide; neither, apparently, could Tierny.

Harry stepped onto the curb.

Tierny was a step behind. "Let's deal this case out and get rid of it. One count of prostitution, three months suspended, a five-hundred-dollar fine, and a year's probation."

"You offered me that yesterday afternoon. Has your case improved since then? Has Officer Renngert recalled new facts?"

"Come on, Harry."

"I'm actually looking forward to his testimony. It takes a man of strong character to admit his efforts to lure Miss Mulcaney into propositioning him with sex for hire were aborted when his willie refused to stop impersonating a compass dead set on aiming south."

"She got paid by *everyone*, Harry. She's one of Giardino's sex girls. Out at the big boss' house on the lake for a swing."

Harry browsed a bookstore window stacked high with the latest techno-thriller. "What if I let you surrender with honor?"

"You're talking about a stet?"

"Inactive docket for one year on the condition she obeys all laws and then you dismiss it. If she fails to toe the line, then we have our trial and listen to Officer Renngert's tale of woe."

"I can't do it, Harry. Jacobs is afraid the papers will get wind of any sweet deal and infer it's because Giardino's involved."

"Paranoia reigns supreme over practicality in your office. No wonder the caseload is impossibly backlogged. What are you and poor Ed Jacobs going to do in five years when the daily crack murders start spreading from the city to our lily-white county and all the rich people who complain now about outrageous taxes are afraid to come to our pretty streets for dinner?"

"Just like a good defense attorney to diffuse the issue by confusing the issue. Besides, you talk about city scum moving out to the county, look at Giardino."

Ducking low branches of a maple tree, Harry stopped to peer over a group of office workers crowding a hot dog vendor. A kosher dog with fried bologna on a steamed bun would be good . . . then again, maybe not: all that cholesterol. Harry walked on. "Giardino's not on trial—and he wasn't home that night."

"We know. He was down in Grand Cayman laundering money or some such thing. We checked with the FBI."

"He was on vacation with his son's family."

"Harry, please."

"My client should not be punished because she happens to be in the house of a man the state and federal government have on their most-pursued list."

"She was going down on a roomful of men for money, Harry." The *willfulness* of the act seemed to alarm Tierny Wells more than its illegality. "And she's got priors."

"Arrests, no convictions."

"Shoplifting, eight years ago."

"I stand corrected . . . but I still like a stet."

"Jacobs wouldn't let me if I wanted to."

Spotting a ray of hope, Harry stopped in the middle of the sidewalk and brandished a triumphant fist, encouraging her. "Make a field decision, Tierny. Strike out on your own. Don't let your life— your career—be run by a political mole like Ed Jacobs. No one should have to take orders from a man who wears such really awful, awful suits."

Tierny laughed. "You're bad, Harry."

He relaxed his hand and gestured a momentary truce. "I try." At an intersection crowded with lunch-hour pedestrians, Harry started down the hill. "Can you be bribed into joining me for lunch at the mall? The Chinese place in the Food Court makes pretty good Szechuan string beans."

Tierny groaned. "My stomach can't take that stuff."

"Won ton soup, then?"

"Do they use MSG?"

"We'll ask."

Tierny hesitated too long for such a simple decision.

"Surely Ed Jacobs can't object to your having lunch with me."

Towsontown Center—a one-time outdoor shopping center, then called Towson Plaza—had been renovated many times over the past twenty-five years. The most recent and expensive effort was a half-successful attempt to transform a run-of-the-mill retail center into a palatial mall.

On the third of four levels was the Food Court: mini-eateries in a modernized version of the sawdust-floored market stalls Harry's father took him to as a boy. The chairs and tables were of indestructible metal. Trompe l'oeil clouds and sky painted on a too-low ceiling tried to compensate for a lack of windows.

Seated on a metal chair at a white veneer table, Tierny Wells induced a plastic bowl of egg drop soup (no MSG) to cool by twirling a smallish spoon through thick yellow broth. At a stalemate in their case negotiation, she decided to discuss what truly interested her. "So, Harry, how do you get to work for a mobster? I must have missed that class in law school." She asked her question timorously, focusing on an unspecified point between her soup and Harry.

"I don't work for a mobster."

"Sam Giardino?"

"I don't represent him."

"Maybe you would if we managed to get him into court. Investigations against Giardino have a way of going nowhere, which we might feel bad about if the feds were more successful."

"Ellis Rubin's firm does Mr. Giardino's corporate work." Harry emphasized *corporate* because Tierny was correct. Sam Giardino

◆ 6 ◆

had not come under indictment since the late sixties. "I don't represent him."

"But you represent his people. His street people."

"No."

"You're telling me your Little Miss Fellatio in court this morning doesn't work for—okay, strike that. You don't represent his people." Tierny went along with him. "Then you represent his . . . acquaintances."

"That some people I represent happen to intersect paths with Sam Giardino is not a matter of pre-set arrangement so much as word of mouth. A client thinks I do a good job, she tells other people, who tell other people, and so on. For someone who includes criminal law in their practice, it's nice to know criminals who know other criminals. *Alleged* criminals." Harry smiled at his own slip, then became more serious. "Just so they're not dopers or rapists."

"You're telling me you have a pious side?"

Harry chewed a spiced and crunchy string bean. "Dopers are uninteresting people who don't see how fascinating life is without chemicals. Rapists commit perhaps the most psychologically damning crime in our society and later attempt to hide behind a defense that their victim consented, which is a second crime as far as I'm concerned. Not to say there haven't been cases of deliberate false accusation, but our court system, adept at it is in some ways, fails miserably when it comes to rape. And since I consider involvement as endorsement, I don't take those cases."

"So if Sam Giardino walked into your office with a suitcase full of hundreds and said it was your partial retainer to defend him on a rape charge, you'd turn him away?"

"If you've ever seen my office, it would be *incredibly* clear I've turned away lots of people. Or else they've turned away me." Harry's beeper sounded a quick chirp. "Sorry." He shook his head, reaching inside his suit jacket. "Damned annoying things, I know." He squinted at the digital readout on the pager's skinny end. "Either the batteries are wearing down or I *do* need glasses. Can you read this?" Harry held the beeper across the table.

Tierny recited the numbers; it was Harry's office.

"Young eyes," Harry commented.

"Give me a break, what are you, thirty?"

"Thirty-four, but I hear the clock ticking. And see these grey hairs?" He touched his temple.

There were a few strands of grey mixed in with short-cut dark-blond.

Harry pushed back his chair. "You know where the phones are? I liked this mall better before they enclosed it."

Tierny pointed him in the right direction and, as Harry started off, she couldn't help wondering if his shift between extreme confidence and subtle helplessness was sincere or a ploy to soften her up; if he needed assistance reading a pager and finding a phone and she gave it, was it that much of a stretch to stet Jennifer Mulcaney's prostitution case?

Crossing the Food Court, Harry noticed a young woman in a Chanel suit. Last year's style, he recalled from runway photos in Italian *Vogue*. Alena would be envious; a highly competitive women, it drove her crazy when someone outside Manhattan could afford clothes that luxurious.

Harry placed his beeper to the phone and caused it to sound a digital playback of his last page, dialing the number automatically. The seven tones beeped clearly, indication the battery was fine; it *was* his eyes starting to go. Damn.

"Law Offices," Marcie answered on the third ring.

"It's me, what's up?"

"Harry . . ." Marcie sounded surprised, although she shouldn't have been, having just paged him. She hesitated, then stammered briefly, "I've got some papers for you to look at—that you need to sign."

"For what?" Nothing on the tickler system had come up as time-sensitive for today.

"The, um, Dickerson divorce."

"The Dickerson divorce?"

"I'll . . . I'll bring it down if you're short on time. I don't mind."

◆ 8 ◆

"Don't leave the phones. George gets nervous when you leave the phones. He's sure that's when he'll get that big personal injury case he's been waiting for."

"George said it's okay."

She'd already asked George if she could leave? "Marcie, what's wrong?"

"Nothing. I'm coming down."

"All right." He saw no sense debating the point. "I'm in the Food Court by the elevator."

Marcie hung up.

Harry went back to his table.

"Problem?" Tierny asked, reading his expression.

"I think our secretary is losing her mind." Harry sat down, concerned. "She's usually quite dependable. Someone under thirty who actually enjoys work."

"I'm under thirty."

"You work for Ed Jacobs. You can't possibly enjoy your work."

Tierny set off defending her boss, albeit without gusto: a subject on which they remained engaged until Harry observed his secretary crossing the Food Court.

Something *was* wrong. Marcie wasn't carrying any papers for him to sign. And her expression—her tight mouth and neck, her sympathetic eyes. "Harry . . ." she forced a grim smile, ". . . I'm so sorry."

He almost said Alena's name, but didn't dare, as though such an utterance might make it true.

Marcie grasped Harry's hand. Her skin was cool. "Harry, your brother was killed this morning. He was shot."

When his vision turned white and hazy, Harry realized he wasn't breathing.

"Your nephew called with the news. He's taking a train up from Georgetown tonight."

Harry nodded as though drugged. He didn't realize his eyes had welled until a warm tear rolled off his cheek.

♦ 2 ♦

Alena Marlacova slid open the glass door and stepped onto the sixteenth-floor balcony. The summer night was warm and still. "I thought I'd find you here. How are you holding up, Harry?"

Slumped back in the chaise, wearing sweatshorts and nothing else, Harry Walsh lifted a hand from his lap; the effort was not so much a wave as demonstration he was alive.

"How about your sister-in-law? Have you seen her?"

"I stopped over at her house. The place was a zoo. Neighbors, women from the Fraternal Order of Police, counselors from the police department—including some psychiatrist who looked like a burned-out Timothy Leary. The phone kept ringing. And Connie . . ." Harry looked up into the dark sky ". . . she's in shock. She kept saying she knew that something bad was going to happen."

Alena hugged him. "I'm so sorry, baby."

Harry held onto her. "And then I got to play the heavy when Connie said she didn't want all those people in her house. I had to get thirty people out the door without insulting them, and most just plain didn't want to go. It was like herding cattle from a field of fresh grass. The looks I got . . . Some folks *love* a good tragedy. They *wallow* in it. Especially the creep psychiatrist, he kept saying Connie needed to identify with her grief."

"Everyone sends their sympathy." She smelled faintly of smoke and martinis from the dinner party she'd left early and Harry had missed. "Are you hungry? Do you want me to fix you something?"

Harry managed a sad chuckle. Alena did not cook. "No. Thanks. I ate part of some casserole thing a neighbor brought to Connie— for the life of me I don't know what was in it."

Alena moved back and stood against the ornate iron railing. Long, sandy blond hair, swept back off her face and stylishly mussed, draped her shoulders. Her work clothes had performed double duty at the dinner party: a breezy bronze-tone Kamali blouse and chartreuse skirt.

Alena's taste ran from glamour to funk, and she had the beauty for the entire gamut. Despite an exotic name, her looks were midwest America: pure heartland made spicy by a creative urge and occasional wild streak. Her skin was flawless; her eyes clear as gemstones.

Harry still wasn't used to how men looked at and came on to her. There had been run-ins with would-be young studs in the loud nightclubs Alena was sometimes in the mood for. A couple times the run-ins turned to fights. Harry couldn't believe he'd actually pummelled a guy over Alena; he hadn't been in a fistfight since college. But Alena's all-consuming lure fit his nature: Harry was either involved to the limit or not at all. Only he'd never felt that way about a woman before Alena, and what worried him was making it last.

Even now, he wondered if something so intense could survive? Against the day's events, Alena drew him in.

She looked out over the night lights of Towson, a suburban metropolis stretching across the once-fertile hills and valleys of hunt country. "Do you want to talk about it? Or try to forget it?"

Harry wished she knew him well enough not to ask; but eighteen months wasn't much time. They hadn't really moved in together; they shared this jointly leased condo on weekends, but otherwise lived in their own places. Harry had a two-bedroom apartment a few blocks away and Alena co-owned a beautifully renovated house in town. More and more, however, Harry spent time here and figured not to renew his apartment lease when it came up next month; he hadn't, however, confessed this to Alena lest she think he was pressuring her to do likewise.

She sat at the end of the chaise and massaged his bare foot. "You're feeling guilty about not patching things up with him, aren't you?"

Harry nodded, although "patching up" was not exactly what his relationship with his brother required.

◆ 11 ◆

"It's not your fault, Harry. He was much older. You grew up in different eras. He went to Canada instead of Vietnam—you never had to worry about anything like that. He was married and has children—you don't. He was a policeman, you're a lawyer. You were very different. Almost opposite."

"I know." Harry exhaled slowly.

Alena continued her massage. Her hands were strong for having such slender fingers.

Harry said, "I've been thinking a lot about my Dad."

She pressed along the pads of Harry's foot.

"When Marcie told me Tucker was dead, I heard her say, 'Your brother is dead,' but inside my mind, I saw the guidance counselor from elementary school. She got me out of class with the same look on her face Marcie had today. She said almost the same thing: how she was sorry to tell me there was terrible news. That my father had been killed." Harry shook his head. "Jesus, it never stops hurting. It never stops."

Harry didn't sleep well that night. His dreams were bizarre. He was in a building with countless corridors and overlapping hallways, many of them so small he had to crouch to gain access. The elevators ran inside shafts at twenty-degree angles and stopped between floors, forcing Harry to crawl out, hoping he was free of the doors before the elevator started moving and crushed him.

The entire time—searching the faceless, windowless building—Harry saw glimpses of his father, but only from behind. Twice, going into a room without any other access, he was sure he'd caught up, but when Harry got there, Jack Walsh, the father he'd lost when he was ten, was gone.

Friday morning, Harry showered and shaved in the condo. Alena, a sound sleeper, did not stir. Harry left a note about getting together for lunch.

He drove to his apartment for a new suit and something to eat. He toasted a bagel, but tossed it to the birds after two bites; it tasted metallic.

◆ 12 ◆

A few times he thought he was going to break into tears—the pain ebbed and flowed like waves of nausea—but ultimately he held it back. He felt better outside than indoors, especially in the car.

Harry drove a 1965 Mustang convertible painted Triumph racing green. The bucket seats were champagne leather; the custom dash was burled wood. It had been his father's car, a weekend toy Harry was taken for drives in as a boy, only there hadn't been enough rides before his father's death.

The car was one of his Dad's few possessions Harry had been able to talk his mother into keeping. It sat in a friend's garage for six years until Harry was old enough to drive. He was the only member of his high-school lacrosse team never to have a wreck; the car meant too much to chance its ruin in a race or running red lights.

Before going to the funeral home, Harry stopped by his office. Unlike lawyers on TV, Harry's practice did not occupy spacious quarters in a glass-and-steel spire with a fabulous view. As with the vast majority of real-life lawyers—of whom there was a statewide influx of nine hundred new faces every six months—Harry's office was modest in size, furnishings, and equipment. He shared the space and a secretary with another lawyer and they were looking for a compatible third.

Twenty years ago, the clapboard two-story had been a private residence, but sprawling commercialism inspired profitable zoning changes and the room where a family had once enjoyed Sunday dinners was now a conference room where criminals, accident victims, and angry spouses conferred with their lawyers.

Part of the neighborhood remained private homes. Older residents who declined offers to sell sat on their front porches, tended gardens, and mowed lawns, while young suited professionals parked car-phoned Jaguars and BMWs along the elm-lined street and hustled to their offices. The conflicting nature of retired living and earning a buck sparked occasional feuds over traffic, defecating dogs, and a lack of parking, but generally, the coexistence was peaceful.

When Harry opened the screened front door and walked into

the living/reception room, Marcie Hall was at her desk, plugged into the Dictaphone. She was a conscientious worker, who managed to handle two lawyers without causing delays. Harry had difficulty imagining her life beyond this office. Plain and unassuming, she would have been the perfect secretary were it not for the occasional client she scared away with an eclectic assortment of desktop Christian paraphernalia—crucifixes, rosaries, and prayer cards.

Marcie immediately came around her work-station and hugged him. "I'm so sorry, Harry." Despite her youth, her embrace was matronly. "You don't have to be here. I canceled your appointments. Everyone understood. Tierny Wells called and said Mulcaney was taken care of."

"Thanks." Harry eased away.

His message slot was jammed with pink phone slips.

"A lot of condolences," Marcie said as Harry went through them.

Very little actually registered beyond numbers and letters on each page. "I didn't know this many people knew Tucker was my brother."

"Most of them saw it in Eisenrich's column. Everybody says you should sue him for what he wrote."

"What are you talking about?"

"You didn't see the morning paper? I assumed you had." Marcie was fearful of his reaction. "Barry Eisenrich's column?"

Harry's pulse increased. "He wrote something about my brother?"

Regretfully, Marcie said, "He mentioned your father, too."

Harry went through the conference room to the stairs that led down to George Patterakis's office. His feet pounded the wooden steps. In case that wasn't warning enough, he rapped the stair wall. "George. Coming down."

George Patterakis was not in. He'd either overslept again, was lingering over high-test coffee at the Bel-Loc Diner, or actually had a court case. The *Morning Sun* was folded on his desk exactly the way he liked it.

◆ 14 ◆

Harry tore to the editorial page. A sketch of Barry Eisenrich's bust—twice as large as any other columnist, per his contract with the *Sun*—glared pompously beside his bold-type name and the headline, "OFFICER GOES DOWN" IS OPPORTUNITY FOR IRONY.

Harry read 750 words of pure malice. His anger prevented him from taking it all in the first time, so he read it again. His pulse elevated further, filling his throat so that it was difficult to swallow. After a third read, he reached for the phone.

The Sunpapers' receptionist said Barry Eisenrich wasn't in, was there a message?

"This is Harry Walsh. Tell that fat bastard I better not find him in any dark alleys." He slammed down the phone and tried to settle his breathing.

Harry didn't want his sister-in-law to see him upset, so he delayed his arrival at the funeral home half an hour. He hadn't completely cooled by the time he walked through the double wood doors, but the sweet smell of flowers and somber music took effect as though injecting a warm anesthetic.

Harry hated these places. His first visit to a funeral home had been for his father. The family was in such shock, no one had thought to prepare him beyond neatening the knot of his tie and making sure his shoes were shined.

Laid out in an expensive coffin lined with white silk, his father had looked like a figure in the Gettysburg Wax Museum, only he was wearing a black suit with a carnation in his lapel instead of a Union soldier's uniform. At the time, Harry thought it *was* a wax replica in the coffin and that his father had already gone to heaven. He had no frame of reference to anticipate that dead people were actually displayed.

He'd cried when he'd been told his father had been killed, but not again until his father was buried. That was when stark realization set in. While a wake was taking place downstairs, Harry cried for hours in an empty bedroom of a neighbor's house. No one ever looked in to see if he was all right. Not his mother, certainly not his brother—who was in Canada—not distant aunts, uncles, or cousins who'd come to the house. Harry knew that day that no one was ever going to check on him again; that had been his father's job.

The funeral director seemed to drift across thick red carpet as though riding a cloud. Elbows bent, his hands were folded somberly above his waist, a pose Harry had never seen outside a funeral parlor.

The man was paunchy and ruddy-tanned. His suit fit without an improper wrinkle or strained seam. His smile expressed all the mock warmth and compassion deserving of the $11,000 bill he'd send Tucker's estate. "Are you Mr. Walsh's brother?"

"Yes."

"Good. I'm Lawrence Jameson." He shook Harry's hand with a firm grip, then shifted his hold to Harry's elbow. He led Harry down the long center hall, the substantial width of which, Harry realized gravely, was to accommodate the moving of coffins.

The walls were papered in rich red-and-cream paisley. Globe table lamps, turned on low, sat on Chippendale tables outside each of eight viewing rooms.

"My assistant just called your office. We were told you were on your way."

"Is something wrong?"

"Your sister-in-law is very distraught, Mr. Walsh. Her son is not making matters any better. And her daughter . . ." Jameson tried, but could not conceal his disdain, ". . . this would be your niece. She is . . . well—I am no expert, Mr. Walsh, and please don't take this the wrong way—but I believe she is stoned."

Harry hadn't known what to expect; before yesterday, he hadn't seen Connie in almost a year, and even that visit had been stilted and brief, not the way it used to be.

The largest viewing room was at the end of the hall. Floor-to-ceiling divider screens had been opened to annex adjacent rooms. There would be a lot of people at Tucker's service: hundreds of police officers from across the state, others travelling from neighboring—even far away—states, and the media: Barry Eisenrich, et al.

Harry ground his jaw.

◆ 16 ◆

Padded chairs were being unfolded and set in rows like church pews by a pair of young men in ill-fitting black suits. No older than twenty, they pretended not to overhear the argument carrying out to the hall; nor did they want to be caught eyeing the outlandish sight that was Harry Walsh's sixteen-year-old niece, Carla.

"Mrs. Walsh." Lawrence Jameson sped the pace with which he delivered Harry to the melee. "Mrs. Walsh!"

Connie and her son Craig were toe to toe with a wiltingly nervous older man Harry assumed was Jameson's assistant.

"*Mrs. Walsh!*"

Connie's face was streaked with tears. She clutched a damp handkerchief. "Harry! Harry!" She hurried desperately into his arms and sobbed his name.

Connie was a tall, strong woman. She was pretty, though her face was lined with anxiety that pre-dated her husband's death. Her thick hair was colored dusty blonde to hide the grey, and cut into a practical wedge.

Harry ran a soothing hand across her back.

Craig, arms crossed, glared at them for reasons Harry assumed he would soon find out. Craig's sister, Carla, sat diagonally across a padded windowseat wearing a black miniskirt and tight black turtleneck; her shoes were somewhere besides on her feet. A stunning young girl, she smiled idiotically, peeking out light-blocking curtains and asking no one in particular why they didn't open the windows to let in some air and sunshine. "It's soooo depressing in here."

"Harry. They won't let me see him." Gripping his arms, Connie leaned slightly back from their embrace. Her face was puffy and oily; dark rings shaded her red eyes. "They won't let me see Tucker. And I want to see him. I want to see him, Harry!"

Harry looked at Lawrence Jameson.

Standing beside his assistant—who seemed greatly relieved by Harry's presence—Jameson's mouth tightened regrettably.

Harry traced the pad of his thumb across Connie's cheek, wiping away tears. "I'll talk to them."

◆ 17 ◆

"Harry," Connie pleaded quietly, "I want to see him. Please, make them let me see him."

"I'm going to talk to them right now." Breaking Connie's embrace, Harry made eye contact with Craig. "Take care of your Mom, okay?"

Craig glowered silently to show his protest or independence— Harry didn't know nor for the time being care which.

Jameson and his older employee followed Harry from the room.

In the hall, Harry said, "What's the problem? You didn't lose the body, did you?"

"Certainly not." Jameson took offense.

"I'm sorry." Harry immediately and sincerely apologized. "This is . . . this is a difficult day. I'm sorry."

"I understand."

Harry looked down the hall. The funeral home was empty this morning. There were flowers and caskets in half the other viewing rooms, but visiting hours didn't begin until two. Still, Harry wanted more privacy. "Is there someplace we can go?"

Jameson gestured toward wide wood stairs carpeted by a thick runner. "My office."

The three men climbed the steps, resigned to unpleasant tasks ahead.

Jameson's office was bright and cheerful. His windows were open and offered a view across the shallow valley to the opposite hill, a vista which included the building in which Harry and Alena rented their condo. The warm smells of summer replaced the artificial smell of recycled air and sweet flowers that permeated the first floor.

Jameson opened a small refrigerator and withdrew a jar of almond butter along with a clump of red grapes. He took an expensive salad plate from a wall cabinet. "The problem, Mr. Walsh, and I will be very frank, if I may . . ." He awaited Harry's approval, which he received. "The problem is the condition of your brother's body." Jameson used a silver spoon to dish a glob of almond butter onto the plate. "His death was a massive trauma." Jameson added

◆ 18 ◆

grapes to the plate and offered it to Harry along with a polished silver spoon and linen napkin. "It's good for the blood sugar."

"I'm not hungry, thank you anyway."

"That's not the point. Your color is not good, Mr. Walsh, take it from someone who knows." Jameson's practiced compassion was replaced by firm practicality.

His assistant, yet to utter a word, sat on an uncomfortable cane chair near the door as though waiting to be dismissed.

Harry stuck the spoon into the thick almond butter and ate a third of it. The taste was unusual, but not objectionable. He chewed a grape in the same mouthful and felt foolishly like a child called in from play for a peanut-butter-and-jelly lunch.

Lawrence Jameson sat behind his desk. "Your brother, Mr. Walsh, simply cannot have an open coffin. I also recommend against any members of the family, yourself included, viewing the body."

"Was an autopsy performed? Is that it?"

Jameson glanced quickly to his assistant, then back at Harry. "Yes, an autopsy was performed."

Harry detected the half-truth and anticipated the actual problem. "It's because he was shot, isn't it?"

"Yes."

Harry looked at Jameson's assistant, whose role he now understood; he was the mortician who prepared the bodies. "You can't make him up? Do whatever you do?"

"I could try . . ." The man's voice was small and hesitant, as though wanting to remain hidden in his throat.

"Is it the expense?" Harry asked Jameson directly.

"No." A quiver in Jameson's eyes conveyed what he did not want to speak.

"He was shot *that* badly?"

Jameson didn't nod, but didn't offer any denial.

"How badly?"

Jameson turned his chair to face a point on the pale-peach wall between Harry and his assistant. He held that direction when speaking, as though not enunciating directly at Harry would lessen the blow. "Are you familiar with handguns, Mr. Walsh? The different calibers and types of ammunition?"

"Somewhat."

"Your brother was shot with a nine-millimeter gun firing hollow-point bullets." Jameson paused before proceeding. "A nine-millimeter is very powerful . . . A hollow-point bullet expands after entry into the body and creates an extremely violent exit wound." Jameson turned back toward Harry, hoping that was explanation enough.

"And . . . ?" Harry braced himself.

Jameson's assistant shifted uncomfortably.

"Your brother was shot six times, Mr. Walsh. In the face and head. At very close range."

Harry put down the plate of half-eaten food.

Jameson said no more.

· 3 ·

"Connie..." Taking her hand, Harry knew he was going to disappoint her. "... it's best that you not see Tucker."

Tears spilled from her eyes. "Why?"

Standing against the wall, Craig made a sound of angry disapproval. Carla was no longer in the room—nor were the two chair unfolders.

Harry said, "You're going to have to remember him as he was, Connie. That's the way Tucker would want it." Clichés were the best he could muster.

"I can't, Harry. I'm so empty inside. I have to see him again. *I have to.*"

"There's nothing to see. He's not here anymore."

Connie sobbed uncontrollably, and Harry held onto her.

Craig slammed his fist against the wall and stormed out.

"It's all wrong, Harry," Connie gasped, clutching onto him. "Everything's wrong. It's been so damned miserable. I can't take this, Harry. I really, really can't handle this."

"I know..."

"No, you don't. You don't know how it's been. Tucker so upset all the time. He and Craig always at one another. And Carla keeps vanishing for days at a time. And everything else," Connie said. *"Everything else."*

Harry had imagined them a happy, ideal family: all he never had since his father's death and never considered trying to establish. As young children, Craig and Carla had been overjoyed to see Harry, their unmarried "kid" uncle without children of his own who brought Christmas presents Tucker and Connie couldn't afford.

When Craig was thirteen—seven years ago—Harry had coached his youth-league lacrosse team. For one delightful spring,

Harry's connection to Tucker's family—although not to Tucker—became a regular event. Craig idolized Harry, but their common cause ended with the lacrosse season and, within months, Harry hardly heard from him anymore.

That Christmas, there was no dinner as had become their custom. Connie called and said she and the kids were going to spend the holidays with her parents, who had just retired to Orlando; she said she would really miss seeing him and would call as soon as they got back to "do their own special Christmas." Harry waited until March before mailing the presents he'd gotten for Craig and Carla.

In the intervening years since the Christmas that wasn't, Harry hadn't seen them six times.

Lawrence Jameson raised his crisp jacket sleeve and showed his watch. It was 11:45. "Mrs. Walsh should go home for a while. We have five hours until the viewing. She needs to rest.

Harry nodded.

Flowers were beginning to arrive; beautiful arrangements were carried into the room. "If there aren't enough," he assured Harry, "we have others in the refrigerator downstairs."

Harry thanked him and helped Connie from her chair to lead her down the hall. Stepping outside into warm sunshine felt almost ethereal. Daylight made death a lesser reality.

"The car's gone." Connie stopped at the top step. Surveying the parking lot, she looked as though she might cry again. "Oh, God, why do they act this way, Harry?"

He was quick to calm her. "They probably thought you'd be here longer—probably went to McDonald's or something. I'll take you home."

He drove Connie to where she and Tucker had lived for almost twenty years: an end-unit brick townhouse with a white bay window, established shrubs, and side yard fenced in chain link entwined with tangles of sweet honeysuckle. The neighborhood was solid working class, and the similarity of homes created a sense of anonymity, which residents countered with personal touches such as decorative awnings or flower gardens.

◆ 22 ◆

A car was at the curb in front of the house, engine running. When Harry pulled in behind it, two men in bargain suits—one seersucker, one poplin—emerged from the front seats.

Harry knew them from the courthouse, and they knew him; both were detectives with the county's small but ever-expanding homicide division. Frank Trammell, in the grey poplin suit, fancied himself as homicide's reigning stud and star investigator. At forty-three, he was confident that if only he were in Los Angeles, TV producers would craft a series about him. Sporting the requisite moustache, he was good looking in the dark sprayed-hair way that attracted the same women who swooned at a revving Mustang 5.0.

Trammell's tag-along, Keith Ahlstrom, was a stout farmhand molded awkwardly into a bureaucrat's seersucker suit. His hair— the color and texture of wheat—stuck straight out from his scalp in a long whiffle like an irritated porcupine's. The inches Ahlstrom lacked of Trammell's height, he made up for with his muscular bulk.

Connie didn't notice them until they came in step beside her.

"Mrs. Walsh," Frank Trammell began, "I'm sorry about your husband. Tucker was a very good man."

Numbed by condolences, Connie nodded thanks. She kept her head lowered as Harry escorted her up the cracked walk to the door. They stepped over countless flower arrangements and fruit baskets left on the porch.

Trammell and Ahlstrom followed. Harry felt their anomosity toward him like the sun's heat on his neck.

Trammell was aggressive and hungry. As low man on the homicide pole ten years ago, he'd completed law school at night and passed the Bar on his first attempt. Rather than moving into the office of the State's Attorney (with whom he had feuded since his days in patrol) or going into private practice, Trammell chose to remain in homicide. His ego further inflated by his law degree, he quickly—and with Machiavellian keenness—ascended to second in command; a title that all but placed him in control of the division, given how Major Kinoviki thought heading homicide was an honorary post as opposed to a real job.

Trammell had lost cases because of his brashness, a few of them to Harry, and the sting of those defeats did not easily wash away.

Trammell said, "Mrs. Walsh, I'd like to come inside and talk for a little while. It's very important."

Connie fumbled in her pocketbook. Her keys made a jingling sound, but she couldn't find them.

"Mrs. Walsh?" Trammell repeated.

Harry asked, "Could this wait until later?"

"We won't take long," Trammell replied sharply.

When Connie finally located her keys and unlocked the door, Harry nodded the detectives inside.

The living room was warm and smelled faintly of indistinct cooking odors and cleaning agents. A fat grey-blond cat jumped from the bay window, raced along the back of a moss-tone sofa, and disappeared into the dining room.

The cat startled Harry; Tucker and Connie had never owned pets before and he hadn't seen it yesterday. Otherwise, the house was remarkably the same as in years past, only he'd expected—as with his previous annual visits—to see a Christmas tree in the corner.

"Just a few moments, Mrs. Walsh. I promise not to take a long time today."

To take a long time today, Harry thought. But not tomorrow, or the next day, or the next. It would be an extended procession of phases, each more grueling than the last. The impact of Tucker's death would be heightened by sensational publicity attached to a policeman's murder; the search for his killer, already under way, would be another harsh dose of anguish; but worst of all would be the trial.

And there *would be* a trial. The police would track down the killer of one of their own.

Harry couldn't imagine Connie surviving the rigors of watching a man tried for gunning down her husband; being face to face with him every day in court for weeks. The last time a policeman was killed in the state, the defendant, having been found guilty, gave the victim's wife the finger in the courthouse hall and snarled obscenities at her. Twenty minutes later, that same man took the witness stand and cried remorsefully so the jury wouldn't give him the death penalty. The jury gave him life.

Connie sat on the sofa with her hands folded.

Beside her, Trammell leaned forward. "I only have a few questions, Mrs. Walsh—may I call you Connie?"

She nodded.

"My name's Frank. I'm going to leave my card. Call anytime you like." He withdrew a card from a slim brass case and set it on the coffee table. "Connie . . . this may be very difficult . . . and I am sorry to have to ask . . . but there are certain things we need to know. Is that all right?"

She nodded automatically.

"When did you last speak to Tucker?"

"I don't know . . . He was working midnight . . . so I guess . . . around ten-thirty or eleven, whenever he left the house." She wasn't crying, though her eyes remained watery and sad.

Harry set off in search of a tissue and overheard the conversation from the kitchen.

"How was he feeling when he left the house?"

"How was he feeling . . . ? I don't know. What do you mean? He wasn't ill."

"Was he upset or angry?"

"I don't know . . . he was just . . . I don't know what he was . . . He wasn't mad about anything I don't think. Carla—our daughter—was late coming home—she was supposed to have been at a friend's house, but wasn't—but that wasn't anything new."

"Was Tucker upset about that?"

"We resigned ourselves to her behavior some time ago."

"Was there anything else going on, financial troubles, health or family matters? Anything that might have been distracting to Tucker?" Trammell was very smooth in his questioning. "And I'm sorry to be so personal, but was there anything at all he might have been upset about? *Anything?*"

"No . . . not that I can think of. Why?"

"It's routine," Trammell assured.

◆ 25 ◆

Connie didn't dispute Trammell's statement, but Harry knew it was a lie. He found a pocket-size container of tissues in a drawer and took them to her.

"So nothing was troubling Tucker?" Trammell double-checked. Wiping her nose, Connie shook her head. "No."

"You're sure?"

When Connie nodded, Trammell stood. The wrinkles in his trousers remained. "Thank you for your time." He tapped the coffee table with two sturdy fingers. "Remember, my card's right here if you need to call . . . if you think of anything."

Ahlstrom, who'd remained by the door, went out first. Harry followed them, careful to pull the door shut. Halfway to the curb, he said, "How did it happen?"

"He was shot during a traffic stop." Trammell responded curtly and without breaking stride.

"Wait a minute." Harry moved in front of him, and Trammell stopped impatiently.

Ahlstrom paused a few paces ahead and looked back with disdain.

"I'm asking how my brother was killed and all you tell me is what I already saw in the paper?"

Trammell glared at him.

Harry had seen the look before.

Trammell's anger, suppressed for Connie's benefit, boiled over. "I knew Tucker for seventeen years. He was *my* supervisor when I was on patrol. I've seen *you* around for a while, too, but I never saw you and Tucker talk to one another—ever. This morning is the first time I knew you were brothers. And I guess I also know *why* I never knew you were brothers. Why Tucker didn't *want* anyone to know."

"Terrific—you read one newspaper column and you know my life story."

"What part are you gonna deny?" Trammell glanced up and down at Harry's suit. "Nice threads. Too bad the pockets are crummy with mob money."

◆ 26 ◆

Harry remained after the detectives drove away. Sweat ran down the back of his neck.

Connie opened the door and looked out. "Harry? Harry, what's wrong?"

He turned toward her and put on a false face. "Nothing."

Her shoulders sloped as though weighed down. "I'm tired, Harry. I'm going to lie down for a while."

"Do you want me to stay? I'm happy to."

"No." Connie leaned against the door frame. "You go on."

Harry concealed his relief. Though concerned for her, he didn't want to sit still right now. He wanted to see someone. "I'll be back to pick you up at four."

Harry slammed down the hall to Ed Jacobs's office and hit the door so hard it flew back against the wall and rattled picture frames and objets d'art on a brass étagère.

"Jesus Christ!" Jacobs's assistant, Tom Davison, jumped out of his seat as though rammed in the buttocks with a railroad spike. "What the hell's the matter with you, Walsh?"

As was common practice in dealing with the State's Attorney's Office, Harry bypassed the round inefficiency that was Tom Davison and leaned over Jacobs's desk. "I want Trammell off my brother's case."

Safely behind Harry, Davison shouted, "You can't just plow in here like that, Walsh."

Alerted by Harry's angry charge through the halls, a small assemblage of office workers and assistant prosecutors gathered outside Jacobs's door and peered into the small sunlit room.

"Get out of here, Walsh!"

"Tom," Jacobs said quietly.

"Walsh, you're a goddamned maniac! You can't—"

"*Tom!*"

Davison—Ed McMahon to Jacobs's Johnny Carson—quieted at his boss's command and waited further instruction like a well-trained—albeit overaged—pup.

◆ 27 ◆

"Close the door, Tom." When Davison hesitated—his orders incomplete—Jacobs added, "Stay or go, whatever you want."

Davison left. Confrontations made his armpits sweat huge rings in his suits, which was one of many reasons he had chosen office administration over litigation.

"Sit down, Harry. *Settle down.*" Jacobs was a light-skinned man with thin curly hair that formed a pale widow's peak against his smooth forehead. Almost diminutive in stature, his strongest presence was his voice. He often joked that his vocal cords belonged to someone else.

Thirty years ago, Jacobs's law career began as a public defender, shield bearer of the poor and unrepresented. He'd been a wild-haired liberal who then had seen his dreams of a better world shot to hell by a long line of indigent repeat offenders who weren't able to relate to Jacobs's post-trial pep talks about improving their lives. They'd looked at him and wondered what the hell this young Jewish kid from the suburbs was talking about—when the hell had he ever been black and poor?

Like any rebuffed zealot, Jacobs turned strongly against those he had once fervently represented. He became the toughest prosecutor the city had ever known. He was a headline maker; a natural for the party machine to run for State's Attorney in his home county; a post Jacobs had held for eleven years running. His name plaque had been on the door now only three months less than the record set by the man who held office while Spiro Agnew was Baltimore County Executive.

"Harry, sit down." Jacobs remained calm, as he'd made a successful effort to behave since he'd been diagnosed with hypertension at forty-seven. "You're going to have a stroke. Your systolic's about one-*ninety*."

"Get rid of Trammell, Ed."

"Harry, that's a police department decision. Besides, Trammell practically runs homicide now. What can I do? I don't have any authority—"

"Bullshit. If it comes from *you*, they'll do it."

"Do what? Promote someone from radar to homicide? Or from

missing persons? Frank Trammell *is* homicide, and he's good at it."

"He's reckless. He goes into a feeding frenzy at the first whiff of blood, and those kids he's got under him follow suit. Today he had Ahlstrom with him, his iron-pumping rube who's only in homicide because when Trammell says jump, Ahlstrom just about drives his head through the ceiling."

"Ahlstrom's a good young cop. Just because he didn't go to a fancy college doesn't make him stupid."

"Goddamnit, Ed, Trammell thinks there's some merit to that crap Barry Eisenrich wrote in his column—like wouldn't it be fitting irony if someone I got off on a criminal case turned out to be my brother's killer."

"Eisenrich took a cheap shot—no doubt about that—but he's an old-timer, and he and your father never got along. You've got to consider the source."

"Meanwhile, what he writes has the cops glaring at me. I want to know what's going on, Ed! All Trammell said was Tucker got shot on a traffic stop, but he's asking Connie if Tucker was upset about anything, if there was some reason he could have been distracted. It sounds like he thinks Tucker did something reckless that got him shot."

Resting the elbows of his horrendous green suit jacket on the desk, Jacobs held both hands palms forward and gestured downward. "Sit down and calm down. I'm going to help you. All right? All right, Harry? But I *don't* want the paramedics carrying you out of here hooked to oxygen."

"I'm all right."

"The idea of you hemorrhaging over my desk is not appealing." Jacobs reached for his phone. "Sit down, Harry, goddamnit! You're worse than my kids. It irritates me when people don't listen."

Harry remained standing.

Into the phone, Jacobs phrased his order as a question: "Can you come over here right now? I got Harry Walsh about to have a stroke."

◆ 29 ◆

◆ 4 ◆

Tierny Wells and Harry went outside and sat on a sturdy bench in the shady courtyard.

Suit jacket removed and shirt collar loosened, Harry felt his anger gradually overtaken by sadness.

Tierny said, "I nol prossed Little Miss Fellatio."

Yesterday's case felt like months ago. "What'd Jacobs say?"

"He doesn't know yet. But I figure I'll kick ass so hard on your brother's case, he'll forgive me." Tierny nodded. "I'm coordinating the investigation between our office and the police, and when we get him, I'm prosecuting it. Whoever did it, I'm frying them big time. *Major* big time."

Suddenly, an adversary was an ally. The legal world turned on an odd axis.

Tierny wore khaki slacks, polished penny loafers, and a Talbot's blouse; her casual in-office attire was tasteful, but bland. Her perfume, however, was the expensive same: Sung.

"What we've got so far," Tierny reported, "is that the last radio contact Communications received from Tucker came around 6:15 a.m. He was back-up on a DWI stop on the Beltway. He stayed with the arresting officer through the field sobriety tests, but once the driver was cuffed, Tucker left the scene.

"An hour and a half later, a commuter who decided to take the day off was driving out near the reservoir when he found Tucker's squad car. Tucker," Tierny added with remorse, "was inside. The coroner says he died immediately upon being shot. He didn't suffer."

Harry felt obliged to nod, because a lack of suffering was supposed to make a difference.

"Tucker's ticket book is missing, so we figure he stopped a car for a traffic violation and was in his cruiser writing out the citation when it happened. The shooter would have taken the ticket book if Tucker had already written his name or car tag in it. What's unusual is that Tucker didn't call in the stop. Usually, before an officer gets out of the car, he radios Communications to run the tag. But not always, especially if the driver looks safe—someone older and well-dressed, or maybe a kid . . . or it could have been a woman. Lots of guys don't call in a woman." Tierny paused, somewhat reluctant to ask her next question. "Was Tucker happily married, Harry?"

Was Tucker happily married? Such an easy question. "I don't know."

"If he was the type . . . Well, one of the troubling parts of our scenario is how Tucker allowed someone to get so close with a gun. He was shot at near point-blank range. Someone would have had to come up to the cruiser with their hands concealed, or had the gun on them already if they were in the car while Tucker was writing the ticket. We're waiting for reports now on trajectory as to the shooter's position, but, however it went down, a nine-millimeter weapon is no small object to hide. But if Tucker was distracted, if a woman was flirting with him . . . well, it's cliché, but we're considering it. Along with many options," Tierny added. "We're also not sure why he was outside his grid.

"Each patrol team is assigned to certain map grids. An officer can be called to any area in the county, or go into another area on their own, but, generally, they remain within a certain radius. Being a supervisor, Tucker had more leeway, but he was found ten miles outside his grid. If he was following someone suspicious he'd first seen in-grid, he waited a long time to pull them over."

Harry couldn't draw any reasonable conclusions from that fact alone. His query took a different lead: "He was shot six times?"

"That's right."

"All in the head?"

Tierny hesitated briefly, concerned about her answer's impact. "Yes."

"From the front, back . . . ?"

◆ 31 ◆

"Front and side."

"Were only six shots fired? Or did some miss?"

"All hits."

Harry went back to his apartment, an undersized two-bedroom walk-out now sparsely furnished since he'd moved his few better items to the condo. The walls were scattered with black-and-white nature photographs in plastic box frames, remnants of his college days, when he was going to be the next Ansel Adams. An oversized artist's pad on the cluttered coffee table was half-filled with sketches of dress designs he and Alena pretended they were going to exhibit in Paris when they quit the rat race and started their own fashion house.

The view through patio doors was a tranquil Sierra Club landscape of deciduous trees and mature evergreens. Angled to take in that woodland vista was the most comfortable sofa he'd ever known: high-backed, extra-long, and reupholstered in a soothing southwest print Alena had gotten a deal on; its sumptuous cushions induced sleep.

Harry lay down and within minutes exhaustion swept him away. He slept, although excess mental activity didn't allow his internal clock to fully appreciate the passage of time. What felt like fifteen minutes was actually two hours.

He was awakened by a warm kiss on the forehead. Alena. "I was worried about you." She smoothed back his hair where lying against a pillow had stood it on end.

He started to sit up, but the firm pressure of her hand kept him in place.

"We have a little time. It's just three-thirty." Alena was gentle with him.

"I forgot to call you about lunch. Sorry."

"Don't worry about it. I had another crazy day. I couldn't have made it." She pulled out the back cushions and moved Harry over so there was room to lie beside him, with her head on his chest. "That's better than last night—your heartbeat. I thought I was

◆ 32 ◆

sleeping with a freight train. Cha-boom, cha-boom. Your poor heart was angry."

He caressed her long hair and stared at the chalk-white ceiling, waiting for the sleep-dulled ache of his brother's death to turn back to searing pain.

He checked his watch. "I told Connie I'd pick her up at four."

Alena didn't lift her head. There was still time. "How's she doing?"

"As well as can be expected. Her kids, though . . . I thought they'd be older versions of what they used to be, but, it's as if completely different people jumped into their skins. Carla was so stoned even the funeral director knew it."

"How old is she?"

"Sixteen? Seventeen? She dresses like a slut. She had on a cheap black turtleneck and no bra. You could see the outline of her nipples across the room."

"You like it when I dress like that."

"Just not when you have appointments with horny contractors." She moved on top of him. "What about Connie's boy?"

"Craig's twenty. He goes to Georgetown and plays lacrosse. I don't know what his problem is."

"Maybe he doesn't have one."

"No," Harry said definitely, "he has one all right."

"No kids, Harry. That's why I had my tubes tied when I was thirty." Alena rolled off and pulled him upright. "Come on, let's get you looking presentable." When his stomach growled, she added, "And get you something to eat." She started for the kitchen. "Any of that pizza left over?" Alena was going to cook.

Through the bay window, Harry saw Connie sitting on the end of the sofa. She looked up, so instead of knocking, he waited for her to come to the door.

Her eyes were puffy and red, though no longer tearing. She wore an inexpensive black dress bought for the funeral of a friend's father three years ago, never imagining it would be worn so soon after to bury her husband.

On the front porch, Harry took her hand. "Connie, this is Alena."

"Hello, Connie. I'm very sorry about Tucker."

Connie nodded wearily. Condolences were tiresome, each seeming to drive a spike deeper into the wound, hammering until the nail was buried and the wound began to heal over the pain that would always be kept inside.

Harry asked about Craig and Carla.

"They came home about an hour ago and left again." Implied in Connie's tone was that she didn't know where they were now.

Harry and Alena each took Connie by one arm and guided her to Alena's Lexus. Across the street was a county squad car dispatched to watch the house; a second was in the alley that ran between Tucker's yard and the homes behind.

Harry drove. Alena sat beside him, but turned around to talk with Connie. "There will be a lot of people at the funeral home. You won't know most of them and they'll all want to pay their respects. A lot of other police officers will be there and they'll be angry and upset just like you're going to be for a long time. The newspapers will be there, and the TV stations. Reporters will want to ask questions. They'll pretend to be outraged and compassionate, but they're whores. I suggest you don't talk to them. Okay?"

Harry was stunned by Alena's directness. He expected his sister-in-law to be reduced to tears.

She wasn't. Connie said, "I don't want to talk to any reporters. They've been calling the house all afternoon." Her voice was firm.

Alena caught Harry's glance. "What makes you think she can't be tough?" She wasn't accusing him as much as she was teaching him; she was always teaching him something, it seemed.

As predicted, the media lay in wait at the Jameson Funeral Home. A policeman's murder was not only the top state story, but with the competing syndicated tabloid shows paying big money for good footage, everyone wanted to be there.

Oddly, the paparazzi had been corralled like high-tech cattle. Sequestered with their telephoto lenses, minicams and satellite vans in the late shade of a huge oak tree, they were encircled by an aggressive length of orange tape on which was printed in bold lettering: PRIVATE PROPERTY, NO TRESPASSING.

Harry searched the media pack for Barry Eisenrich, wondering if the Pompous One would have the nerve to show in person or if he was going to hide behind his byline. Harry didn't see him.

He turned his attention back to the driveway just in time to brake for the man acting as sergeant at arms.

Luckily for Alena's Lexus, Harry didn't hit him. The man was a giant. At six-seven, well over 250 pounds, his jet-black skin glowed like polished ebony. His hair was trimmed to an even quarter inch over his massive skull. His shoulders looked as wide as the car, while his waist was equal to Harry's thirty-four inches. His white shirt was heavily starched; his pleated black trousers finely stitched of summer worsted wool.

"Mr. Walsh . . ." The black man spoke through the car windows, in a South African accent sounding almost British, ". . . if you'll pull around to the back door, sir, I'll get you inside and away from these people."

Harry proceeded as directed.

The black man jogged alongside the car like a single Secret Service agent running point. At the stone building's rear door, out of view of the imprisoned media, he scanned the row of white birch and poplar trees that screened the Jameson Funeral Home from adjacent properties. He snapped open Connie's door, then Harry's. "Someone is prowling around in those trees, Mr. Walsh, but I'll get them."

Harry searched between the peeling paper trunks of birch trees, but didn't see anyone.

The black man opened Alena's door. "The car will be here for you, sir. No one else is coming in or out this way besides family."

"She has a son and daughter," Harry said. "And parents," he suddenly remembered. "Connie, are your mother and father up from Florida?"

◆ 35 ◆

"Tomorrow," she replied passively.

"Tomorrow," Harry repeated unnecessarily to the big man.

"Okay, sir. You can go ahead inside. Just leave the keys on the seat." He started deliberately across the paved parking lot toward the stand of trees, from which there suddenly sounded a mad scurry of escape.

At the top of a short set of steps, ruddy face washed in filtered sunlight, Lawrence Jameson stood looking concerned. After nodding a solemn greeting to Alena and Connie, he guided Harry aside and whispered, "Mr. Walsh, do you know who he is?" He nodded toward the black man heading to flush reporters from the wooded area.

"I assumed he worked for you."

"No. No, sir, he does not."

"Do you want me to—?"

Jameson started nodding before Harry could finish the question.

Harry took a deep breath and started toward the birch trees. He saw patches of white shirt moving adroitly between the trunks before the man finally emerged, brushing leaves from his sleeve.

"It's all right, Mr. Walsh. They're gone."

"Thank you." Standing beside the modest giant, Harry fully appreciated just how big the man was. "Who are you?" Harry asked him.

"Terrence Davis." He offered his hand, which enveloped Harry's in a firm grip. "Call me Terry. I'm sorry about your brother, Mr. Walsh."

"Did you know him?"

"No, sir."

"Then why are you here?"

"I'd be pleased to be considered a friend of the family."

Harry understood. He released the man's hand and went back to where Lawrence Jameson waited nervously inside the red doors.

"Friend of the family," Harry assured.

Inside, Harry saw the glorious arrangement of angelic white roses; dwarfing countless bouquets alongside his brother's bronze

◆ 36 ◆

coffin were six dozen Concetta's Innocence roses, a gift of sympathy forwarded by the same man who dispatched Terrence Davis.

The outpouring of compassion shown Connie was overwhelming. Surviving spouses of other officers killed in the line of duty provided the greatest comfort; they consoled Connie that the healing process was slow and painful, that there would be nights that seemed to last forever, but that while her life would never be the same again, it would get better. She would live again, but she had to give it time, even more than she might consider reasonable. They printed their home phone numbers on sympathy cards and told her to call.

Connie appeared to gain visible strength and resolve.

Harry spent the first half hour at her side, then moved across the crowded room, where Alena was attracting the hello of every man in the place, married or not.

"Connie's doing well," Alena commented. It was warm and the swell of her perfume carried through the aroma of thousands of flowers to Harry's nostrils.

"It's unthinkable," he said, close to her, "just *what* I'm thinking right now." How much he wanted her came in an inescapable rush, and he felt guilty.

Alena hugged him about the waist. "More of these people will go home and have sex tonight than couples in night clubs. I read an article once that funerals are aphrodisiacal. Reminders of death spark the need to experience life."

His hand eased up her torso. The smooth silk of her black blouse slid softly over her bra. "I love you, Alena. I love you a lot."

"I love you, too."

"Then I guess," he said quietly, "you better let go of me before this turns into a spectacle."

"Yes . . ." Alena glanced over his shoulder, ". . . besides, someone wants to talk to you. Do I have competition?" She eased away with a teasing smile.

Harry turned and saw Tierny Wells looking at them. She'd

changed from her casual office slacks to a plain dark-grey dress and heels.

"I didn't mean to interrupt."

Harry flushed slightly. "This is my . . ." He never knew how to describe Alena; *girlfriend* sounded juvenile, *lady friend* too new age, *fiancée* too presumptuous, *lover* too *Cosmo* magazine. "This is— was . . ." he corrected as Alena walked off to consider the white roses, ". . . my fiancée." It was easier using that term when Alena wasn't there to amend that she was his *almost* fiancée.

"She's very pretty." Tierny cocked her head, looking around Harry. "God, what gorgeous hair. Is she a model?"

"Interior designer."

"Guys kill for women with hair like that, don't they?" Tierny pushed a hand through her own short locks. "And I've got this. Oh, well . . ."

"I like your hair."

"Because it reminds you of the tomboy you played dodgeball with in elementary school, right?" As the number of bodies filled the large room even closer to standing capacity, Tierny gestured Harry toward the hall.

Other rooms of the Jameson Funeral Home were not in official use, but the overflow from Tucker's viewing spilled into them. Down the hall, the front doors were open and bright minicam lights glared into the foyer. Terrence Davis had released reporters from their pen to interview the County Police Chief who was taking advantage of the forum to belch rhetoric about mean streets and bringing renegade criminals to task. "We have to take justice away from the dangerous criminals and their *slick lawyers* and give it back to the hard-working people who are our community."

Tierny Wells said, "It's cheap shots, Harry, but they're going to take them. That your brother was a cop and you're a lawyer is too easy a mark to resist."

Harry swallowed a nettle-ish sting of anger and showed Tierny to the stairs. Unhooking a purple velour rope, he proceeded ahead of her.

The second floor hall was empty and quiet save residual conver-

◆ 38 ◆

sation and undertones of dreary piped music from downstairs.

"The crime scene team filed their preliminary report," Tierny informed. "The first bullet entered at a downward angle, striking just in front of the right ear, which fits the scenario of Tucker looking down, writing out a traffic ticket, when it happened. The shooter was definitely outside Tucker's patrol car when he opened fire."

Harry experienced a sudden chill. Tiny specks of white light crossed his vision.

"Harry, are you all right?" Having reduced Tucker's death to provable elements, she'd lost sight of the fact that Harry might not be ready for the gruesome details.

"Give me a minute." His fingertips were tingling.

"I'm sorry."

After a few deep breaths, he felt steadier. "What else have you got?"

"The road shoulder was hard gravel, so there weren't any tire tracks. The shooter was calm enough to retrieve all the spent shells from the nine-millimeter, and the smear marks made in . . ." she checked his color ". . . Tucker's blood show the shooter was wearing gloves, so fingerprints are likely to prove negative. We're trying to get a better fix on where your brother was between the time of the DWI stop he assisted on and his death, by checking lottery ticket agents in the area."

"Lottery agents?"

"The M.E. took a sample from under Tucker's fingernails and found a silvery matter he couldn't identify at first. It's inker's paint, what you scrape off instant lottery tickets to see if you've won. We figure Tucker stopped for coffee and bought a few jackpot tickets. He mustn't have won, though, because no tickets were in the car."

Harry never pictured his brother as the lotto type. Then again Harry didn't think of himself that way, either, yet he'd had the 7-Eleven clerk snap off a few instant game pieces more than once.

"We also have a theory as to why Tucker may have let his guard down a little . . ."

So they were pursuing that idea, Harry thought.

◆ 39 ◆

"Tucker had traces of Valium in him, Harry. Not a lot, but it was there."

"Valium?" The possibility seemed absurd. Harry thought of his brother as the type who wouldn't take so much as an aspirin.

"A few months back, Tucker made an appointment to see the department's stress therapist. The guy's not a real psychologist—he's an RN with therapy credentials. When Tucker found out he couldn't prescribe tranquilizers, he walked out and never went back . . . but he went to someone to get the script." Tierny adjusted her stance. "Has his wife said anything about him taking Valium?"

"We haven't really talked about it."

"Did he ever say anything to you?"

"We weren't close, we didn't really . . ." Harry decided to come out and say it. "My brother didn't like me very much."

◆ 5 ◆

Harry drove back to Tucker's house alone. He parked in back of the police cruiser stationed across the street and approached it from behind. He saw the patrolman, one he didn't recognize, watching him in the rearview mirror, and made certain to keep his hands visible.

"I'm Tucker's brother," Harry said into the opened window. "His wife forgot something." He displayed the set of keys he'd taken from Connie's purse before leaving the funeral home.

The cop nodded. "Okay."

"Appreciate your watching the house."

"Sorry about your brother."

Harry nodded. He had to wait for a few passing cars before crossing the street.

Inside the house, he proceeded directly to the small master bedroom. The room felt old and lifeless. Curtains that had been hung fifteen years earlier were still in the windows. Inexpensive veneer furniture had been chipped and amateurishly repaired.

Harry circled the bed and flicked on the bathroom light; two bulbs behind an opaque bend of glass barely cast his shadow. Slightly larger than a closet, floored in small square tiles, the room had just enough space to accommodate a plain ceramic toilet and sink. The medicine cabinet was mirrored glass, meager and inexpensive but extraordinarily clean. The rest of the bathroom was equally spotless and smelled faintly of Lysol.

Harry slid open a cabinet door on its smooth track. The sight of his brother's disposable razor was slightly disorienting. Tiny flecks of dark beard littered the shelf. Harry touched them with his fingertip, and when bits stuck to his skin, examined them closer to the light. "Tucker . . ." He whispered his brother's name without

◆ 41 ◆

thought, but his tone was clearly one of apology: asking forgiveness for many misunderstandings, but, mainly, for this intrusion.

There was no Valium in the medicine cabinet, nor in the vanity beneath the sink. Harry turned off the light and backtracked to the bedroom.

That the house was so clean saddened him further, as though Connie worked extra hard to make up for what they didn't have. There was obviously little money for household goods. The bath towels were thin in spots; the bedspread unravelled along one edge. Wallpaper peeled away near the ceiling and repeated efforts to reglue it had left mottled stains on painted plaster.

Harry opened dresser drawers and searched gently, though unsuccessfully, through folded socks and underwear for a bottle of Valium.

Tucker's clothes were in the bedroom closet. His pants were cotton/poly blends; most of the newer purchases were styled to be larger through the seat. There were only three suits, all polyester, in plain dark colors; Harry had seen Tucker wear them to court.

His brother always appeared self-conscious in a suit, but his testimony remained solid whether delivered in plainclothes or uniform. Sometimes, Harry used to go around to the judges' hall and watch his brother's testimony through a side door, experiencing pride when Tucker came through rigid cross-examination without a hitch.

Harry left the bedroom light on and eased down the hall to Carla's room. Opening the door, he stepped into a melee. A small desk was piled so high with clothes and shoes it would likely require carbon dating to ascertain the last time pencil had touched paper anywhere on that surface. The walls were covered with posters of hard metal rock bands tacked at rakish angles. Harry felt older than usual when he failed to recognize a single group. The posters' common denominator was a shirtless long-haired lead singer, generally with his head wrapped in a bandana, and boasting a noticeable protrusion in the front of his pants; these young men appeared half erect, perhaps, from the beseeching, arm-waving teenagers in the front row who reached for them with desperation,

◆ 42 ◆

as though all that was wrong with their lives could be cured by violent music.

Carla's twin bed was unmade. An excess of black silk sheets, designed for a double, was tucked haphazardly between the mattress and the wall against which the bed was positioned.

If Connie had never made a search of this room for teenage contraband, Harry could hardly blame her. The energy required was of marathon level, and where would you start? Just grasping the handles of bifold closet doors, Harry got the impression the overstuffed contents would fly out at him like a sprung booby-trap if he dared look inside.

How, he wondered, could the past six years have made so much difference in this girl? How did that metamorphosis take place? The change in interests from stuffed animals to rock-and-roll animals with socks stuffed in their pants? How could the rest of Tucker's house look the same and his daughter's room be so different? It was as though elements of change were rationed per family, and Carla and Craig had willfully claimed the entire allotment, and not spent it wisely.

Harry would have been surprised had his brother *not* been disturbed by it all. How could you not?

Still, Harry couldn't imagine his stalwart brother reaching for Valium. As a young man, Tucker had not avoided the Vietnam draft because of fear, but as a snub against their father. When he returned from Canada, it was not under an amnesty plan; he crossed the border in Michigan and turned himself into the U.S. Attorney's Office. Tucker had been ready to go to jail. He faced a federal magistrate and told him as much, only the magistrate had imposed a more fitting penalty.

Tucker was sentenced to work five hundred hours of community service, time he served in a tumultuous section of downtown Detroit during violent struggles for civil rights. He'd been in the riots and saw how the national guard and police used excessive force.

Maybe that experience motivated Tucker to become a cop, or maybe he'd still been rebelling against his father, long since dead in a puddle of blood on a Baltimore street corner. At least those were Harry's best guesses, and guesses were the best he could do. Tucker had never said.

Harry went back to the funeral home, his detour to Tucker's house having taken no more than forty minutes, round trip.

He felt guilty returning Connie's keys to her purse. There wasn't any reason he couldn't have come out and asked about Tucker taking Valium, it was just his excuse to be alone in the house—to get a feel for what life had been like for them the past six years.

"I can't believe they never showed up. Their own father . . ." In the back of Alena's Lexus, Connie stared out the window at the storefronts of car dealerships and fast food outlets on Joppa Road. She held a handkerchief in her hand, but rarely used it as more than something to clutch.

"That was a lot of people, Connie." Harry's instinct was still to defend them. "Maybe they couldn't handle it."

Alena gave Harry a nice-try glance, then turned toward Connie. "You might want to consider a counselor—someone to help the three of you through the next couple of months. It's going to be hard and there's no sense going it alone. I'll ask around for you if you like. My office should be good for a dozen names. Someone I work with is always in therapy for one thing or another."

Harry was again struck by Alena's directness, and Connie's response:

"We've tried with Carla, but it's gotten so she can outsmart the psychiatrists. She manipulates them so it ends up that Tucker and I are the bad guys. It's all *our* fault.

"She smoked marijuana at twelve. Did LSD at thirteen. Lost her virginity in there somewhere and has been on the pill for the past three years. She drinks. She stays out all hours of the night. Tucker has chased more than one boy—*boy*, listen to me, some of them were *men*—away from the house. One night we heard a noise in the club room and thought it was a prowler. Tucker went downstairs and nearly shot Carla. She was with a man Tucker's and my age." Connie's voice turned mean. "They were doing it on the linoleum floor."

Harry didn't want this to be how life had come to treat his brother's family, because they were *his* family, too, the only family he had. His parents were dead, he had no other siblings. Random and distant aunts and uncles were no more than barely recognizable faces; some at the funeral home tonight had needed to remind him of the connection.

Alena asked, "Is she still doing drugs?"

"She says not, but probably." Connie sounded beyond hope. "She's good at hiding whatever she does . . . It's like living in the house with a spy. She tiptoes in and out, squirrels away things in cubbyholes and boxes all over her room." Connie wiped her handkerchief under her nose and, after a few moments, started crying again.

She was still sniffling when Harry helped her to the front door. More baskets of flowers and fruit were on the concrete porch, pushed back against the wrought-iron railing.

Connie unlocked the door and went into the darkened house, leaving the baskets on the porch. Harry took them in for her and kissed her cheek goodbye.

She turned toward the stairs, but stopped and looked up, exiled by a policeman's killer to spend many nights alone.

Harry turned on the lights. "You want me to stay?"

"I want none of this to have happened."

Hands stuffed in his pockets, rolling his neck to loosen a stubborn knot, Harry walked back to the car.

When he got behind the wheel, Alena squeezed his hand. "You're being a good brother, Harry."

"You're being a good almost sister-in-law. Tough, but good."

"You don't approve of my advice to Connie?"

"I wish I'd thought of half the things you said." Harry shifted into gear and looked over his shoulder to pull from the curb. "Are you going back into the city tonight?"

◆ 45 ◆

"It's Friday."

"Thank God." He'd lost track of the calendar.

Before Alena, Harry had hated weekends. He found the unmarried scene more grueling and insincere than the courtroom, and had almost become a Saturday-to-Sunday recluse until Alena entered his life and pulled him into the vivacious orbit of her social life.

It was a clear shot down Joppa Road to the Ridgely Towers. Harry slipped out the security card from Alena's visor and put it into the slot for the underground garage door. Their pair of reserved spots was near the elevator bank.

Riding up to the sixteenth floor, Alena was unusually quiet.

The doors opened to a lavish hall that split from the elevators in three separate wings. The carpet was so plush, all but the angriest footsteps were absorbed to silence. Thick walls were papered in muskmelon watermark silk and lit by the muted light of shell sconces. If Alena wasn't paying more than half the rent, Harry would go broke trying to live here.

Inside the condo, Alena turned on recessed lights and tossed her bag to the marble dining table. The kitchen, dining, and living rooms flowed together in an open floor plan designed to provide optimum views through wide balcony doors.

Alena turned back to Harry and laid her face against his chest. "I'm a little scared, lover." Her voice didn't sound afraid, but her hands were cold, pressing through his shirt. "I get to feeling desperate when people die. I want to do everything I've postponed right away. Like if I don't do it now, I never will." She stroked his back. "And right now I want to love you, Harry. I really want to love you." Her one hand held his, leading him to the bedroom; the other opened her blouse.

When she unbelted his pants and touched him, Harry was surprised how quickly he responded, and was once again glad for the way Alena so completely engulfed him with her spirit.

◆ 46 ◆

6.

Harry loved their condominium. Not because it was the most expensive place he'd ever lived in, but because being there with Alena felt like home, and it had been a long time since he'd experienced that fond sensation.

He loved the way morning sunshine spilled through the windows, enveloping the bed in a soft haze. Natural light brought out subtle details in tropical print wallpaper, adding depth to countless hues of green and pink.

Saturday, he lay naked on his side, facing Alena, and watched her sleep. He held his hand against the sunlight and moved shadows slowly from the slender curve of her shoulders to the smooth skin of her breasts. He made a circle with his thumb and forefinger for the sun to stream through onto Alena's soft nipple.

He was aroused by the sight of her now and by memories of her the night before. Her lovemaking had been intense and tireless; she took him to the edge of a climax numerous times only to ease back and rebuild the pressure; each time his response was more vigorous, as though she drew out that which was buried within him. When they finally reached orgasm, it was explosive; Alena had been on top, golden hair splayed wildly across her shoulders and breasts. Straddling his hips, she had taken him deeply, completely captivating him with her slick tension.

Now, his phallus half erect, Harry eased out of bed and stepped to the walk-in closet. The smell of cedar shelves and Alena's lavender sachets intensified his desire for her. He explored hangers holding her dresses, blouses, and skirts. Individual pieces invoked distinct memories of times she'd worn them like certain songs reminded others of a favorite moment. He was immensely attracted to the way she looked in silk blouses, how the fabric slid over her breasts, sometimes grasping her erotically, other times flowing so freely the actual lines of her body became mysterious. Silk was an especially nice contrast with faded blue jeans and worn loafers.

He picked out a moss-green blouse and jeans with ripped knees and set them over the antique valet for Alena to get the hint. His own day would start in thick sweatshorts and a rich-orange Eddie Bauer T-shirt.

Grateful for how Alena braced his soul against the harsh phantoms of the outside world, Harry went into the kitchen to start the coffee.

Harry and Alena were snuggling on the sofa, sharing Jamaican Roast and the latest issue of *Allure*, when the intercom buzzed. Harry made his way to the front door, stretching out the residual muscle aches of sleep. "Yes?" he asked into the intercom.

"Mr. Walsh?" It was Ginette, vigorous front desk matron on weekends, who prided herself on keeping unsolicited pests from the residents' doors.

"There's a man to see you who says it's very—"

"It's about your brother, Mr. Walsh." The caller spoke over Ginette. His tone was officious.

Harry would have preferred to know more of his caller's intent before committing himself to a face-to-face meeting—especially if he was a reporter—but he also didn't want the entire building to get wind of whatever this was about; and Ginette, queen gossip, could spread rumors with the speed and maliciousness of a brush fire. Harry said he'd be right down.

He changed into a white dress shirt, jeans, and Bass docksides without socks. His stomach knotted slightly, his heartbeat elevated: his date with reality was beginning. Keeping it at bay had been nice while it lasted.

The caller wasn't a county policeman. His haircut was too precise, suit too freshly pressed, shoes too recently shined, and posture too rigid. His eyes expressed a benign detachment; his lips were thin slivers of ice. "Good morning, Mr. Walsh." He extended a bureau-

◆ 48 ◆

cratic greeting, pumping Harry's hand efficiently and releasing. "I'm sorry to disturb you on a weekend. I won't keep you long." Aware of Ginette eavesdropping from her desk, he gestured toward the front door. "It's a beautiful day. Would you mind if we talked outside?"

"That's fine."

Harry's caller went first through the revolving doors. He was correct about the weather. The humidity was down, persuaded away by a gentle breeze that rippled the silvery leaves of ash trees along the Ridgely Towers's serpentine driveway.

The man stopped near a stone garden thinly shaded by a weeping cherry tree. "Is this all right?"

Harry said, "FBI?"

"No, sir. ATF."

Alcohol, Tobacco, and Firearms: another overlapping octopus-like arm of federal law enforcement. He offered a vellum card.

"Daniel Hemingway—no relation to the writer." He smiled uncertainly. He seemed unsure whether such a remark was even slightly humorous. "Baltimore office."

Harry examined the card and assumed it was legitimate.

"Mr. Walsh, I'd like to be frank with you . . ." Hemingway was a big man used to bending over to speak confidentially; he leaned forward now. ". . . I am a bit compromised by your being a defense lawyer, Mr. Walsh, because while I am hopeful you have information helpful to me, I am aware information *I have* may be potentially useful to your clients."

Harry crossed his arms. "That's your decision."

Hemingway's lips drew tighter together. "Were you aware, Mr. Walsh, that your brother had been deputized by our office?"

"Tucker was working for ATF? No, I didn't know that."

The arrangement wasn't unique; federal agencies often deputized local policemen for select assignments.

"Then the two of you wouldn't have discussed any cases he was working for us?"

"No."

"Did he . . ." Hemingway stopped. He extended his hand.

◆ 49 ◆

"Thank you, Mr. Walsh. Sorry again to interrupt your weekend."

Harry stared at him.

Hemingway withdrew his hand. "Goodbye, Mr. Walsh."

"What the hell do you guys think I'm going to do, use information about investigations into my own brother's murder to help his killer? You boys should get back in the real world."

"I'm not investigating your brother's murder. My assignment is a post-mortem debriefing."

"Jesus, you guys . . . Who comes up with those terms? A post-mortem debriefing. What the hell is that?"

"Tucker was not a regular agent, so he did not file regular reports. His contacts with me were on an as-needed basis, and since some time had passed since our last contact, there may be developments of which I'm not fully informed."

"Yeah." Harry's anger seeped out. "Like someone put a gun to his head and blew him away."

"Yes."

"Yes?" Harry mocked him. "Yes." He shook his head and flipped his hand as though backhanding Hemingway across the street. "Go to hell, pal. Go-to-hell. Whatever you had Tucker working on for you, I hope it was a lesser waste of time than most of your investigations."

"I'm sure Mr. Giardino would prefer that." Hemingway's smile may not have recognized humor, but it fully appreciated irony. Hemingway had set him up, feigning a proper attitude while saving Sam Giardino as a parting shot.

"My brother was investigating Giardino?"

"I didn't say that. I merely made the reference as an example."

"Try a straight answer for a change. It's contrary to federal procedure, I know, but you'd be amazed at its effectiveness."

Hemingway stood as though waiting to address the Cabinet.

Harry said, "Was my brother investigating Sam Giardino?"

Hemingway rocked slowly from heel to toe on polished size-thirteen wingtips. He chose his words as carefully as he might move chess pieces against a grandmaster. "Your brother was investigating a pattern of crimes which we believe may include an on-going

◆ 50 ◆

criminal scheme of Sam V. Giardino, yes. Beyond that," he continued, cutting off the follow-up question Harry was about to ask, "I am not at liberty to divulge details. Given your relationship to Mr. Giardino, I think you will agree that is entirely appropriate."

"I don't represent Sam Giardino."

"You go out of your way to give that impression, Mr. Walsh."

Borrowing a quarter from Ginette, Harry placed a call from the phone booth in the lobby. A man answered whose only response after saying "Hello" was to take a message.

Harry went back upstairs and waited. His call wasn't returned before Connie phoned two hours later. She sounded stronger than yesterday. "The man from the police insurance fund is here, Harry."

"I'm on my way."

"I can take care of it myself if you're busy. It's—"

"I'm on my way. Give me ten minutes." Harry hung up and headed for the bedroom to tell Alena he was going out. She emerged from the cedar closet wearing the green blouse and ripped-knee jeans he'd set aside.

She kissed him. "Mind if I tag along?"

"I'd prefer it."

In the elevator, Alena said, "I'm not asking, just letting you know that whenever you want to talk about what the man said this morning to upset you, wing it by me."

Harry put his arm around her and watched the indicator check off floors toward the lobby.

"Mr. Walsh . . ."

Harry disliked the Police Department representative as soon as he saw him. He was a ball-shaped sweaty fellow with a circular head shaved to pink skin like a pig. He could have been a young forty-five or old thirty-five. His wrinkled shirt-tail bunched loosely at his waist inside the spread of a black polyester suitcoat with as much shine as his head. His hand was small, cold, and damp; his voice so sickeningly sweet it dripped like stringy cotton candy.

◆ 51 ◆

". . . I'm so very sorry about your brother. It's a true tragedy. Horrible." He finally withdrew his hand. "My name is Scott Mayes, County Policeman's Fund. I've been talking with Connie about some of the generalities of Tucker's benefit package, but I'll gladly go over it again for you—and so she can hear it again, too. It can be a little complicated at first blush." If Mayes was any more inflated with his own sense of his expertise, he would have exploded.

Behind Mayes's round back, Alena rolled her eyes and mouthed, "Who is this bozo?"

Connie appeared similarly unimpressed. She sat on the sofa wearing a conservative church dress, holding on her lap a weighty stack of fine-print forms that looked as exciting to read as the phone book.

Mayes settled into the bend of the sofa as though preparing to make a day of this discourse. He rambled on for almost ninety seconds without taking a breath before Alena cut him off:

"Maybe we could skip over all the wherefores, foregoings, and hereinafters—that stuff that doesn't mean anything—and let's get to the bottom line."

Connie grasped Alena's hand and squeezed thanks.

"How much? That's all we want to know. How much does she get and when?"

As Mayes swallowed, a toilet was flushed upstairs, and the simultaneous actions seemed an appropriate duet. He finally said, "A one-time benefit payment of one hundred twenty-five thousand dollars, plus a two-thousand-dollar contribution to funeral expenses, plus seventeen thousand dollars per year, payable monthly for life, with cost of living increases calculated annually."

Alena said, "What about health benefits?"

"They cease within six months of the death of the primary insured. A notice will be sent."

Harry looked at Connie, who kept hold of Alena's hand. "Do you have any questions?"

"Probably. I just can't think what they are." She wasn't helpless, just overwhelmed by the onslaught of a new system of bureaucracy with which she'd have to deal.

"There is also the will." From his accordion stack of papers, Mayes withdrew the short document, folded in thirds and bound in a blue cover page. He flattened it on the sofa cushion that separated him from Harry. "You are named as personal representative, Mr. Walsh. That's what they call executors in other states. It means you are authorized to submit the Estate for probate with the Register of Wills and—"

"I know what it means," Harry said politely, seeing Alena about to interrupt poor Mayes if he didn't. "I'm a lawyer."

"Oh." Mayes's rounded shoulders straightened with indignity. "I'm surprised your brother didn't have *you* draft his will."

Harry deflected the implied insult with a considerate smile. There was no sense in prolonging this visit. "You've been most helpful, Mr. Mayes. We appreciate your taking time out from your weekend."

Mayes was not appeased. "It's my job."

Harry showed him out. Closing the door, he turned toward Alena and said, "You're mean."

"He'd have had us here all day!"

Although somewhat painfully, Connie started to laugh. "Harry, I don't know where you found this woman, but you definitely have to keep her."

For the first time since his brother's death, Harry saw a glimmer of hope in Connie's eyes.

And then Craig came down the stairs.

Craig Walsh, Harry's twenty-year-old nephew, wore a team practice T-shirt with the Georgetown lacrosse logo ironed onto the chest. Left untucked over dark blue athletic shorts, the grey tee had been hand-ripped around the collar to give the impression of muscles bulging through the confines of stitched cotton.

Craig was a good-sized young man, fit and formidable, though somewhat flush with youth's misdirected rage.

At the bottom of the stairs, he began a turn toward the kitchen; completing the motion, he made a sweeping visual survey across the living room, casting sour disapproval.

◆ 53 ◆

When Craig was in the kitchen, Connie said sarcastically, "Welcome to our home." She moved Mayes's papers from her lap onto the coffee table. "I'm sorry, Harry . . . but this is how it is around here now."

Harry headed into the kitchen.

Craig was at the sink drinking a glass of orange juice. He was looking out over the rear yard where a sturdy climbing tree was far too large for such a small patch of grass.

The cat that surprised Harry yesterday offered an encore performance in statuesque pose from the dining-room hutch. Its feline stare made it seem a doubting juror waiting for Harry's re-introduction to his nephew.

"You doing okay?"

"Not really." Craig spoke to the window.

"How about Carla? How's she doing? She seemed a little . . ." he debated how to describe her condition ". . . lost yesterday."

Craig shrugged.

Harry leaned against the linoleum table that had belonged to his mother. "I appreciate your calling my office the other day, letting me know about your father. Sorry I wasn't there. I had this joke of a case in court. A woman charged with going down on about half a dozen guys for money." Harry felt extremely awkward trying to establish rapport, and wasn't at all certain this was the proper tack until Craig grunted disapprovingly.

"Sounds like someone ol' Tuck would have arrested . . ."

Ol' Tuck? This was how he referred to his father?

". . . he was a bit too hard in the hard-ass department, wouldn't you say?"

"He was conservative," Harry agreed, eager for common ground.

"Conservative. Hell, man, Ronald Reagan was conservative. Tuck Walsh made the Nazis look like a fun crowd." Craig gulped the remains of his juice and banged his glass into the sink. "Good talking with you." He pasted on a fake smile. "But I gotta go pick up Mickey and Minnie at the airport."

"Who?"

"The two old-fart dwarfs. Grandma and Grandpa Kittle flying up

◆ 54 ◆

from Orlando with Disneyworld sweatshirts for everyone." Craig threw his hands outward, mimicking glee, having spoken his crack loudly for Connie's benefit.

His purpose was achieved; he'd reduced his mother to tears.

Heading back to the condo, Alena said, "I see what you mean about Craig. A lot of anger there. You don't know what that's about?"

"The last I saw him, he was your average fifteen-year-old. Impressed by cars, money, beer . . ." Harry lifted his hands from the steering wheel and made them quiver ". . . and hot babes. There wasn't any indication he and Tucker weren't getting along. Not that I saw them together more than a couple of times, but my brother loved that boy. You could see it. Craig was progeny. He was his kid. They even look alike, which is tough. Back at the house, I'm standing in the kitchen looking at Craig and I see my brother. Only when Tucker was a little older than Craig, he was my hero, my big brother who'd gone away, but at least he was still alive. He was out there somewhere. Which meant a lot to me. Now . . . I don't know. I don't even know how to talk to Craig . . . what to say."

"They aren't your clients, Harry."

"What's that mean?"

"Oh, boy, okay . . . What's that mean . . . ?" She patted her hands against her jeans-clad thighs. "Okay . . . what it means, Harry, the man I love . . ." she turned toward him ". . . is when you talk to most people, you talk to them like you're in court. You stand back and watch them and you wait to react, but it doesn't look as though you feel anything. You hear words, you look between each phrase for hidden meanings and inconsistencies, but you just deal with the words, you don't deal with the people."

"That's not true. Are you saying I talk that way to you?"

"You used to. You get this plain, noncommittal expression on your face, it's like you're bracing for bad news, or a damaging answer, and even when it kicks the wind out of you, you don't react. Like you're afraid the jury will see you hurt."

Harry leaned toward her with a doubtful look. Smiling, uninsulted, he teased, "Is this what you and the gang downtown—the therapy junkies—talk about over lunch? Psychobabble."

Alena directed his attention back to the road. "Drive the car, Harry."

Alena was right, to a certain extent. Harry knew the "face" she was talking about: his courtroom face. By purposefully disconnecting the tension points at his temples and jaws, and slightly tilting back his head to ease his neck muscles, Harry could maintain a passive expression against an onslaught of damning news.

It was a critical trait for a litigator. Revealing panic or unplanned concern to a jury was detrimental to a client. At pivotal moments in a trial, jurors, especially if confused by testimony, looked for a lawyer's response. If the lawyer was affected, the jury added importance to the point made. If the lawyer remained intent, but unexpressive, the subliminal message was that an answer to a rival's volley was forthcoming.

Harry's father had mastered the mannerism, so it may have been something Harry unconsciously picked up from him. Interestingly, Sam Giardino was also adept at the neutral response, so it may have been learned from a man eagerly sought by federal authorities.

◆ 7 ◆

The phone call came in at 3:13 P.M., Saturday afternoon. A volunteer answered: "Metro Crime Stoppers."

There was silence at the other end, a common response. Many people who phoned into the crime tip line had last second reservations. The handbook said to wait a few moments, then calmly repeat: "Metro Crime Stoppers."

"You're not taping this, right?" The caller sounded anxious.

"No sir, and all calls are anonymous. We do not tape the call and we don't trace it."

"What about that Caller ID thing?"

"No, sir, we don't use that. This call is to remain *completely* anonymous. If you choose to apply for a reward, you will be issued an anonymous ID number—"

"I don't want no reward."

The man's bad grammar sounded unnatural, but that wasn't unusual either; many callers altered their speech pattern in case they were being taped after all.

The volunteer waited patiently, pen and paper at ready.

"I found something," the caller said.

"You found something?" The volunteer kept his tone casual to make this seem like ordinary conversation.

"A police officer's traffic ticket book. And it's got blood on it."

Connie's parents, George and Esther Kittle, were handsome, self-assured people whom Harry hadn't seen since Tucker and Connie's wedding, during which George Kittle had tried vainly to express a joy that was not in his heart.

They met again at the funeral home Saturday afternoon. A gathering for family only.

On a small tapestry sofa, Connie sat beside her mother, nodding forlorn response to Mrs. Kittle's quiet assurances.

In contrast, George Kittle, a robust, leather-tanned man of sixty-seven, hands and face marked with liver spots, was not in a consoling mood. His sharp eyes failed to diffuse restless anger. "You smoke?" he asked Harry louder than necessary.

"No."

"Good for you." The statement was not complimentary. "Maybe you'll join me outside anyway."

Harry and Alena shared a what's-this-about glance before Harry followed Mr. Kittle out to the carpeted hall. Connie's father was not a tall man, but his strides were aggressive and kept him evenly ahead of Harry's longer legs.

Outside, they were alone on the steps. Although tomorrow would be a newsworthy event, there were no reporters on Saturday.

"Harry," Mr. Kittle began, sharply tapping a Lucky Strike from a soft pouch, "I'm a man who believes that which begins bad ends bad. And I think this . . ." He produced a disposable lighter and flicked substantial flame to life. With a small fire dancing in a gentle breeze, George Kittle puffed his cigarette until smoky passion billowed from his mouth. "I think this," he repeated, snapping away the lighter, "proves me correct. I told Connie the day she and your brother decided to marry it was a mistake. They were rushing into it. That it would ruin her life." Cigarette in his mouth, Mr. Kittle scanned blue sky as though on watch for enemy aircraft. "Now she might never get over what's happened, and that would be a shame. She's got good years ahead of her, but not unless she puts this behind." George Kittle spoke of his daughter as though she was a racehorse. "Her problem is, she never staked out on her own—always had to depend on someone else. Not like her sister, Kelly. Kelly's a go-getter. She works in Orlando—executive for the biggest TV station in the market. Connie couldn't do something like that. She always had to have someone to rely on. Tucker was *her* choice to marry, and that's history. What happened twenty years ago is as unchangeable as what happened yesterday. But she's got to get on now before another twenty years goes by—before she makes another mistake."

Drawing hot smoke deeply into his lungs, exhaling as he spoke, George Kittle said, "I'm in excellent health, Harry, although actuary tables show I don't have a lot of time. It's enough, though, for me to get Connie straightened out and back on track so the rest of her life is better than what she's been living. I can't do it if she stays up here. I want her to move to Florida with us, and I want her to do it soon. Help me convince her it's the right thing to do."

Despite George Kittle's none-too-subtle attack on his brother, Harry felt obliged to civility for Connie's sake. "I'll talk to her." The vague response produced an agreeable nod from Mr. Kittle, who, prematurely believing he had drawn Harry's alliance, stalked off on a walk around the building, cigarette clenched firmly in his lips.

By 6:15, people had stopped coming to the funeral home. Most relatives had come the day before. Connie appeared exhausted. Esther Kittle remained postured with the tireless resolve of a woman who had managed to raise two children and remain married to George Kittle, which Harry perceived as no small feat.

George Kittle restlessly checked his watch and announced, "I don't think anyone will miss us if we leave a little early."

Connie was about to object, but her mother spoke for her. "The children, George. The children." Craig and Carla were yet to arrive.

George Kittle grumbled and left the room, reaching for cigarettes.

Ten long, silent minutes later, Lawrence Jameson appeared in the doorway. "Phone call, Mr. Walsh. A Ms. Wells for you."

In the anteroom near the front entrance, the phone laid off the hook. Harry picked it up and heard commotion at the other end: rustling papers and urgent voices. "Tierny?"

"Harry." She sounded energetic to the point of hyperactivity. "We got him, Harry. We got your brother's killer."

◆ 59 ◆

*   *   *

Harry was issued a visitor's badge at the front desk and led quickly through winding fluorescent halls that felt like subterranean catacombs.

The cadet escorting Harry was a chatty young man whose light mood Harry attributed to not having yet taken an "unknown disturbance" call that would bring him face-to-face with a murder victim hacked to death with a butcher's knife.

They proceeded to the second, middle floor, where Homicide Division occupied cramped quarters. Undivided floor space was sectioned by desk modules.

The six people in the office when Harry arrived were six more than normal for Saturday. County detectives worked regular hours—no swing shifts—and had the relative luxury of weekends with their families.

At a conference table pushed against a blue-painted wall, Tierny Wells stood behind the unbearably arrogant Lt. Frank Trammell as he efficiently tapped the keys of an IBM Selectric. Tierny's hands were braced tensely on the hips of her pleated skirt. "Goddamnit, Frank, I'm telling you what I want in the warrant."

Trammell shook his head and frowned.

"Frank, listen to me." Tierny forced her voice to remain composed as though recalling a moot court professor's admonishment not to become shrill against frustration. "This warrant's trouble. I want background on the informant spelled out. How many times you've used him, what his success rate has been—"

Trammell backspaced to correct a typo, and recited brashly, "*Illinois v. Gates* gives me all I need. So *re*-lax. Besides, I've been filling out search warrants since you were slapping some boy's face in the back seat of his father's car in high school. So - give - me - a - fucking - break. Okay?" His spelling error corrected, Trammell cranked the warrant to the bottom line and tapped in his name. F.V. TRAMMELL II.

When Tierny attempted to continue her argument, Trammell stood and brushed by her, leaving her little choice but to move aside.

◆ 60 ◆

The five men in this room, though they would be her witnesses at trial, were not her brethren; certainly they were not Harry's.

Keith Ahlstrom and the other detective on hand had been picked by Trammell to join homicide. The two mountain-sized officers in uniform were part of the Special Situation Unit summoned to assist in what Trammell like to call a "yank," to wit: taking a suspect off the street.

Trammell's force took him past Harry into the hall without acknowledging him.

Tierny's greeting was a grim smile. Together, they trailed Trammell down the hall.

"Problem?" Harry asked over the echo of aggressive footsteps.

"I hope not."

"Me, too." Harry tried to remain objective, although since receiving Tierny's call, he had thought about nothing other than a face-to-face with his brother's killer. But the shooter was not here; what Tierny had meant was they *knew* who Tucker's killer was; they didn't have him, as such. Harry asked, "So who is it?"

"Someone named Ronald Showels."

"From the city?"

"We've got an address in Sparks."

"Sparks?" Harry didn't envision a policeman's killer living in the northern end of the county, where sprawling horse country was being rapidly bulldozed for new bedroom communities. "Are there warrants out on him? Drugs? What?" Harry ran off the standard causes that found patrolmen murdered on routine traffic stops.

"No record. All I've got's the name and address."

Trammell opened the stairwell door and started down to the commissioner's office.

Tierny quickened her pace to keep up.

"So how the hell'd you get him?"

"The Gallant Lieutenant Trammell," she replied derisively as the stairwell door closed. Two steps later, Tierny grasped the door handle. "Tipped by an informant. A reliable one, he says." She pulled open the door. "I know, Harry, I don't like it, either, but off

◆ 61 ◆

we go. The search warrant's for Showels's car and house. A tech team's on standby for prints and fibers."

"Jumping pretty fast aren't you?"

"They're hungry for him, Harry." Tierny entered the stairwell. "I'm sorry this isn't working out better. I'll call when we get him."

"Let me come with you."

Tierny laughed sourly. "I'll be lucky if they take *me* along." She hustled down the stairs, an unwanted guest determined to crash the party.

8

The pearl-white Lincoln limousine waited in the Ridgely Towers's secured underground garage.

Harry scanned the area before altering his course from the elevator bank. The long car's windows were covered with darkening tint, so when Harry looked at the glass he saw only himself.

Waiting until the automatic locks fell, he opened the rear door. The artificial scent and chill of freon-cooled air greeted him as he ducked into the spacious rear compartment.

"Sonny." Turned sideways, Sam Giardino embraced him fondly. "My thoughts have been with you, Sonny." Giardino's strong hand held the back of Harry's neck, tightening his hug before releasing. "He's with your father now, so they can make their peace." Giardino leaned back into a deep corner of leather seating.

The lack of interior light caused his features to partially disappear in shadow, but still visible was his flattened boxer's nose: a width of cartilage nearly pushed inside the lines of granite cheekbones and a jutting jaw. The damage was the result of numerous defeats in the ring when, as a union hall boxer in the late 1950s, Sam Giardino fought up two classes in weight for an extra twenty dollars per bout. He claimed were it not for his nose he'd look like Paul Newman (there was a vague resemblance, especially in stature).

Giardino's nasal passages were almost completely blocked by scar tissue, requiring breathing through his mouth; at times, at age sixty-three, the process appeared labored until one realized the strength with which his chest rose on each breath.

"I think always about your papa, Sonny, about what a good man he was . . . how many times he saved me. You know if I could change what happened, if I could have been in his place, I would."

Harry nodded.

Giardino's hands, rough and bent as a stone mason's, lay against the knees of beige poplin trousers. Missing from the top knuckle up were the tips of two fingers on his left hand. "I still see that car a thousand times in my dreams, Sonny. I see the window down. I know right away it's too cold a day to ride like that . . . I see the gun . . . I grab your father's arm—we've just come out of Sabbatino's— I want to pull him to the ground . . . but Jack thinks I'm joking with him—we were always sparring like schoolboys . . . He pulls away . . . and by the time I call to him, it's too late. The bullets are fired. I feel the burn in my shoulder, but worse is the pain in my heart when your father is hit." Giardino's enunciation was practically without accent, affected more by obstructed nasal passages than heritage. "The things that happen in life, Sonny . . . You've been through a lot for a young man."

Harry sat back. Through the soundproof slide, he saw the anonymous hatted head of Giardino's driver and knew the man was listening through an open intercom.

"The roses," Giardino said, "were all right?"

"Yes, thank you. Also for supplying Terrence. He's very good at keeping people under control. It was nice not having microphones jammed in our faces."

"As much as I wanted, I didn't think it would be right to come to the funeral home. There will be too much attention as it is. Please tell your sister-in-law."

"I will."

"She's doing okay? She needs something?"

"It's hard for her, but her parents are here now."

"That's best. They're in good health?"

"I think so."

"Good. If she needs anything, you'll let me know?"

Harry nodded again. In a way he felt like a boy around Giardino, protected and secure, although at the same time guarded. For while he loved and respected this man, the bridge between them was not a blood bond, but one of honor, obligation, and business, which meant there was always a price, even if a reasonable one.

◆ 64 ◆

Giardino sat forward, emerging into the light. He placed a hand on Harry's shoulder and squeezed, believing admonishment was best delivered with reassuring contact. "This is going to be a hard time for you, Sonny, but you need to keep your head about you. Calling this newspaper and making a threat to their writer was not smart. You had a right to be hurt by what he said, but don't react that way. No one worries about the threat they hear. They know the words are all that will happen to them. You threaten someone, it makes you look weak. We've talked about this: how you deal with people, how you *handle* them. You know better." He shook Harry's shoulder firmly and sat back. "So what do you need to talk about?" Giardino was referring to the message Harry left for him earlier.

"An agent from ATF stopped by to see me."

"What's his name?" Giardino asked, seemingly unconcerned.

"Daniel Hemingway."

"When?"

"Late this morning. Right before I called you." Recognizing a need for tact, Harry proceeded carefully. "He told me Tucker was working with them on—"

"Working for ATF?"

"Yes. He'd been deputized by them." Harry made certain to look directly at Giardino. "Hemingway inferred Tucker was involved in something that had to do with you."

"Well, then, there's nothing to worry about."

Harry knew from Giardino's tone there would be no further explanation. Giardino was master of the ambiguous reassurance.

"Okay?"

With forced agreement, Harry said, "Yes."

"Good." Giardino nodded and shifted positions, his physical motion signalling mental movement as well; he was ready to move on to other matters requiring his attention.

An active man, Giardino headed a small, but powerful political action committee, BUYUSA, the name of which was embossed on his vanity license plate. His purpose was to influence manufacturers to use American materials and labor, and he was responsible for a massive print and billboard campaign that had originated in central Maryland and soon thereafter spread its patriotic message north to Pennsylvania and south to D.C. and Virginia.

"By the way," Giardino added as a parting note, "your girl wasn't sure when you'd be home, so she went to a party downtown. She left you a note, but if I can save you the trip upstairs . . ."

Harry knew he was not supposed to be offended that Giardino routinely entered his apartment and office.

Giardino cocked his head toward his driver, ". . . what was the person's name, Lenny?"

"Alexandra," came the reply through the speaker.

"That's it." His memory refreshed, Giardino nodded. "That's who's giving the party. When you see her, Sonny, you tell her to let her boss know that job she bid on—decorating the new office tower in the harbor?—they're going to get it. They better hire some new people . . . and give your girl a raise. Okay, Sonny? You tell her that, it'll be a nice surprise." Giardino patted Harry's arm and sat back.

Time for Harry to go.

When Harry was thirteen, a limousine—black in those days—waited for him one bleak winter afternoon outside of school. It sat amidst a long line of ugly yellow school buses.

Standing at the sleek car's long hood was a huge man in a dark suit. Looking as though he stepped off a mountain and seemingly oblivious to the pelt of icy sleet, he moved through a scurry of children heading for their buses, and came directly for Harry. He was so big even his teeth were large, and Harry was scared by the man's smile—but his voice was surprisingly gentle.

"Harry," he said, speaking in a coddling tone as though Harry were six, not thirteen, "you see that big car over there?"

Harry had seen it. So had most of the other kids; they stared at it through circles they wiped clear in fogged bus windows.

"A man who was your father's best friend would like very much to talk to you. Would you like to talk to him?"

"What's his name?"

◆ 66 ◆

"Mr. Giardino. Do you know who he is?"

"Yes." Although his mother had tried to keep the newspapers from him, Harry had seen the front page photographs of his father's murder: Jack Walsh's body sprawled lifelessly in a pool of blood on a downtown street. The headlines had been bold and dramatic: LAWYER GUNNED DOWN IN ATTEMPT ON GANGSTER. Sub-headline: REPUTED MOB BOSS SAM GIARDINO ESCAPES ASSASSI-NATION ATTEMPT.

"Would you like to talk to him, Harry?"

Although the big man never touched him, Harry believed he didn't have any choice but to go along; but that was all right, he wanted to go. There were already rumors in school about his father having been a member of the Mafia. *The Godfather* had recently opened in the movies. Being thirteen, any cause for celebrity was worthwhile, so Harry squinted against the sting of sleet and walked to the limousine. Two hundred kids he went to school with saw him get into the back of the long sedan.

Harry had never met Sam Giardino in person, but he recognized him from the newspaper; still, it took a few moments to adjust to meeting a larger-than-life figure. What struck Harry immediately was that the back of the limousine smelled like his mother's bathroom, very feminine. The scent came from a white rose in Giardino's lapel.

"Do you like flowers?" Giardino asked, noticing Harry's stare.

Harry at once shifted his glance to Giardino's mouth, surprised by his slight speech impediment. A boy with a harelip in his class sounded something like Giardino and everyone made fun of Kyle; Harry doubted anyone insulted this man for how he talked.

"I talk this way because of this," Giardino explained. Making scissors of his rough fingers, he pinched shut his own nose. "You lose a lot of fights, this is how you end up." He kept his fingers clamped on his nose while he spoke. "This *schnozzle* is so worthless they may as well cut it off—like these." He held up his left hand with the missing fingertips. Then he laughed. "Don't be scared, Sonny. I'm just joking around." Giardino nodded, appraising Harry. "It's very good to meet you like this. Man to man. Very

◆ 67 ◆

good." Unlike the big bodyguard who now sat up front alongside the driver, Giardino spoke to Harry as though he was an adult, not a child.

Slowly, his expression dissolved to seriousness. "This is a very important day for me, Sonny. Very important. You know your father, he was special to me. He was my best friend. I'm sorry, very sorry, that I didn't die instead of him. If I could do it again, I'd put myself in front of your papa and let them fill me with bullets." Giardino made a fist and punched himself in the chest; the resulting sound was as stiff and sharp as slapping a heavy side of beef onto a butcher's block.

"When I visited your father in the funeral home to pay my respects it was before anyone else saw him, before your mother saw him. I kissed his forehead and vowed I would watch out for you, Sonny. That best as I could I'd take care of you like my own son. You've been getting good grades and I'm proud of that. You stay out of trouble and that's good, too. You respect your mother, and that's best of all."

Harry didn't think to ask how Giardino knew these things; he just accepted the statements as true, because they were.

"I respect your mother, too, Sonny, and that's why you can't tell her about our meeting today. I've waited three years to talk to you to make sure you'd be old enough to understand. I think you're old enough now."

Harry didn't immediately realize that was a question. "I am," he finally responded.

"Good." Giardino grasped his shoulder and squeezed so firmly it caused pain.

Harry knew he was not trying to hurt him and fought the urge to wince; men like this, he thought, did not respond to physical pain.

"Your mother believes it is because of me that she no longer has your father. She has been hurt by me, Sonny, and there is nothing I can do to change that. So whatever I do for you always has to be just between us. You understand, Sonny? Your mother can never know, because I don't want to hurt her any more. I don't want her to *worry* about you. She has suffered enough."

◆ 68 ◆

"I won't tell her," Harry agreed, not asking what would happen if he did.

Giardino looked out the window. The last classes were being excused; kids splashed through puddles of icy rain that collected along the curb; some stopped to stare at the limousine, but none came closer to look inside. "We don't have much more time today, Harry, but I'll see you soon." He gripped Harry's shoulder again, but didn't apply pressure. "How is your memory? You're not so good in math class, only B's this year, but can you remember numbers? A phone number?"

"I think so."

"Look at me now. Look in my eyes." Breath rasping through his mouth, Giardino waited until Harry's look met his pale-blue irises. His thumb and fingers dug into Harry's shoulder as though physically implanting the phone number he slowly repeated three times.

Harry's eyes were nearly watering by the time Giardino released hold of him, but he never forgot that phone number, nor Giardino's instructions: "Whoever answers the phone, tell them where you are, nothing else . . . I'll get to you as soon as I can. Don't call a second time and don't say anything except where you are. Understand?"

Harry nodded.

Exiting the limo, Harry walked to his bus through stinging sleet and barely lowered his head against the hard rain. A part of him that had felt empty since his father's death was suddenly full again.

The music and laughter were loud, bordering on riotous. Whoever answered the phone left it off the hook and was calling for Alena with thespian flair. "Ah-leeee-na! Dahhhling! Ah-leeee-na! Telephone, dahhhling! Tele!"

Harry heard quick footsteps cross a hardwood floor and ice cubes clink into a glass; he assumed the phone had been picked up in the kitchen.

Alena was slightly breathless by the time she came on. "Harry? Is everything all right?"

"They haven't arrested him yet, but they know who he is."

"Oh, my God . . . That's good, but it's scary, isn't it?"

"Yes." He was on the condo balcony with the portable phone, looking over the lighted valleys of Towson.

"So what happens now?" Alena spoke loudly against the party noise.

"Assuming they have enough to arrest him, they'll interrogate the hell out of him, at which time he either confesses, denies it, or asks for his lawyer which cuts off the discussion—or *supposedly* cuts it off. He'll go before a commissioner to see if he can be released on bail pending trial. Given the crime, the commissioner will deny it, which means a judge will review the case Monday morning. If the guy has a lawyer, he'll be there—along with a few dozen reporters—and maybe bail is set, maybe not."

"What about the trial?"

"That's nine or ten months down the road, at least. Longer if his defense counsel is any good."

"Oh, God."

Harry leaned against the railing. The abhorrent length of time it took a case to proceed from arrest to final appeal no longer affected him; it was a given. "How's the party?"

"Terrific, why don't you come down? We haven't had much of a weekend so far, and God knows you could use the reality break. Jeanna's here."

"Say hi for me."

Jeanna was a young woman in Alena's office who admittedly had "the terminal hots" for Harry; she flirted with him boldly, making daring comments about how she could do things for Harry Alena never dreamed of.

"So you're not coming?"

"I'm waiting for a call from the ASA."

"You're not mad at me for being down here, are you?"

"Not at all. It's just that Connie invited me to dinner with her parents, but I couldn't bear it. Her father is a real—pardon the expression, love—asshole. He tells Connie he'll take her wherever she wants to go and says to pick someplace nice for a change—like she only eats at McDonald's if Daddy's not paying. Connie's not really hungry—you can tell she'd just as soon go home—but instead of saying something, she picks a restaurant and her father just about bites her head off. He says he told her to pick someplace nice, not a greasy spoon. The guy's unbelievable."

"No wonder Craig didn't want to get them at the airport."

"Absolutely."

Harry sat on the chaise. "I miss you . . . but have fun. If you get drunk, stay over in town and I'll pick you up in the morning."

"Drunk, *moi?*"

"I've got to go, in case the ASA's trying to get me."

"You can call her by name, Harry," Alena said with amusement. "I know she's a woman. You don't have to homogenize it for me— but it's cute that you do."

"I love *you.*"

"I love you, too. Stay sane out there, Harry."

"Always." He switched off the phone and wondered what Alena was wearing until a different image came to mind: two police cars speeding north along dark, tree-lined roads; the lead car driven by Lt. Frank Trammell, search warrant stuck in his pocket; the trailing car operated by one of the Special Situations men, with Tierny Wells jammed in the back seat. A small assault team heading to investigate his brother's killer.

By midnight, Harry had yet to get a call from Tierny Wells.

Restless, darkly curious, Harry retrieved the phone book and tried the various spellings for Showels. Ronald Showels, Tierny said the suspect's name was. Schoals, Shoals, Shols, finally finding a listing for Showels, Ronald T. in Sparks.

Harry debated whether what he was about to do would have any impact on Trammell's "yank," and finally decided it wouldn't. It was a simple act: picking up the phone and dialing.

The line rang three times before being answered by a machine. A man's voice played on the taped message. He sounded mid-to-late thirties; educated; mildly irritated, possibly from needing to record his greeting numerous times to get it right if he was like most pencil-and-paper people in the rom-and-megabyte world. Maintaining an awkward monotone, as though self-conscious about the machine, he announced, "Hi. This is Ron Showels. If you're calling for me, wait for the beep. If you want Mary Anne or Missy, they have a new number . . ." With a hint of sadness, Ronald Showels carefully read off seven digits.

Harry guessed Mary Anne and Missy were his wife and daughter, and they were recently separated. Harry's divorce clients recorded similar messages on their answering machines, though many were not as hospitable. One angered husband venomously charged, ". . . if you want that bitch, Christie, she's probably at the Red Iron Bar coming on to guys half her age." Divorce law was truly a lovely and rewarding business; Harry hated it.

He set down the phone and pictured Ronald Showels preparing that tape, imagining, from his voice, a man of average size and height, a white-collar executive who was probably a little overweight and in the early stages of balding. If Harry was half close to being correct, this was hardly the sort of man who would shoot a

◆ 72 ◆

policeman at close range which was probably why Tucker had not been suspicious of Showels and fatally lowered his guard.

Alena wasn't home nor had Tierny Wells called by 2:30 A.M. Harry worried about them both.

Since he and Alena had become "serious" and leased the condo together, she had never shown signs of infidelity, though given her spirit, Harry found it difficult to imagine her being totally satisfied with one man. That she was still out wasn't a sign of anything, he reasoned. By downtown party standards, the night was young; besides, he'd told her not to drive if she drank too much. Still, he couldn't help picturing her ultimately succumbing to one of the many come-ons to which she was constantly subjected. Perhaps it would be one of the artisan house painters who frequented her social scene, always talking about their "real works" on canvas and how they'd love to paint Alena, how her hair and eyes and cheekbones did such wonders with light. Harry had photographed her and knew that appraisal to be correct.

Tierny Wells he worried about for equally selfish reasons: that something had gone wrong with the search; that Frank Trammell, seeing the headline opportunity to have Tucker's killer in hand before the funeral, was in the process of committing a hasty mistake that would prove ruinous to the State's prosecution.

When a dull ache pushed behind his eyes, Harry went into the bathroom and took two aspirin. Turning off the water, he heard the phone.

He grabbed the bedroom extension.

"Harry . . ." It was Tierny.

"What happened?"

She was pumped with adrenaline. "Showels wasn't home, but instead of going in, Trammell had us stake out the house and wait. Showels came home about two hours ago. Trammell got him in the driveway as soon as he pulled in. You should have seen it, Harry. Trammell's good." Tierny's reluctant admiration couldn't conceal her enthusiasm; the physical rush of police work was a completely different thrill from the mental tension of a court trial. "Showels pulls in, nothing seems out of place. Ten seconds later—I'm not kidding, *ten seconds*—he's down on the driveway, surrounded by cops. They searched the car and we got a gun. A nine-millimeter under the driver's seat—recently fired. The clip holds thirteen shells, a fourteenth fits in the chamber . . . there were only eight rounds left in the weapon. Your brother was shot six times, Harry."

Harry tried to remain calm. "What about the ticket book?"

"Not in the car, but once we had the gun, Trammell aborted the search. He arrested Showels and is going to file for a more detailed warrant for the house to expand what we're after."

"Did Showels make any statements?"

"He was so stunned, he couldn't talk at first. He rambled something about the gun not being his, then he shut up and wanted to talk to his lawyer."

"Who's he got?"

"Mark Gesser."

"Gesser? He doesn't do criminal work."

"I've seen him handle a few DWI's. I thought maybe he worked in another county."

"He's local. Very successful, but does personal injury and divorce work."

"That's good for us then."

"Maybe."

"Sure it is. I'll blow him away, Harry. Watch me."

"Tierny—even if it's the right weapon, you need more than that gun to make it stick."

"We will. Fibers and Prints are doing the car. I'll let you know. Right now, I gotta crash. I'm exhausted."

Harry figured that, tired as she might feel, Tierny would be lucky to fall asleep by dawn; if she was anything like him, it would take that long to stop trying the case in her head so her eyes could stay closed.

Shortly before dawn, in the deep stages of REM sleep, Harry dreamed about his father again. It was his father as Harry had seen him in old black-and-white photographs during his first years as an attorney: young, dauntless, flashy in double-breasted suits with wide lapels and cuffed pants; leaning against the railing of his walk-up office on a winter Baltimore street, smoke from heat grills rising behind him. Jack Walsh brandishing a confident smile, cigarette held between two strong fingers. A pose Harry often copied as a boy.

In the dream, instead of Harry looking for his father, Jack Walsh was the one on a search. Harry, ten years old again, called out to his father, "I'm over here, Dad. Here, down here!"

Jack Walsh didn't respond. He kept moving away, hands stuffed in the pockets of a slick, baggy suit, puffing his cigarette.

Harry ran after him, but couldn't catch up by the time his father got into the back of a black limousine and was driven away.

Oddly, then, and in the abrupt impressionistic segue dreams are made of, Harry was suddenly in a car with Alena and Jeanna. Jeanna was naked. Alena was watching her seduce Harry. She took him in her hands and got him hard, laughing how she was going to make him want to leave Alena. When she sucked him with her mouth, Harry very vividly felt the softness of her lips.

"It's okay . . . It's okay . . ." Alena's voice.

Harry was awake. The dream was over.

". . . It's okay." Alena had pulled back the sheet and taken down the sweatshorts he slept in. She was naked; her body glowed faint pink in streams of dawn coming through the bedroom window. Crawling seductively on top him, she kissed the taste of martinis into his mouth. "Don't mind me . . ." she smiled—mildly drunk— just getting home at 6:10 ". . . but I just have to have you." Reaching between them, she fingered his erection in line with her vagina and eased firmly on top of him. Drawing his hard-on deep inside her, she groaned pleasurably.

Harry clutched her thighs and tensed his hips.

Alena tossed back her head, whipping warm air with her hair. She arched her back and moved.

◆ 10 ◆

Sunday morning, a jogger discovered the body. Twenty minutes later, the police arrived.

The boy, seventeen, slender, with long brown hair, hung from a backstop at a state park softball field. He was naked, his head cocked awkwardly to the side, neck snapped by a noose made from yellow nylon rope strung through the overhang of the chain-link backstop. His toes, pointed toward the ground, aimed at a trio of concrete blocks toppled over in dry dirt.

The crime lab technician collected a sample of viscous fluid puddled on the concrete and sealed it into a cellophane bag. "Semen," he commented to the Medical Examiner looking over his shoulder.

"Crazy kids." She'd seen it before. Masturbation asphyxiation: a cheap thrill brought on by depriving the brain of oxygen at the point of orgasm in order to intensify the rush.

The M.E. measured the three concrete blocks and estimated that, end on end, they would have made a platform high enough for the boy to stand, noose around his neck, *without* hanging himself; but once the top blocks toppled, he fell the two feet necessary to break his neck.

The M.E. was adding these measurements to her notes when a sudden thought caused her to look up and search the ball field. "Where's his clothes?"

The technician shrugged. "Maybe in the woods."

Within forty minutes, the deep woodlands that formed a heavily shaded horseshoe around the baseball field were being combed by county police officers.

They found the boy's clothes.

They also found a pair of girl's cotton panties, but no body to go with them.

*   *   *

Alena fought her hangover with orange juice, Extra-Strength Tylenol, and vitamin B_{12}. She showered, did her make-up, and tied her long hair in a thick braid. She dressed in a black Lauren blazer over a black tank top, with a matching below-knee chiffon skirt: an ensemble as close to funeral somber as she allowed her wardrobe to venture.

In the time she did this, Harry managed only to pull on the pants of a formerly retired suit that no longer fit him well. The waist was tight and the legs flared a bit too much, but black was not a color he kept current, because juries, Alena said, didn't like black; it reminded them of funerals.

Sitting at the foot of the bed, Harry stared at his feet as though expecting them to get him through the day on autopilot.

Alena said, "It's ten-forty, baby. We should be there by eleven."

Harry's eyes suddenly teared. "I miss him so much."

Alena secured him in her arms. She knew he was talking about his father.

Just inside the funeral home driveway, Harry stopped and rolled down the window for the well-suited parking attendant. Leaning forward, the man asked with mouthwashed breath if they were family or friends. When Harry said, "Family," he was directed to the rear of the building: the area so ably guarded by Terrence Davies Friday evening as a present from Sam Giardino. Terrence was not there today, nor was there need for him; even the most obnoxious reporter had manners during a funeral.

Connie's 85,000-mile Taurus station wagon was parked near the building in the shade of a weeping fir. Harry pulled in behind it.

Alena let herself out of the car—as was her habit—before Harry came around to open her door. She adjusted the black coat on him, leaving it unbuttoned. "You look handsome even in this old rag." Her eyes were considerably clear and reassuring for someone with four hours sleep.

Inside, the smell of flowers was so potent a swell of nausea crept through Harry's stomach. When he drew a series of deep breaths, Alena asked if he was all right. He nodded.

Lawrence Jameson strode dramatically toward them, greeting Harry with patented mortuary flair, taking Harry's hand between both of his. Even though they were alone in the wide, cool hall, Jameson whispered to lend churchly credence to his ornate, steepled building. "We'll begin the service in about forty-five minutes. A chaplain from the police department will say a few words, and I wasn't sure if you wanted to say anything or not, so before I—"

"I won't be speaking."

"That's fine." Jameson, at long last, released Harry's hand, and gestured to a side door. "Family is through there, Mr. Walsh. Please show yourselves in. I need to attend the foyer. People are beginning to arrive." He bowed slightly and stepped back. In a dark way, funerals were theater and Jameson appreciated his major role.

By arranging movable walls along a series of ceiling tracks, a private section for family members had been created at the head of the large viewing room. Connie sat with her mother on a stiff needlepoint sofa, their posture identical to the way Harry had last seen them. Connie appeared drawn and weary. Her swollen eyes were burned around the rims with red, and shadowed by deep, dark circles.

When Harry went to her, she clung to him with a child's desperation and whispered urgently, "Take me away from here, Harry, please. *Please!*"

Esther Kittle rubbed a hand across Connie's back, a contact that caused Connie to further tighten her grasp around Harry.

"Please . . ."

"It's all right. It'll be all right."

She wouldn't let go of him.

"It's all right."

"Harry, please . . ."

When he finally eased away, Connie collapsed against her mother and wept.

From a corner of the anteroom, George Kittle glared at Harry as though Harry was to blame. Perhaps he expected Harry to have talked Connie into moving to Florida by now.

Although Harry's profession inured him to the discomfort of facing adversaries at close quarters, the walls suddenly seemed too constricting to suffer a forty-five-minute wait with George Kittle. Not directing his question to anyone in particular, Harry asked where Craig and Carla were.

"Outside," George Kittle said angrily, even less successful at hiding his mood today than at Connie and Tucker's wedding.

Harry turned and left. Alena joined him. In the hall, she said, "I'd just say something to the old fart we'll all regret later."

Craig was stretched out in the backseat of the Taurus. His eyes were closed; his hands folded behind his head.

Harry rapped on the window.

Craig tilted his neck back and peered over his forehead. "It's open," he announced unenthusiastically.

Harry sat down up front and left the door open. It was warm inside the car. "Where's your sister?"

"Went for a walk in the woods."

Alena, standing outside the car, nodded toward the birch trees to let Harry know where she was going.

"Hot," Craig said, pulling himself up by his knees.

"Yes, it is."

"I mean her." He watched Alena cross the parking lot.

Harry recognized youth's compliment. "At least we still have something in common. Like when we used to sit on the hill before games and watch the girls."

"Yeah." Craig didn't sound especially nostalgic.

"So how's Georgetown?"

Craig sighed, bored and restless. "It's all right. Beats living at home. But what doesn't?"

"You taking summer classes?"

"Nah." Craig stretched as though just awakening. "Living in the frat house. It only runs me five hundred for the whole summer. I got a lifeguard job at a rich bitch country club down there. Pheww. Lot of money, Harry. *Lot-of-money* down there." Craig loosened his knit tie. His sports jacket was tossed back in the trunk compartment. "Girls' fathers own international businesses, banks, factories. Unbelievable. Growing up around a shithole like this, who even knew there were people like that out there? And so many of them . . . Shit. The parking lot at the club looks like an exotic car showroom. So much wax on those Benzes and Jags you could start a candle factory."

Harry felt as though his own status in Craig's life had been reduced by comparison in the net worth standings. This, however, didn't seem like a good time to lecture on money and happiness. "I take it you and your father weren't getting along."

"Ol' Tuck threw me out of the house. He was done with me, and I was done with him." Craig reached for his jacket. "Yep, good old *Dad* threw me out just like he told Mom not to invite you over anymore." Craig struggled into his coat and ran a hand through his hair. "I hear they caught whoever shot him. Some reporter called the house in the middle of the night to ask Mom how she felt about that. I wish I'd've answered the phone. I'd tell 'em I'd like to run right over and shake the guy's hand, say, 'Hey, bud, you're my wish come true. Maybe there is a God.' " Craig got out of the car and slammed the door.

Harry caught him halfway up the steps and grabbed his strong arm. "Look, Craig . . ." Harry spoke firmly ". . . don't do anything to upset your mother. All right?"

He exhaled a sour laugh. "Why not? What's she done for me? Ol' Tuck walked all over me—hell, walked all over *you*—what'd she ever do to defend us, huh? You know, that's why I wanted them to let us see the body, see old Dad shot to pieces, see him for the piece of shit he was."

Harry snapped, "Don't be a jerk." Enough was enough.

Craig exhaled the trademark sigh of insolent youth. "You didn't know him."

"He was my brother."

"But you *didn't* know him."

Harry couldn't deny that.

Craig maintained eye contact. "You know, I liked playing lacrosse for your team. I liked being with you. I used to pretend you were my father, because my father was such an asshole. I used to *hope* something would happen to him so you'd have to take care of me, so you'd be my father! Shit. Now he's finally gone, and it's too late. Well fuck him, Harry. *Fuck him!*" Craig yanked his arm free and walked away hard.

Harry sat along the shady side of the stone steps where it was cool.

Behind him, the thick red door sealed the somber music and floral scents inside the funeral home like shutting a tomb. Around front, people continued to arrive; car doors closed, footsteps clicked across macadam; and voices carried quietly on the breeze.

Alena emerged from the birch trees and came over to sit beside Harry. "I was going to ask how's Craig, but now I'm more concerned about you."

Harry sighed.

The doors opened behind them and Lawrence Jameson stood at the threshold. "We're ready, Mr. Walsh."

Alena said, "We're waiting for the daughter . . ."

"All right then."

". . . and here she comes."

Carrying sandal-like shoes by the heel strap, Carla ambled out of the birch trees as though strolling a sunny lane. Her dark hair was windblown, her gaze unfocused. She wore a pullover black dress that hung from her shoulders like an oversized artist's smock. "Uncle Harry!" She ran to him gleefully, as though still twelve— only she was sixteen and stoned.

The anteroom "wall" was opened shortly before the service began.

From his seat, Harry could only see the first five rows, but there was the Chief of Police in full regalia, and a host of other dark-suited officials with plans to make mercenary use of news minicams set up outside.

Harry assumed State's Attorney Ed Jacobs, Homicide Lieutenant Frank Trammell, and Detective Keith Ahlstrom would also be in attendance. An election was never so far away as to dim one's concern about image; voters would remember Jacobs as the man who either won or blew the case against a slain police officer's killer; Trammell and Ahlstrom—but especially Trammell—could always stand a little glow of the limelight, because one day the Chief was going to retire, and picking a successor from among the ranks was preferable.

Harry was relieved when the depressing music was finally cut off, only the minister who took up position behind the podium proved equally droning. His eulogy was delivered slowly; each word hung in the air like an old rug draped over a line waiting for new life to be beaten into it.

Harry was overcome with the feeling that this was all wrong; *everything* was wrong. Now he understood what Connie talked about the other day.

Look at them. Look at this family:

Connie stared mournfully at Tucker's closed coffin, comforted by her mother. Florida-tanned George Kittle checked his watch and shook his head in disgust. Craig had slipped on wayfarer sunglasses, which could have been seen as covering reddened eyes, except that his posture imparted disdain, not sadness as he slouched with his legs outstretched and ankles crossed, hands stuffed in his jeans' pockets. Only Carla—courtesy of whatever controlled dangerous substance she had imbibed—managed a few sniffles.

How had they come to this? This was their father's funeral goddamnit. Their father had been killed. *What was wrong with them?* Why weren't they sad? Or was the question: what was wrong with *him?* Why wasn't he crying? This was his *brother's* funeral and his eyes were dry.

For thirty-six years, he had a brother, now he did not. Focusing on the soft bronze patina of Tucker's coffin, Harry slowly came to understand just how right Craig was: Harry had *never* really known Tucker at all. He had turned Tucker into a fantasy, telling himself that if he'd needed Tucker, he could call him, and Tucker would be there; only there wasn't a tangible piece of evidence beyond hopefulness to support that wish. His brother had been as beyond his reach as his dead father.

It was that realization that caused Harry to lower his head. For the moment, he was the only one crying, but, soon, tears escaped silently from behind Craig's sunglasses.

The service passed with such relative speed it seemed almost inconsequential ceremony. Harry felt there should have been more; perhaps he should have spoken—but to say what?

Lawrence Jameson escorted the family into the hall and whisked them outside where two limos, engines and air conditioners running, awaited with opened doors.

Connie and her parents got into the first car. When Jameson directed Craig and Carla after them, Craig—his sunglasses back on—said, "No way in hell," and strode to the second limo.

Carla bent forward to look inside the lead car. Curled hair hanging in her face, she announced cheerily, "I'm going with them, okay, Mom." It wasn't really a question.

So there they were, sharing the back of a limousine: Harry, Alena, Carla, and Craig. Waiting for six police pallbearers to place Tucker's coffin in the hearse that would start the ten-mile procession to the cemetery.

Carla put down the power window and cocked her head outside. Eyes closed, she smiled and basked in sunshine.

In uniform step, the police officers placed Tucker's coffin into the hearse and closed the tailgate. The long, dark car pulled slowly around the side of the building. Tucker's coffin was concealed from view by dark purple curtains over oblong windows.

Carla, sadly, but detached by chemicals, said, "There goes Daddy."

The hearse was escorted by two police motorcycles, lights flashing. A long stream of cars fed slowly from the Jameson Funeral Home, turned north onto York Road, and entered the Beltway at a cloverleaf interchange.

Harry looked out the rear window at the seemingly endless parade of cars with their headlights on; many of them police cruisers, flashers turning silently on a bright sunny day. It reminded him of his father's funeral, when he had spent the entire ride to the ceme-

◆ 83 ◆

tery on his knees looking out the limousine's rear window. The number of cars was even greater than today. He'd felt like his father was a hero, so many people had come to honor him. Harry had not known at the time that his brother, a thousand miles away, felt Jack Walsh had been anything but heroic.

Now, as Harry turned around in his seat, Carla was looking at him. He smiled solemnly.

"Uncle Harry . . ." she began, and then paused ". . . do you believe in heaven?"

"Sure," he answered reassuringly, thinking she was concerned for her father.

"I don't," she said definitely. "I don't believe in God, either. I think that when we die, it's as dark and endless as before we were born, and we go back to the nothing we came from."

Harry held his smile. "What a cheerful thought."

"It's not a downer. Really. Not if you think about it. It means if this is all we have, we should *enjoy* every day, and not get caught up in all those society kind of tensions. That's what I tried to tell Dad—if he didn't like his job anymore, he should quit. We could live off the *land* like early settlers."

"Early settlers," Craig cut in, sunglasses aimed at the limo roof, "got bitten by rattlesnakes and mauled by grizzly bears. And the only people who live in tents are losers who can't cut it in the real world."

"God!" Carla swore. "Mister Junior Achievement businessman. Maybe if Dad wasn't laying out fifteen grand a year for you to party at school he'd've been in a better mood at home."

"Yeah, right. It's all my fault. You're so perfect."

Alena patted Harry's thigh and stated clearly, "Aren't you glad I had my tubes tied?" Her statement was mean, but accomplished the desired effect: Craig and Carla remained quiet for the rest of the drive to the cemetery.

· 11 ·

ou going to get drunk?"

"I'm thinking about it."

Alena found Harry in a corner of the dining room in Connie's neighbor's house. After such a large turnout at the funeral, only a few dozen people attended Tucker's wake. Liquor had been bought in anticipation of a considerable crowd, and Harry had taken to consuming the no-shows' share.

"Looks like you're beyond the thinking stage to me." Alena sat on a rented folding chair beside Harry and hung her arm over his shoulders.

Harry considered his plastic glass of melting ice and squeezed lime. "I think I remember why I don't drink . . . It doesn't help." He tossed down the remainder of his vodka/tonic all the same. Ice sloshed to the lip of the cup and spilled down his chin.

"Time for this one to go home," Alena decided, slipping a hand under his arm. In nine months, she had never seen him drunk, rarely seen him consume more than three beers at a time.

Harry slurped the remaining ice from his cup and set it on the sideboard. "What a lousy day."

Providing a steadying hand, Alena led him to the living room. Offering goodbyes, they circulated the modest floor plan that was a mirror reverse of Tucker's home next door. Given the overall amount of drinking that had taken place, Harry managed to pass for sober in the eyes of most.

Their final goodbye was to Connie, who sat in a reupholstered chair near the front window, numb from yet another volley of condolences. Esther Kittle remained at Connie's side, a sturdy dock for her daughter's listing ship.

"If you need anything," a man Harry didn't know offered her kindly, "you call us, okay?"

Connie forced one more smile and nodded.

"We will," Esther replied.

When Harry moved in front of her, Connie stood and threw her arms around him, clutching even harder than at the funeral home. She didn't say anything, just held on and released tears withheld since they were at the grave site.

From her seat, Ester Kittle caressed her daughter's back and said, "Thank you, Harry . . . for everything." She spoke politely, but with a sense of completion, as though Harry wasn't needed anymore.

"You'll be okay," he whispered to Connie. "You'll be okay."

She managed to pull away, nodding emptily before hugging Alena.

"You're tougher than you think," Alena reassured.

"Will I see you?"

"Of course."

Alena stepped back and moved Harry toward the door. Connie was sobbing quietly when they left.

Outside, afternoon sun was hot on Harry's face. He was sweating in his old suit. "I'm throwing this goddamned thing away," he complained, suddenly angry as he shed the jacket. "Goddamned black. Juries hate black." He started down the sidewalk, then turned toward Connie's house. "I gotta pee."

"Okay, Harry."

None too gracefully, he crossed the small lawn, grabbing the iron handrail in the nick of time to save a humiliating fall. He climbed the front steps and went inside. His footsteps were heavy on the stairs, his grip on the banister desperate. "What the hell am I doing drinking?" he muttered to himself. "Jesus, what an asshole."

At the top of the stairs, the door to Carla's room was open. She was on her hands and knees, fishing around under her bed. The skirt to her smock dress was raised high and revealed her lack of underwear.

Harry looked at her in spite of himself.

Carla pulled out a shoebox and shifted onto her rump like a little girl rooting through her Barbie clothes, only Carla eventually produced a prescription vial, opened the cap, and rolled a pair of yellow pills into her palm. She popped them dry before Harry could react. When she saw him looking, she waved casually with the bottle. "Dad's Valium. He probably figured I was the one swiping his scripts, but he never caught me. Want some?"

Harry took the small bottle and read the label imprinted with Tucker's name. "I think I should keep this."

"Sure. I've got more."

"You shouldn't take this crap."

Carla focused on him quizzically, then laughed. "Uncle Harry, are you drunk?"

He leaned against a wall that wasn't there and stumbled a few steps before catching himself.

Carla shrieked with amusement. "This's great. We should have a party." She ran into the hall. "Craig! Hey, Craig!" She banged hard on her brother's door, only George Kittle appeared, not Craig. "Ooops." Carla tried to smother her laugh. "Forgot."

George Kittle saw Harry perched on the edge of Carla's bed, in obvious need of support. With a look of disgust, he slammed the door.

"I made a real fool of myself. I have six drinks a year, this year I just happen to have them all in the same day, and it's around family I hardly see. They'll think I'm a goddamned drunkard." Harry was mad at himself. He was mad at Tucker's family for being in need. He was mad at Tucker for getting shot. Mad at his father for taking bullets meant for Sam Giardino.

Alena stopped for the red light. "Harry, it's no big deal. This is a traumatic time, you're entitled."

"No . . ." he shook his head ". . . no. It's embarrassing. Christ, the look on Connie's father's face."

"Who cares?"

"*I do.*"

◆ 87 ◆

"Okay . . ." Alena saw there wouldn't be any reasoning with him now ". . . you'll make it all better in the end, Harry. That's your style."

Alena stayed with Harry in their condo until near midnight. Harry gradually sobered, turning back a headache with straight aspirin. They lay on the living-room floor, sketch pads and colored pencils between them, working on the Harry/Alena line of fashions. Harry had gotten pretty good at drawing reasonable likenesses of Alena, and used her as his favorite model.

"So what's this blouse made of?" Alena asked, hugging close.

"Something thin . . ." Harry sketched a hazardously unbuttoned top ". . . *very* thin. See through." He drew in the soft circles of her nipples.

"Mmm, I like it. So where would we go with me dressed like this?"

"Someplace exotic."

"Far away?"

"Very."

"And hot?"

"But not too." Harry shaded the drawing, providing details that brought his paper Alena to life.

"South America?"

"Rio."

"Would we go nightclubbing?"

"Yes. And I'd have to beat up a dozen hot-blooded Brazilians who tried to seduce you."

"You'd be exhausted."

"But not too." Harry smiled, drew some more of her short skirt, and said, "My brother was buried today."

"I know."

An hour after Alena left, Harry's sobriety turned to anxious restlessness.

His mind raced in anticipation of tomorrow, when he would see the man who killed his brother. Ronald Showels would have his bail review. He'd stand before a district court judge with his attorney, Mark Gesser, and probably Gesser's co-counsel.

Gesser would love the headlines of representing a cop killer, but capital crimes were over his head; he'd bring in another attorney, someone qualified but relatively unknown, who Gesser could keep in his shadow and make it look like he was doing all the work.

Harry hoped Tierny Wells would be prepared. Unmindful of the hour, he called her at home.

Tierny didn't answer; her recorder did.

"Tierny, Harry Walsh . . ." he hoped she was monitoring her calls and would pick up ". . . something you should know about my brother." Harry paused, but Tierny didn't come on the line. He spoke quickly, unsure how long the machine would give him. "Tucker was working with ATF. Remember what you said about Tucker being outside his grid when it happened? This could be why. If Showels was tied to the ATF investigation, Tucker could have followed him anywhere, even outside the county. Maybe you should talk to ATF before the bail review. Special agent's name is Hemingway. If you want to talk about this, call me anytime. Otherwise, I'll see you tomorrow morning in court." Harry hung up.

The more he thought about Ronald Showels, the faster his mind worked. But there were so many unknowns, he kept coming up with more questions and fewer answers.

He waited half an hour for Tierny to call back—she didn't—then he dressed and went for a ride, telling himself he was just going to drive by the place, that was all, just drive by.

The trip from metropolitan Towson to rural Sparks took thirty minutes. It was 2:15 A.M. when Harry arrived.

Showels's house was a substantial rancher, recently built, faced in dark stone that so overly dominated the home's one hundred-foot length it created the effect of a fortress wall. Situated on a rolling acre of ground that backed to a cluster of poplars and oaks, it was neither the prize nor spoil of a pricey development favored by upper managers unafraid of a long commute.

Unlike energy-conscious neighboring homes, Showels's was well lit. A pole lamp midway down the driveway cast a round specter of light across a trimmed lawn. Ground lights along the house front shone through shrubs and ornamental grasses.

Harry made two slow passes before parking across the street in front of a new home under construction. A dog barked in the distance; crickets and frogs sang quiet night cadence; otherwise, there was quiet.

Harry exited his car and jogged cautiously to the side of the stone house. He proceeded quickly around the back and promptly encountered a duo of halogen lamps splashing white light across a multilevel redwood deck. At one end, the woodwork encircled a fanciful brick barbecue pit; at the other was a spacious hot tub.

Further toward the trees, where the light remained powerful enough to throw shadows, an elaborate cedar swing set/playhouse stood upon a wide base of sand. The Showelses appeared to enjoy suburban luxuries.

Emerging from shadow, Harry crossed the deck, quieting his footfall. He stuck his hand inside his dark T-shirt and tried every doorknob. Each was locked. He shaded his eyes and peered inside a kitchen window. In dim light he saw dishes piled in milky sink water. Empty boxes of frozen dinner entrees and rakish piles of newspapers littered a colonial-style table.

Although the size—and corresponding value—of the house was a surprise, the rest of the setting was the upscale suburbia Harry anticipated from the address. The crime, however—killing Tucker—remained very much an enigma: how had a man at this station in life come to shoot a policeman?

A snapped branch caused Harry to turn abruptly toward the trees. Keeping still, he waited, but heard no further motion, only frogs and crickets now that the dog had quieted.

He replayed the snapping branch in his mind's ear, trying to estimate how large an object had caused it. The sound had been high pitched, a smaller twig, easily broken by a groundhog or possum. Unassured by that logic, he felt exposed.

The landscape no longer seemed sprawling enough to conceal

him in its vastness, but confining as though there was nowhere to hide. Heading back toward his car, Harry cursed his restlessness for bringing him here. There had been little to accomplish and, he estimated, he had fallen short of even that.

·12·

The Towson District Court was not housed in a multiservice center like most other districts, but occupied the small ground floor of an office building.

Monday morning, it was the scene of chaos. The normal crush of landlord/tenant cases and serious traffic violations stacked defendants and lawyers into the hall, which left no room for the onslaught of media and court hangers-on wanting a look at a policeman's killer.

Although Ronald Showels would be tried in Circuit Court, the Maryland Rules—long known for illogical and inconsistent interpretation—put bail reviews in the lower District Court where courtrooms were smaller and security nonexistent.

Maneuvering through the fray, Harry located Tierny Wells in Courtroom One. She leaned over a scuffed trial table and worked tensely on her notes.

Slouched beside her, half concealed by a stack of files, was a bored Junior Assistant State's Attorney assigned the repetitious and highly unsexy task of handling twenty DWI cases on the morning docket.

Harry reached over the flimsy railing that sectioned the trial area and touched Tierny's arm. "I called you last night and again this morning. Did you—?"

"I can't talk to you now, Harry."

Her curtness surprised him. "Did you get my message? About Tucker working on a case for ATF?"

"Harry. We *can't* talk." Her severity was more than pretrial stress.

"What's wrong?"

Tierny faced him hands on hips. "You tell me. You were seen at

♦ 92 ♦

Showels's house last night, Harry." She spoke with quiet anger. "I don't know *why* you were there, *what* you were doing, and it really doesn't matter right now."

"God*damnit.*"

Tierny sat down.

Harry leaned further over the rail. "I went out there—"

"Harry . . ." she turned in her seat ". . . you want to see what happens here, fine. But that's all I can do for you." Her voice remained severe, but her eyes relayed a different message, one she couldn't speak.

Harry backed away, thinking, Lt. Frank Trammell: he must have had Showels's house staked out. What a mistake to have gone there. Now Trammell, who already thought Harry dirty because he was a defense lawyer, had circumstantial evidence to add credence to that ludicrous notion: Harry *had* been at Showels's house in the middle of the night. Why had he gone there? Well, they'd never know, would they, because Harry had been chased away by a sound. That's how Trammell would see it.

Harry found an open spot to stand against the wall and unbuttoned his suit jacket.

After a fiscally conscious weekend without air conditioning, the courtroom was hotter than outdoors. The body odors of those summoned to appear who hadn't showered hung sourly in still air.

Harry waited for court to begin. The law was such a glamorous profession.

Harry had been uncertain how he would react when Ronald Showels was brought in. He'd been in court so many times—usually representing one of those in the line of recent arrestees—that being there in any other role didn't seem real. *The process* didn't seem real, and, for a moment, Harry couldn't grasp this was how it was done. It suddenly seemed ludicrous.

Eleven men, all wearing ill-fitting detention center greys and soft ankle-cuff slippers, stood before the bench and Judge Stanley Morganstern.

While the courtroom buzzed with conjecture over which de-

◆ 93 ◆

fendant was the cop killer, Harry spotted him right away.

Showels was medium height, though his pudgy build made him seem shorter. Thin strands of brown hair were dirty and combed against his skull as though painted by an untalented artist. His thin mouth, pinched feminine nose, and small eyes reminded Harry of a rodent that would invade the dark burrows of smaller mammals to consume their young.

Showels looked scared, intimidated by the other weekend arrestees, all of whom were bigger, most of whom were black.

Now Harry knew how he felt seeing Ronald Showels. Perhaps it was a sixth sense developed from a lifetime in courthouses—first tagging along with his father, then as a law student, now as a lawyer—but there was something about this case. Even at this early stage, Harry could feel it: something was wrong.

Judge Morganstern did not bother to quell courtroom chatter before launching into the docket. An efficient bureaucrat without false pretense as to his duties, Morganstern handled the docket like a grocery checkout clerk faced with a very long line. He rang them up and got them out, unconcerned as to potential errors left in haste's wake.

He disposed of a third-time DWI bail review and started the next case in one sentence: "Five thousand, ten percent cash, next, Ronald Showels. Step forward from the line, Mr. Showels, are you represented by counsel?" The question was for the record, because Mark Gesser was already beside his client.

"Mark L. Gesser for Ronald Showels, Your Honor." Gesser's sculpted golf-pro looks were more fitting for the lady divorce clients he wooed than criminals. He was sprayed, starched, and suntanned for his morning appearance. His custom grey silk suit cost more than most used cars.

"Morning, Mr. Gesser, Madam State's Attorney, what've you got to tell me?"

"Tierny Wells for the State, Your Honor." Already standing, she clasped her hands behind the back of her police-blue single-breasted suit. "Ronald Showels is charged with first degree murder in the shooting of Sergeant Tucker Walsh of the Baltimore County. Bail was denied by the commissioner. The State requests no bail be continued. Ronald Showels has a history of violence that—"

"Objection."

Tierny replied, "This court has twice issued orders for protection from domestic violence against Ronald Showels at the request of his wife."

"The court will keep in mind the *ex parte* nature of domestic violence proceedings, continue Miss Wells."

"Ronald Showels was twice charged with assault and battery against his wife, but both time charges were dropped at the request of his wife. Mrs. Showels is present in court today, Your Honor, should the Court choose to question her as to those cases."

Harry, like the rest of the courtroom, looked for Mrs. Showels. He found her not because hers was one of the only heads not turning, but because she was seated beside one of the county's more aggressive and notorious divorce lawyers, Sheila Parks, a/k/a Suicide Sheila.

"This is a capital crime, Your Honor. Given that Ronald Showels is a danger to society as well as a risk to flee, the State requests continued no bail pending trial."

"Mister Gesser?"

"Judge . . ." The time it took Gesser to utter that single word made evident he was going to make more theatrical use of center stage than did Tierny Wells. Gesser expanded his slight southern drawl almost to the point of song, a tack which sometimes swayed jurors who expected attorneys to perform like a trial was TV, but uniformly annoyed the hell out of judges. ". . . Mr. Showels's *alleged* history of violence is the product of a mercenary divorce suit filed against him by his wife and her attorney, Sheila Parks. Ms. Parks, I note for the record, is in court this morning seated alongside her client."

Mrs. Showels, wearing a plain churchgoing dress, shifted uncomfortably at the attention and accusations focused her way. Sheila Parks, however, remained undaunted. A tall, strong woman, unmarried at forty-seven, Sheila had long been smeared by envious male counterparts as a man-hating lesbian, a label Harry knew was untrue.

"Just as," Mark Gesser continued, "*all* previous criminal charges against my client have been dismissed before trial for a lack of merit, I suggest this case will be dropped as well."

Tierny Wells violently kicked back her chair and stood. "Your Honor, I assure you, on behalf—"

"Mr. Gesser," Judge Morganstern interrupted, tilting forward at an angle of reproach, "do you mean to suggest this case has been concocted by a fellow member of the Bar? Or by the State's Attorney's Office?" Ethical consequences were left dangling like a noose.

"Judge, I did not state—nor do I mean to imply . . ."

Although clearly he did, Harry thought.

". . . anything about how these charges came to be presented, however, the search warrant was based upon statements by an *unnamed* informant."

"Which can be addressed to the Circuit Court upon the proper motion."

"But it's important at this stage as well, Your Honor. My client is entangled in a difficult divorce case. Marital property issues of *significant* financial impact are concerned, and my client being imprisoned is most helpful to his wife."

Harry couldn't believe it. Gesser was skirting as close to the line as possible, claiming Sheila Parks had orchestrated Ronald Showels's arrest. No wonder Gesser was braving this case solo, no criminal-defense-wily co-counsel at his side. He thought he was handling a collateral issue in a domestic matter.

"Further, Your Honor, my client has an alibi witness—a *reliable* alibi witness, not an unnamed informant like that used by the State—who will account for his whereabouts from ten P.M. Thursday evening until Friday noon the following day. The victim in this case was killed approximately six A.M. Friday, according to the police report, a time during which my client was in the company of our alibi witness, Nicole Matson."

◆ 96 ◆

"Spell the name, please," Tierny Wells requested, feigning minimal concern.

Gesser rattled off his reply, making Tierny write quickly, as did the reporters, though they reacted to this revelation with far more intrigue than the Assistant State's Attorney.

"Further, Your Honor, my client's ties to the community are strong. He has been a county resident for *twenty* years. His business is located in the county. He is the president of a financial brokerage firm, East Coast Equities, with annual loan processing that has averaged ten million dollars per annum over the past three years. His daughter, who he visits regularly since his wife's abandonment of the family home and *in spite of* his wife's lack of cooperation, resides in the county, and Mr. Showels very strongly wants not only to keep contact with her, but to be awarded custody—over Ms. Parks's objections, of course." Gesser couldn't resist a final jab.

Harry shook his head. Unless this was a ploy of misdirection—and it certainly seemed not—Gesser didn't know what the hell he was doing.

Alongside Gesser, Ronald Showels stood in pained trance. Harry wondered if Showels knew lack of competent counsel was grounds for a successful appeal from a criminal conviction.

Judge Morganstern waited through a brief pause. "That it, Mr. Gesser?"

"On behalf of the defendant, I respectfully request personal recognizance pending trial."

"Defendant continued on no bail, next case, Jermaine Taylor, assault with intent to maim, step forward, Mr. Taylor."

Taylor, a slight black man, sauntered forward. Ronald Showels had to be guided back in line by the Sheriff.

Mark Gesser moved behind his client, whispering assurances before leaving the courtroom.

In the hall, Gesser was immediately placed in a tug of war between print reporters wanting first crack and TV personalities desirous to move him to awaiting minicams outside. Gesser, who had TV looks, opted for outside.

Jimmy Hawkes, an AP reporter who had been in law school with Harry for a year but quit due to a "violent reaction to hypocrisy," locked a supportive arm around Harry. "How you holdin' up, old friend?"

Harry watched Gesser outside through the glass wall and double doors. "Okay . . ."

"Too bad it was your brother got shot, man. 'Cause right about now, that guy Showels needin' a lawyer like you, not that suit. But, hey, Mr. Suit's my story, right." Hawkes shrugged and headed out into the foray.

·13·

The longest, most demanding part of lawyering was preparation. Endless hours were spent in the office, which was why Alena had transformed Harry's formerly bland second-floor quarters into a comfortable setting of neo-wilderness funk.

She'd selected a sturdy wheat-colored twill fabric for Harry to reupholster the corduroy sofa that opened into a queen bed. A chipped antique desk had been stripped, repaired, and refinished in washed oak. Hardwood floors were cleaned, polished, and topped with a "reasonable" moss rug. Plaid wallpaper was steamed off and replaced with a freestyle southwest pattern the color of Sedona red rocks.

Harry had to admit, pleasant surroundings made even tense tasks more enjoyable. Or maybe having Alena's decorating touch was second best to the actual touch. In his office, he never felt she was that far away.

Turned from his desk, feet crossed and propped on the window sill, Harry rested his elbows on the chair arm and tapped his fingertips together. He kept rehashing Ronald Showels's bail review. Apprehension that this case was going to hit a rocky course wouldn't let him quit. Over the years, he'd learned to pay strict attention to those nagging concerns; experience showed they were subconscious warning buoys.

By 1:15, he'd phoned Tierny Wells three times and hadn't gotten a return call. He grabbed the phone and tried a fourth time, thinking it might be the winner. Tierny Wells was still not in.

Across the lawn, Harry watched a young working couple share a basket lunch on the patio of an office/house owned by a mortgage-banking service. He wished Alena worked nearer by. Mondays were the worst. During the work week, he sometimes went into the city and stayed with her; less often she came out to the county. Her career was extremely important to her, and Harry respected her drive. Alena had come a long way from a small Ohio town: promoting herself, receiving raves in decorating magazines, emerging as one of the premiere "small" designers in the city.

Part of what was exciting about their relationship was the fire ignited by those parts of their lives they didn't share. Maybe if they got married, the flame would be snuffed out. Maybe not.

Harry watched the picnicking couple with envy. When they folded their checkerboard napkins and went inside, Harry dropped his feet from the sill. Leaving his suit jacket across the sofa arm, he headed down the stairs.

Marcie, who had been holding his calls waiting for Tierny Wells, shook her head when Harry pointed to the pink message slips in his slot. "No one who can't wait."

"Thanks."

Outside, Harry loosened his tie and followed the cooler, shady side of the street to a phone booth. He dialed a number and left a message with the man who answered.

From there, he took an original of his brother's will to the Register's Office and set about the methodical task of opening the Estate of Tucker Walsh.

The clerk, a fixture in the office for as long as Harry could remember, said she was sorry about his brother. "I just hope the person who shot him doesn't hire some slimy lawyer to get him off. No offense, Harry."

He shook his head. "None taken."

Harry was halfway up the front walk to Tucker's house when he heard shouting. He should have called first, but the prospect of Connie's father answering the phone had deterred him. Harry didn't like the man and figured he could better steer around George Kittle and get to Connie face to face. But now this . . .

Through opened windows came George Kittle's roar. "The problem with you goddamned kids is you don't respect anything. Don't respect your mother, your grandmother, or me, and certainly not

◆ 100 ◆

yourselves. You're selfish goddamned brats, spoiled and mollycoddled all your lives. Well, welcome to the *real world*. Spit out your pacifier and start acting like a young adult."

"You're full of shit!" Craig yelled.

George Kittle slapped Craig's face.

"You think that hurts?" Craig's voice toughened with defiance. "You think *you* can hurt *me?*"

George Kittle's fist struck toward Craig's face, but Craig swiftly deflected the blow with his forearm, and grabbed his grandfather's fist and threw it aside. Craig had let himself be hit the first time—not again. He pivoted toward the door and kicked open the screen, storming outside. Seeing Harry, he shouted, "He's all yours."

Harry grabbed him. "What the hell's going on? Where's your mother?"

"She and Grandma Minnie Mouse went out somewhere. I guess to buy new bathing suits, because guess what . . . ?" Craig shifted his voice to mock a TV announcer. "Hey, Craig Walsh, your father's been gunned down in the line of duty—what're you gonna do now?" Craig made a sour smile and returned to his own voice: "Well, shit, bub, we're going to Disneyworld."

Harry gestured toward the house, "Is that what this is about? Going to Florida?"

"That's the point—I'm *not* going." Craig was jittery with nerves; the confrontation with his grandfather had him riled. He looked as though he'd like nothing better than to hit something. "No way am I going down there with *them*. And Carla took off as soon as Grandpa Mickey gave us the word, so I doubt they'll see her by flight time." Craig bounced on nervous legs.

Harry tightened his grip. "Settle down, all right?"

"That old fart in there wants to fight me, you believe that? My own grandfather," Craig accused mockingly. "He goddamned tried to punch me out."

Harry roughly pulled his nephew close and the momentum nearly pulled Craig over. "He's an asshole, all right," Harry whispered harshly. "And what you do with assholes is you stay away from them, you don't put your nose up against one, right? *Right?*"

Craig was visibly surprised by his uncle's strength. "Yeah, yeah, okay . . ." He calmed somewhat.

"Go sit in my car, I'll be right back."

Craig hesitated.

"Do it."

Harry waited for Craig to get in the Mustang before going inside the house.

Connie's father was in the kitchen. Leaning against the counter, he poured himself a shot of Jack Daniels from a recently opened bottle. His hand shook. "Goddamned kids," he muttered, glancing at Harry from the corner of his eye. "*God*-damned kids." Breathing uneasily, he downed the whiskey hard.

To his surprise, Harry felt sorry for him. George Kittle was a once-strong man who had just been demoralized not just by a much younger man, but his grandson; he would likely never forget how the last five minutes made him feel old and defeated. "Are you all right?"

"Fine. *Fine,*" he repeated forcefully when his first answer didn't sound strong enough. He sat down at the kitchen table and his raspy breathing eased.

"You're sure?"

"Yeah, fine."

"When Connie gets back, please have her call me."

"What do you need to talk to her about? We got reporters calling every hour. She's got to get away from this place . . . all these bad memories."

Harry lied: "I need information to file an inventory for Tucker's estate. The faster I get it," he added before George Kittle could object, "the sooner Connie has everything in her name."

"So she can sell the house?"

Harry was going to say, *If she wants to,* but, instead, said, "Yes."

George Kittle poured himself another shot. "I'll make sure she calls."

* * *

Ten minutes from the house, Craig calmed enough to admire the polished wood grain of the Mustang's custom dash. "This is a pretty decent car."

"My Dad's. He used to take me for rides with the top down when I was a kid."

Craig was silent a few moments before asking, "What was he like? Ol' Tuck wouldn't talk about him."

Harry smiled fondly. "The greatest man who ever lived."

Harry and Craig went to TGI Friday's for a late lunch. They sat at the bar, one of many offset levels in the wood-and-brass-fixture restaurant. Craig ordered a beer and seemed relieved the stout bartender didn't ask for ID.

"It was great, prowling around downtown with my dad," Harry said, picking up where they left off in the car. "The people he knew were incredible. I saw them all, loan sharks, prostitutes, bookies, enforcers. An incredible group. Absolutely incredible. I was nine and ten, a little pipsqueak kid, going into places even cops didn't know about.

"One night, not too long before he was killed, Dad took me to the basement of the Greenway Hotel. It's gone now, but, back then, the Greenway was a very plush place. Rich people stayed there, and a line of big limos was always out front.

"Down in the basement—a sub-basement, actually, you had to walk down this narrow set of dingy steps to get there—there was an enormous illegal casino set up. Craps, roulette, blackjack—a few high-stakes poker games. There must have been five hundred people. All well dressed. And so much cigarette and cigar smoke you could hardly see from one end of this huge room to the other. A lot of laughing and screaming. Dice rolling. Cards being dealt and chips stacked on felt tables. Women—incredible women, some of them topless—carrying trays of drinks and cigarettes."

Craig said, "Holy shit."

"Dad had the run of the place. Everybody knew him. They treated him like a king. *How yah doin', Jack? Hey, this's your boy. Hey, kid, glad to meet you. Stick with your old man, he's the best.* Even guys he hadn't been able to keep out of jail were glad to see him. This one guy, Jesus, he was enormous, he looked twenty feet tall to me, with arms like watermelons. He told Dad he just got out from a two-year stretch, but it could have been worse, the time was easy, and he thanked Dad for getting the sentence cut to two years.

"I was amazed. First of all, I'm surprised to see a man this big, but I don't think I'd ever known anyone who'd been in jail—so, I'm pretty naive, a little kid, I asked him why he was in jail."

Craig thought that was funny.

"You know what the guy says?"

"No, what?"

"He says, 'I killed somebody, but he was a weasel and deserved it.' He shows me his hands—they're huge—and he says, 'Strangled him, you know.' "

"Holy shit."

"You're telling me. But you know what I said? I looked up at this humongous man—you know, I'm goddamned ten, all I know about people being killed is what's on TV—so this giant tells me he just got out of jail for killing a man and I tell him, 'Neat.' "

"Neat?"

"I was a *kid*. Dad laughed, so did the guy. He tells Dad, I'm going to be okay, that I'll grow up to be a great lawyer just like him. And then he asks if I want a better look around the room. I said, sure. And with the same hands he strangled a man with two years before, he lifts me on his shoulders. I was what felt like ten feet above everyone else, being walked around the room. He's telling people I'm Jack Walsh's kid and they better be nice to me because Jack's not going to be practicing law forever and they're going to have to come to me. One guy in a fedora, smoking a big cigar, puts a five-dollar bill in my pocket and says it's a retainer for the first case I handle for him. Pretty soon, everybody in the room's putting money in my pockets. I walked out of there with almost five hundred bucks."

"What?"

"Five hundred bucks."

"Jesus."

"On the way home, Dad asked if I thought they were nice people. I said, yeah. Sure I thought they were nice. He says it's important to remember that. That just because someone breaks the law doesn't make them bad. It depends on who they hurt. If they hurt innocent people, that's bad. But sometimes the people they hurt deserve to get hurt, just like what the big man, Jolly, said."

"Jolly? The big guy's named Jolly?"

"Like the Jolly Green Giant." Harry drank ice tea and smiled. Craig laughed. "Unreal."

"When we got home, about three hours after we left, supposedly to get ice cream, my mother was furious. She asked my father where we'd been, and he said getting ice cream. She said then why did we smell like smoke? Dad winked at me and told her the ice cream store caught fire."

Craig laughed again, and Harry realized just how much he'd missed being with him, and how sorry he was for the years that had gone by without keeping touch.

At his office, Harry introduced Craig to Marcie and to George Patterakis.

After hellos and condolences, George, the occasionally perplexed and perpetually late-sleeping attorney with the basement office, removed his glasses and gestured wildly with them in hand. "Alan Reinkin got another *juice* PI case, Harry. I could just fucking die. His plaintiff's a Peabody concert pianist, gets broadsided in a car accident by a showroom new Mercedes driven by a major stockholder in BGE. Reinkin says he's looking at high six-figure specials, easy."

Harry started up the stairs. "He tells you these things to make you crazy, George. Don't believe him."

"You don't think it's a real case? He's making it up?"

"I wouldn't doubt it."

"That son of a bitch."

Harry had sorted through his phone messages by the time he reached the upstairs hall.

◆ 105 ◆

"Used to be a house, huh?" Craig said, stating the obvious as he followed Harry.

"Not as flashy as the buildings around the courthouse, but I don't have those kind of clients." Harry sat behind his refinished desk. "I get the less formal—albeit less profitable—work-a-day people. Unfortunately, that's a syndrome of a dying breed."

"How's that?" Craig considered the wall of black-and-white nature photographs in plastic box frames.

Harry reached for the phone. "Lawyering's being swept along a black tide of high-priced specialists and TV advertisers. People who need us the most—folks being screwed by unscrupulous car dealers, negligent realtors, and mail-order swindlers—can't afford the cost of litigation. The bad guys—the big companies—are over-staffed with paper lion litigators who churn out pleadings by the pound, not the page. Going against one of them's like trying to swim out of a whirlpool with your hands and legs tied."

"But there's other cases, right?"

"Not as many as there are lawyers." Harry hit a speed-dial button. "Not like when my dad—your grandfather—practiced. It was a different world then. Being a lawyer was like being part of a big fraternity. Lawyers were rivals, but friendly ones. Now, lawyers steal clients from one another, lie behind each other's back, entice clients to file unfounded legal malpractice cases. It's nuts."

"So why do you do it?"

"I ask myself that a lot."

Craig continued to scan the photographs, touching a few with his fingers as though detailed images would have texture beyond visual depth. "You take these?"

"A long time ago."

"They're good."

"Thanks," then, into the phone: "Hey, Beth, it's Harry."

"What?" She spoke loudly over a pleasant commotion in the background. It sounded like Saturday night's party had started up again, this time in the office.

"It's Harry. Where's Alena?"

"Oh, Harry!" she cried happily. "We're measuring Alena for a throne. She got us the AmeriCenter Tower job. The contracts came over this morning. Can you believe it! The entire place's going berserk. We're going to be rich! *Rich!* She's a genius. There's talk of a coup so she can run the whole shop."

"Is she there?" Harry asked loudly.

"Somewhere! I'll look."

Harry held the phone from his ear. "Celebration over a new job," he explained to Craig about the jubiliation coming over the line.

Alena picked up with an excited, "Whoa! We got it, lover! We're having a party after work. Can you come into the city?"

"I've got Craig with me."

"Really? Is everything all right?"

"I think so, yeah." Harry considered his nephew.

Craig gestured to a case file—could he look at it?—Harry nodded.

"Well, bring him along. We're going to the Wilmington show house. It closed over the weekend, so we're going to trash it."

"I've got biker clients better behaved than you guys."

"The Interior Visions girls ride into the night!" Alena was high from success. Million-dollar jobs weren't just rare—when it came to a modest-sized firm, they were practically nonexistent. For her to land this contract was more than a major feat; she'd be the envy of the city design industry. "Get your buns down here tonight, Harry Walsh. I've got a special something for you."

"I love you, too." After Harry hung up, his ear continued to ring from the noise.

"Sounds like our frat house." Craig smiled, reading interrogatories in Harry's file. He looked surprisingly studious in the curve-backed chair Alena had bought from an upscale leasing company. He read carefully before turning pages.

Harry watched him. "You find that interesting?"

"One of my fraternity brothers' father is a products liability lawyer in Alexandria. Right before Christmas I helped him move into a new office. He had some old case files we had to take to the dump, but he said I could read them if I wanted. I took fifteen

◆ 107 ◆

R-Kive boxes back to the frat house. Still got six to go."

"What's your major, anyway?"

Craig smirked. "Undecided—although not really. I wanted to be pre-law . . . but Ol' Tuck said no way. He wasn't spending fifteen grand a year to have another lawyer in the family." He closed the folder and slapped it back to Harry's desk. "I hated him for that . . . and a lot of other things."

"You want to talk about it?"

"I don't think so."

Harry didn't press the issue—it was too soon. He was reaching for a file when Marcie buzzed him.

"Call for you on two, Harry. She won't say who. You want it anyway?"

"Yeah, okay." He picked up the phone. "Harry Walsh."

"Meet me at six-thirty where we had lunch Thursday."

Harry was about to say her name, wanting to make sure it was her, but she hung up.

◆ 14 ◆

At the entrance to the mall's Food Court, Harry scanned rows of white tables, most of which, at 6:30 on a Monday night, were empty.

"So who is it we're looking for?" Craig asked.

"An assistant state's attorney."

"Odd place to meet, isn't it? Or you have something going with her?"

"She's prosecuting your father's killer." He tossed that out for Craig's reaction.

His nephew blinked, but otherwise remained stoic.

Harry checked his watch. "We're on time, but I don't see her."

"I'm going to get a piece of pizza, all right?" Craig gestured toward the Vettori's stall.

"You need money?"

"No, you got lunch, thanks." Craig headed off between tables.

Keeping watch for Tierny, Harry noticed a young girl wiping tables with unusual determination. She looked at him with recognition. If she was a former client, he hoped to recall her name before she said something. Too late.

"Are you Harry?" Turning over a sloppy towel in her hand, she ambled toward him.

"Yeah."

"I thought so." She nodded, then pointed with her dripping rag into the mall. "Your wife said she was going to Nordstrom's. The athletic department."

"Wrong Harry. I'm not married."

"Well your girlfriend, then, I don't know, she looked like a wife. Said she was supposed to meet you here at six-thirty. Got short dark hair, cute, slender."

Tierny, Harry realized. "Nordstrom's?" he confirmed.

"Athletic department."

"Thanks." Harry nodded toward Craig. "See that kid in the blue T-shirt, getting pizza? Tell him I'll meet him at the car, would you?"

Harry headed for the department store at the far end of the complex, wondering why the need for this surreptitious rendezvous.

The mall was nearly deserted this early in the work week. Mostly, its inhabitants were kids who made it their home away from home, turning it into Summer Camp Consumption as they paid full price for the latest fashions; a luxury borne of low overhead: no mortgage, health insurance, utility bills, but mainly, no kids of their own.

Harry found Nordstrom's athletic department—actually athletic sportswear—but didn't see Tierny.

"Harry?" A sales clerk with bright eyes called his attention.

Was the entire retail world, Harry wondered, operated by those under eighteen?

"Hi." Her smile was friendly. "She's in the dressing room. She wants to see what you think of this tennis skirt. *I* think it's pretty cool. You can go 'head back if you want. No one else's back there." She shrugged. "It's *so* boring."

Along a short hall were six dressing rooms, three on each side. The last door on the right was closed.

"Tierny?"

No response.

"Tierny? It's Harry." He heard a zipper. "Tierny?"

The door opened and he saw her reflection in the wall mirror; Tierny wore a short white skirt with the tags still attached. The tail of a coral blouse hung over the skirt's waist. "Come on in, Harry." She checked over his shoulder as he crossed the threshold.

"What's going on?"

"I'm off the case."

"What?"

"Jacobs pulled me."

"For what? You did great this morning." The cubicle was made for one, and he was immediately aware of close confines. "Showels isn't out, is he?"

"For now, but Mark Gesser filed a writ of habeas corpus in Circuit Court. Hearing's set for tomorrow. Trammell's going crazy trying to find this alibi witness, Nicole Matson. She's not on record anywhere, phone company, gas and electric, no criminal record—state or federal. Trammell even checked voter registration all across the state."

"Why the panic? Almost every client I've ever had claims an alibi. Most aren't credible at all." Harry couldn't help noticing Tierny's legs showing from the short skirt. And that her blouse was untucked, even though buttoned, was arousing.

"Trammell's afraid Showels might get a bail set, and he'll be able to post it. He's got money."

"He posts, he posts, it doesn't mean he's innocent. It's something else . . . Right?"

She combed her hand through short hair. "We've got no motive, Harry. A weapon, but no motive. Nothing at all. And no one shoots someone, especially not a police officer, *six times,* without cause. So why did Showels do it? Except for those domestic violence cases, Showels is clean. And I talked to the assistants who had those domestics . . ." Tierny shook her head. "The wife's spent time in Sheppard Pratt. She's manic depressive. *She's* also got an extensive record for shoplifting. She's got a thing for going into grocery stores late at night and pocketing cosmetics. She's always got plenty of money with her, she just can't control herself. If she was poor, she'd be a thief, but because she's got money and a shrink, it's a mental disease. She's on supervised probation now."

"Maybe ATF has something on whatever Tucker was working on for them."

"I called the agent you met with—Hemingway? He said they didn't have anything to help us."

"What about your informant? How'd he know about Showels?"

Tierny exhaled. "That's another problem. The anonymous witness number Trammell used on the arrest warrant? Get this—it's the generic number they use whenever a call comes in from Metro

Crime Stoppers, that TV phone-in number. They're *totally* anonymous informants. They're assigned a number to call back later to see if they qualify for a reward, but only the caller knows his number. Even Metro doesn't know who they assign the ID to."

"Swell."

"It gets worse." Tierny hesitated. "They think you're involved."

"What?"

"They saw you at Showels's house last night, Harry. What the hell *were* you doing out there?"

"I don't know." He was mad at himself. "I got impatient. You told me the guy's name and I wanted to know what he looked like, where he lived. Hell, before I drove out there I called his house and listened to his voice on the goddamned answering machine. I had to know. I wanted to face the bastard, and short of that, to get a feel for how he lived, who he was. He shot my brother."

"I know, I know . . . but Trammell told Jacobs you were trying to break in. That you had your hand inside your shirt and were trying the doors."

Harry felt like a fool. "He was out there, huh? Trammell . . . ? So why didn't they grab me? Find out for themselves what I was doing?"

Tierny bent her knee and placed a bare foot against the wall behind her. "You're not supposed to know any of this. That's why I wanted to meet you here. They're so paranoid, I wouldn't be surprised if your phones were tapped. They could even be following you." She saw his look of doubt. "I know, I feel a little silly myself—like we're playing spy." She laughed. "But when I called you today . . . well, I was upset, and I guess their paranoia was making *me* paranoid."

"Getting yanked off a case can do that to you."

"I didn't just get pulled from the case. Jacobs suspended me. With pay, because he knows it's without cause, but I'm suspended."

"For what?"

"Because I nol prossed your Mulcaney case last week."

"That has nothing to do with this."

"Jacobs thinks if the press gets wind I dropped a case with ties to

◆ 112 ◆

Sam Giardino and you, and now I'm prosecuting a case where they think you're involved . . . you know, Harry . . . the same bullshit. They'll worry someone thinks I'm getting paid off."

"That's insane . . . I'm sorry."

"Don't be. I was mad, I was going to go to the papers with it, but maybe it's best. You're right about Jacobs. How can I work for a man who wears such lousy suits?" Tierny took her slacks off the door hook. Holding them in one hand, she pulled off the tennis skirt. Her shirt-tail covered all but a glimpse of silk wine-red panties as she tugged on her slacks. Buckling her belt, she turned back toward him. "Guess we ought to get going. I'm surprised they haven't called Mall Security on us already." Tierny opened the door.

"You find her?" Craig leaned against the Mustang's fender, holding a casual pose from a jeans advertisement.

"Yeah."

"So what's going on?" Craig helped Harry put the convertible top down.

"Nothing, really. Technical stuff."

"Oh."

Craig, Harry thought, appeared relieved; maybe he too was worried about the case against Ronald Showels going south.

Driving out of the parking lot, Harry said, "Want to go to a party downtown?"

"Yeah, sure."

"We'll stop back at my apartment to get you a clean shirt."

"Cool. Gotta razor I can borrow?"

"We'll find something." Changing lanes, Harry glanced in the rearview mirror and noticed a nondescript brown sedan ten car lengths back.

Forty-five minutes later, leaving his apartment for the city, he thought he saw it again, but when he turned onto the Jones Falls Expressway, it didn't follow him.

Great, he thought, now *I'm* getting paranoid.

◆ 113 ◆

· 15 ·

Craig was impressed when Harry turned into the "millionaire's neighborhood," an area three miles inside the city line that used to be considered country when downtown's premiere industrialists bought the land in the late 1920s and erected sprawling mansions and elaborate gardens.

Craig was even more impressed when Harry pulled down the oak-lined driveway to Wilmington House. "Who lives here?"

"It used to be owned by a big-time tea merchant. The guy died twenty years ago and placed it in trust for his heirs. The last one died, so now it goes to charity. But before the remainderman sells it, they're letting city decorating firms use it for a showcase house. Designers do the place up for publicity. People pay to go through it, and the proceeds go to a hospice service. Works out pretty well for everyone."

The Mustang's tires rumbled easily over a brick-paved drive edged with moss. Twenty cars were parked near the front entrance. Harry pulled in next to Alena's Lexus.

"Some place," Craig said. "Makes the houses I've seen around campus look like 7-Elevens. And I thought *they* were big."

Wilmington House was an overpowering sight: a massive Tudor with intricate stone and molding around a plethora of interesting windows, doors, and multiple roof lines. No single architectural line stayed a straight course for longer than twenty feet lest the eye become bored.

In the final hour of sunlight, countless gardens glowed in a saturation of pink-orange color. The front lawn, precisely trimmed and raked between hundred-year-old trees, appeared as a lush, rolling mattress of green.

Harry hiked up a dozen marble steps to the imposing front door, ignored the SORRY, THE SHOWHOUSE HAS CLOSED sign, and went in. Craig followed. Their footsteps were swallowed by a thirty-foot-high foyer. A monolithic chandelier sparkled bits of gold light against marble floors and cherry walls. Three arcs of circular stairs wound into the massive body of the home.

Harry had been here countless times with Alena during the showhouse planning stages and had never gotten used to its sheer size. The manpower necessary to construct it, not even considering the money, was unthinkable. Ultimately most impressive, however, was not the mammoth proportions, but the finite attention to detail put into every square foot.

Harry made his way toward laughter and music at the rear of the house. The celebration was in the music room, the original two-thousand-square-foot greenhouse that had been converted to passive-solar living space. Champagne corks popped like firecrackers. One of the artisan house painters tickled the ivories of a baby grand piano, leading an off-tune sing-along of an Elton John number.

"Hello, Harry." Cleo Lane, Interior Visions's owner, a stalwart woman of fifty-five, gave Harry a sweet champagne kiss on the cheek. Cleo was attractive because of her obvious strength, not in spite of it. "This is an incredible day for us thanks to Alena. I didn't even want to bid the job, as bad as things have been. And she goes out and gets it. Maybe I'm too old, Harry, what do you think?" The question was purely rhetorical. Cleo would never leave the company's helm, nor should she. "Armand would have loved her, you know. Loved her to death. It's too bad he didn't live to meet her, or see this day. Truly, *truly* our finest hour."

"You still have to do the work," Harry reminded fondly.

"Work, wonderful Harry, is easy. *Selling* is the bitch." She touched his hand. "Have fun, Harry. Get drunk. Everyone else is." Waving a long arm overhead as though casting confetti into slow-twirling Casablanca fans, she announced loudly, *"We'll be driven home in limos!"*

Revellers cheered.

"Harry!" Jeanna emerged from the partying throng and threw

◆ 115 ◆

her arms around him. She was the freest, most sincere woman Harry had ever known; "a few ticks past thirty-five," as she described her age, Jeanna's youthful playfulness was born of an exuberance for life, not a mask of emotional hurt. "I've got you all to myself. We're going to do nasty things, Harry." Jeanna's blouse was splashed with champagne, as was the front of her skirt. "Quick," she tried to pull him from the room, "before Alena catches us."

Harry laughed, resisting. "Where is she?"

"She's fled the country. I made her leave so I can have you to myself."

"Je-an-na," Harry warned, enunciating each syllable of her name.

"You're no fun!" She pushed him away in mock anger. "How come the only men who believe in fidelity are the ones I don't date? How come—my God, who's he?" She saw Craig, who had remained near the arched threshold, a bit intimidated by the older crowd. "I know I'm drunk, but I don't see double. He looks like you."

Harry motioned to him and Craig ambled over. "This's Craig—my brother's son."

"Oh . . . oh, God," Jeanna's voice turned quickly sad, "I'm sorry about your father—so sorry."

"It's okay."

Jeanna looked between them again. "You two *do* look alike. Hasn't anyone told you that?"

Craig said, "We haven't been around each other in a while."

"Actually," Jeanna said, continuing the comparison, "I think you're better looking." Craig was mildly embarrassed, more so when Jeanna put her arm around him. "And stronger." She butted his chest firmly with the heel of her palm, testing his pecs. "Harry, love, I don't know how to tell you this, but it's over between us. I'm in love with another man."

Unsure how to react, Craig put his arm loosely around Jeanna's waist.

"He's only twenty," Harry kidded, "watch yourself."

◆ 116 ◆

"I believe, counselor, sixteen is legal in this state." She led Craig into the melee of the party, a course he accepted somewhat awkwardly.

Harry smiled at his young nephew. "I won't leave without you."

Wrapping both arms around Craig, Jeanna announced, "Alena's upstairs, Harry, having a little dirty time with Loey, I suspect. I wasn't going to tell you, but who cares now."

When the Wilmington Showhouse rooms were originally assigned to decorators, Alena captured the prime appointment: the master bedroom. Not about to disappoint, she went all out, using her own money to exceed the budget Cleo set.

"Louis the Fourteenth's Opulent Decadence," she called it. The tower room was done in sultry reds and dark greens. The centerpiece was a raised verde-iron canopy bed that subliminally suggested a stage for indecent performances to be viewed through any of the dozen floor-to-ceiling windows covered only in sheer lace.

The room's intent was so bold that around the office the decorators had coined the phrase, "going to do a little Loey," when anticipating an amorous night.

By the time Harry climbed the stairs to the fourth floor, the concerns of his day became partially submerged by the overwhelming anticipation of Alena. She was like a sweet narcotic, concealing in a haze all that which he sought to avoid.

Harry opened the heavy wood door and looked inside. Sunset's blush pressed through lace curtains of the west windows, casting long rose rectangles of light across the raised bed.

Easing into the room, he looked for Alena.

"Don't turn around, Harry." She spoke quietly from behind him. "Just walk over to the bed . . . and let me watch you undress."

He smiled. Walking slowly from her, he pulled his shirt from his pants and unbuttoned it.

"That's it," she whispered softly, "do it slow . . . nice and slow."

His shirt came off . . . he stepped from tasseled loafers . . . unbuckled the Coach belt . . .

◆ 117 ◆

"You've got a nice back, Harry. Nice shoulders."

. . . he pushed down his pants, taking off a sock in the same motion that freed each pants leg . . .

"Only one thing left, lover . . ." Alena sighed. "Mmm, let's see it . . . that nice ass. Oh, yeah, Harry," she muttered obscenely. "I've got you now. Turn around . . . slow . . . and let me see you . . . let me see—oh, yeah, look at you, Harry. Look at you!" Alena was already naked. Leaving the bedroom door open, she came for him. "Maybe," she warned, glancing at heavy cording draped over the canopy bed, "you better hang onto something."

"I was thinking you could do that." He pressed against her, his erection rubbing her stomach as they kissed.

"Should I?" she whispered. "You want to tie me up?"

"Not exactly." His tongue slipped into her mouth, tasted champagne, and withdrew. "I was thinking of something more . . . athletic."

"Mmm-hmm . . ."

He boosted her up three steps to the bed platform and had her grip the top arch of the sturdy iron canopy. "This is the tricky part." He slipped his hands under her ass and lifted her.

Alena cried with surprise.

"Hold on," he grinned.

"I'm holding!"

He supported her legs as though she was sitting on his shoulders, only doing it backwards. The fuzz of her pubic hair brushed softly against his mouth. "Maybe," he suggested, before pressing forward with his tongue, "you better hold on tighter."

"You're feeling guilty about having a good time—I can tell."

Harry poured Alena more champagne from an open bottle on the liquor cart, sticking to Coke for himself. They stood away from the crowd in the music room. "It's been a strange few days."

"I'm glad you came." She kissed him. "It wouldn't be right for you not to be here. This celebration has as much to do with you as me."

"Not really."

"I'm not naive, Harry, I know Sam Giardino had something to do with us getting this job."

"Don't underestimate yourself."

Alena sipped champagne and considered that. "I hope you're right." Changing the subject, she observed, "Party's quieting down. Gone from that rowdy drunk stage to just plain drunk. But not Cleo. Look at her." Alena was full of admiration.

Interior Visions's majestic owner, her posture erect and powerful, continued to circulate among her employees and guests. She was a mother *and* father figure, at once calculating and compassionate. When she took over the company fifteen years earlier, after her husband Armand's death, she had never made a single business decision; since then, she had made thousands, most of them correct.

"She's as drunk as the rest of us—*most* of us—she just refuses to show it."

Cleo caught them watching and strode directly over, champagne glass in one hand, cellular phone in the other. She wore an expensive Vittadino dress, attractive and businesslike. "Are you plotting my overthrow, Alena?" she asked with fond regard. "The troops would likely fall in behind you tonight."

Without releasing Harry's arm, Alena kissed Cleo's cheek. "It's a great party, Cleo. *You're* great."

"Notice," Cleo commented to Harry, "how she avoided answering my question."

"Because it doesn't deserve an answer," Alena said. "The day you're not running the company, I'm out the door."

Cleo's deep blue eyes, sparkling a bit from champagne, glowed with appreciation. She did not demand unquestioning loyalty, but certainly appreciated it. "Your nephew is a handsome boy, Harry. He seems very nice."

"I haven't seen him for an hour—and I'm afraid to go looking. I told Jeanna he was only twenty."

"Twenty." Cleo recited the age with amazement. "What any of us wouldn't give to be twenty . . . and how little those who are appreciate it."

"Today's as young as you're ever going to be, Cleo."

Cleo groaned. "Get him something stronger to drink, Alena. Harry's turning into a Hallmark card."

An hour later, most of the guests were shuttled home in taxis, summoned and paid for by Cleo. Craig and Jeanna eventually found their way back to the music room, arm in arm, Jeanna admonishing Harry, "Don't give me that look, we just talked."

Craig offered a boyish smile that reminded Harry of times past. Maybe a little of the old Craig was left after all.

"We should get going." Harry checked his watch; it was closing in on midnight.

When Craig didn't object, Harry was certain he and Jeanna *had* gone to bed; Craig was too interested in Jeanna to leave without a struggle if any sexual tension was left to be spelled out.

"Call me," Jeanna told Craig, kissing him goodbye.

Oh, yeah, Harry thought, they've definitely gone to bed; a suspicion Alena echoed, whispering her goodbye kiss to Harry's ear: "Looks like we weren't the only ones having a good time tonight."

Craig lingered at Jeanna's side.

Harry said, "Let's go, kid."

"He's no kid, Harry. He hasn't been a kid for a long, long time. Kids aren't that good."

Craig blushed slightly.

"Bye, guys," Alena said, amused.

Craig followed Harry through the house. Most of the interior lights were off, making the expansive rooms seem even larger.

Outside, descending the front steps, Harry couldn't hold back. "Nice going, Craig. Real nice going. Jeanna, too. The big time."

Craig exhaled appreciatively. "She's great. I mean, she's . . . I don't know how to describe it."

"Experienced. And interested."

"No, not that way. We didn't screw."

Harry looked at him doubtfully as they got into the car.

"Really, we didn't. We messed around a little bit, but mostly, you know, we just talked. But it was incredible. Like she knew me already. Like we've been through some of the same things."

Craig's expression glowed under street lights as Harry turned onto Charles Street and drove north. "I felt for the first time in a long while somebody really gave a damn about me, and it's somebody I don't even know."

Harry felt caddish for assuming the only thing that could have put Craig in such a relaxed mood was sex, but that concern was soon displaced by another. He checked three times to be certain, but he *was* certain.

The car he thought had been following them earlier was back.

A brown sedan stuck close for a few miles, a few turns, then disappeared. Five minutes later, it returned, which meant he was being followed by two cars, maybe three, switching off to make their pursuit less obvious. Which meant it was the Feds. The county police didn't have that kind of manpower budget.

♦ 16 ♦

Back at Harry's apartment, Craig looked at photographs hung on the wall—black-and-white nature prints similar to those in Harry's office. "How come you don't have any pictures of your father?"

Harry tossed a spare pillow and blanket on the southwest-motif sofa. Craig was spending the night. "My dad was killed before I learned how to use a camera."

"You don't have any pictures? Even ones someone else took."

"No." Harry parted vertical blinds to check out the front window. There weren't any cars he didn't recognize as his neighbors', but with his building this far at the end of the complex, the cars tailing him wouldn't have to get close to watch him come and go: there was only one way out.

"You don't have *any* pictures?" Craig asked again. "None at all?"

Harry shook his head and gestured down the hall. "I'm going to call it a night. Help yourself to whatever you want."

"Tuck had pictures of him," Craig said, referring to his father for the first time without the *Ol'* precursor. "Pictures of the two of them together, and others with you and Grandma. You were at the beach, standing on the boardwalk in front of the Breakers."

Harry barely remembered the vacation, but knew the pictures. He had only been three or four at the time, which made Tucker thirteen or fourteen. It was probably the last time they went on vacation as a family. Soon after, his father stopped venturing that far away from the city or his new client, Sam Giardino. Giardino became Jack Walsh's family.

"Tuck had a whole book of pictures of him, a lot from before you were born, I guess. Some with Tuck at Little League games. Your

♦ 122 ♦

father had on a baseball cap in one of them. It looked kind of funny on him."

"Dad didn't look good in hats."

"Tuck also had newspaper clippings in this book. When your dad started getting his name in the paper for representing, you know, mob people. It was like Tuck was proud of him, but then there was a long gap in dates on the newspapers . . . until the one where he was shot. That page was just stuck in there."

Harry couldn't imagine his brother keeping a scrapbook of their father's life.

"Tuck came into my room one night, real pissed, and asked if I'd been going through his things. I said no, what was he talking about, but I knew he meant the pictures. He was mad that I'd seen them. I looked for them a couple days later and they were gone. I never saw them again."

Harry understood Craig was asking a question—what happened to make Tucker react that way? Harry didn't have an answer.

Tuesday morning, Harry showered, shaved, and fixed himself a poppy-seed bagel, which he ate on the back porch. His activity didn't awaken Craig, who slept the deep slumber of youth, snoring quietly in a contorted position on the sofa.

By eight, Harry was out the door, careful *not* to look for evidence that whoever had tailed him had moved closer to his apartment. It had been a while since he'd been placed under surveillance, and the feeling, while uncomfortable and aggravating, was one he adjusted to like the return of chronic pain.

The first time he had been tailed was by the FBI. Outraged, he'd confronted them; when they wouldn't roll down the window, even on a ninety-two-degree day, he'd slammed his fist on the roof of the dark cruiser until the two white-shirted men drove off.

When Harry had related the incident, Sam Giardino thought it funny. "Just like your papa," he'd said. "A hothead. That's what I liked about your papa, Sonny. That inner rage and determination. But you can't let it control you. *You* have to control the rage, store it for the right moment, then you unleash it like a torrent and put your enemy on his knees."

For Jack Walsh, that "torrent" was cut loose in the courtroom. The first time Harry watched his father try a case, his heart felt as though it would burst from his chest. Harry had only known his father as a mild-mannered, easy-going man, a dad who could wink while offering a white lie about an ice cream parlor catching fire. In court, Jack Walsh was the meanest man Harry had ever seen, and it scared him.

Jack's typically quiet voice roared with accusation, cross-examining a police officer. He called the cop a liar and picked at details in his story, hitting hard on seemingly minor points that gradually combined specks of inconsistency into such a large thundercloud of doubt that the policeman's credibility was destroyed. And Jack Walsh won.

After court, Jack Walsh took Harry's hand to help him through a crowd in the hall, and felt how cold his son's fingers had become from fear. "It's just how court works," he explained softly. "It's nothing to be frightened of."

"But that was a policeman," Harry said, recalling lessons in school about respect for men in blue.

"There are a lot of good policemen," Jack Walsh told his nine-year-old, "and some bad policemen. No one group of people are all good or all bad. And it's my job in court to make sure the bad policemen don't lie. That policeman you saw today is a liar. And he's a thief. And he's not the only one."

Vaguely reassured, Harry went with his father to Burke's for lunch and tried to wash away lingering uneasiness with a root beer served in a frosted mug.

Harry spent an hour in his office dictating on the day's files and making phone calls; most of the time was wasted rehashing medical bills with a paranoid insurance adjuster who thought every personal injury claim was fraudulent and every medical bill severely inflated. Thanks to TV-advertising lawyers who made having an auto accident sound akin to winning the lottery, it was becoming next to impossible to get realistic compensation for a legitimate plaintiff.

At 9:20, Harry headed down the steps, and mouthed, "Circuit Court," to Marcie who, on the phone, nodded okay.

Harry gave a cursory left/right glance along the street before turning toward the courthouse. He didn't see any suspicious sedan—hadn't seen anyone trailing him from his apartment either. Either they'd been called off or were concealing themselves unusually well. In due time he would find out what they wanted.

Heading down the block, Harry began to perspire. The humidity hinted at the commencement of steaming dog days: high temperatures and blank white skies; the sort of weather that caused his phone to ring late at night with calls from clients who'd snapped under the heat and let aggressions—and fists—fly.

Those waiting to pass through security into the courthouse slung jackets over their shoulders and fanned their faces with files or court notices. Harry showed his pass and avoided the delay.

He checked the docket and found SHOWELS, RONALD - WRIT. Courtroom #7, Judge Abbott.

Nyle Abbott was one of the youngest judges on the bench, and considered an outsider. He hadn't risen through the ranks of the county bar association, but had received his appointment from the Governor for a decade of excellent work in the U.S. Attorney's Office. Although clearly capable and learned, Abbott's appointment had been fought by most of the locals because he wasn't "one of the boys"; he hadn't accumulated or wasted favors through years of practicing alongside those he would soon rule over. Nyle Abbott, as a judge, was a clean slate, and for the carousers and bullshitters who relied upon the sharp edges of friendship to win cases, Abbott was not a welcome sight.

When Harry reached Courtroom 7 and opened the door, instead of finding a repeat of yesterday's judicial fracas, he found an empty room.

"Postponed, Harry." Lenny Beck, a retired police sergeant turned court bailiff, had been on his way to lock the door when Harry walked in.

"Why?"

"Ask Gesser. It was at his request. Judge Abbott asked when he wanted it reset . . ." Beck cocked his shaved head ". . . Gesser said he'd like to leave it open."

"Who's got the case for the State?"

"Tommy Birchette."

"Anybody with him?"

"Frank Trammell, that was it."

"They didn't object to the postponement?"

"Tell you the God's truth, Harry, they looked relieved."

"What about Gesser?"

"He was in here eight-thirty this morning to meet with the judge before court—didn't look like he'd slept all night." Beck laughed. "Hell, he even had a hair out of place."

The Towson Commons Tower shared a multilevel garage with its companion shopping mall. Permit parking occupied the top three decks. On the middle reserved level, Harry located the red late-model Mercedes 560SEL. He committed to memory the window sticker's five-digit ID, then retreated to an enclosed stairwell and headed to ground level. At the exit kiosk, Harry approached a serious black man in a guard's uniform.

The man looked up from his clipboard.

". . . up on level four, some kid just ran a key down the door of a red Mercedes."

"Shit." The man angrily slapped down his clipboard. "You get a look at him?"

"Not really. White kid, sixteen, maybe, had a baseball cap on backwards. Carrying a skateboard."

The guard slid open the kiosk door.

"I got the parking permit number off the Mercedes's windshield if you need to let the owner know."

The guard jotted down the numerals Harry recited, compared them to a master list, then picked up the phone. Dialing, he mumbled, "Red Mercedes . . . *shit.*"

* * *

Harry watched from inside the stairwell as Mark Gesser and the guard re-examined the high-gloss finish of Gesser's car. Gesser was notably relieved; the guard also, but he was clearly puzzled why someone would have given him a false report.

This ploy may have been unnecessary—Harry was yet to detect anyone following him today—but he had wanted to make sure what was about to occur happened without witnesses.

When the guard departed for the elevators, Gesser remained by his car, checking the Mercedes's side panels from every conceivable angle to make sure no potential nick went undetected. Maybe it was due to concern that his precious car had been dinged, but Gesser did not look his usual well-coiffed self today. His finely tuned persona looked to be striking a few sour notes.

He was still examining his car, very intent, when Harry approached him from behind, and said firmly, "Let's take a ride."

· 17 ·

A re you threatening me?" Mark Gesser's bloodshot eyes darted side to side. Harry's rumored association with Sam Giardino, generally written off as so much supposition, suddenly seemed less fabricated.

"Get in the goddamned car. It's about your client."

"What about him?"

"Get in the goddamned car before someone sees us and figures I'm feeding you the State's case."

"What's going on?"

"Open the goddamned car!"

"All right, all right." Gesser fumbled with his keys and unlocked the driver's door; the passenger door unlocked simultaneously.

Harry got in.

Gesser kept his door open and leaned away from Harry as though preparing to escape. His voice worked hard to conceal tremors of nerves. "If this is because Ron Showels is charged with shooting your brother, I'm reporting you to the Ethics Commission."

Harry took a calculated gamble. "I'm not sure he did it."

"What?"

"I don't think your client did it."

"What do you know? Who've you been talking to?"

"I can't tell you . . . directly."

When Gesser's expression lit with intrigue, Harry knew he had him. Gesser thought he was Woodward *and* Bernstein, and Harry was Deep Throat. Harry said, "You can't find your alibi witness, can you? That's why you postponed the hearing this morning."

"I've got three PIs on it. We've been up all night for Christ's sake."

◆ 128 ◆

"Trammell can't find her either. And they're probably looking harder than you."

"Do you know where she is? Do your contacts know?"

"Not yet," Harry ad-libbed, thinking, *Gesser, you schmuck, no one can find her because she doesn't exist. Your guy made her up. They all do. If you'd handled a few criminal cases you'd realize that.*

Gesser said, "I've got the bar staked out where Ron met her, but the bartender said he'd never seen her before, so we're trying to run down the other regulars to see if they know her. I also had an artist do a composite sketch we're taking around. We've been checking the local hotels, thinking she's from out of town."

"Your man spent the night with her and doesn't know where she's from?"

"She didn't say." Gesser wiped his forehead. "Christ, it's hot." He started the car and turned on the air conditioning. Within moments, cool air blasted through the vents. "Ron says she only wanted to talk about him. She said she was 'looking to forget herself for the night.' "

"That's pretty convenient."

"Pretty *lucky* for a guy like my client. Poor Ron . . ." Gesser shook his head, regaining confidence ". . . Christ, I've known this guy six years, Harry, since he first started having trouble with his wife—and she's cuckoo, I tell you. He's always had *real* bad luck with women. He's not that attractive, still, his luck . . . One time, *once*, I swear to Christ, he calls one of these escort services. About two years ago. His wife's driving him nuts, so he needs a little breather. A woman from the service shows up, he tried to get to bed with her, offers money when she hesitates . . . and you know what? Turns out she's a cop. Busts him for solicitation. Charges got dropped, I expunged his record, but it's that kind of thing. A few months later, he had a new secretary. They're working late closing some loans, just the two of them. It's been a long day so he asks if she wants to go out for dinner after. They do, she gets a little drunk, so does he, he makes a pass at her, they fool around—consensual sex, *no question*—but the next day she quits and files a sexual harassment suit. Turns out her boyfriend found out she was with Ron and put her up to it. I got that dismissed, too, but you see what I'm talking about, bad luck? *Now,* he spends the night with this woman and comes home high as a kite and gets popped for a murder he doesn't know a damned thing about."

Gesser told a plausible story, but that was the difference between winning cases and losing them.

Harry said, "What about the gun?"

"The gun?" Gesser made that sound preposterous. "Have you seen the ballistics?"

"No."

"State won't produce the test. You know what I think happened? I think that bitch wife of Ron's and Suicide Sheila had Ron followed. They see him with this other woman and figure to do a screw job on him. Sheila gets someone to call in an anonymous tip, probably that fag secretary of hers, and a very eager bunch of cops jump on the first lead they get. Ron ends up smeared in the press and will have to admit he was with another woman to prove his alibi. Only now it's working better than either of those two bitches could have expected because we can't find the goddamned alibi!" Gesser continued to sweat despite the air conditioning. "I'm telling you, Harry, Ron Showels did not kill your brother. I doubt he can even fire a gun. I know this guy. I'm telling you straight. He didn't do it. You want to help find the person who did, you'll get everyone you know looking for this woman. *Everyone* you know."

Harry left his impromptu meeting with Mark Gesser more unsettled than he would have ever anticipated. His goal had been to get involved with the case through the back door. Since the State was cutting him off him from their end, he had chanced conning Gesser to let him see the defense side. The ploy was a risky one, but Harry had to know what it was about Ronald Showels's arrest that was so disturbing.

He'd been looking for a small detail, the golden loophole so often sought and rarely grasped. According to Gesser, however, it wasn't a slight defect, it was an obvious flaw: Frank Trammell had yanked the wrong guy.

Ballistics, Harry thought. He had to see the ballistics results. Tierny said the gun found in Showels's car was a match, but had she *seen* the test result, or merely been told of it?

And motive. There was *always* a motive—a reason for pulling the trigger.

Harry wondered if the people following him last night had a theory. Why else would they be following *him* unless they suspected he fit into the plot? Special Agent Hemingway said Tucker was investigating something for ATF that had to do with Sam Giardino. Maybe Tucker had gotten too close to something. And now he was dead, killed very much execution style. Six shots to the head. But, Harry wondered, if he was a suspect, where were they late this morning?

He walked back to the office for his car and took the Mustang out for a circuitous drive. He stopped for coffee at a 7-Eleven, then crossed roads and pulled in for gas five miles later. Still unable to pick out a tail on him, he headed out a lonely stretch of Dulaney Valley Road to hit a quick bucket of balls at the driving range.

After, his shirt sleeves rolled up, having broken a very mild sweat, he put the clubs back in his trunk, and scanned the open parking lot. If they were there, they were very good.

Harry rapped on the screen door, alerting George Kittle.

Connie's father stood at the foot of the stairs checking his watch. He was not happy to see Harry. His jaw pushed back and forth as though chewing mean words he was about to spit out. "Plane leaves in two hours," he yelled up the stairs. Saying that, he glared at Harry as though having just announced checkmate.

When George Kittle didn't open the screen door, Harry let himself in. A trio of suitcases sat against the sofa. Two were part of a matched set; the third was not.

"She's going to Orlando with us." Connie's father dared Harry to object.

"What about the kids?"

"They can do whatever they want. They want to come down, I'll buy them a ticket. Right now, who knows, seeing as we can't find either of them."

"Craig stayed with me." Harry's tone was defensive and he immediately regretted sounding as though he and George Kittle were fighting over Tucker's family.

Connie came hurriedly down the stairs, breathless by the time she reached the bottom step. Her eyes were frightened and panicky. When she saw Harry, she froze as though caught in a crime.

"Let's go, Esther," George called up the stairs.

Harry said, "You're leaving?"

"I just told you she was," her father cut in.

"It's all right, Dad," Connie said. "I have to get away for a while, Harry." She brushed back blown-dry hair with an unsteady hand. "I need to think. Get myself together." Her entire body seemed to be trembling.

"I wish we could talk before you go."

"I'll be okay." She couldn't stand still.

George Kittle grabbed the banister and leaned forward. "Come on, Esther!" he bellowed, adding a grumbling, "Goddamnit," as he checked his watch again.

Harry took Connie's hand. Her skin was like ice.

"I'm all right," she assured, withdrawing from his touch. "I just keep seeing him, Harry. He's everywhere in the house. But he's not. I can't be here by myself. I'll go crazy, I know I will."

"You should see someone, Connie. Talk to Alena. Let her get you the name of—"

She shook her head rapidly. "I just need to be away for a while. For a rest. Things have been hectic for so long. So tense. I just can't take it anymore."

"What about Craig and Carla?"

Connie's expression turned almost wild with desperation. "What about them! They're *never here*. And Craig attacked Dad yesterday!"

"That's not true."

◆ 132 ◆

"The hell it's not!" George Kittle stuck out his forearm as though mortally wounded, displaying a faint bruise along the underside of his wrist. "That's what the bastard did to me!"

Harry assumed Connie's father was taking a blood thinner for hypertension; otherwise there would have been no mark. "You tried to punch him, George. He let you smack him once—"

"Enough!" Connie screamed, covering her ears. "I can't take it, Harry! Please . . . *please!*" She looked ready to cry, only there were no more tears. She faced away from him, arms crossed tightly, looking up the stairs through painted balusters.

Harry felt his presence torturing her. "I'll take care of the kids . . . until you get back." He added those final four words as a hopeful afterthought; in truth, he didn't think she was coming back.

Craig was awake, reading a law textbook delegated to provide bookcase ballast, when Harry returned to his apartment.

"Your mother's going to Florida with your grandparents."

"Shit."

"You and Carla can go down if you want. Your grandfather says he'll pay for the tickets."

"Forget it," Craig snapped.

Harry desperately wanted Craig back in last night's good mood. "Why don't you take a shower and shave and we'll have lunch. There's someone I want you to meet."

They drove into the city with the top up and air conditioner running, because, Harry told Craig, he wanted him looking presentable, not a sweaty mess. Harry hoped that didn't sound too fatherly; if it did, Craig didn't object.

Harry liked being with his nephew again. It was different, a little awkward, but at its core that powerful bond he'd first felt when Craig was a boy remained; a feeling Harry hadn't had for anyone other than his father. It was too bad he was distracted from that fine sensation halfway into the city. The team of alternating sedans was following him again.

◆ 133 ◆

.18.

Vazinni's maitre d', Giorgi, a barrel-chested man of fifty-five with a full head of dark hair, was as well-armed as he was accommodating. Opening the door to greet Harry and Craig, he observed the brown sedan pull along the street and gave Harry a nod that said, *I see them.*

As they were escorted through the busy dining room, Harry knew cameras were whirling from third floor windows overhead. The car—more likely, *cars*—that had followed him were being photographed. By the time espresso was served, Harry would know who they were.

Craig grinned expectantly as Giorgi led them down the narrow hall, past the active kitchen. Despite Craig's persistence, Harry had refused to divulge who they were meeting. Likely, Harry thought, Craig was hoping for dancing girls, a wild harem scene from a college fantasy.

When Giorgi rapped twice on the door before opening, Craig tried to peek inside for a preview. The empty room changed his eager expression to disappointment, but when Sam Giardino walked in from the brick-walled garden holding six clipped roses in gloved hands, Craig stopped in place. He'd seen enough newspaper photos to know the man by sight.

Sam Giardino, blinking the sun's brightness from his eyes, focused questioningly on Craig, then beamed with pleasant surprise. "It's Tucker's boy," he announced to Giorgi. "That's who this is. Look at the size of this boy." Giardino handed the roses to Giorgi and removed thick garden gloves.

Craig stood half a foot taller than Giardino, but appeared dwarfed by him. The presence of age and experience towered over raw naiveté.

"Big boy." Giardino's smile broadened as he clapped strong hands above Craig's elbows. His exhilaration caused his voice to push through scarred nasal passages with a harsh rasp. "What a wonderful surprise. Jack Walsh's grandson!" Giardino released Craig and turned to hug Harry. "This is a wonderful surprise, Sonny. Magnificent. A tremendous treat. Tremendous." Giardino gestured for them to sit at the square table covered with red linen.

The private room was lit entirely by natural light spilling in from the garden; muted reflections of sunshine splashed across pale walls.

Giardino had "moved into" Vazinni's shortly after the murder of Harry's father. The one-time rowhouse in Baltimore's Little Italy section, previously gutted and remodelled for transition into a seventy-five-seat restaurant, had been further renovated for Sam Giardino. A window wall overlooking the small backyard garden was replaced by the same bulletproof glass that protected presidents. Dark-green English ivy was planted and run along trellises to conceal piercing barbed wire coiled atop the garden's twelve-foot brick wall.

Though substantial in nature, the improvements were made unobtrusively, allowing the restaurant to conduct business as usual for a steady clientele of legitimate business people and tourists who made the trip from the more populated Inner Harbor.

Giorgi ran the large white roses—Concetta's Innocence— through a thorn clipper and placed them in a crystal vase on the table.

"All these years," Giardino exclaimed, "I wait to meet the grandson of the man who saved my life. I am *honored.*" He sat with his back to a solid wood wall which was reinforced with steel between sections of two-by-fours. The garden was to his right, the entrance door left.

Giardino noticed Craig looking at him oddly because of his voice, so he smiled and hit his own nose hard with the butt of his hand—a similar trick to that he'd played on Harry many years ago.

Craig flinched.

◆ 135 ◆

Giardino laughed. "It's just there for decoration—doesn't serve any useful purpose."

Craig was embarrassed.

"And these . . ." Having fun with the boy, Giardino offered his missing fingertips. ". . . I lost grinding meat. Other than that," Giardino grasped the sides of the table, "all my parts are in working order." He banged the underside of the table with his knee as though able to do that with an erection.

Craig didn't understand at first, then laughed, put at ease.

"These kids, Sonny," Giardino told Harry, "you gotta give them time to catch on. They're slow."

Harry was pleased to have made him so happy.

Giardino continued to study Craig. He spoke slowly, as though admiring classic artwork. "This's a good looking boy, Sonny . . . Looks like you and his grandfather." Giardino's mouth tightened suddenly. "You got Jack's eyes, don't you, son?" That quickly, Giardino's eyes began to water. "I miss your grandfather. He was a great man."

"I don't know much about him." Craig spoke timidly.

"Your grandfather and your father . . ." Giardino made a deflecting gesture as he unfolded a linen napkin ". . . sometimes this happens between fathers and their sons. What should be a wonderful union becomes a battleground. But how wonderful your grandfather would feel to see you today. Jack would love this boy, Sonny. He'd love the two of you so much." A single tear fell across Giardino's cheek. "Ahh, look at me, a sobby old man." He wiped perspiration and tears from his face with a wide brush of napkin.

Harry hoped Giardino was right: that his father would be proud.

Craig wasn't sure what to make of the side dish of linguini served with the veal piccata; there was no tomato sauce.

"It's in garlic and oil," Harry said.

"Oh." Craig didn't want to seem impolite, still, garlic and oil? "I better not."

"He's afraid of indigestion," Giardino appraised, eating zestfully. "Not used to Italian food. Like his grandfather at first. Raised on canned spaghetti with dehydrated garlic. Prison food. *Real* garlic won't do that to you. Here, look." Giardino fished a half clove of garlic saturated in virgin olive oil from strands of al dente linguini. He dipped a hunk of thick crusted bread in the oil, then wrapped the moist dough around the garlic and popped it in his mouth, chewing as though in ecstasy. "Italian candy."

Craig braced himself as though preparing to dive into icy water. He stuck his fork to the midst of oily pasta and began to twirl; eventually Craig managed to induce a small portion of pasta onto his fork—Giardino refused to let him cut the linguini into bite-size pieces, feigning heart failure at Craig's suggestion. Craig enjoyed the dish enough to eat half but, after four slices of veal and lots of warm bread, couldn't force down another bite. "That was really good."

Giardino said, "We'll get him some calamari next time."

"I'm up for anything." Craig was enthusiastic over the celebrity-level attention Giardino was paying him.

"Calamari it is," Giardino confirmed. "Next week we'll get together again."

"Great."

"This's a good kid, Sonny. A good boy." Giardino removed the napkin from his shirt collar. "But, son, if you'll excuse your uncle and me for a few minutes, we have some business to talk about."

"Sure, yeah." Craig pushed back from the table, very eager to please. "I can, um, take a walk for a while, whatever."

"I don't want you out on the street just now. Why don't you let Giorgi show you downstairs. We got all sorts of pinballs and videos down there. Costs you nothing to play."

"Great."

As though cued, Giorgi opened the door and greeted Craig with a smile. "Got your flipper fingers ready, kid? I'll challenge you."

Going out the door, Craig said, "I'm better at the video games than pinball . . ."

Giorgi slapped his back. "Whatever you want."

When the door closed, Giardino waited a few moments, then, in a much less celebratory tone, said, "It's ATF outside. *Three* cars."

"I figured as much."

"Goddamned federal boys got so much money they don't know who to harass next."

"I don't know why they think I'm worth following."

"They don't need a reason, they just do it. Like going fishing. Who knows when you might catch something, forget how much bait you waste when there's no fish."

A knock on the door preceded a waitress bringing in espresso. Her delivery was efficient and without conversation. Once she left, Giardino continued, "You called yesterday, Sonny—something wrong?"

Harry sat forward, elbows of his white shirt on the table. "I'm not sure, but a lot's happened since then."

"So tell me."

Harry filled Giardino in on Showels's bail hearing; that Tierny Wells had been taken off the case for stetting Jennifer Mulcaney's charges; and that Mark Gesser believed his client's innocence.

"Sonny . . ." Giardino began, ". . . you can't be surprised by any of this, especially by the State Attorney blocking you out. You're on the *other* side. You're *not* a prosecutor. You can't be."

"But I don't want them to screw up, and I've got this bad feeling they're going to."

"They screw up all the time. They're the *government.* The government can make a thousand mistakes, any of which gets you or me fired, but the government *can't* be fired. It goes on forever, getting worse and worse." Giardino sipped espresso. "You have to let them do their job, Sonny, and you do your job. You can't be partners with the State Attorney."

"I understand, but if this case is blown . . ."

"Sonny . . ." Giardino's tone drew a firm line ". . . why are you involving yourself like this? You think finding who killed your brother brings your papa back? If that were true, I'm with you—a *hundred* percent. But this has nothing to do with what happened before. The police never found out who shot your father, but *I* know who shot him. *I* took care of it, but not by running to the police." Giardino looked closely at Harry. "Is *that* what you think

◆ 138 ◆

you're going to do, Sonny? You think *you're* going to get whoever did it?"

Harry didn't answer.

"Don't get in this case any deeper, Sonny, because maybe you can't finish it."

"He's my brother."

"Who you barely knew . . . who you talked to how many times the last ten years?"

"That's not the point. He's my family—"

"No." Giardino firmly thrust the air with a single finger. "He was *related* to you. But he left your family when he broke your papa's heart and ran to Canada. You don't know how that hurt him, Sonny. You were too young. Your brother left to try to devastate your papa, and he was almost successful. And he did this without concern for you or your mother." Giardino grew angry. "A goddamned *hypocrite*, that boy. You don't know the things he got into when he was a kid. He got into trouble like most teenagers, like you almost got into but you knew I'd have beaten your ass. Only when heat came down around your brother, all his lying, he blamed your papa. Because Jack was my lawyer gave your brother the right to do whatever he wanted—so he thought. He wouldn't stand up and face the punishment he deserved. He ran."

"What are you talking about?"

"It's over. You don't need to know."

"How can you say that? This is *my family.*"

"Sonny, your family is you and that boy downstairs and his sister. Your papa, God rest his soul, is dead. Your mother and brother are dead. I promised your father I would watch over you until the day I died, but I can't do *everything*. Don't get involved in something I can't get you out of."

"You know what happened to Tucker, don't you?"

"No."

"Then how do you know it's something you can't get me out of?"

"I don't. Maybe it's nothing. Maybe the police have the right man, maybe they don't. What I'm saying, Sonny, is if there's more to it than it seems, if Tucker got himself into something again—"

◆ 139 ◆

"Got into what again?"

"Don't make me break my promise to your father."

Harry summoned the courage to do something he'd never before attempted: to challenge Giardino. "You know, don't you? Who killed him?"

"No." Giardino held eye contact, unwavering. "Do you believe what I tell you, Sonny?"

"I want to."

That was the wrong answer.

"It hurts me, Sonny, that I've lost your trust. After all these years."

"You haven't lost my trust. Not at all. But you're keeping something from me—you don't deny that, do you?"

"No."

"I respect your desire to protect me, but I want to know what's going on. If it had something to do with what happened between my father and Tucker."

Somberly, Sam Giardino said, "Sonny, I promised your father—the man who died for me . . . I can't let anything happen to you."

"And if I find out what happened to Tucker something could happen to me? That's what you're saying?"

"Sonny, when people go where they don't belong they get into trouble. Why would you take that chance? You have a lovely girlfriend, maybe you'll have a family of your own one day. You don't take a risk that outweighs the return. That's all I'm telling you."

·19·

On the drive back to the county, Craig spoke admiringly about Sam Giardino until realizing Harry had nothing to say in response.

"It's business," Harry said, belatedly excusing his shift in mood; thinking how ironic it was that he could outline a complex criminal case for a jury of strangers, but couldn't offer more than nebulous explanation to his nephew. "I've got to take care of some things this afternoon. I'll call tonight. We need to tell Carla what's going on with your mom."

"I'll let her know. She'll be cool about it."

Harry nodded. Later, in front of Tucker's house, he said, "Touch base with me so I know what you're doing, all right?"

"Message on your machine okay, or you want me to page you?"

"Either's fine."

Craig began to swing his legs out, but stopped. He leaned back and put an arm around Harry, hugging him much as Giardino had. "I had a great lunch. Thanks a lot."

Kids, Harry realized, were expected to accept the temperament of their elders without explanation, while having to justify every downturn of their own feelings in infinite detail to parents worried about drug abuse and teenage suicide. Was that really fair?

Craig looked back from the front door and waved before entering the house.

Harry waved back and pulled abruptly from the curb. He was angry at Sam Giardino for withholding information on the basis of undefined good cause, and he was mad at himself for allowing Giardino to manipulate him. He took out harsh feelings on the Feds following him.

He took three abrupt turns, ran a red light, and, two miles later, congratulated himself for leaving a trio of ATF cars in the dust.

◆ 141 ◆

Even if it was a minor victory—they'd find him at his office or apartment soon enough—knowing they'd be speculating as to why he'd thrown their tail was perverse pleasure.

Back at the office, a handful of phone messages and a fax were stuffed in Harry's slot. The fax was from ASA Tierny Wells; it was a copy of her resumé to which she'd applied a Post-It note before transmission. The note read boldly: I QUIT.

"Make sure to call Alena," Marcie reminded as Harry started up the stairs. "She said it was important."

"All right." Harry scanned his phone messages and checked the FedEx package on his desk to find overdue answers to interrogatories from a nasty divorce case he was sorry he'd taken. Maryland law had finally modernized past the nineteenth century to allow for no-fault divorce, but there was still no such thing as a "no-lose" case. Usually, it was an "all-lose" situation.

"Call Alena," Marcie reminded again through the speakerphone.

"Doing it now." Harry speed-dialed Interior Visions. There weren't any whoops of celebration from the designers' offices today; work and life were back to normal.

Alena picked up quickly and from her apprehensive tone, he knew something was wrong.

"Bad day?" he asked.

"I got a call about three hours ago from Mr. Giardino . . ."

Harry tensed; Alena shouldn't talk about him over the phone.

". . . he wants to schedule a meeting with Cleo and me, and . . . I'd like to talk to you about it first."

"You should have paged me, I was just in the city."

"I'll come out, but it might be late. We're swamped with the new job already. Some of the installation dates have been moved up and the contract has deadline charges if we're late. Cleo and I have been with the lawyers most of the day seeing if we can't make some revisions before signing."

"Let's meet halfway. How about Mount Washington? We'll get

◆ 142 ◆

something to eat, and late's okay. Say nine?"

"Chen's?"

"I'll call ahead so we can have the duck." Harry could tell Alena wanted to talk about whatever had come up right now, and the delay was frustrating her. "If you need to change the time, just call."

"Okay . . . but no duck. I don't think I'm going to be that hungry."

"A real treat," he said, trying to brighten the mood, "seeing you twice during the week."

"I love you, too."

"Bye." Harry hung up and thought how wonderful life could be if business didn't interrupt.

He opened his bottom drawer and lifted an empty file; beneath it was a black-and-white photograph he'd taken of Alena when they'd only known one another a month. She'd stood by the walk-out door of his apartment and dropped the robe she was wearing. Smiling coyly, she covered her breasts and bent her leg to partially conceal the triangle of her pubic hair. He'd been infatuated by her then and was even more so now.

He slid closed the drawer and walked to the window. One day they'd get out of here, away from business.

After an hour of dictation, Harry went back to the window and looked outside to see if his ATF shadows had caught up. He didn't see them, but was still looking when Marcie announced, "Tierny Wells," through the speaker.

Harry reached for the phone, but no lines were lit.

Marcie said, "Okay to send her up?"

"Sure."

Harry made certain he'd put away the picture of Alena as Tierny's light but determined footsteps ascended carpeted steps. Harry went into the hall and smelled a whiff of perfume before Tierny turned the corner.

"So this is private practice?" Tierny surveyed Harry's less-than-

◆ 143 ◆

glamorous accommodations. "You're right, it does look like you've turned away some clients. And I thought that was a self-serving sales pitch."

"You prosecutors are so jaded."

Tierny was without the usual touch of make-up, and her face shone slightly with perspiration. Her smile was forced to conceal worry.

Harry said, "I got your fax."

"How about that, huh? I walked right into Jacobs's office and tendered my resignation. I typed it up and laid it on his desk and said, 'See yah.' Just like that."

"And you were scared when he didn't try to change your mind?"

Tierny's shoulders drooped slightly. "Was he *that* glad to get rid of me?"

"Hardly. That's just how he does it. You can go into work tomorrow morning like it never happened if you want. You could probably go back next week without apologies. Ed's forgiving that way. He knows the job stinks and you have to blow off steam."

"I'm not going back." Tierny regained determination.

"Maybe you should tour a few more offices like mine before you decide."

Tierny pushed her fingertips into the center of a sofa cushion to see if it was as soft as it looked. "I think this set-up's fine, besides, it's time. I've got to move on." She gestured toward the window. "And you've got a view. It's nice."

But not what she expected, Harry guessed.

"Okay if I sit down? Am I keeping you from something?"

"Not at all."

"You're not going to stop being nice to me now that we're not dealing cases?"

Harry shook his head.

Tierny chose one of the round back chairs facing his desk. The sleeves of her loose-fitting blouse were rolled to her elbows; her checked skirt looked picnic-casual. "You know, Harry," she admitted awkwardly, "I want to apologize for flashing you last night in the dressing room. I don't know what the hell I was thinking about.

Actually, it was two vodka tonics that kept me *from* thinking."

"It was hardly offensive—certainly not pornographic by contemporary community standards."

"I haven't flirted with anyone since tenth grade and, well, it's stupid. You've got a fiancé and, actually, I guess that's why I did it. Because I knew you'd be safe, and wouldn't tell half the world about it. I've just been so jammed up from work the past few years . . ."

"I don't think you have to worry about turning too wild. And I won't tell anyone."

"I'm not worried about that . . . well, maybe I was worried a little." She crossed her arms. "Shit, I am *so* nervous about quitting this job. How come it seemed like the right thing to do this morning? Ed Jacobs yanked me off the case. I'm sick of his politics."

"You'll do fine. A big firm will jump at the chance to have you. You're an experienced litigator, a hard worker—"

"How much you want to bet Jacobs blackballs me as a reference? He'll tell people I was fired for nol prossing a mobster's case and I'm on the take."

"Then you'll sue him for slander and move to the islands with your damages."

"Damnit." Tierny tapped her middle finger rapidly against her elbow. "I would have nailed Showels, Harry. I'd have made that case. I *deserved* that case."

"I know." He let her seethe a few moments, then said, "I talked to Gesser this morning."

Tierny stopped her finger drumming. "You're kidding? Why?"

"I want to see his case."

"Christ, Harry, what'd he say? Did *he* talk?"

Harry nodded. "He thinks Showels is innocent."

"He's dreaming."

"Could be . . . Did you see the actual ballistics test on Showels's gun, or just the conclusions?"

"I had the whole thing. The gun's a match. Not only that, Trammell thinks he can track down the anonymous informant."

"How?"

◆ 145 ◆

"The caller said he saw Showels put Tucker's ticket book in a trash can at the race track—that's where he said he found it."

"Has it been turned in yet?"

"No, but that's not the point. Pimlico has security cameras all over the place, inside and out, and they keep the tapes. Trammell was down there first thing this morning, and he went back after the writ hearing was postponed. They've got Showels on tape at the track. He was there alone. Looking very skittish and betting big. Five hundred dollars a race minimum. He dropped four grand and change."

"Helluva hit."

"Tell me." Tierny ran her hand through her hair. "It was easy finding him at the betting windows. Now Trammell's going through the other tapes, trying to pick him up during the races. It's four hours of activity to cover, but they'll piece it together."

"They need Showels tossing out the ticket book, or carrying it around with him."

"They'll get it. You know, I was never a big Frank Trammell fan, but once you get past his ego—"

"No easy task."

"No, but he is damned good, Harry. If I had to bet, I'd say he'll find Showels dumping the ticket book. We have that, the jury will be hungry for him."

"Motive would still be nice. Why does he pull a gun and shoot six times?"

"He's got a history of violence against his wife," Tierny countered as though still prosecuting the case. "He blows up when he's angry. Maybe he was at the track the day before the incident and lost a few grand then, too. He's driving around mad when a policeman catches him for speeding. He's had all he can take, and he loses it."

"That's *real* thin. Besides, the shooting is at dawn. That's twelve hours after the track closed."

"So maybe he was at an all-night poker game."

"Gesser says his alibi witness will testify otherwise."

"Has he found her?"

"Not as of a few hours ago." Harry flipped absently through his phone messages as though rereading them. "Tell me something . . . how close are you to Tommy Birchette?"

"You mean can I keep getting information about how the State's case is going?" Tierny tilted her head side to side as though physically weighing the question, then nodded. "I think he'll tell me. He was against Jacobs pulling me off."

"He won't be suspicious of your interest?"

"I don't know. Tommy's pretty straight." Tierny tilted sideways and leaned her elbow on the chair arm. "So what's going on, Harry? Are you bringing me over to the other side? I'm out . . ." she checked her Timex ". . . five hours and already I'm doing defense work? Feeding Mark Gesser information?"

"No . . . I'll be the one doing that."

"Jesus, Harry, why? Showels killed your brother."

"You've got a lousy case without a motive . . . and if Gesser will give me Showels's motive . . . I'll give it to Tommy Birchette."

"That's *very* tainted evidence."

"Not if it comes from an anonymous informant."

"Jesus, Harry."

"If you don't want to do it, don't. I'll find another way."

"No . . ." Tierny considered him ". . . I'll do it. I'll do it," she repeated as though to quell her own disbelief.

"Whatever you find out, don't call on the phone, and don't come by here."

"And I thought *I* was being paranoid yesterday after a couple drinks."

"I *am* being followed."

"Trammell?"

"Alcohol, Tobacco, and Firearms. Three cars." Harry smirked. "I really rate."

"Are they out there now?" Tierny turned toward the window while leaning away from it. A rectangle of sunshine through the glass reached as high as her knees.

"They come and go."

"That would scare the shit out of me. What do they want?"

◆ 147 ◆

"Like I told you the other day, Agent Hemingway said Tucker was working a case for them . . . he said it had to do with Sam Giardino . . . but I don't know."

"I talked to Hemingway before Showels's bail hearing and he said they didn't have anything to help us."

"Maybe you should ask him again."

"Give me the phone." She held out her hand. "Here, give me the phone, I'll ask the son of a bitch."

"Not this phone." Harry took a quarter from his pocket. "There's a pay phone at the corner."

· 20 ·

Ronald Showels's wife's divorce attorney, Sheila Parks, earned her nickname "Suicide" two years out of law school when she walked into the management company of what was then the tallest office building in Towson and signed a lease for the most expensive corner of the penthouse. She hadn't tried a single Circuit-Court-level case when she put her name to a contract personally obligating her to what was, by current dollars, a ten-thousand-dollars-per-month rent.

The manager didn't want to authorize the lease, but said *maybe* he'd try her out for three months if she'd go to bed with him. In an era before such advances had even a hint of illegality attached to them, Sheila Parks left the office without a word and returned the next day with a cashier's check for the entire year.

Immediately making enemies for her aggressive tactics, Sheila found the mostly male Baltimore County Bar waiting hungrily for her to fail. Jokes abounded: Where can you find more balls than in the Orioles' equipment room? Between Suicide Sheila's legs.

The smug old boys used to walk the street in front of Sheila's building looking up, expecting her to throw herself from that top story window once her grandfather's trust fund—bravely staked on the year lease—was exhausted, and Sheila was broke.

On the twelfth month, they almost got their wish. Sheila's first year in private practice barely covered expenses. She was three months behind on her apartment rent. Her car had been repossessed. She had a dozen good personal-injury cases, but since those fees came at the end of the case and not before, her male opponents did all they could to postpone settlement, figuring they could force her to take less than the case was worth, or, better yet, put her out of business.

◆ 149 ◆

Sheila refused to sell her clients short, but started calling other attorneys in contemplation of turning over her cases to them, because she was thinking about getting out and cutting her losses.

She made an appointment with her building's new owner, and even as her hand turned the doorknob to enter his office, wasn't sure if she was about to cancel her lease option or try to negotiate a better rent. Word was the new owner was a bastard and raising rents through the roof.

When she walked in, the owner was all smiles. "Got your check," he said. "Nothing like a tenant that pays a whole year in advance, even if she does con me out of two months for free."

Sheila was stunned and searching for explanation when she noticed the other man in the owner's office, a man with a white rose in his lapel, who looked at her and in a frightening raspy voice, said, "You don't let those bastards beat you."

When she found out who he was, Sheila was afraid of what Sam Giardino wanted in return for guaranteeing her lease for another year, but all that was ever required was her signature on a note with interest at 17 percent. She signed the note and paid it off by year's end. Sam Giardino said it wasn't a favor, it was an investment. Seventeen percent was a good return on his money, and he knew she was going to make it.

She did. Five taller office buildings had been built in the area since, and Sheila moved to the top floor of each one. Her nickname took on a new turn, Suicide for her style in negotiations. She was steely and dealt with other lawyers as though they'd both jumped from an airplane at the same time, and the winner was the one who opened the parachute last—and survived.

Harry had clerked for her for two years while he was in law school. He'd been twenty-two; Sheila, thirty-three. He was there a year before they fell into a brief, torrid affair that flared like a comet and burned out, leaving Harry hurt, but not bitter, when she ended it. Sheila never for a moment considered he'd been in love with her.

* * *

Sheila Parks's inner office was bigger than Harry's entire apartment. Occupying a glass corner of Towson's most prestigious—and highest—building, her work and conference areas were sectioned only by the arrangement of antique furniture; there were no dividing walls. Two rolltop desks, expertly crafted to house computers, were for Sheila's paralegal duo: honor law students representing both the state's schools.

When Harry arrived at 6:15, Sheila was the only one in residence. "They're at bar review," she said of her assistants' empty work stations. "The February pass rate was sixty-two percent, so they figure theirs will be horrendous. They're probably right."

Sheila favored tailored Anne Klein suits in pale browns, bucking the trend for "jury blue." Her shoes were simple, but expensive, bought at Nordstrom for full price because good women's size 11's did not go on sale and the tall shops assumed women of height lacked taste.

She was a big-boned woman, and the approach to middle age had added a few pounds, but she held herself with a confident repose that didn't exaggerate her stature; unless, of course, she wanted to use her height to loom over shorter male attorneys and intimidate the hell out of them.

"I saw you in court yesterday." Sheila sat comfortably erect behind her massive desk, the top of which held numerous modern artifacts subliminally designed to make whoever was seated in Harry's spot feel as though before a firing squad. "You looked worried."

Despite the aggressive artifacts, Harry was comfortable; he always had been around Sheila. He said, "No motive."

"Hmm. Harry thinks Ronald Showels is innocent. You and the not-half-as-smart-as-he-thinks-he-is Mark Gesser make two. For little Ronnie's sake, you better end up on the jury, otherwise . . ." Sheila drew a sturdy finger across her throat. "Of course, if a jury acquits him, I'll have the honors then won't I? The first death penalty divorce case."

◆ 151 ◆

"No motive," Harry repeated as though saying it again might not make it so.

"Harry, *you're* the primo criminal lawyer, the State doesn't need a motive to make their case."

"It helps."

"And so you're here to find out what I know about little Ronnie." Through the window walls behind Sheila's desk, fading sunset cast a pink summer glow over the countryside all the way to the dusty line of skyscrapers in Baltimore, fifteen miles south. "Am I being asked to breach client confidentiality?"

"Is Showels in financial trouble?"

"No comment."

"I'll take that as a yes."

"Take it however you want."

"Does he have a gambling problem? I'm asking because maybe I have information you might want to trade if he does."

"Such as?"

"Videotape of Showels dropping five grand."

"And you have this tape?"

"I know where you can subpoena it."

Sheila liked the offer. "Ronnie is allegedly up to his ass in gambling debt, and with some reputably mean people. Where's the tape?"

"Pimlico Race Track security tapes, last Friday."

Sheila picked up her solid gold pen and jotted beautiful penmanship across a legal pad, making notes.

"Does Showels owe any of Giardino's people?"

"That's an off-the-wall question," Sheila responded, still writing.

"You have an off-the-wall answer?"

"Did you ask Sam?"

"He doesn't agree with my looking into the matter."

"Why?"

"He won't say . . . exactly."

"What does he say un-exactly?"

"That I might get in over my head."

◆ 152 ◆

Sheila rocked her chair, intrigued. "That's an odd thing for him to say, isn't it? What are we missing here, Harry? What's little Ronnie into?"

"Sam claims not to know. His warning was hypothetical, or he's trying to make it seem like that. He said I can't be a prosecutor."

"Just as well. The pay's lousy." Sheila made another notation. "So why *do* you care about this? Are you going to be your brother's savior, Harry? If the parts were reversed, if you were the one killed, would Tucker do the same?"

"I hope so."

"Harry . . ." Sheila spoke firmly, though with sympathy. "All those Christmases . . . you went to his house with presents for his kids and he was never there. His wife told you—what?—that he got called into work. And you believed her, because you wanted to believe her, but the lie was so obvious."

The memory was painful, but Harry stared through it. "He was my brother, and why ever he acted the way he did doesn't change that. Besides, what about his wife and kids, don't they deserve justice?"

"Oh my God, listen to you. Justice! You sound like the naive law clerk who used to complain about Sheppardizing cases for me. We've both put criminals back on the street. Lots of them. We do it in the name of protecting rights of the innocent, but the rationale doesn't necessarily forgive the contradiction. We tell people a verdict of not guilty doesn't mean innocent, it just means the proof of guilt wasn't clear, or that procedures were breached, but the result is the same. This is a business, it has nothing to do with anything besides making money."

"If you believed that, you wouldn't take cases where your clients don't have money—divorce cases where you don't charge a fee. That's why you really scare the shit out of the rest of the Bar, Sheila. You take nickel-and-dime cases because someone should do it, and you win the hell out of them because they deserve to be won. Some good is done by *all* of us."

"Just causes are like sneaking out of a smoke-filled room for a breath of fresh air. Eventually, we all go back to the smoke."

◆ 153 ◆

"I want whoever killed my brother to go to the gas chamber."

"Harry . . . this is ridiculous." Sheila grew impatient seeing he was not to be dissuaded. "Fine. Your conscience aches, you want to serve up a rare slice of justice, go out there and find a worthy client who can't afford the system, get your breath of fresh air where you can help someone who's still alive, someone who won't look the other way when you pass them in the courthouse halls. Your brother is dead, Harry. You making sure his killer pays isn't going to make him love you."

Harry got up from the cushioned antique chair and turned to leave.

"Four years ago," Sheila announced when Harry was at the door. "Ronald Showels and his wife were driving around Acapulco when a young Mexican boy almost ran them off the road with his jeep. Showels drove after him through the hills like a maniac. Mary Anne thought they were going to be killed. They played high-speed cat-and-mouse until Showels saw his chance and took it. He ran the boy off a cliff, Harry. He killed him. The police never found out. Showels threatened his wife that if she ever told anyone about it, he'd kill *her*. He's a tyrannical son of a bitch, Harry. He's beaten up Mary Anne half a dozen times. Last winter, he gagged her and took her out back to their little girl's playhouse, and tied her up and sodomized her on the goddamned lawn. I've got the medical reports from that one. The bastard had to take her to the doctor because of all the bleeding. He's a maniac, Harry. Don't let Mark Gesser tell you otherwise."

"Did you tell the State's Attorney?"

"I can't risk it. This information is my leverage to a settlement for my client. This goes to the State for criminal prosecution and the money I think Showels has hidden overseas is gone forever. My client and her little girl get nothing. I'm giving you this so *you'll* know what's going on, but you can't use it. I'm trusting you, Harry, so you'll know the police got the right person."

·21·

Harry's pager sounded as he exited the elevator into the marble and chrome lobby of Sheila Parks's building. Closed in a phone booth, he had the pager sound-dial his caller.

"That was quick." It was Tierny Wells. "Where are you?"

"Pay phone."

"I called ATF and bluffed my way to Hemingway's secretary. He's out of town . . ."

Even the Feds take a holiday, Harry thought.

"And Tommy Birchette? My worthy replacement on the Showels case? When I called him, he asked me out on a date—said he's been wanting to go out for three years, but couldn't because of our employee dating policy."

"You like him that way?" Harry wanted to make sure she wasn't doing this just to get information.

"Yeah, he's cute. But, you know what else? Conning law enforcement is kind of fun, isn't it? I think I've found my niche." Tierny's patter was revved with excitement; perhaps she saw her alliance with Harry as avenging her dismissal from the Showels case. "I'll call you later."

When Tierny broke the connection, Harry phoned his answering machine. He had two messages.

Alena: "It's just me." She sounded tired and antsy. "I can't concentrate and felt like talking." She exhaled frustration. "Marcie said you'd gone out, but didn't say where . . . I didn't want to page you because it's not that important, and, what the hell, lover, it's not *that* long until nine. See you at Chen's."

The second call was Craig, sounding much more upbeat. "Jeanna called me. We're going out. Hot shit, hot shit, *hot shit!* Anyway, Carla's here. She's cool about Mom being gone, like I

♦ 155 ♦

said. I told her you wanted to talk and she said she'll be around tonight, so, whenever . . . As for me, don't wait up . . . Dad."

Ronald Showels's office was on the main highway that cut through Timonium, an established suburban area of shopping centers, four-bedroom colonials, and apartment complexes. Just north of Towson, it was an easy commute from Showels's home in Sparks.

Showels's company, East Coast Equities, was in a renovated bungalow sided in beige-painted wood and topped with a new cedar shake roof. Planter boxes bursting with gardenias were attached beneath paned windows for a homey look. The side yard had been covered in asphalt, creating a parking pad nearly filled with a half dozen cars, five of them belonging to the Baltimore County Police.

Lt. Frank Trammell had kept the building under surveillance since shortly after Showels's arrest. No one had come or gone except the secretary, an attractive young woman five months out of secretarial school. She dressed the barfly part and was allowed to come in late so long as she worked seven hours, which she logged from eleven-thirty to six-thirty, leaving in time to make happy hour at any of the local bars.

When Frank Trammell and his men confronted her in the parking lot with the search warrant, she was not pleased. Tuesday, the American Café spread out a free Mexican buffet from six to seven-thirty.

Chewing a stick of freshen-your-breath gum, she said, "This is going to take a while, isn't it?"

"Maybe you could point us in the right direction and save us all some time."

The woman unlocked the door and led them inside.

It took over a dozen phone calls before Harry found a contact in the financial community who knew Ronald Showels.

Just after 7:00 P.M., Harry put the top down on the Mustang and drove north on I-83, exiting on Shawan Road and winding along wooded back roads toward Oregon Ridge and the Hillside Country Club.

Hillside was founded during World War II by bankers and real estate developers who'd come roaring out of the depression with hand carts overflowing with money. The thieves and pilferers of capitalism created a monument to themselves, a mansion club house of stone and wood, with high ceilings, Oriental rugs, and chandeliers. Private conference suites were leased yearly to corporations with the means to pay the tab, and having a "room" at Hillside was as revered as holding a seat on the world's largest stock exchanges. Deals may have been dreamed up in downtown offices, but they were consummated here.

When Harry's father first brought him to Hillside, it was Christmastime. Young women dressed in cleavage-boosting Santa outfits put on a show of decorating a twenty foot tall tree. In the bar overlooking the snow-covered eighteenth green, Jack Walsh handed Harry a wrapped cigar box and directed him across the room to where fat Judge McKintock sat by the window carousing with his buddies.

The Judge was a ruddy man whose shirt buttons fought violently to contain his massive stomach; he wore short sleeves even on the coldest of days, claiming only freezing temperatures comforted his atomic blood pressure.

Harry made his way to Judge McKintock and gave him the cigar box. The judge ran his hand through Harry's hair and laughed deeply, "Bet you've never seen anyone fat as me without a Santa suit, eh?"

Ten years later, well after Jack Walsh's death, Judge McKintock was removed from the bench for taking bribes. He died from a massive stroke two weeks before his trial was to begin. Among the allegations was that he accepted bribes in wrapped cigar boxes.

Corruption notwithstanding, Harry thought of the late judge with great fondness; he reminisced about McKintock and others as he crossed Hillside's ornate threshold for the first time in years. Being his father's son had been so comfortable and simple.

◆ 157 ◆

Of the current longstanding Hillside survivors, Harrison Tyler was one of the oldest. A retired banker, Tyler continued to earn enough money sitting on the boards of local and national corporations to maintain a suite at Hillside. A widower, he spent his days and most nights at the club.

Harry found him in the card room, surveying a gin rummy game. Tall for his age, Tyler was thinner than Harry had last seen him and his color wasn't good. With a keen eye on the cards being played, he stood with his hands braced on the back of a sturdy chair. His fingernails were buffed and trimmed. His shirt and trousers were custom tailored; his Johnston Murphy shoes polished without fault.

Tyler greeted Harry with a firm handshake; even that mild exertion made him tremble. His eyes were bright, but at the same time, sad: the mirror of a sharp mind imprisoned in a declining body. "Wonderful to see you."

"You, too."

"If only I didn't look like hell. Doctors . . ." He shook his head. "Worse thing you can be is sick and rich. They give you every test they can think of to pay for all the drug addicts they have to treat for free. If you're sick, be poor, they'll mistreat you out of your misery." Tyler walked with noticeable effort to a leather sofa pushed back against the far wall.

The card room's walls were of the same rich wood as when originally built, cared for with the meticulousness attended to the golf course's plush greens. Tables and chairs were of heavy wood, padded with dark-red leather.

Tyler laid a thin arm along the sofa back. He struggled to cross his legs and didn't bother lowering his pants cuff when bare white shin was exposed above brown socks. "You're working with the police about your brother?"

"Not directly."

Considering the implications of Harry's statement, Tyler touched two fingers to the underside of his mouth and firmly rubbed his lower lip. Briefed by Harry's phone call to him, he got to

◆ 158 ◆

the point. "Ronald Showels," Tyler reported dismissingly. "Typical hustler. He started as a finance officer for a couple smaller banks and lending companies. He moved around a lot before going on his own, brokering mortgages. He set up when housing prices were going through the roof. He arranged loans at triple prime—homeowners, mostly—but he was way off line with his numbers. His appraisals were high to begin with, and he was loaning up to a hundred ten percent of value. His argument was that the house would appreciate to the mortgage value within a year, so the investor would be covered, but that was assuming housing prices would keep soaring, which we all knew they wouldn't."

"Did you have any dealings with him?"

"No." Tyler sounded as though that would have been crazy. "A few of the Four Tiger boys gave him a couple shots, but most didn't stay long." The Four Tigers were Asians from Korea, Hong Kong, Taiwan, and Singapore. "I heard he picked up some East European money, even a few petro-dollars lately—hooked up with a retired foreign service big shot from the Carter administration with all kinds of oil contacts—but I think he's in trouble. I hear Marion Greenbaum's been handling Showels's settlements and foreclosures and says it's like a waterfall, all this bad paper coming down on him." Tyler paused. "Does this help?"

"I don't know. Showels doesn't sound like he would have had anything to do with my brother."

"Maybe he didn't. Fate plays terrible games, Harry. Sometimes bad things just happen. It's nice to have a sense of order, but look at me: cancer takes my wife and now it wants me. I suppose there is some connection, but all I know is I'm getting weaker and it scares the shit out of me. Your father was too young, but in his own way, he cheated death." Tyler made a fist that shook his failing muscles. "He didn't see death coming, and robbed her of that perverse pleasure of pulling him under inch by inch." Tyler's quivering hand dropped hard on his thin leg.

"You'll beat it."

Tyler appreciated the encouragement, but his expression was

grim. "I don't think so." He looked back toward the card game where the announcement of gin was met with an opponent's loud expletive. "I'll ask around for you, Harry, to see if someone knows more than I."

·22·

You look great." As Alena swiveled off the padded barstool, Harry placed his hand along the back of her neck and eased her nearer. Her lips were warm and tasty with gin.

The man who'd been coming onto Alena before Harry's arrival watched their kiss enviously in the gold-flecked mirror behind rows of liquor bottles. When Harry caught his reflection, the man looked away.

"You want to bring your drink to the table?"

"Leave it."

Harry smoothed out her long hair. He loved touching her, especially when they'd been separated for a while; twenty-four hours apart often felt like a lifetime.

They entered Chen's dining room, a long, narrow area, plainly decorated, with booths along both walls and a row of tables between. A waiter emerged from the kitchen with a sizzling platter, and the aroma of peppers and sesame beef swirled potently.

Alena slid into a booth, struggling slightly when her long denim skirt wouldn't glide over a velveteen cushion.

"You want to talk first, or order?"

"What does Giardino want, Harry?"

"What did he say?"

"That he wanted to meet—as soon as we could make it—to discuss the project."

"That's it?"

"He's not on the AmeriCenter list of contractors or consultants. He wants *something*." Alena held her voice low. "Does he want a kickback for getting us this job?"

"*You* got the company the job."

"Come on . . ."

◆ 161 ◆

"You did. If your presentation hadn't been first class you'd have been rejected."

"First class? But not the best, right?"

"You've won awards, Alena, you've made a name for yourself. A big job like this is the next logical step."

"So if *I* got the job for the company, we can run it however we want. If he wants us to do something, we don't have to do it."

"That's right."

"*There's* a qualified tone of voice if ever I've heard it."

"Why don't you talk to him first . . . before you get bent out of shape."

"I *want* to be prepared. I *want* some idea what this is about." Tension constricted her usually smooth flow of speech. "Let's not play semantic games, okay. Don't negotiate with me like I'm a client. I'm in love with you, Harry, talk to me like you love me."

"I do."

She shook her head. "You hold back what you think I don't want to hear. You weigh everything before you say it. It's a calculation. It's not honest."

"I don't lie to you."

"That's not what I'm saying. It's not about lying, it's about letting me in. There's part of you inside *you* that doesn't always come out, and I want to know everything. I don't want to be protected."

Their waiter came over, order pad in hand even though their menus had remained closed. Harry ordered shrimp toast to start and the waiter departed.

Alena leaned closer. "Do you understand what I'm saying? That not lying and honesty aren't necessarily the same?"

"An example comes to mind."

"Which is . . . ?"

"I'm not renewing the lease for my apartment." When Alena didn't respond, Harry said, "Now who's the one *not* saying what the other person might not want to hear?"

Alena's expression initially reflected guilt, but was quickly replaced by honest determination. "I'm not sure I'm ready to move in

◆ 162 ◆

with you. I don't know if I know you that well."

"What don't you know?"

"Basically: one question."

"Going to be a toughie, huh?" He wanted her to smile.

"Are you a mob lawyer, Harry?"

After dinner, they kissed for a long time on a dark side street in the small historic town of Mount Washington. The Falls River moved quietly through a culvert, partially covering the conversation of residents sitting on front stoops around the corner. Nearby, a radio broadcast an Orioles game.

The feel of Alena's flesh, moist from summer humidity, left Harry longing for more. He leaned her against the side of the Lexus and pressed close. She allowed him to unbutton her denim halter and push it back from her breasts. She felt him hard in his suit pants and, between kisses, gasped, "Maybe we better get in the car."

A playful hour later, Alena headed back into the city. Harry drove to his brother's house.

On his way to Tucker's, Harry checked routinely for the Feds on his tail. He hadn't seen them all afternoon, and they weren't there now.

Maybe they'd all gone on vacation with Agent Hemingway. Maybe running with the bulls in Pamplona. If he saw the humorless ATF agent again he'd ask him that and see if Hemingway picked up the reference. Probably not.

Harry turned his worries to other matters, namely, the "speech" he'd rehearsed for his niece a few times over the past couple days. He wanted to set Carla straight, convince her to stay off the Valium (and whatever else she was taking), and to be a grown-up version of the six-year-old he had adored. What he wanted, he realized, was a magic wand. Despite situation comedies and made-for-TV movies, the world possessed relatively few problems ready to be cured by a polished monologue delivered within a thirty-min-

◆ 163 ◆

ute block of time. Sam Giardino once told him if you dated a difficult situation to its roots, you'd need three times that long to resolve it.

So when Harry pulled into a parking space two doors from Tucker's house and saw Carla outside, waving to him in the glow of the porch light, he wasn't surprised that his semi-planned discussion suddenly seemed nonsensical.

Carla ran to the car, crossing in front of the Mustang's headlights wearing a windbreaker and short skirt. Her dark hair was curled and wild over her shoulders. She was without make-up, but smelled sweetly of cheap perfume that stung Harry's nostrils as she bent over to talk. "Hey, Uncle." She tapped his arm with a soft fist. "I need a ride. Craig's got the domestic wagon train."

"It's kind of late," Harry protested mildly.

"Gawd, you sound like Mom." She circled back in front of the car, pausing to do an uninhibited tap dance in the headlights. She laughed, getting in the car. "Think I'm ready for Broadway?"

Harry didn't know her at all anymore. "I told your mother I'd watch out for you while she was gone."

"Come on, Uncle Harry . . ."

"Does she let you go—strike that—never mind."

Carla laughed again. Harry didn't know if she was on something or not; if anything, it wasn't Valium; she wasn't in a haze like the other day.

"It's not far," Carla said. "You know Fox Chase? Out Dulaney Valley Road. I'll show you." She turned on the radio and spun the dial through endless static and occasional squawk. "Oh my God, *what is this?*" She squinted at the dial. "AM?" She shrieked with amusement. "You only have AM? How old is this car?"

"About twice as old as you. It was my father's."

"Yeah? And it still runs? That's pretty cool, I guess." She switched off the radio and sat back, half throwing herself against the seat. Her skirt rode up, revealing slender thighs. "Warm out tonight."

Harry didn't say anything.

◆ 164 ◆

"Go up here and take a left, then go back down Joppa to Dulaney Valley Road and . . . what? You're looking at me weird. Is something wrong with my hair?"

No, Harry thought, *everything* is wrong with you—just like Connie said after Tucker's death. "What if I don't take you to this place?"

"I'll call a cab, or get a friend to pick me up."

"What if I asked you not to go?"

"Would you ask nice or like an order?"

"Nice."

"Nice, okay . . . you ask nice and I'd say okay, I won't go, and then I'd pretend I was going to bed, and in about an hour I'd climb out my back window and get a cab."

"What if I *ordered* you not to go?"

Without malice, Carla said, "I'd walk out the front door and come back in a few days."

"I figured as much." Harry shifted into gear. "Tell me, did you only pull this shit on your mother, or did my brother fall for it, too?"

"I guess that depends when you're talking about. Dad used to raise holy hell, then, lately, he'd go with me."

"He went with you?" Harry asked doubtfully.

"He got really cool in the end. It was clearing out his mind."

"What was?"

"Fucking teenagers."

Harry didn't flinch, but his stomach felt that same angst as when a witness hit him with a damaging answer. "What are you talking about?" In court that would have been the wrong question; the first rule of examination was that if you didn't know the answer, don't ask the question.

"You don't know what 'fucking' means?"

"It means a couple things." Harry tried to maintain his composure. He turned onto Joppa Road at the light. "Fucking *over*, for example . . . or intercourse."

"Oh . . ." Carla was having fun with him ". . . well, we're talking the, uh, how did you say it . . ." she feigned a proper tone ". . . *intercourse?* It would be that kind of fucking." She laughed, and Harry saw inside her.

He fell into silence.

"It wasn't like rape, or anything," Carla said.

Silence was a prevaricator's enemy; it kept her from knowing how her prey was reacting, and it *was* possible to go too far. Some people might just write you off, then you couldn't use them any more.

Carla said, "She was willing—she wanted to do it with him . . . and she was old enough."

So now it was only one girl, not plural. Perhaps the whole line was a lie. Harry let her talk, waiting for more contradictions.

"I hang out with older people. You know, most of them are in college, or old enough to be." She crossed her arms defensively. "It wasn't like anybody got hurt or messed up. It was just a good time, and Dad sure needed it. He was so bummed."

Harry couldn't resist a question. "About what?"

"Work," Carla said quickly. "He hated his job. The lousy pay and hours, and he said court was a joke. That all the crooks got off. That people like you got them off."

"He talked about me?"

"Yeah . . . He didn't like you."

Harry believed this to be true.

"He said people like you could get away with anything, and people like me, I'd do one thing wrong and get busted."

"Interesting disciplinary approach," Harry commented sarcastically. "I see it worked." He glanced over his shoulder before changing lanes. "Besides, possessing someone else's prescription is a crime and I don't see you behind bars."

"I'm not holding anything."

"The Valium the other day? You did say it was your father's?"

"Oh, yeah."

A mile down the road, she pointed excitedly to a 7-Eleven while reaching into her jacket. "Turn in here. I've got to cash this lottery ticket." She pulled out an instant game piece that looked like it had been through the wash. "Twenty-five bucks."

"Congratulations."

"Dad said the only way people like us ever get anywhere is to hit the lottery. This past Christmas he gave me a hundred tickets. It was really cool. He said why give me clothes I'd wear out in a few years when he could give me a shot at a real future. It was cool scratching off all the tickets together."

Harry pulled to the front of the convenience store and hoped one of his clients didn't have the cashier tied up in the back to rob the place; it was empty inside.

"Pass," Carla said.

"It's all right." Harry saw the clerk now, a middle-aged woman doing a cigarette inventory.

"No, pass. Bad vibes."

"You already won. You get bad vibes about *cashing* a ticket?"

She turned toward him with wide eyes of perturbed explanation. "I was going to get some *more.*"

It was 11:30 and Harry didn't have the time or stomach for this. Still, he backed out of the lot and headed for Dulaney Valley Road, only to have Carla direct him to a Farm Store half a mile later.

"Please . . ." she begged childlike when he glared at her ". . . please."

The store was packed. Harry waited while Carla worked her way to the cashier like a floor trader on the commodities exchange. A hassled kid at the register handed over her winnings and moved to the next customer.

"I thought you were getting more tickets?" Harry said when Carla got back in the car counting cash.

"Shit, I forgot."

When she reached for the door handle, Harry grabbed her arm. "This is taking long enough as it is. Some of us have to get up in the morning. We work for a living."

"Ow, that's spooky."

"Work?"

"No, Dad used to say that, about waking up to go to work for a living. But I don't think that's what he said *you* did."

◆ 167 ◆

Harry let it go. He followed Carla's occasionally haphazard directions to a respectable home in upscale Fox Chase. In the driveway, he said, "Call and let me know where you are, okay?"

"I'll be here," she said, smart-assed, pointing along the curving stone walk that led to the front porch.

"Call tomorrow anyway—in case you need something."

"Okay, Uncle Harry." Suddenly, she was the innocent Carla again. Harry half expected her to skip to the front door.

Driving home, Harry thought about divorce clients who'd come to the office with wild kids like Carla, the same uncontrollable teenagers he'd represented in juvenile court. He always thought those parents should do something about their kids, discipline them, do something. Suddenly, he appreciated their powerlessness.

Back in his apartment, the answering machine greeted him with its lonely blinking light.

Only one message: Tierny Wells. Harry played back the tape and heard dishes clanking in the background; he assumed she'd called from a restaurant. "I'm with Tommy Birchette and I've got news. Ronald Showels is taking a lie detector tomorrow morning. Trammel's running it. Unless Mark Gesser found a way to test polygraph him at the detention center, he's taking one hell of a chance. I'll let you know . . . can't talk long . . . my date's waiting." Tierny sounded to be enjoying the subversion.

· 23 ·

The naked boy found hung to death, dangling from the State Park backstop, wasn't identified until Wednesday morning, three days after he was cut down. Missing persons profiles and morgue photos passed around squad room briefings had failed to produce an ID; fingerprint results finally caused JOHN DOE to be properly re-named EDWARD THOMAS LAUREL.

Eddie Laurel, seventeen, was a high-school dropout with a brief, unspectacular history of drug abuse and drug-related arrests: theft, breaking and entering, possession, possession with intent to dis-tribute.

When uniformed officers appeared at Eddie's trailer park home Wednesday morning, his parents assumed it was to tell them Eddie had been arrested—again.

Informed of their son's death, Mrs. Laurel collapsed against her husband and muttered frail desperation she hoped would serve as final appraisal of her young son: "He was a good boy . . . really . . . in his heart."

Mr. Laurel shut the door and went back into the dirty kitchen for his beer and *Easyrider* magazine.

Back in the Homicide Office, Frank Trammell closed the case he hadn't wanted to deal with in the first place. Fortunately, the media was still enamored enough with Ronald Showels that Eddie Laurel barely made the papers beyond a tiny, titillating article: UN-IDENTIFIED TEENAGER FOUND HUNG, NAKED, IN STATE PARK. Just another kid gone bad.

"She doesn't see very well," the nurse's aide told Harry, "and you have to speak loudly into her left ear."

Seated by the wide sunny window was a beautiful woman with

surprisingly youthful skin for seventy-six. Her hair was the color of grey-white summer clouds, cut short and well-kept by weekly appointments to the retirement home's visiting beautician.

The aide crossed the small, pleasant room ahead of Harry. "Mrs. Travers, you have a visitor."

Back hunched by scoliosis, Phyllis Travers stood and turned slowly.

"Hello, Phyllis," he said loudly, "it's Harry Walsh."

She made a quiet sound of surprised pleasure and gestured him near. Her eyes—fogged with cataracts—continued to search for Harry's approach.

He clasped the hands that had processed files in the Circuit Court for forty years, a procedure that began on pen and paper and evolved into computers. Phyllis Travers's handwriting was legendary in the land records books: beautiful cursive letters stroked consistently on thousands of pages from the late 1940s until the early '80s when computers came on line.

"How did you find me?" Her voice carried a strength her eyes had lost. "I thought when they put me in here, they threw away the key and kept my friends from knowing where I was." Her tone was unusually spry, a surviving trademark of undaunted independence.

The nurse's aide leaned near. "I'm leaving, Mrs. Travers. Let me know if you need anything."

"Thank you, dear." She kept hold of Harry's hands and looked up with eyes aimed slightly below his. "I'll pretend you look marvelous, because I'm sure you do." She reached toward his face. "Do you still have your hair?"

He ducked his head to her palm and she caressed it.

"I knew you would. Your father had such beautiful hair. Such a handsome man. I still remember what he looked like."

"I think I do, too, then I see a picture of him and he looks different than I expect."

She smiled with memory. "Look in a mirror and you'll see him."

Harry helped her back to her chair and thought how time was pulling hard at his lifetime friend much as it was Harrison Tyler. Harry's father would have been almost seventy had he lived, and

◆ 170 ◆

Harry wondered how painful it would have been to care for him had his health deteriorated. How incredibly difficult it must be to age gracefully while failing physically. He often heard older people say they'd grown tired of living when he suspected they were really saying they'd grown tired of aging. Life offered enough diversions and change to keep one's interest for a millennium; it was the diminishing body that wore down the mind's endurance.

Facing the bright window, Phyllis gestured outside and said, "See my pond?"

There was no water, only traffic, a shopping center across the street, and a car dealership on the corner.

She tugged Harry's arm to clue she was kidding. "I only see light, mostly, and some movement, but I pretend it's my pond from home. My son sold the farm, you know. They've built houses on it. So now, this is my pond."

"Johnnie said you won't let them operate on your eyes."

"To see what? This place? Please, Harry," she laughed. "I can smell the food, I *have* to eat it, I think that's torture enough, don't you? I certainly don't want to see it."

"What about reading?"

"They have books on tape, and television is lousy so I don't have to see that. No, thank you, my memory is very good. My mind remembers things exactly as they were, and that's all I need." She patted his hand. "I'm fine."

He felt remorseful. "I should have come sooner."

"You're here now, and that's wonderful."

Harry glanced to the hall. Attendants and staff passed by the door, as did other residents, some of whom stared at him spitefully, jealous of visitors. Conscious of how loudly he needed to speak, he asked if it was all right to close the door.

Phyllis said it was, and her expression acknowledged an underlying purpose to his call.

In six normal strides, Harry crossed the room. There were few furnishings around which to negotiate, only a single bed already made at this early hour, a small TV on a stand, and an inexpensive dresser. "Do you hear the news?" Harry asked, back at her side.

◆ 171 ◆

"About your brother?" Her guess was without condolences for Tucker's death.

"You know he was shot?" Harry pulled a second chair to Phyllis's good side and sat.

"Ronald Showels."

"I should have known you'd still follow the courthouse."

"It's in my blood. It keeps my veins clear. The woman across the hall reads me the newspaper, including Barry Eisenrich's column. He's still a fat old prick, isn't he?"

"Yes . . . he is."

Phyllis tilted closer to Harry. "But you know *that*. Who you probably don't know about is Ronald Showels."

Harry marvelled at her intuition. Showels was half of what he wanted to discuss.

"Ronnie Showels used to file financing statements with me when he worked in the auto loan department for First Maryland. He was a liar—I knew the first time I saw him. And he was a thief. He was fired for embezzling. They kept it quiet so as not to damage the bank. The board of directors were afraid they'd get the boot for allowing such terrible accounting practices—and this was long *before* the banks started failing, so you can imagine . . . After that I saw him now and again, but I never saw Showels as a killer, although people change and usually not for the better."

"He's taking a lie detector today."

She shook her head. "He'll pass it. A lifetime liar can break a polygraph in a snap. Am I telling you anything you don't know?"

"Yes."

"How pleasant to be useful for a change."

Harry checked his watch; the State's Attorney was holding a case for him in District Court. "Phyl, I heard something yesterday about Tucker. That a long time ago, before he left for Canada, he tried to lie his way out of some jam—and from the way this person made it sound, it wasn't something small."

"You think whatever this was—if anything, so many years ago—has to do with why he was killed?"

"I doubt it."

◆ 172 ◆

"So do I." She slouched deeper into her chair. "Are you still involved with Sam Giardino, Harry?"

"Yes."

Phyllis nodded. "He's who told you about something in Tucker's past?"

"Yes." Again, Harry thought, her intuition . . .

Phyllis said, "When Tucker was seventeen, he was arrested for selling drugs."

Harry was stunned.

"Your father had been working for Sam Giardino a few years and was gaining a lot of notoriety. He was very good at keeping Giardino out of jail, and the police hated him for it. They started following your family. Your father was followed, and so was Tucker. The police saw he was a wild boy. It was his age coupled with the fact that he was good looking, and that his father was a mob lawyer. Tucker thought he could do anything. He saw your father defending known criminals and must have figured this allowed him to do whatever he wanted. If he got caught, your father could get him off. And he did get caught. He was selling LSD.

"How it started is a matter of some question. The police claimed Tucker actively sought out a source. Tucker claimed the police set him up, that a plant kept offering drugs and showing how he could sell them and make a lot of money. It was the money that got him, because your father, and maybe you were too young to know, but he was very frugal. He didn't make a lot of money from Giardino and he lived conservatively, at least that was how it was represented. Cash was surely passing hands, but under the table.

"But as for Tucker, he was arrested, as a juvenile, for distributing a substantial quantity of drugs. Your father was outraged, not at the police for any misconduct, but at Tucker for being so stupid. Your father refused to help him. If Tucker had done something that dumb, he deserved to be punished. Your father was going to let him go to juvenile detention."

"I can't believe this."

Phyllis nodded. "Tucker ran away. He went to Canada and stayed until after your father's death. He only came back when he

◆ 173 ◆

knew the State couldn't make its case against him, by which time he was in violation for not registering for the draft. He handled that in federal court somewhere out of state."

"I knew about that . . . but I thought the reason he left *was* the draft."

"No."

"No one ever told me." Harry tried to imagine all that had happened when he was too young to know. "The LSD case—what was it?—how did it happen that the State couldn't make their case?"

"The plant and an undercover officer who would have testified against Tucker were killed during a raid. Supposedly, someone set up an ambush."

Harry walked into Courtroom 2 of the Towson District Court at 10:15. Judge Harold Harlow was yet to take the bench and the defense lawyers were grumbling; most handled misdemeanor cases for a flat fee as opposed to billing by the hour, which meant every minute spent waiting was a loss.

Amanda Yin had the docket for the State's Attorney. She was three years out of the University of Baltimore Law School, and establishing herself as a prosecutor on the rise. Like most new ASAs, she'd come to the job with a hard-on for every criminal case she was assigned, but acclimated quickly to the practicalities of her office and understood that, at least at the lower-court level, the scales of justice weighed the crime against the time it would take to try the case, and if the balance was skewed, she took a plea to get on with the next case.

She was especially skillful in dealing with the obnoxious old-boy lawyers who made their living dealing "nothing" cases. She mostly ignored petty comments they thought were funny, like Roland Tanner wisecracking every time he had a case with her he had the urge to get extra starch put in his collar, or Alfred Morrison calling her Amanda "Egg Foo" Yin.

Harry once asked Amanda why she put up with their crap, and she calmly said it was like working with ornery children: pay as little attention as possible and they soon go away.

◆ 174 ◆

This morning, Amanda sat alone at the trial table, having already talked with every lawyer and unrepresented defendant scheduled for the 9:15 session. Her legal pad was sectioned into columns much as Harry set up his juror's grid during voir dire. Amanda's cases were organized like an ER nurse triaged patients: postponements and jury trial requests would come first, followed by pleas, then trials.

Except for two defendants yet to appear, Harry's was her only case left undefined.

Harry nodded to his client, a career car-parts thief, and gestured he was going to talk to the prosecutor. His client, gold earring in his left lobe despite Harry's pretrial warning to lose the jewelry, nodded complacently.

"Morning, Harry." Amanda Yin wore a stylish black suit jacket over a white blouse and matching skirt. The aquamarine ring on her left ring finger was new.

"Engaged?" Harry asked of the ring.

"Thinking about it." Her almond eyes were clear and smart; her make-up was sparse and tasteful, nicely highlighting pale olive skin tones. "I'm sorry about your brother. I had some of his traffic cases last month. He was a good policeman."

"Thanks." Harry sat in the chair beside her, the one to be occupied by police officers who would read statements of fact in cases being pled out.

"How's his family? I was at the funeral. They looked very sad."

"It's going to be a long struggle."

She nodded sympathetically. "My father was killed in an accident when I was little. It's such a shock." She folded her hands. "Were those your parents at the funeral?"

"No, his wife's, my sister-in-law's." What a pleasant discovery, Harry thought: the young attorneys didn't all know of his father's ties to Sam Giardino.

Amanda pulled out a case file. "So what are we doing with your Mr. Mackey? Mr. Car Parts 'R Us."

"Your witness here?"

"On call."

◆ 175 ◆

Harry sighed. "I really don't have time for this today."

"Guilty to one count of theft, one year, ten months suspended."

"So he does two months . . . he'll be out in six weeks . . . ?"

"Give or take."

"Probation?"

"Two years, normal conditions."

"He really hates probation."

"He should be used to it. He's forty-two and spent half his life reporting."

"It gets so old . . ."

Amanda spent an easy smile and bartered, "One year probation."

"How about he does ten weekends and *six* months probation?"

"I've got a solid case."

"I know."

"And with his priors I could ask for five years and probably get it. He's a career thief. He's going to be back, Harry."

"They all come back."

"One month in, one year's probation, that's the best I can do."

"Can you get me out of here by eleven o'clock?"

"No problem."

"Deal." Harry went back to his client and sat down.

Arnie Mackey was a gristly veteran of court and jail whose claim to fame was that he really never committed any crimes serious enough to get a judge really hot. Arnie stole parts off luxury cars and sold them to friends who owned repair shops. For his court appearance, he wore jeans and a wrinkled white shirt. Engine oil was embedded under his fingernails. "What's the deal counselor?"

"One year, eleven months suspended, one year probation. Can you handle that?"

"On my head."

Harry nodded toward the rear doors. "I'll be right back, okay. Sit tight."

◆ 176 ◆

"Yep."

Harry didn't have anywhere to go, he just left the courtroom to wait in the hall. Some days he couldn't bear sitting next to his clients.

◆ 24 ◆

When Harry called in for messages, Marcie said, "Alena wants to make sure you'll be at the lunch meeting at one."

Harry checked his watch: 11:05. Amanda Yin had kept her part of the plea bargain and gotten him out of court posthaste. "I'll be there. Call her for me?"

"Sure. You've also got a new client who wants an appointment ASAP."

"Give it to George."

"He was very specific about wanting to talk to you, Harry."

Which could mean it was a referral from Sam Giardino. "Okay, set him for tomorrow sometime."

"Also, Harrison Tyler . . . ?" the name was new to her ". . . he wouldn't say about what. And the Westlaw salesman stopped by again."

"Did Tyler leave a number?"

"He said he was at the club? You know what that means?"

"Yeah, okay, thanks. That it?"

"Everything else can wait."

"Nothing from Tierny Wells?"

"No, are you expecting her?"

"She's got my pager if it's important." Harry checked his watch again, becoming apprehensive about the remainder of his day.

Marcie asked, "When will you be back?"

"I'm not sure how long I'll be downtown, but go ahead and page me if something urgent comes up."

"Okay."

Harry left the District Court lobby by the rear police exit. His client had been taken through the same doors five minutes earlier

◆ 178 ◆

and placed in a barred sheriff's van for transport to the Detention Center half a mile away; it would be easy time, and by defense practice standards, Harry had negotiated a "winner." Despite the impression left by TV movies that sought to outrage as opposed to inform, the vast majority of criminal defendants were found guilty and did time, so a defense lawyer's won-loss record wasn't predicated upon guilt or innocence, but the deals he put together.

Harry walked the sunny alley and crossed two parking lots on a shortcut to his destination. He entered the office building through revolving doors and immediately found the air conditioning a welcome relief from the increasing humidity. He passed the newsstand and closed himself in a phone booth.

His call to the Hillside Club was put through promptly to Harrison Tyler's business suite. Tyler answered on the third ring, announcing his name forcefully, as though his every physical act was a defiance of debilitating disease.

Harry pictured Tyler at his Edwardian desk, framed against a backdrop of tall windows fashioned with ornate swags and jabots. The view behind Tyler would be the serpentine fairway of the long par-five seventh hole. "It's Harry."

"Good morning to you." Tyler rustled a few papers. "I discussed Showels with one of the Four Tiger boys I mentioned to you—a Korean national. He took a dozen mortgages brokered by Showels three years ago. Most were seconds, some thirds. Total value just over half a million. The interest rate was five points above the banks, and every mortgage went into arrears within sixteen months. My friend turned the mortgages over to his attorney for foreclosure, but was advised a sale might not cover the principal and the borrowers weren't good candidates to collect on a deficiency decree."

Even speaking slowly, Tyler needed to pause to regain his breath. "My friend was understandably upset—probably more upset with himself for not better investigating his borrowers—but when he approached Showels, Showels was apologetic. He said he'd just worked out a new deal and offered my friend two options.

Showels would buy back the paper at face value, or, if my friend would drop the interest rate two points, Showels would arrange the monthly payments to be delivered in cash."

"Cash?"

"Yes. My friend took the deal, but just for three months. He became jittery—worried Showels was running a sting operation against foreigners for the IRS. That these cash payments, which we know are appetizing because they're untraceable and theoretically tax free, were setting him up. My friend also got word that Showels was in trouble from gambling debts, and the mortgages were a complete fraud. He checked some of them and found a few had never been recorded with land records. Showels blamed the Clerk's Office, but my friend suspected—and was probably right—that Showels was charging transfer and recordation taxes to the borrowers and never paying the monies to the State."

"Your friend . . ." Harry asked ". . . I assume he doesn't want to be known."

"Foreigners doing business here are carefully scrutinized, Harry. Tax fraud is grounds for deportation."

"Would your friend let me talk to him . . . ? Anonymously?"

"I'm afraid not." Tyler's breathing became more labored. "If there's something else you need to know, I'll gladly inquire for you."

"I'm trying to link Showels to my brother."

"Yes, you said yesterday."

"Does your friend know anything about that?"

"I asked if he knew of anyone else dealing with Showels and he said no. Only that he had heard the same rumor as I: that Showels had connected with Middle East money and it was being arranged through a former diplomat who wined and dined the sheiks."

"What about Showels's gambling debts? Who did he owe? Who did his bookies work for?" Harry feared the answer was Sam Giardino.

"I'm not sure my friend would know that . . . but I didn't ask." There was a long, heavy pause. "Do you *want* me to ask?"

◆ 180 ◆

Harry inhaled. When he breathed out, his chest ached. "Yes, I'd like you to ask."

"I'll call you," Tyler said, and hung up.

Outside the phone booth, office workers began the early exodus to lunch. They passed through revolving doors into bright sunshine and heat. The tasks of their jobs left at their desks, none seemed engrossed by problems.

Harry plunked in another quarter and phoned Mark Gesser's office, telling his receptionist, "This is the parking attendant. Please advise Mr. Gesser his Mercedes has been scratched . . . again."

As soon as Mark Gesser stepped out of the elevator and started across the parking garage, Harry knew Ronald Showels had passed the polygraph.

Harry forced a co-conspirator's smile. If he was pretending to be Gesser's ally, he should be pleased for Showels's good fortune. "Successful morning?"

Gesser unlocked his Mercedes and arrogantly gestured Harry inside—he seemed intrigued by this covert-meeting scenario. "I've got a bucket," Gesser said, pseudo-southern accent running thick today, "full of Frank Trammell's sweat and piss. It was beautiful, Harry. The lie detector. Trammell's asking the questions—he thinks he's such hot shit. He's nailing Ron with tough questions, real bombs, blam-blam-blam. Ron's squirming, hooked up to all these wires and sensors. Trammell sounds ready to pull Ron's lungs out his throat, but I watch the meter, the gauge, whatever they call the thing that prints out the results, and it's steady as a perfect heartbeat, bip . . . bip . . . bip . . . Not so much as a fucking blink. And Trammell sees it, too.

"The steadier Ron's answers read, the more Trammell sweats. He looks at his polygraph guy like there's something wrong with the machine, and the guy shrugs. Trammell pounds Ron for an hour and then I finally can't resist, I say, 'Satisfied. He didn't do it.' Trammell's so goddamned mad, he storms out. An hour later, I get a call. Trammell. He says, maybe—get that, *maybe*—my guy didn't

◆ 181 ◆

do it. But if he didn't, whoever did had some cause to want to set him up, and Trammell wants to know who. I say he gets a decent bail set, maybe we'll give him a name."

"Do you have a name?"

"Yeah, hell, his crazy-assed wife and that lesbian bitch Suicide Sheila."

"Come on, Mark. Sheila Parks isn't murdering policemen to frame opponents in a divorce case."

"I'm not saying she *did it*, I'm just saying she's the one who made this 'anonymous call' setting up Ron."

"So where'd she get the gun?"

"It's a ruse. I bet my mortgage the gun doesn't match."

"I got word it does."

"Harry . . . Harry . . . if it did, would they consider cutting Ron lose on bail?"

A prudent cop wouldn't, Harry thought, but Frank Trammell might as an act of desperation. "The State's Attorney," Harry lied, "has been working on another theory. That Showels has serious gambling debts."

"No way. He's making a mint in the mortgage business. That's lots better odds than the Orioles giving two runs against K.C."

"He goes to the track," Harry pointed out. "They've got race-track surveillance tape of him there just like the informant said."

"Okay, yeah, he goes to the track."

"And he's dropping a few grand."

"Look, Harry, this is off the record, okay, but Ron knows some guys who own horses and they get certain tips now and again. You understand what I'm saying? You know these guys, right? So you take a flier on ten, twelve to one. It's a hobby, a lark, not an obsession. And believe me, Ron Showels can afford to drop a few grand at the track—it hurts less than getting nicked shaving. Besides, the day you're talking about, Ron wasn't betting just his own money. He had a hot tip and called a few friends, myself included. I know, it's stupid, cost me five hundred bucks, but you know what? The time before that, I made ten grand." He slapped Harry's thigh with the back of his hand. "You like horses? I'll call you next time."

◆ 182 ◆

"Sure." Harry went along at playing Gesser's newest best friend. "Why not. You know, if Showels is doing that good brokering mortgages, I might have some investors for him."

"You and everybody else. Ron's doing *real* good. Better than anyone knows, although his wife and Sheila suspect something. They know he's got lots of loose cash floating around. He's getting some fees in cash. Again, this is off the record, but I'm telling you because I want to make sure you know damned well he did *not* kill your brother. There's no possible reason for him to do it. What's their theory? He gets pulled over for a traffic stop? He's mad about a traffic ticket?" Gesser smirked. "It's not even original."

"If he's got dirty cash on him . . . ." Harry omitted telling Gesser that Tucker had been deputized by ATF and may have been after Showels for reasons other than speeding.

"You got the cash part right, but it's not dirty. I've run the numbers for him through one of the big firms downtown. Their international department cleared the procedure. Ron's completely legit on his source of funds. Now how Ron's investors get money out of their home country . . . ? That may be another story, but as far as Ron is concerned, he's spotless on his sources of money. In and out. He's clean. He's not laundering or anything like that. It's up and up investments."

"That's good, because this case could open a can of worms for him if not. Someone in the State's Attorney's Office is looking into allegations Showels isn't recording all the mortgages and is pocketing transfer taxes."

"Absolutely not. A couple times recordation was pulled, but that's because the courthouse is running three months behind processing deeds, and . . . all right . . . yeah, I know what you're saying." Gesser's tone turned confessional.

So much, Harry thought, for the up and up.

"It's probably happened six lousy times. Sometimes Ron holds off recording the mortgage as long as payments come in okay. For a few months, he makes some float interest on the transfer tax money. Some scratch."

"Somebody gets a hard-on for him, he'll get banged for it."

◆ 183 ◆

"I appreciate it, Harry. Thanks for the tip. Owe you one."

"Enough to let me talk to Showels?"

"About what?"

"Ask him face to face about my brother?"

"If that's what it takes to convince you one hundred percent, yeah, sure. No problem. But we wait until he's out, right? You go to the detention center, someone sees you're helping us out."

"He getting bail?"

"We're talking about it—in exchange for Ron giving the name of who set him up."

"Suicide Sheila?"

"And the bitch wife."

Trammell, Harry thought ruefully, was about to get conned by an amateur.

Gesser pulled a folded sheet of copy paper from his jacket and opened it to reveal a composite sketch of a gypsy-looking young woman. "This's Ron's bar date. He says this looks just like her, except for the eyes. Ron says they're real deep green, mesmerizing, fuck-you-till-you're-dead eyes. You look into them, you're in love. We're still looking for her in case the State stays insane and tries to prosecute."

"They might. They don't always believe lie detectors."

Gesser laughed. "Tell that to the sweat under Frank Trammell's armpits."

◆ 184 ◆

·25·

"No friends today." Giorgi checked the street for federal agents in plain cars as he opened the door for Harry.

"They'll be back. They always are." Entering Vazinni's, Harry was overcome by the wonderful smell of onions, olive oil, and garlic.

Giorgi nodded his large head toward Sam Giardino's private room. "Everybody else is here already."

Harry checked his watch. He wasn't late. It must have been Cleo's idea to arrive ahead of schedule. Alena would have wanted to wait for him.

Harry walked through the restaurant, which was crowded with tourists and business people. Conversations were animated and loud, taking on Italian spirit by osmosis. In the back hall, he knocked on Giardino's door and entered on Sam's boisterous, "Come in."

Once inside, he was welcomed by Giardino's customary hug. Any animosity from yesterday seemed forgotten. "Hello, Sonny. Now you're here you spoil the odds. I had your lovely lady and her lovely boss all to myself. Two of them and one of me." Giardino laughed.

Cleo and Alena sat at the room's only table. A white Concetta's Innocence rose lay across each of their place settings. Both women dressed with her own signature style. Cleo wore an elegant Adrienne Vittadini suit and estate diamond jewelry. Alena went funkier in a colorful Norma Kamali ruffled top worn off her shoulders with multiple strands of heavy black beads.

Cleo toasted Harry with a glass of champagne. Alena's smile wasn't so sincere.

Harry kissed her and whispered, "Relax." He sat to her right at the large table.

"Sonny," Giardino said, pouring him champagne, "I was just telling Cleo and Alena how wonderful it is for them to get this AmeriCenter job. How of *all* the big firms bidding for it, their small company pulls it out. Masterful. They are the envy of the city. And they are the best." He raised his glass. "To the best design firm in the city. May you soon be the best in the country."

"Or at least," Cleo added, "the most profitable."

Giardino laughed easily, in high spirits. "Yes, yes, the most profitable—far more important than just being best. I like this woman, Harry. I like *both* these women. Where were they when I was their age?"

"Kindergarten."

Giardino grinned scornfully. "Ow, such a terrible boy, this Sonny of mine."

Alena shifted uncomfortably at the possessive phrasing of Giardino's statement.

Lunch was served at a leisurely pace. Mussels marinara as antipasto, veal piccante as the entree, black pepper fettucini in lemon basil oil as a side dish. A moderate Italian wine replaced champagne. Espresso was served with raspberry cannoli for dessert.

Conversation was dominated by Giardino and Cleo; Giardino flirted with Interior Visions's owner and asked countless questions about the history of her business. He responded with appropriate sorrow when the timeline covered the death of Cleo's husband, and corresponding adulation when Cleo spoke of taking the company's helm and riding into profitability.

Harry reached under the table and patted Alena's knee whenever he sensed her anxiety about to explode with a direct and ill-timed question as to the purpose of this lunch. Alena was not the chatty type with business pending, a trait that sometimes offended business clients used to being wined, dined, and flattered before drawing nigh to the bottom line.

As the final bite of cannoli was finished, Giardino reached for his napkin, wiped his mouth, and, still chewing, said, "So tell me, what ideas do you have for the job?"

Cleo said, "That's Alena's department," and turned toward her for input.

Giardino held his small espresso cup in the hand with missing fingertips. "I'm excited to hear."

"What do you want to know?" Alena remained defensive.

"Everything! Designs, colors, fabrics. Not so much details, you understand, but the overall vision. I want to see it in my mind. Such an exciting project."

Alena responded tentatively, beginning with actual construction changes being discussed with the architect, ways to improve the visual feel of necessary walls, adding glass and smoothing out deliberate angles. There was discussion as to a possible mosaic for the lobby floor, a patriotic theme, nothing so routine as a flag or eagle, but a striking image that when viewed from atrium balconies above would be breathtaking.

Giardino said, "Wonderful," a compliment repeated constantly over the next ten minutes whenever Alena took a breath. His praise increased to an appreciative, "Wonderful, wonderful, wonderful," when she finished. "Simply wonderful." He pointed to Alena and told Cleo, "This young woman deserves a raise."

"We're seriously talking about it."

"Good." Giardino placed his boxer's hands on the chair arms to stand, but didn't. As though an afterthought, he said, "Do you happen to have a list, a—what do the young people call it?—a database of your subcontractors and suppliers?"

Before Alena could ask, "Why?" Cleo said, "Would you like to see it?"

"I may know some people who could get better deals for you, or supply labor at better rates. All of them American companies, naturally. Did you know I'm the one who pays for all those billboards . . ." Giardino painted a bold square in the air with his hands ". . . BUY USA."

Cleo said, "It's an effective campaign. It's made me very conscientious about reading labels."

◆ 187 ◆

Cleo was good at playing the game, Harry thought. *Reading labels*, sure, but probably not paying much attention to them. He didn't think Adrienne Vittadini sewed many stitches in the U.S. And Cleo had obscenely expensive—$350-plus a square yard—French tapestry carpet in her home.

Giardino said, "And I know the perfect painting company for the job. They're magnificent."

Alena said, "We have very good painters."

Cleo never broke stride, saying, "I'd love to talk to your people," and her enthusiasm wiped Alena's words from the air as though erasing a chalkboard.

Giordino beamed. "This is going to be wonderful. Wonderful! The crown gem building of the city." He stood and graciously held Cleo's chair. "Sonny," he said, ushering them politely, but directly, to the door, "this wonderful lady of yours is going to be so rich, you'll probably be able to retire." His firm hand lay atop Harry's shoulder and squeezed, applying pressure that reminded Harry of yesterday's conversation.

Harry allowed Cleo and Alena to go out ahead of him, then turned back toward Giardino, who stayed behind. Harry offered the composite sketch Mark Gesser had given him.

"What's this?"

"Ronald Showels's alibi. I need to find her. Showels passed the polygraph. The cops are in a panic."

Giardino looked down and smoothed his hand over tonic-slicked hair. "Sonny . . ." he commented with disappointment. After a few breaths through damaged nostrils, he met Harry's eyes. "I'm wasting my breath, aren't I?"

"Help me find her. Whatever happens, I excuse you from any promises made to my father."

"If only it was so simple."

Outside, Alena and Cleo waited for Harry at the curb.

Cleo was beaming from champagne, prestige, and soon-to-be-made money. "He's a wonderful man."

◆ 188 ◆

Alena stood defiant. "I don't want to be told how to run my jobs. Who to hire, who to buy from."

Cleo laughed. "Oh, dear, my now highest-paid employee and future part-owner is an idealist. Heaven help us."

"We're a good solid company. We've always done things our way and it's worked well."

Pleasant, but serious, Cleo said, "Alena, if that man can find us good talent for less cost, people to hang wallpaper at three dollars less per roll than Maxine's company, do you know how much more profit that puts in our pocket? We'll hand out bonuses equal to salaries."

"The contractors we've been using have been good to us for years, Cleo. We can't ditch them."

"We'll have more other new business from AmeriCenter publicity than they'll be able to handle. Besides, my guess is by the time we get back to the office, the contract and deadline snags we've hit on this job will be solved. What do you think, Harry?"

He'd stayed back half a step, trying not to interfere. "I think you can stop worrying about the contract."

Cleo grasped Alena's elbow with reassurance. "You always wanted the big time—so did I. Welcome to it."

Harry's pager sounded. He shaded the read-out from the sun's glare, held it farther from his eyes than he used to, and saw his office number.

Cleo asked Alena, "You want to go back to the office with me or have Harry drop you?"

Alena exhaled obvious disgust over the turn AmeriCenter had just taken.

"Harry, she's yours." Cleo unlocked her Jaguar, which was illegally parked in front of Vazinni's.

He hugged Alena. "It's going to be okay."

She was stiff in his grasp.

Harry tapped on Cleo's window. "Use your car phone?"

Cleo started the engine and air conditioning while Harry called the office.

◆ 189 ◆

"It's me," he told Marcie. "I'm still downtown."

"Harry, I got a strange call from someone named George Kittle. He says he's your sister-in-law's father?"

"He is."

"This is really odd, but he says he's calling from Florida . . ."

"That's right. He lives down there now."

"Well, your sister-in-law's been arrested."

◆ 26 ◆

George Kittle was mad, but he was also scared. "She was with her mother, shopping. And all of a sudden these guys grab Connie on the street and say she's under arrest."

"Slow down. What guys?" Closed in a phone booth, Harry covered his ear to block out street noise.

"They were federal."

"Marshals?"

"Christ, I don't know. Esther said they were federal agents."

"They must have said something else. ATF?" If Harry had to bet . . . Special Agent Hemingway talks to him on Saturday, now Wednesday, Connie is arrested by federal agents, and Hemingway is out of town.

"Esther," George Kittle bellowed away from the phone, "what the hell did the guys say they were? Did they say ATF?"

"Department of Alcohol, Tobacco and Firearms." Harry clarified, spelling out the acronym.

George Kittle replayed this to his wife.

Harry heard Esther's voice, but not the words; she sounded shaky. Connie's father came back on the line. "That was it. Alcohol and Firearms. What the hell's going on, Harry?" Implying this was Harry's fault.

Harry banged his fist against the phone booth wall and shoved open the door. It was like a sauna in there.

Delta had the earliest open seat to Orlando, but it was a connection—like every other Delta flight east of the Pacific Rim—through Atlanta. And a close connection at that. Harry passed and booked a later flight on USAir that was direct. Scheduled time of arrival in Orlando was 5:45.

He packed a few things back at the apartment while waiting for Richard Manning to pick up the phone. Manning was an Orlando attorney with a federal criminal practice; Harry got his name from the National Association of Criminal Defense Lawyers' roster.

Harry didn't know Manning beyond the listing and hoped the guy was good. His secretary seemed efficient, which was a positive starting point.

Manning came on the line as Harry put a second suit in the hanging bag. He sounded smart and aggressive.

Harry kept his introduction brief and thanked Manning for taking his call. "I've been on the phone with ATF for the past half hour getting the runaround."

"What else is new?"

"My sister-in-law's been picked up down there, and I can't find out a damned thing."

"They like to be mysterious and keep defendants from their lawyers to induce deals they'll cheat out of later. Don't sweat it. I've got some contacts. I can run her down for you."

"I'd appreciate it. Her name's Connie Walsh."

"Give me a number where I can get back to you."

"I'll call you. I'm flying down. I've got a flight in two hours."

"I'll have someone pick you up at the airport. Give me your flight number."

"Don't bother."

"No bother, we're set up for it. Give me the flight."

"Mr. Manning . . . Richard . . . I've got to be frank. My sister-in-law doesn't have a lot of money, and I'm not exactly wearing thousand-dollar suits, either."

"So you'll return the favor one day. We stick together, Harry. It's what the NACDL's all about. Otherwise these federal bastards'll grind us into the ground. Have a safe flight. We'll talk when you get into town."

While he was in the air, Harry wondered if he should have told Craig and Carla what was happening. He'd decided to keep their mother's arrest from them until *he* knew what was going on. Maybe that was wrong.

Alena promised to check on them—if only by phone—until Harry got back.

The flight seemed interminable. Normally a bit claustrophobic on planes, Harry found the purpose of this trip made him more restless than usual. He couldn't imagine what the hell had gone on in Orlando, George and Esther Kittle's new home town where Connie's life was supposedly going to be wonderful.

By the time the 727 landed, Harry was wired with energy. He was one of the first passengers off the plane, hanging bag over his shoulder.

At the gate, a good-looking man, late twenties, blond and tanned, wearing a hand-tailored suit, held a laser-printed sign: HARRY WALSH. In his other hand was a portable cellular phone.

Harry went directly to him. "I'm Walsh."

"Richard Manning's associate, Alex Gregory." They shook hands; Alex's grip was like taking hold of a graphite tennis racket. "We're going this way," he directed, serious but friendly.

They proceeded along the concourse toward the monorail that would take them to the main terminal. Disney music and motifs prevailed, priming wallets and pocketbooks for a big hit at the theme parks.

"Have you found out anything?"

"Yes, sir. Your sister-in-law's being held for five counts under USCA Section Eighteen, Article Four-seventy-two."

"You don't have to impress me with cites, just give me the offense."

"Sorry. It's the federal counterfeit statute. She deposited bogus currency at four local banks and had more in a satchel when she was arrested."

"Counterfeit money?"

"Yes, sir. Almost a hundred thousand dollars worth."

"I don't believe this."

"Well ATF sure suspected her, because this bust didn't come on any local tip. They followed her down from Maryland."

"I do *not* believe this."

They stopped and waited for the monorail. It whisked into the ministation moments after a computer-generated voice announced its arrival. Small children jumped up and down with excitement, wanting to see Mickey Mouse.

Harry's head began to pound. Boarding the electric train, he gripped the support post as doors slid shut and they headed for the terminal.

The young Orlando attorney saw him suffering.

Harry said, "I'm sorry for snapping at you back there about the statute. It's been a bad couple of days. My brother, her husband, was killed last Friday. He was a policeman."

"I'm sorry, sir."

"You don't have to call me sir."

"Mr. Manning's rules."

Outside the airport, in oppressive heat, a white Lincoln Town Car and uniformed driver waited. The driver was a hard weight-lifter type in a starched white shirt and crisp black pants.

Harry wondered if his luck was changing, striking this kind of gold picking a name out of a lawyer's directory.

The car's interior was cooled with bracing air conditioning and tinted windows. Harry had never been to Florida in the summer and leaving the heat of Maryland for even worse heat in Orlando seemed absurd. He couldn't imagine anyone voluntarily living here year round.

Traffic on the expressway and I-4 was horrendous. The efficiency with which tourists were whisked around Epcot Center was only a dream on the highways. Apparently Disney's desire to move people expediently was limited to shooting them from one Disney-revenue spot to another. On public roads, it was everyone for himself.

The limo driver was aggressive, but patient.

Alex Gregory asked Harry if he wanted aspirin.

◆ 194 ◆

"Thanks, no." Harry looked north across flat glades toward the city, never conceptualizing Orlando having a real downtown area. "Has bail been set?"

"Not yet."

"When will that happen? I confess to being a little stale on my federal procedure."

"It wouldn't matter if you weren't. Every circuit seems to 'interpret' the rules differently. But it may be that no bail is set."

"For a hundred grand in counterfeit they're denying her bail?"

"That's not what I mean. Your sister-in-law hasn't been officially charged. As of now, she's merely being held in custody."

"What are they waiting for?"

"It seems, sir, they're waiting for you. I spoke with an Agent Hemingway. He said he was expecting you."

As a result of booming tourism, Orlando was a growing city. Its boundaries sprawled across a grid of mixed business, industrial, and residential uses. Its former low-rise landscape was dotted with office towers put up by big regional and national banks. The air was clean, darkened only by thunderheads almost every day in the summer, not smog.

Harry and Alex Gregory went through metal detectors in the lobby and took an elevator to the ATF offices. A pleasant receptionist paged Special Agent Hemingway by intercom. An assistant took them to a conference room further inside the windowless, fluorescent-lit hive.

Their path intersected Hemingway's in the hall. The tall agent wore a smug grin. "Hey, what a coincidence. Harry Walsh, the lawyer who *doesn't* represent Sam Giardino." He snapped his fingers. "I knew I recognized you from somewhere."

Hemingway unlocked the conference room and turned on lights to reveal less-than-homey office space. Fluorescent tubes flickered behind faded ceiling inserts. The walls were plain, panelled white, no windows, no artwork. Deficit correction, it seemed, began with cutbacks in decorating.

◆ 195 ◆

Hemingway sat on one of ten metal-backed chairs positioned around a cheap conference table. His weight released a puff of air from a vinyl seat cushion.

Alex Gregory pulled back two chairs across from Hemingway for himself and Harry.

Hemingway said nothing. He folded his hands in his lap and crossed his legs like a cowboy on the saloon's front porch: his demeanor was a far cry from his first meeting with Harry, but some people reacted that way when they were winning. It went right to their head. Finally, he spoke, nodding toward Gregory. "Who's your friend?"

The attorney introduced himself, adding, "From Richard Manning's office."

"Don't know him."

Gregory removed a legal pad from his hard-sided briefcase. "That's because you're not local."

Hemingway sat forward, leaning directly toward Harry. His smile was erased. "I've got Connie rock solid on five counts of uttering and/or possessing counterfeit currency. She's looking at fifteen years per. I get one ounce of shit from you and she goes before the magistrate. You cooperate, you get *her* to cooperate, and she walks with no record, not even an arrest."

Harry stayed cool. "Contrary to your impression, I don't know what you're talking about."

"That's one quarter of an ounce of shit, three more quarters and we're done here."

"Look," Harry suggested diplomatically, "let's not talk like we're in the movies." It was warm in the office and Harry began to perspire. "I don't know why you've arrested my sister-in-law, don't know what you think she's done, or what you think she's part of. But I'm pretty sure I know where you're leading and you're as wrong today as you were Saturday. I do *not* work for Sam Giardino, and if this has anything to do with him, you're wasting your time."

Hemingway sat back. "Then we're finished here. I guess it was just a coincidence your brother's wife gets arrested and you're here within . . ." he checked his watch ". . . ten hours."

"I'm here *because* you arrested her. Why she was arrested, what she was doing, I have no idea beyond what you've said so far. Which isn't much. As far as I know, the whole deal's a ruse you figure to use as leverage to get me to talk about Giardino. Just like the not-so-subtle inferences you made that Giardino *may* have something to do with my brother's murder."

"It's not just an inference."

"Nice try. The State's Attorney's Office called you for information about my brother's killer, and you said you didn't have anything."

"We said we *couldn't* help them. Not that we didn't *have* information."

Harry's anger emerged. "You know who killed my brother?"

"You want to make a deal?"

"You bastard! You've got material information on a policeman's murder and you're withholding it? That's unconscionable."

"I've got a hip-deep investigation into one of the most sought-after mob bosses in the mid-Atlantic region. I make my case, I'll go back and set the record straight."

"That's swell. That's real swell."

Alex Gregory scribbled on a legal pad in his lap as he had throughout the exchange. Harry noticed the young lawyer was calmly taking down the conversation in shorthand.

"Are you telling me," Harry repeated, intent on making a record for Gregory's transcription, "that you know who murdered my brother?"

"I have information." Hemingway was no longer smug. He was anxious and mad, which told Harry the agent didn't want to walk out of this meeting empty-handed. Hemingway thought he was close to making his case, whatever that case was, but he needed something from Harry. Something he was going to swap for Connie.

"You know *who* killed my brother?" Harry pressed.

"Who actually pulled the trigger? No. Who ordered the killing? Definitely."

"You think it was Giardino?"

◆ 197 ◆

"I *know* it was Giardino."

"Why?"

"Uh-uh. I'm not handing you my case, Walsh. No way. But I'll tell you this—it's a good case."

"So why aren't you making it? Why haven't you picked Giardino up?"

"Because it's only *part* of my case. And I want the whole thing. I want your daddy's best friend in Allenwood until he's so old he's pissing his Depends every half hour."

"What do you want from me?"

"Information."

"On Giardino? You can't be serious."

"Seventy-five years behind bars for sis-in-law says I am."

"You framed her."

"Uh-uh. She screwed herself. Monday, back home in Towson, she and grandma go out on some errands, one of which is stopping by a bank on Joppa Road. Connie goes in empty-handed, gets into a safe deposit box your brother opened in joint names less than a year ago. She comes out with the money, brings it down here, spreads it around four banks."

"You're out of your mind."

"You know about Giardino, Harry. *She* knows about Giardino. Things I want to know."

"I don't know anything."

"Bullshit. The guy's been your father figure since *your* father was killed. Which makes me wonder why the hell you want to protect him in the first place? Your father's dead because a bullet meant for Giardino killed *him*. Sure, Giardino puts you through college, he pays for your law school, he tosses in some spending money. That's real gracious of him, paying for your father's death like that. Don't look so surprised . . ."

Harry didn't—and wasn't.

". . . you think we don't know all this? We've been watching Giardino for *thirty* years, Walsh. Since I was thirteen years old someone in this office has been watching Giardino, from back when putting fake revenue stamps on liquor bottles and cigarette packs was his main source of income."

"I'll tell you again: I *don't* know anything about his business. I'm not his consiglieri."

"You know—and sis upstairs knows." Hemingway reached for the phone. "Let me show you something." He dialed a three-digit interoffice number and asked someone to wheel in the VCR. Hanging up, he told Harry. "You'll like this."

The tape was surveillance footage shot from across the street of Vazinni's restaurant. The digital date-and-time image in the lower left corner, which could have been altered, was from last November. People on the street were bundled up against the cold. Snow flurries danced in the air. Harry recalled an early cold snap last November and figured the date stamp was probably legit. The start time was 9:17:33 A.M.

Alex Gregory made shorthand notes about what appeared on the tape.

Harry's stomach turned acidic, going on no food and considerable anxiety. He watched the tape expressionlessly, as though a jury might watch for his reaction. In this case, the jury was Hemingway.

When a Ford Taurus station wagon entered the frame, driving by the restaurant, Hemingway stopped the tape. "Recognize it? Look close."

It was Connie's car. Tucker was driving.

Harry felt strange seeing his brother. He swallowed a lump of sadness that filled his throat.

Gregory said, "What are we looking at?"

"My brother," Harry said plainly, "driving his family car."

Gregory added to his notes.

Hemingway fast-forwarded the tape four minutes worth. "Nothing happening in here . . ."

Harry would have to take his word for it.

". . . but here we go."

The tape played at normal speed. Tucker came back into the

♦ 199 ♦

frame, on foot this time, carrying an athletic bag in his hand. Harry thought, "Oh, God, no," when Tucker ascended the steps to Vazinni's and knocked on the door.

The time was now 9:22:49. Vazinni's didn't open until 11:30.

Giorgi opened the door and ushered Tucker inside.

Hemingway stopped the tape just as Tucker crossed the threshold. "See the bag he's carrying? It's got 'Mizuno' written on the side?"

"Yes." Harry's reply was partially choked in his larynx.

Hemingway kept the tape freeze-framed and went to the file cabinet. He unlocked and opened the top drawer, pulled out a Mizuno athletic bag, but thousands had been manufactured as a promotion; it could have been a duplicate. This one was bagged in clear plastic as evidence, with Connie's name, a date, and case number inscribed in permanent ink in the corner. Hemingway tossed it onto the table. It slid across the veneer, stopping just short of Harry.

"This is what she was carrying the money in. One hundred fifteen thousand dollars in counterfeit twenties and fifties. She dropped her mother at a doctor's office this morning, and proceeded to drive all around town, opening four new bank accounts in four separate banks. Twenty thousand per bank.

"We got calls in to all the bank managers in time to keep them from checking the bills for authenticity. We told them the money was bad and we were about to make an arrest. Everyone cooperated. They made sure Connie sat with an accounts officer with a good security camera aimed at their desk. Made sure everyone was happy and smiling, that all the papers were processed quickly, and the deals were consummated. Three of the managers have already given us depositions. The fourth is due in tomorrow morning.

"We waited until Connie went back to pick up her mother at the doctor's to arrest her. The shock value works so much better that way. She still had over thirty grand counterfeit in the bag."

Harry had a lot of questions, but none of them were for Hemingway. "I want to talk to her. Alone. No microphones in the room, no eyes."

"I'll have her brought down."

◆ 200 ◆

·27·

As soon as she was led handcuffed into the conference room and saw him, Connie began to sob. She fidgeted helplessly as the marshall unlocked the cuffs and, once freed, rushed into Harry's arms. Her tears were warm against his neck. "Harry, get me out of here, please! I didn't do anything. What do they want? What's happening?"

"Okay, settle down. Take it easy." He stroked her back, glaring over Connie's shoulder at Hemingway and the sturdy federal marshall who remained at the threshold. "You want to take a few steps back and shut the door," Harry demanded angrily.

They did. Shadows of their feet remained outside, showing under a crack in the door for a few seconds before they walked off.

Alex Gregory looked out to make certain they'd gone. The marshall sat across the hall, sidearm holster unsnapped, posed as a deterrent as though Harry and Alex might actually try a rescue. The uniformed man glared at Gregory, daring him to challenge his right to be there, finally saying, "She's a prisoner, okay, pal." The marshall wanted an argument in the worst way.

Gregory closed the door. "Let's sit down here." He motioned to the end of the table farthest from the door.

Harry put two chairs at right angles to one another, seating Connie in one as he took the other. She wore a summery short-sleeve top, shorts, and tennis shoes with white socks, looking like any other recently arrived tourist except for red handcuff marks around her wrists. Her knees touched Harry's as he sat forward and took her hands into his. Her skin felt as though held under cold water. Every few seconds, she shivered as though iced with fear.

He couldn't help thinking about their Christmas dinners together and how time had changed them. Much in the same way

◆ 201 ◆

Craig admitted fantasizing Harry was his father, Harry had experienced similar daydreams: at times having imagined he and Connie were married, that Craig and Carla were their children. Warm, idle thoughts that were only familial, not passionate, although there had been occasional unthinkable urges Harry had immediately driven away.

Now, those separate chapters of their lives seemed incongruous. There was no logical course from there to here. Somewhere along the line, like the onset of cancer, normal paths had been nicked by flaws and the divergence had metastasized.

"Connie . . ." He spoke unaccusingly, but to the point. "Where did you get the money?"

She wept. "I don't know."

"Connie . . . You got it somewhere."

She pulled a hand from Harry's grasp and wiped her eyes. "I don't know where he got it."

"Where Tucker got it?"

She nodded.

"How did you find out about it?"

"I don't know . . ."

From her tone, Harry understood she did know, but didn't want to say. He waited.

Connie's hands manipulated a handkerchief that wasn't there. "I think he was taking bribes."

Harry was laden with a terrible sense of loss, more so than when Marcie told him his brother was dead.

"It all went wrong so fast, Harry. We had a nice life. I thought we did, anyway. But then . . ." she looked up into faintly flickering ceiling lights ". . . I guess I did have on blinders. That's what Tucker always used to say: 'Get those blinders off, Connie, see the real world, see what's really happening out there.' I don't think I wanted to see . . . because I knew I wouldn't like it."

"Connie, did you know the money was counterfeit?"

"No," she replied desperately, repeating a denial already offered dozens of times to Hemingway during interrogation before Harry got there.

◆ 202 ◆

"Why did you go to different banks to deposit it?"

"My father—"

"Your father?"

"Before coming down here . . ." she spoke slowly, offering each phrase as a mistake made ". . . when I found the money in the safe deposit box, I told my father about it. I hadn't expected it to be there. I was looking for life insurance papers, or anything else . . . I told Dad I didn't know where Tucker got the money. I didn't want to say anything about what I thought—about him taking bribes— but Dad's eyes lit up and I think he suspected, because he said, 'Maybe the loser didn't leave you so bad off after all.' " She lowered her head. "The first nice thing he ever says about Tucker . . . not that it was really nice. But the first compliment . . ." She wiped her eyes.

"I wanted to tell you about it, Harry. I thought we should take the money to the police, but Dad said no. He said they'd cut off Tucker's benefits to me if it was found out Tucker was involved in something. I'd get nothing. So he said to pack up the money and bring it to Florida. That if the police started looking around—if Tucker was suspected of anything—they might look in banks at home, but not in Florida."

Harry rubbed his forehead. Perspiration made his fingers slide across his skin.

"So I put the money in the bag that was in the safe deposit box." She gestured to the Mizuno satchel in the clear evidence pouch. "I carried it on the plane. And put it in the bank."

"But why the *different* banks?"

"Dad said it would look suspicious putting it all in one place. That they might think it was drug money. But if I put twenty thousand in different banks, I could tell them it was money my parents had been keeping under their mattress because they didn't trust banks, or that I'd been given the money as a gift. He said twenty thousand dollars was the most you could deposit without the bank having to report the transaction to the IRS."

Harry shared a look with Alex Gregory. George Kittle only

◆ 203 ◆

missed the IRS reporting regulation amount by $17,000. A real international caper artist, old George.

"Harry, what's going to happen to me?"

"The agent who arrested you . . ." Harry paused, unsure he wanted to know the answer to what he was about to ask. "The agent who arrested you thinks you have information about the source of the money."

"Harry, I swear to God, I don't know. I told him."

"But you *thought* Tucker was taking bribes?"

"It was just a bad feeling . . . whenever I saw him with extra money. But it was never *that* much. Not *thousands* of dollars."

"Okay."

"Ma'am," Alex Gregory interrupted politely.

She looked at him, for the first time questioning his presence.

Harry explained: "Alex is a local attorney. He's here to help."

Connie nodded.

"Ma'am, what makes you think your husband was taking bribes? Even small ones? Did he ever say anything to you? Did you overhear conversations? See anything suspicious?"

"Sometimes he'd come home with money in his pockets or in envelopes. More money than he made at work."

"How much money?"

"I don't know for sure, but maybe a few hundred. It always looked like a lot because it was in smaller bills. Twenties, sometimes fifties."

"Did your husband say where it came from?" Alex Gregory questioned Connie as gently as tweezing a splinter from a young child's finger.

"That he won it playing the lottery."

"You have legalized lotteries in Maryland," Alex assumed, turning to Harry.

"Daily, weekly," Harry confirmed. "The whole deal."

"Ma'am, did you ever see him buy lottery tickets?"

"We didn't go out that much together, so I didn't see him actually buy them. But he had them around the house all the time.

Carla—our daughter—she loved scratching them off with him. The instant tickets."

"Did you ever see them win?"

"Lots of times."

"A lot of money."

"Twenty-five dollars mostly, five dollars, two dollars, sometimes more. On the rub-off cards."

"What about bigger amounts?"

"He said he won bigger amounts on the Saturday or Wednesday lotto. The drawing. I didn't pay much attention to it. I didn't think it was a good influence on the children, really. Our son got mad when Tucker gave Connie a hundred tickets for Christmas. He said they were both stupid and stormed out." Connie spoke sadly, and sarcastically. "It was a wonderful holiday." She smiled remorsefully at Harry. "Not like our old Christmases."

Harry wiped sweat from his forehead to conceal sudden tears rising in his eyes.

"So it's possible," Alex surmised with some suggestion, "it's *logical*, for you to believe this money found in a safe-deposit box could have come from lottery winnings."

"I guess."

"Did you and your husband file joint income tax returns, Mrs. Walsh?"

"Yes."

"Did you read them and sign them?"

"Yes. We went to a tax service and the woman always read over every line with us."

"Were lottery winnings ever listed?"

"No." Connie answered vaguely, as though unsure whether that was the right answer or not.

"So it's understandable why you would have thought your husband would have put winnings in a safe-deposit box and not put them in a bank where records would be kept. Lottery winnings are taxable income. He wouldn't have wanted there to be a record."

Alex was at once selling and coaching Connie, but it was a thin

◆ 205 ◆

argument. A jury might buy it, though, if properly packaged and rehearsed.

"Connie?" Harry held her hands firmly and backtracked the line of questioning. "Why do you *think* it was bribe money? Not direct evidence, nothing you saw that was suspicious, but in your heart. What makes you think Tucker was taking bribes?"

She took her time answering. She pushed away sweaty locks of dark-blond hair that fell around her eyes. "Not long after the money started showing up, Tucker became depressed. The same way he got depressed if he missed my birthday or forgot our anniversary or got passed over for a promotion. He always wanted more money, Harry, and here it was in his hands and he wasn't happy about it. I took the blinders off, Harry. Tucker was upset about the money because of how he got it."

"Did Tucker ever mention a man by the name of Sam Giardino?"

Connie looked at him as though summoning the answer to a quiz. "The man your father was with when he was killed?"

"Did Tucker mention anything about talking with Giardino? Meeting with him?"

Connie said, "No," and was immediately horrified by realization. "Oh, God. It's mob money, isn't it?"

Harry and Alex Gregory remained in the conference room after the marshall took Connie back to a temporary holding cell upstairs. Harry had been shaken by the sight of his sister-in-law in handcuffs. He tried to consider her as any other client: a logical but impossible ploy. This was Connie, a part of what little family he had left. He had to get her out.

Alex Gregory spoke quickly, not knowing how much time they had before Hemingway would rejoin them: "We've got a strong argument she didn't know the money was counterfeit, Mr. Walsh. They have to prove knowledge. It's an element of the crime. It can be inferred by conduct, but I think we're okay on that. Who deposits counterfeit money in a bank? It's passed on the street or sold."

Harry considered the young attorney. "You're saying we hardball them? Tell Hemingway to stick it?"

"Absolutely."

"Which leaves Connie locked up or posting bail."

"What's our option? She's got nothing to give them."

"*I* could bluff them. Make Hemingway think I'm going to help him if he lets Connie out."

"You could get hit with obstruction of justice."

"I'll take the chance if he cuts her loose. I don't want her in here, Alex. I want her home."

"We can probably do that anyway. Mrs. Walsh wasn't arrested under indictment or complaint or warrant. She'll be taken before a magistrate, probably tomorrow, maybe the next day if Hemingway wants to stall. They'll hold a probable cause hearing. We'll raise the knowledge issue, but likely won't prevail. We'll make the decision, with your input of course, as to whether to waive indictment and let them proceed under an information. And pretrial release will be considered. Mrs. Walsh seems a likely candidate, maybe not for recognizance, but a moderate bail."

"How moderate?"

"Under a hundred thousand," Alex estimated.

"But maybe more, right?"

"Perhaps her parents could raise—"

"No. George Kittle tried taking care of her. He blew it in forty-eight hours. I'll take it from here." Harry thought of Connie as a client—for the moment it took him to reach a decision. "Tell Hemingway no deal. She didn't know the money was phony."

"Yes, sir."

"I'm going back to Maryland. Connie may not have known the money was counterfeit, but someone does."

Harry tried to call from Orlando, but Alena wasn't in the office and no one seemed to know where she was other than to say she took the afternoon off. Harry tried her twice more via skyphone en route, and again upon arrival at BWI. All he got were answering machines at Alena's townhouse in the city and their condo in Towson. He wished she'd answer; he wanted to see her that night.

By the time the plane landed, Harry's stomach was in knots from anxiety and hunger. His digestive tract needed solid food to diffuse the acid. The sports bar at the head of Pier D was the only eating spot open at 9:30.

Harry was one of six patrons: all tired businessmen with briefcases and draught beers, settled amidst memorabilia of the city's golden age of sports, when the Orioles reigned supreme and the Colts played outdoors on turf at Memorial Stadium, not on polyethylene in the Hoosier Dome four state lines west.

ESPN was usual fare on the minisaloon's four wall-mounted TVs, but once auto racing came on, the bartender grazed the channels via remote control. Maryland may have been on the Mason-Dixon Line, but only her hillbillies liked car racing.

The bartender stopped on Channel 13. Sally Thorner was doing a fifteen-second tease for the 11:00 news.

"I got the hots for her," the bartender said to anyone listening.

A patron said, "Nope. Lynn Russell on Headline News any day. Those jackets she wears—it looks like she doesn't have on anything underneath."

Sally Thorner broadcast: "And in local news, the alleged killer of a Baltimore County police officer goes free on bail. Details at eleven."

* * *

"Mark?"

"No, this is Harry Walsh. I'm calling for Mark Gesser."

"He's not here."

"Are you Mark's wife?"

"Yes." She sounded mad, not necessarily about being Gesser's wife, but that he wasn't there.

A small child in the background said, "I want to talk to daddy."

"It's not daddy, honey."

"Late again," the little girl chirped mynah-like, echoing her mother's oft-spoken words.

Marriage to an attorney tended to be a lousy life.

"Do you know when Mark will be in?"

"No. Neither does the broiled chicken. It's been on the table so long it thinks it's family. It asked for its allowance half an hour ago."

"I need to talk to Mark as soon as possible. Would you have him call me, please?"

"Assuming I don't kill him first."

Harry left his pager and home numbers.

Just before Mrs. Gesser hung up, the little girl started squawking, "Late again, late again, late again."

Harry didn't bother going back to the bar for the kosher dog and kraut he'd ordered. He suddenly wasn't hungry.

He got his car out of long-term parking and drove the Beltway to the Joppa Road exit. He kept checking the rearview mirror to confirm he wasn't being followed. For whatever reason, he no longer seemed of much interest to the Feds. Maybe now that they had Connie, their manpower was diverted. It was impossible to figure out federal law enforcement strategy, and you could drive yourself insane trying to deal with it logically.

Harry arrived at Tucker's house just after ten. It was dark inside until Harry flicked on a standing lamp.

Alarmed by the intrusion, the grey cat jumped off the TV. The quick, silent motion startled Harry; he kept forgetting they owned a pet. The grey tabby dashed softly across worn carpet into the

◆ 209 ◆

kitchen, leapt onto the counter, and toppled an empty plastic cup with his tail.

Harry called, "Hello," and checked upstairs to make sure neither of the kids were home. They weren't. He started going through the house, opening drawers, searching through envelopes and folders, looking inside empty cans in the basement and shoe boxes in the closets.

Going through their home before Tucker's funeral had been only a cursory search in comparison to his current attempt.

He found bank papers. Connie wrote checks from a joint account for the mortgage, groceries, utility, car, and Visa bills. Cancelled checks and recent statements were rubber-banded in a desk drawer in the dining room hutch. In the basement, Harry opened an old metal cabinet and began assembling files containing other bank and insurance records, tax returns dating back seven years, college and financial aid information for Craig, and three editions of review materials for the Baltimore County Lieutenant's exam along with results.

The most recent test was taken two years ago. Tucker scored an 89. Promotions came from 95 or higher, except, according to a nasty letter of objection Tucker wrote to the review board, in the case of minority applicants, one of whom was promoted with a 75, another with an 81. A copy of Tucker's complaint was stuck crumpled in a file along with a letter from Darwin Ellis, a respected county lawyer specializing in employment law, who advised in lengthy legalistic fashion that Tucker did not have a basis to file a reverse discrimination suit against the county.

Bank statements and correspondence revealed even greater frustration than Tucker's hopes for promotion. Checks had been returned for insufficient funds. Mortgage late fees were routine, not exceptions; twice their house had been listed in the newspaper as a foreclosure for nonpayment. Checks were made payable to George Kittle marked: *Repayment of money lent.* A home equity loan taken out three years ago for debt consolidation nearly did them in at 22 percent interest. That loan, apparently, was what George Kittle paid off for them, and Connie and Tucker were repaying George

◆ 210 ◆

$100 a month. How humiliating it must have been to go to Connie's father for money; how George Kittle must have rubbed Tucker's face in it, punishing the bad dog he'd warned everyone was a rotten puppy.

But worst of all, seven months ago, two months after the ATF surveillance tape caught Tucker leaving Vazinni's restaurant, Tucker and Connie Walsh's long-term money troubles began turning around. Bills were paid on time. Credit card balances were steadily, but not abruptly, reduced. The Taurus was paid off in full. All this, even though according to last year's tax returns and this year's pay stubs, Tucker's salary hadn't even been increased to cover the cost of living index.

Tucker, Harry analyzed with great remorse, had either gotten very lucky, or very dirty. Harry sat among the brief physical evidence he had collected and considered destroying it. It would have been an act of denial, little else. The records here were easily duplicated by the concerned banks and credit agencies. Tucker hadn't been very careful.

Harry leaned back against the cool concrete wall and closed his eyes. He was worn out. Long day. He thought about Alena.

Pulling himself up, he crossed the small cellar to Tucker's workbench by the back door. A phone was mounted to the wall. Harry dialed Alena's downtown number.

He got the answering machine again, and tried not to worry why she wasn't home yet. Instead, he worried about where Tucker had gotten all that money.

◆ 211 ◆

❖ 29 ❖

Thursday morning, Alena's answering machine picked up again. Thinking she might have been in the shower, Harry tried back thirty minutes later. Answering machine again.

It left him with an empty feeling. She would have checked for messages since yesterday afternoon, which meant, for some reason, she wasn't returning his calls.

He wished there was time to go downtown and look for her, but he had an unknown deadline to meet in Orlando: to get Richard Manning and Alex Gregory enough information to blow Special Agent Hemingway out of the water with Connie's case.

As best he could, Harry forced his personal life aside, hoping there was a reasonable explanation. He started off on his day.

Marion Greenbaum ushered Harry inside her private office and closed the door. She was at work early, as always, bolstered by expensive coffee blends delivered by an exotic and overpriced java-of-the-month club.

Her real estate title office was tastefully decorated in conservative solid woods that offered a feel of stability, as though Marion had been there forever and would be there forevermore.

She was a short, solid woman with a pleasant round face and nose she'd had redone for her forty-fifth birthday. Her main client was a family-run S&L with assets over five million dollars. The family owners happened to be Marion's family. Lined across her credenza were settlement papers for the five mortgage refinances scheduled for today.

Harry sat when Marion offered a chair. He wore a rich olive-hued suit; an Alena present.

❖ 212 ❖

Settled behind her sturdy desk, Marion thought a bit longer about Harry's proposal.

"The police," Harry prodded, "could subpoena your records."

Marion's expression reflected professional courtesy, but real estate was that type of practice: nonadversarial, concerned with liens and flaws in titles, not impeaching the liars and fools put forth as opposing witnesses at trial. "You don't have to threaten me, Harry."

"I didn't mean it that way. What I need I could probably get at the courthouse—it's all public record—but you could save me a lot of time."

"Ron Showels is a client, Harry. I'm bound by confidence, you know that."

"So you do handle settlements for the mortgages Showels brokers?"

"Most, not all. Some of his mortgagees use their own counsel."

"I'm looking for one of Showels's investors with an Asian name. Korean. He would have been the source of money for about a dozen mortgages, probably done close together, twelve to thirty-six months ago."

"Business has been crazy with the damned prime rate yo-yoing all over the board. I'm doing thirty settlements a week on average." Marion was trying to bow out gracefully—if Harry would let her.

"Marion . . . somehow, some way, some*thing* links Ronald Showels to my brother. I need to talk to someone who was doing business with Showels. I have a line that Showels hasn't exactly been operating straight and narrow, and if Tucker was investigating something about Showels's activities, then I have the link the police can't find."

"I'm sure Ron didn't do it."

"Well, like you said, he *is* your client."

"My *real estate* client. I don't represent killers."

Harry contemplated telling Marion about Showels using a car to run someone off a cliff in Acapulco. A fanciful angry-spouse-told tale, but sometimes the wildest stories turned out to be true. He decided against it, though, for fear of revealing his source. Instead, he proffered, "I'll make a deal with you."

"Title attorneys don't plea bargain."

"Give me the investor's name. I'll tell him I got it at the courthouse. I'm only going to ask him about the mortgages going bad and how Showels offered to have P & I payments made in cash."

"You could ask *me* if anyone's brought cash to the settlement table."

"That would breach a confidence."

"It concerns my reputation, so I'll answer: my settlement funds come by bank check only. I read the warnings about money launderers, Harry. Bank checks only."

"I didn't doubt *you.*"

"Just in case." Her polite expression showed traces of concern. "You think Ron Showels is laundering money through real estate loans?"

"It's just a question, not a theory. You give me the investor's name, maybe I can find out."

Harry left his car in the small lot behind Marion Greenbaum's office and walked three blocks to the courthouse.

Grey clouds laden with moisture from the Gulf of Mexico had made the slow trek up the eastern seaboard, inclined to hover over central Maryland today. Office workers stepping out of doors first checked the sky to consider the prudence of umbrellas before proceeding on their errands.

The low clouds erased shadows and glare, and smothered the small metropolis's traffic sounds, making horns sound hollow as trumpets played in a faraway room.

According to his secretary, Mark Gesser had a Master's hearing scheduled for 9:15. Harry displayed his courthouse pass and circumvented the line at the entrance metal detector at 9:05. He took the stairs instead of the elevator, and halfway to the third floor wished he hadn't. His legs were heavy from a lack of sleep. His breathing came much more heavily than usual.

Gesser was in the outer hall with his client, another in an end-

◆ 214 ◆

less line of bitter husbands with deep pockets and even deeper desires for revenge against a soon-to-be-ex-wife. Gesser often said that about half of his fees were for legal work, the other half to put party opponents "through the ringer."

In the crowded hall, Gesser looked to be priming his client like a trainer going over last-minute instructions with his heavyweight contender. He offered a slight nod to let Harry know he saw him.

Harry impatiently checked his watch. There was so goddamned much to do today. He'd been falling behind at the office before yesterday's detour to Orlando, which really set him back. Marcie was spending far too much time covering for him, seeking extensions on time-imposed matters and filing motions under his signature when allowances couldn't be agreed upon with opposing counsel.

Gesser made Harry wait ten minutes. He sat his client in a spot he deemed beyond swinging distance of his wife or her lawyer, and made his way to Harry.

"Did you get my call last night?"

"Yeah, but I didn't get in until two."

Harry led Gesser into the enclosed stairwell, which afforded stark surroundings, but privacy. They spoke quietly so their conversation wouldn't carry along hard concrete walls like ping-pong balls. Gesser was only half into his phony southern accent this morning:

"One of the dicks I got looking for the alibi woman thought he had her last night. A guy at the bar the night Ron met this girl gets around. He saw her night before last at the Sheraton and called us. He's an enterprising guy, going after the five grand reward we've got on the table to find her. He strikes up a chat with this honey and says he'd like to go out with her. She says, get this, 'Bring your wallet and I'll be there.' She's a hooker."

"So what happened?"

"Guy's there, we're there, we wait until after midnight . . . She doesn't show."

Harry shook his head. "This guy's jerking you around. He probably hit on you for a couple hundred bucks for his effort."

◆ 215 ◆

"No . . . Not really."

"Not really . . . ? He asked for pocket money, right? For the drinks he spent at the bar the night he supposedly saw her?"

"Fifty bucks."

Harry laughed sourly. "Christ. He suckered you, Mark."

"No he didn't," Gesser said defensively. "He got her, but she was scared off."

"By what?"

"After she didn't show last night, these two dicks went out looking for her. People they'd talked to the last couple days about her—bartenders, other carousers we paid a couple bucks to because they said they'd keep an eye out—all of a sudden they don't know *anything*. What girl were they talking about?" Gesser's mouth tightened. "Somebody's out there shaking the weeds, trying to scare this chick off."

"Let me talk to Showels. He's out now, right?"

"I told you it's no problem." Gesser grinned broadly through his concerns. "Told you I'd get him out, too, didn't I? Who knows, I might dip into this high-profile criminal stuff more often. Goddamned newspapers are ringing my phone off the hook."

"Let me talk to him today."

Harry called Marcie from a phone booth outside the courthouse. He tapped the glass door waiting for her to answer. Four rings, five rings . . . come on, Marcie.

"Law offices."

"It's me. You hear anything from Alena?"

"No, but I've got Alex Gregory on hold long distance from Florida. You want a conference call?"

"Tell him I'll call him right back."

"Okay." Marcie shifted some papers. "I rescheduled your new client for one. I couldn't put him off. He was very insistent. I'm sorry."

"Pain in the ass." Sometimes Giardino's referrals were obnoxious; they found being arrested a major annoyance.

"I'm sorry, Harry. He was really insistent."

◆ 216 ◆

"It's not your fault. I'll be there. See you at one. Tell Alex I'm calling him back right now." Harry hung up and went into his pocket diary for the card the young Orlando attorney handed him yesterday in the limo.

Richard Manning's receptionist answered promptly and immediately put him through.

"Mr. Walsh, good morning." Alex Gregory sounded well-rested. Harry was envious. "I'm in Mr. Manning's office with him. We're going on speaker phone if that's all right?"

"Fine."

After a few electronic clicks, Alex's voice echoed annoyingly through the speaker system, but remained clear. "Mr. Walsh?"

"I'm here. What's going on with Connie?"

"Harry, Richard Manning." Manning's voice came through stronger; likely he was closer to the phone. "I appreciate your calling back, but we're glad to pick up the long-distance charge."

"There's an outside chance my office phones are tapped. The Feds followed me for a while after my brother's death."

"If that's true, we've got a circuit judge down here who loves to chew up agents for misconduct. He even encourages lawsuits for invasion of privacy."

"I'd like to meet him sometime. How's my sister-in-law?"

"I spoke with her half an hour ago, Mr. Walsh, she's holding up all right."

Harry couldn't imagine that; then again, "all right" was a subjective term.

"Her father," Richard Manning said, "is a different story. He's raving mad about her still being in custody. He said if I couldn't get her out he was going to find another attorney. I told him it was because of his wonderful advice Connie was in jail in the first place. And if he did an encore and found a lawyer as smart as he is, Connie could be in jail until she's a hundred. That shut him up."

"No small miracle," Harry complimented. "What about the probable cause hearing?"

"That's what we want to talk about. I don't assume you've been able to find anything helpful so far."

◆ 217 ◆

"No, but with one exception, that's *all* I'm planning to do the rest of today. How much time do I have?"

"Under normal scheduling in this district, Harry, the hearing would be today, but Alex and I have been giving the matter a lot of thought, and we're advising the hearing be held off until tomorrow or even Monday. We'll need to waive on the record, but that can be done by written motion."

"And Connie sits in jail until then?"

"Hemingway has made arrangements for her to remain in the temporary detention quarters in the federal building instead of going over to the state pretrial system. Connie's alone and she's safe."

"You've talked to Hemingway?" Harry was surprised.

"I took the liberty, Mr. Walsh. We spoke yesterday after you left and again this morning."

Harry became uneasy.

Alex said, "Hemingway is amenable to holding off on the hearing, which is beneficial to Connie if evidence can be found quickly to establish her innocence."

"I don't want to leave her in custody to take that chance. Let's go ahead with the hearing and get bail set. Once she's out—"

"Mr. Walsh . . ." Alex interrupted, and then paused not in hesitance, but as a gesture of manners so as not to seem accusatory. "Mr. Walsh, I don't believe your sister-in-law was being entirely honest with you yesterday."

"Did Hemingway say something?"

"No, sir. But, Mr. Walsh, her story is not entirely logical. If I have the time table incorrect, please tell me, but according to your and her statements, last Friday, six days ago, your brother was murdered. A mere four days later, Mrs. Walsh says she went to a bank safe-deposit box to, and these are her exact words: 'I was looking for life insurance papers or anything else.' Earlier in our conference, she said she suspected your brother was taking bribes, but never confronted him with it." Alex again offered polite pause. "Most people who have safe-deposit boxes know what's in them. And if your brother was taking bribes and keeping it a secret from

◆ 218 ◆

Mrs. Walsh, would he have put it somewhere she knew about?" When Harry didn't respond, Alex said, "I don't think she was looking for life insurance papers, Mr. Walsh, I think she was looking for the 'anything else.' And I think she found it."

Harry's instinct was to object, until he thought about the round-headed man from Baltimore County who visited Connie last Saturday to explain and leave copies of *insurance papers* and Tucker's will. Alex Gregory was right: Connie had no reason to look in a safe-deposit box for insurance papers that had been hand-delivered to her.

"Now, Mr. Walsh, please understand, I'm not saying I believe your sister-in-law was involved, but I think she knows more than she's saying and she's afraid to tell us."

"Maybe if I talked to her alone."

"Maybe," Richard Manning contributed, "if she sits in a comfortable, *safe* cell for another day, Harry, and thinks about what a string of years behind bars would be like, she'll be a bit more candid. Solitude," Manning added, "induces reflection, but we'll run it however you want, although let me advise you this: our firm bills five hundred an hour for criminal work in federal court. We get that because we win. So far, we're not charging you dime one. This is professional courtesy, Harry. Return the courtesy and do yourself a favor, take our advice. You're too close to the case to see it objectively."

"She's not lying to me."

"All right then, let's look at it this way. Maybe she needs time alone for other reasons. If she's not in jail, she's around her father."

"You're fairly perceptive, aren't you?"

"Schmucks don't bill five hundred an hour."

Harry left the phone booth and walked up the hill to his car. Next stop: Dr. Connelly, the psychiatrist who'd prescribed the Valium Tucker had lingering in his bloodstream when he was killed. Connie said Tucker had been depressed; Dr. Connelly might know if it had to do with a hundred grand plus in counterfeit money in a safe-deposit box.

◆ 219 ◆

◆ 30 ◆

Your brother wasn't a patient of mine."

Dr. Brian Connelly was a slender man with a thick head of dark curly hair and a pleasant face. His sunny office, not far from where Harry and Alena met for dinner at Chen's, was a converted upstairs bedroom in an elegant townhouse.

Dr. Connelly believed seeing patients in his home offered a greater sense of security and warmth than being behind just another door in an office complex.

"I saw my brother's prescription bottle for Valium, doctor. It had your name on it."

"You're sure?"

"I'm positive."

"Then that's very troubling." Connelly spoke in the pseudocomforting monotone of a therapist, offering words without underlying emotion. His brow, however, knotted slightly with concern. "Last winter, I was burglarized. Very little was taken. So little, at first I thought nothing was gone, but then I noticed a few missing pieces. Some of the Avalians." He gestured to the glass cocktail table where small colorful carvings were positioned like Dali-esque chess pieces on an abstract board. "They're from Haiti. Not at all valuable, but I like them. The artist has been missing for two years, believed to have perished attempting to boatlift into the states."

"This has to do with my brother?"

"Besides some art pieces, prescription pads were taken, but only a few. I didn't know any were missing until a pharmacist friend from Cross Keys called to verify a prescription. I didn't know the patient and hadn't written the prescription."

"You notified the police?"

"Immediately. So did my friend, but whoever was passing the

prescription must have become suspicious because they left before the police arrived."

"Was it my brother?"

"A younger man, I believe they said. Scruffy looking."

"I'd like to believe my brother didn't break into your home."

"I'm sure he didn't." The reassurance was more familiar than simple reflex. "I *did* know your brother, Mr. Walsh. We spoke a few times. He impressed me as a concerned man—worried, but no more so than most fathers of teenaged children."

"You said he wasn't a patient."

"He wasn't. But his daughter—I guess that would be your niece—Carla. I saw her a few times. She was having trouble at school. Nothing serious. A teacher met with your brother and his wife at a parent conference and recommended me."

"Her mother said Carla had seen a few therapists. She said she was good at conning them."

Connelly smiled as though recalling a fencing adversary to whom he'd lost a few jousts. "She's a very manipulative young lady. And her grades don't reflect it, but she's quite smart."

"But is she also a thief?"

"Well," Connelly hedged, "kids don't see it that way. They take something . . . it's not really stealing from someone else because they don't understand the sense of loss that comes from being robbed. It's more of a lark. Kids perceive the immediate moment. Their thinking is extremely short term. What can I do *now* for fun—*right now*. They spend very little time considering consequences and their consciences are remarkably slippery—not much sticks to them."

Harry tried to drive a defining spike through the mumbo-jumbo. "You think she took your prescription pads?"

"If your brother ended up with a Valium prescription supposedly written by me, which I didn't write . . ." Connelly shrugged, still unwilling to place blame, á là, there's no such thing as a bad person, just good people who do bad things.

Harry never thought much of that theory: he knew a lot of bad people.

* * *

Harry left Dr. Connelly, thinking how much fun Carla must have had with the mild-mannered therapist. If her conversation in the car the other night, boldly announcing Tucker had been having sex with teenagers, was any indication of her intent to shock, she must have been able to tangle Dr. Connelly in Freudian knots.

Connie was arrested with over a hundred thousand dollars in counterfeit money, but it wasn't her fault.

Tucker had Valium from a stolen prescription, but he didn't steal the pad or fraudulently obtain a narcotic.

Sam Giardino had been visited by Tucker last November, but that he withheld this fact from Harry was not an implication of Giardino and Tucker being involved in any common schemes.

Ronald Showels was found in possession of the weapon that killed Tucker, but he didn't do it.

Tierny Wells leased a one-bedroom apartment in a circa-1970 complex of stucco-and-wood buildings called The Colony, a one-time haven for the swinging singles set where "mod" and "disco" divorcées used to flock for action as soon as the separation papers were signed.

The times had changed radically. There were no more Nehru jackets and love beads, but The Colony's reputation for attracting a party crowd lingered in varying degrees of fact and fiction across low California-influenced units built into the side of a gentle hillside.

Tierny's taste for decor was strictly store-bought country, a severe contrast to the vintage Colony look of mirrored walls and playpen sofas. Much as the way she dressed, Harry noted, Tierny's living space reflected a dichotomy of personality between the staid and outgoing.

Not long out of bed and seemingly enjoying her recent unemployment, Tierny let Harry in and retreated barefoot across pale carpet. She settled into an upholstered armchair by the open sliding door. The outside air smelled of rain yet to fall.

Tierny ran her hand through tousled hair in an attempt to flat-

◆ 222 ◆

ten it out, and drew the belt of a white cotton robe more tightly about her waist. "Tommy Birchette," she explained happily, "spent the night." Tierny laughed. "I feel like I should be smoking a cigarette. It had been a while, Harry. Too long. Not that it's everything . . . but it's nice."

Harry thought about Alena. "Yes, it is."

"Tommy," Tierny grinned naughtily, "was *very* late for work."

Harry shared her smile and eased into a country-plaid sofa, resting his elbows on his knees. "What happened with Showels?"

"Trammell got Tommy to go along with a deal."

"Reduction in bail," Harry guessed, "in exchange for Showels saying who he 'thinks' set him up—Gesser told me his game plan. It's a fake. He thinks it's Showels's wife."

"It's plausible. They claim the wife's schizophrenic and sometimes goes off into this fantasy world. They say she's a chronic liar." Tierny didn't sound entirely convinced, but added, "Those times she filed abuse charges against Showels? Tommy looked back at them. It's true, both times she asked that the charges be dropped, but only *after* the prosecutor found medical evidence inconclusive of abuse. One ER doctor even said, off the record, he thought some of her physical trauma was self-inflicted."

"Bullshit. I know Sheila Parks. She wouldn't suborn perjury."

"She might not know. SS didn't represent her back then. And in the divorce case? She's fighting Gesser tooth and nail to prevent a psychological evaluation of the wife."

"You have to. If you go along with the evaluation, your client thinks you're agreeing with the other side that she's nuts. They go ballistic on you."

"Still, consider Showels passed the polygraph. And if you consider the set-up theory, who else would have access to Showels's gun and have keys to his car to plant it?"

"Which would mean the wife shot Tucker? Come on."

"She's got an alibi—a *good* one."

Harry couldn't believe Trammell had been so desperate as to even consider Mary Anne Showels a serious enough suspect to question her whereabouts.

◆ 223 ◆

"And with Showels, we've still got no motive." Tierny referred to the State's position as though still in their employ. "Trammell got a search warrant for Showels's office and house and went through both places. There's nothing incriminating. Nothing that links Showels to your brother. Nothing that even puts Showels near the crime scene. And you remember the snitch who said he saw Showels drop a paper bag with Tucker's citation book in a trash can at the race track?" She shook her head. "Trammell's had one of his men working with Pimlico security piecing together tape from different cameras. Now they don't have Showels coming into the building—not all entrances are covered by surveillance—but they have him inside at one-fifteen, fifteen minutes before the first race, and he isn't carrying any bag."

"He wouldn't walk around with it. He'd dump it as soon as he got there."

"Follow that theory even further, Harry. Tucker is shot before dawn. The race track doesn't open until twelve-thirty. That's six hours—plus, it's a forty-minute ride from the scene to the race track. Why wait that long to dump very incriminating evidence?"

"People do it all the time. They panic. They're not sure about the best place to trash something. It's not always logical. Why do escaped convicts go right from jail to their mother's house where the police are waiting for them?" Harry sat back. "I can't believe Jacobs authorized Birchette to cut this deal."

"If he didn't, Gesser was going to hold a press conference and announce that Showels passed a lie-detector test. This way, Ed got to hold the press conference. You didn't see him on the news last night?"

Harry shook his head.

"He was quite outraged. *Quite* outraged. He blamed it all on the system and slick defense lawyers."

"Wonderful." The police were in full panic.

"Showels is being tailed around the clock, if that helps."

"I doubt he's planning to kill someone else."

"You never know."

·31·

The man seated in the dining/conference room did not look like one of Sam Giardino's usual referrals. The clients Giardino sent were not necessarily more intelligent than the rough-looking man in the jeans and filthy work shirt, but they carried themselves with a certain racketeer's panache.

They were fringe players, bookmakers, con men, and crooks who preferred interesting upscale capers to holding up gas stations; they favored sparkly jewelry and flashy polyester clothes, loved Sinatra and Tony Bennett (even some of the young ones), and were ready to head off for Atlantic City at the snap of a crisp hundred-dollar bill. Impetuous men and women, they often came in with sons or daughters who had been picked up on "some small beef": shoplifting, DWI, a business-licensing violation, or various street scrapes.

The angry man in the conference chair, watching Harry from the corners of slit eyes, was not like that at all. He was far less innocent. At least, Harry figured, he'd be able to make quick work of him. He'd quote a high retainer and that would be that, but he would do it graciously—professionally—even suggesting another attorney.

"Mr. Laurel . . ." Harry slid closed the conference room door. ". . . I'm Harry Walsh." He offered his hand across a corner of the table.

Without moving his squarish head, Otis Laurel turned a sullen stare toward Harry. His thick hands, imbedded with grime, remained folded across the oil-stained lap of his grey shirt. An oval name tag stitched with OTIS, was half torn from a single breast pocket which bulged with a soft pack of cigarettes.

"My son," he said, barely moving his mouth, "is dead." Otis Laurel was not mourning a loss; he was mad.

◆ 225 ◆

Harry awkwardly withdrew his hand and sat across the table. "I'm sorry."

"Why? You didn' know 'im."

"I'm sorry for your loss."

"Yeah—uh-huh," Otis mumbled sarcastically. "Sure." He was probably only thirty-eight, but looked a hard forty-five. He smelled of sweat and engine grease. His black hair was long and slicked back, not with tonic, but with the body oils that accumulate with a lack of bathing.

He was not, Harry realized, one of Giardino's referrals. "How did you get my name?"

"Friend of a friend sort of thing." Otis didn't blink. He held his stare firmly on Harry and a precarious rage quivered tightly in his expression, a bound torment looking for a vent.

Harry knew the warning signs and laid back warily. "Is this about your son?"

Otis emitted a crass grunt.

Harry looked down at his blank legal pad, pen in hand. He waited a patient thirty seconds and stood, speaking firmly. "Mr. Laurel, I don't have time to—"

"Sure, you fuckhead," Otis shouted, suddenly jerking forward. The emotional land mine had been tripped. "Nobody ever has the time! The *system* don't have the time. Not unless *we* do something wrong. Then they're o'er us like flies on shit! Then the system's got a *lot* a time for us. Put the old boys in jail, lock 'em up with the niggers 'cause that's what they treat us like. Boons in white skin."

Harry didn't raise his voice. "Get out."

Otis jumped up, kicking over his chair. His arms cocked aggressively.

Harry's adrenaline surged. He threw his legal pad to the floor and stood. He'd tried diplomacy; if Otis Laurel was a nut who wanted to fight, he'd come to the right place. Six days of severe stress was rubbing raw.

Otis pointed at Harry and yelled. "My son is dead, you fucker! Police say he done killed himself, and I know he didn', but they don't care 'cause of who he *was*. If it'd been that flirt shit whore girl

◆ 226 ◆

they'd'a been all over the place lookin' who killed her like they're lookin' to see who killed your *big-time* cop brother. I'm glad the prick cop got it. Serves his crooked ass right somebody done him. *I'm fucking* glad *they did!* I hope the guy gets away with it."

"What do you know about who killed my brother!"

Otis smirked. "Same thing the police know about who killed my boy . . . Jaaa-ack shit!"

Harry charged around the table, grabbed the man's throat, and shoved him hard against the wall. Otis tried to knee Harry's groin, but missed when Harry's thumbs went into his windpipe.

Marcie opened the door and screamed Harry's name.

Harry let Otis go, and Otis fell hard, face down, coughing viciously.

"Shut the door!"

Her voice shook. "Should I call the police?"

"No. Just shut the door!" Harry stood back, scared at how he was coming undone. Otis had re-ignited a snuffed fuse burned dangerously close to explosion. Otis had no reason to suspect he would encounter a man in the grasp of an even deeper rage than his own.

After a few pained minutes, Otis managed to get onto all fours. He choked up phlegm and spit it out on the hardwood floor, daring Harry to stop him. Harry sat by the door, guarding the way out.

"I'll sue you," Otis spat hoarsely. "I'll get every nickel you got."

"I thought you said the system didn't have any time for you, Otis? Or was that just poor dumb white trash crying?"

Otis spit, "Fuck you." He rubbed his throat and considered coming back at Harry for another round.

Harry heard Sam Giardino's warnings from an earlier age, Giardino telling Harry how to fight: *You hit him fast, hard, surprise him, take him down, and get out. You don't let him get up. You let him up and he's not afraid of you—later, he finds you. And he's got four friends with him. And they beat the shit out of you, Sonny.*

Harry's expression let Otis know if he wanted more to come on.

Otis stayed on the floor.

"Why'd you come here, Otis?"

"To let you know you're shit."

◆ 227 ◆

"You don't even know me."

"I know your stock. I know my boy said you were some big Mafia lawyer, and I said bunk to that. I drove by this place and laughed. This ain't no mob lawyer's place."

"That's right, it's not."

"You know that."

"I'm agreeing with you, Otis, you asshole, so why don't you tell me why you're here."

"I told you."

"You told me you're glad my brother's dead."

Otis chose not to say that again.

"So how do you know my brother?"

"I know his kid. The slut. She had my boy's pecker in such a state he'd follow her anywhere. She used to come 'round the place wearin' those shirts with no bra and if she'd catch you lookin' at her she'd laugh and say, 'Gives you somethin' to think about when you whack off, don't it?' Real teaser, that little whore."

Harry wanted to grab Otis again and slam him harder against the wall this time, but chimes of potential truth rang through Otis's ignorance. As much as Harry didn't want to hear more, he forced himself to let Otis talk.

"All the trouble my boy ever got into was 'cause 'f her. Started when he was fourteen. She let him in her pants and he was lost in it. Both of them fourteen and ballin' their brains out. Sneakin' out at night. She got him to hot wire cars and take joyrides. They started shopliftin' together and doing drugs, then it got to the point all she had to do was want somethin' and Eddie would snatch it for her. Snatch for snatch, I told him he was doin', and he was *stupid* for it. Damn, dumb kid. Told him he'd get caught, he said no sweat, that little Carla slut told him her uncle was a big-time lawyer could get them off if they got caught.

"Well, they got caught all right, only it was cop daddy who comes beatin' on my door, *in uniform*, hauls me out my house in the middle of the night . . ." Otis swelled with indignance ". . . busts me up against the side of the trailer just like you done with me here,

◆ 228 ◆

and says he'll get the kids off, but if Eddie ever comes around his little girl again he's gonna castrate him. I tried to tell him it was her cruisin' for Eddie's goods, not the other way around, and he nearly tore my head off."

Otis kept rubbing his throat. "I told Eddie stay away from the wild-ass cop's daughter, but he wouldn'. Couple times more they got in jams. Never came to anythin', though, which I figured meant the *big-time* lawyer got them off, and maybe the girl didn't tell her daddy no more because he didn't show his ugly face no more. Then this last thing out in Howard County and Eddie gets dumped on."

"What?"

"Like you don' know."

"I don't."

"Bullshit, too. You fixed Eddie good. What'd your brother tell you? To set it so Eddie got screwed? Get his ass sent off to detention camp where he spends nine goddamned months while the whore gets off. He's not out a month and he's dead. I told him not to see that slut again, that he'd get really done up right if he didn' stay away this time. I guess he couldn't help hisself."

"You saw him with Carla?"

"No, bub, I didn't see him with the whore, but I know he was gettin' it from the cock smile on his face, actin' like king of the world 'cause he was gettin' some."

Harry's jaw was tight.

Otis grew righteous. "So now *you* know *I* know my Eddie got done in. Don't care what those asshole police friends of your brother say. Boy didn't commit suicide. Police killed 'im for messin' with the girl 'f one 'f their own."

Harry stared at Otis, said, "Get out."

Otis stayed where he was as long as he dared, then pulled himself to his feet. Standing, he shifted his weight from one foot to the other as though ready to fight. He pulled his shoulders back and cocked his square head defiantly, sticking his chin to the side.

Harry slid opened the door.

Otis sauntered straight for him, trying to make Harry flinch. He didn't. Otis turned away and glared at Marcie on his way out. His odor lingered after he slammed the door.

Marcie asked if it was okay to lock the deadbolt. Harry said it was.

He went upstairs to his office and took two Tylenol. His heart pounded as he stood by the window and looked out at the rain that had begun to fall.

The brick front of Alena and Jackie's three-level townhouse turned dark clay red from the rain. The polished marble stoop shone wetly.

The home sat precariously in a fringe section of the city, where renovation and prosperity tried to push back dilapidation and poverty. For a few square blocks, new and rehabbed homes faced planted trees and grass medians, their backs turned toward surrounding blight.

Crime was a constant threat, fought with alarm systems, private parking spaces, and a volunteer neighborhood watch. Still, not a week went by without numerous muggings or burglaries. Yet the young, liberal-minded city dwellers who craved the pace of downtown remained undaunted.

Walking quickly through a steady drizzle, Harry went around to the alley and peeked in the two-car garage that was the home's basement. Alena's Lexus was gone.

Harry would have gone inside to try calling her again, but he didn't have a key. Though she had a key to his apartment, Alena had not made a copy of hers for him because of Jackie.

Harry hustled to the corner, staring off a pair of lingerers appraising the victim-potential of passersby. He closed himself into a pay phone that had, miraculously, not been vandalized beyond the requisite sprayed graffiti of someone with the unusual desire to paint the word SQUID in numerous freehand fonts.

Harry hated the city for how much it had changed since days spent here with his father—how deterioration marred buildings reminiscent of those times.

◆ 230 ◆

Alena still didn't answer her car phone and wasn't at Interior Visions. No one knew *where* she was. Harry's concern increased.

For the past year and a half, she'd been a constant in his life, a close emotional element that had been missing since his father's death. She was as rock-sturdy as she was beautiful, and he relished that safety like clinging to an anchored buoy in rough waters. Right now, it would be enough just to hear her voice.

The rain fell in sheets against the Mustang's windshield, mocking the fast slap of its wipers. Driving rain beat so hard against the canvas top Harry could barely hear the engine's easy rumble and twice thought the car had cut out on him.

He towelled the inside of the windshield with a cloth he kept under the seat, but no sooner had he cleaned the glass than it fogged again.

Traffic slowed to a crawl. It took half an hour to go the twenty blocks to Vazinni's. Little Italy's narrow lanes were covered with an inch of rain like a poor man's Venice. Harry parked in a red zone and ran across the street to the restaurant's entrance.

Giorgi opened the door. Harry stepped inside and brought the rain with him; a puddle collected around his feet. His clothes were heavy with water and lay against his skin, making him shiver against the cold blasts of air conditioning.

Late lunch patrons, mostly tourists, looked at Harry as if he were a lunatic for being out in such weather.

"I need to see him."

"You didn't call. He's not here."

"Then please get him here. As soon as he can make it."

Giorgi nodded, realizing Harry's desperation. He led Harry down the hall past the kitchen. When Harry's footsteps sloshed over large squares of tile, Giorgi barked orders in Italian for a busboy to clean the floor.

Harry was ushered inside Giardino's private room. The door shut behind him.

Ceiling lights were dimmed, but against the darkness outside, Harry's reflection appeared in rain-streaked glass overlooking the

◆ 231 ◆

brick-walled garden. The image was hazy, yet he distinctly saw himself as a small boy waiting for his father, the father he always had to make an appointment to see, the father he couldn't just drop in on unannounced and expect to be welcomed. These meetings always had to be arranged. Not like with a real father. Not like with *his* real father.

Just as he had imagined Tucker a brother who would be there for him in a time of trouble, Harry now feared Giardino was going to prove to be a similar illusion.

· 32 ·

Giardino entered the room by a side door. He wore a handsome linen suit, pale grey, with polished wingtip shoes. A Concetta's Innocence rosebud adorned his lapel. Wherever he had been, not a single drop of rain had dared to touch him on the way to the restaurant.

Harry had been waiting an hour. His clothes were still damp and hung limply on his strong frame as he stood.

There were no hugs today, but Harry had known how it would be, how it always was when Giardino's rules were violated. He had witnessed others standing where he was now—in the cold.

"What's happened to you, Sonny?" Though Giardino appraised Harry for signs of harm, his tone was tense. "You're not hurt?"

"No."

Giardino nodded.

"Tucker's wife was arrested in Orlando for possession of counterfeit money."

Giardino didn't react.

"She says she found the money in a safe-deposit box Tucker opened."

Giardino offered no comment.

"She says she thought Tucker was taking bribes . . . She says she doesn't know anything about it . . ." Harry suppressed anger and mirrored Giardino's noncommittal look. Giardino was playing the game with *him* now, hiding behind the stone face. Hiding *what?* "She was arrested by the ATF agent who said Tucker had been deputized by them. Hemingway followed her to Florida." Harry's pulse beat so hard it left him somewhat short of breath. "Hemingway showed me videotape of Tucker coming into this building last November. He was carrying an athletic bag. The same athletic bag

Connie found in the safe-deposit box and used to take the money to Florida."

Giardino made certain Harry was finished. Though accused, he did not flinch. He spoke softly and with great injury; delicate words pinched through scarred nostrils. "What have I done, Sonny, to make you lose faith in me? After all these years, tell me what it is that I have done to breach your trust."

"Why didn't you tell me Tucker was here?"

"What would that have accomplished?"

"That's what I need to know."

"We tread upon dangerous ground here, Sonny." Giardino spoke firmly. "What you need to know I've told you."

"I want to know everything."

"Because you no longer trust me."

"That's not what I'm saying."

"Isn't it?"

"No."

Giardino stood at near attention, as though being inspected. *"Do* you trust me, Sonny?"

"Yes."

"Then your questions are answered."

"No—it's not a matter of trust. I want to know what happened. I deserve to know. This is my family."

Giardino became stern. "We discussed this. Tucker is *not* your family. He left your family years ago and chose not to come back because he was a selfish young man. And troubled. And these destructive traits returned after he made it seem they were beaten."

The vague rhetoric annoyed Harry. "Where did he get that money?"

"I don't know." Giardino turned toward the window and looked upon his garden.

The rain had lessened, but continued to fall steadily: fine drops splashed quietly into puddles atop blue brick and cast patterns across the water like expensive lace.

Giardino said, "This is a time of great sadness for me, Sonny. You tell me you trust me, but your eyes give a different answer. I'll

◆ 234 ◆

not look at you now because it hurts me too much to see your true feelings." Giardino closed his eyes. "I'll only hear your words and make myself believe they are true."

Giardino spoke in low timbres that matched the sounds of rainfall, making Harry strain for every word. "Your brother called me last fall, Sonny, and said he would like to see me. He spoke good-naturedly and said he had a surprise for me. I expected good news. I *expected* to have the son of my dearest friend Jack Walsh come into my arms to ask forgiveness for the ways in which he treated your papa, and for how he treated you. I expected a reunion and what I received instead was an insult.

"Your brother came, but never once mentioned your papa . . . never mentioned you. He came into this room, carrying the bag you talk about, and told me he had an incredible opportunity. An incredible deal. I was saddened by this approach, but still gave him the benefit of the doubt, knowing how he had always been, and thinking maybe this was his way, that he wanted to go into a business venture and leave the police force and needed my help. Help I wouldn't have ever given without his first renouncing his conduct toward your papa, but I was willing to listen. Until he showed me what was in the bag.

"He unzipped this little satchel like something he'd seen someone do in a movie. He dumped the money across the table. It wasn't a lot of money. Thirty, forty thousand dollars banded together. Very proudly, he says to me, 'There it is,' and I ask what I'm looking at. He laughs like a *fool* and tells me, what do I think it is. I ask him, what does *he* think it is. He picks up a band of hundred-dollar bills and puts them in front of my face like I'm a *child,* and tells me it's counterfeit money. The *best* counterfeit money in the world. Perfect United States currency, and he tells me there is much more *where that came from.*" Giardino mocked Tucker's words.

"And I tell him, the only thing more where that came from is a jail cell or a coffin. He smirks and tells me he can sell me this money for twenty cents on the dollar, and if I want over a million dollars, fifteen cents on the dollar."

Harry was stunned.

"I told him to leave and Tucker got very angry. He said it was always going to be that way, wasn't it. That everyone else could be involved in schemes, he called them, but that it was off limits to him. That he'd always been kept out of the business just like when he was in high school and sold narcotics." Giardino bowed his head. "Tucker thought he was someone he saw in a movie when what he really was was nothing."

Harry watched Giardino's reflection. "Why didn't you tell me this before?"

"You shouldn't have ever had to know. You were better off thinking well of your brother—not knowing about him like this. It doesn't serve any purpose."

"My brother may have been killed because of that money."

"You know the rules about people who are killed. Some die innocently, and some put themselves in harm's way. If your brother died because of how he chose to conduct his life, then that is the price he paid."

"The police have made an arrest and if it's the right man, they need information to convict him. If it's the wrong man they need to know even more."

"No. You and I have nothing to do with the police, Sonny. That is their business, not ours."

"Not in this case."

Giardino opened his eyes and turned. "Precisely in this case. Because your brother *was* right about one thing. That counterfeit money was perfect. You could take it to the U.S. Treasury in ten years and ask to cash it for new bills and they'd accommodate you without suspicion. The paper and fibers were perfect. The plates had to have been perfect. The dyes ninety-*nine* percent perfect. Whoever printed that money did it with great care. Which means they have a plan and they're part of a very big organization. Very big. And very, very dangerous. Your brother was naive to think he could live very long dealing with people like that. And you're naive to think you can find out who killed your brother and not be killed yourself." Giardino lowered his head. "Now . . . You have

◆ 236 ◆

made me break the promise I made to your father that I would keep you from harm. I have revealed information, and if you decide to act on it, I can't help you . . . because you're putting yourself in harm's way and you're not going to be able to get yourself out."

Rivulets of rain ran along glass walls of the phone booth like tears.

Richard Manning said, "Do you believe him?"

Harry had just related his conversation with Giardino. Sadly, he answered, "No. It's too convenient. I think ATF gave Tucker the counterfeit money to try and sting Giardino. And I think Giardino was interested."

"So why have they arrested Connie?"

"Maybe I should sit down with Hemingway and find out. Can you arrange it?"

"You should be able to do that yourself. Hemingway cancelled a meeting with us less than two hours ago. He's flying back up to Baltimore. But, Harry, I must tell you," Manning warned, "this is a dangerous line you're walking."

"I know . . . I'm stealing a little bit of everyone's confidence, collecting pieces of an inadmissible puzzle that may never be put together."

Harry sat in the Mustang, parked across the street from Alena's townhouse, waiting for her to come home.

He pushed the driver's seat back and stretched his legs. His suit, rained on and dried, hung on him like a sack. He desperately needed a good night's sleep, but that seemed unlikely.

Mark Gesser hadn't been in the office when Harry called, but had left a message for him: no meeting today. Showels was "unavailable." Harry had lost his edge with Gesser. Showels had passed the lie detector and made bail; the police were panicking. Their case was weak and even a criminal defense neophyte like Gesser knew it.

Tomorrow would be a week since Tucker's killing. Each day that passed without solid leads made it less likely the case would be solved. And county homicide, Frank Trammell et al, didn't even

◆ 237 ◆

know about the counterfeit money or Tucker's involvement with ATF, because Hemingway wasn't telling them.

Harry wiped the inside of his windshield when it fogged over. The rain had stopped. Dark clouds turned pale and spread apart. Rays of late afternoon sun reached the streets, making them steam as cool water evaporated off warm macadam.

A few hours later, amber street lights flickered on to begin their night's sentry. Street urchins who better plied their trades and wares against midnight shadows slipped onto the street as though emerging from cracks in mortar of the buildings in which they'd hidden since sunrise.

A lamp switched on inside Alena's townhome, but it was on a timer in the living room. She still wasn't home. Harry pulled away. He'd try again later.

❖ 33 ❖

Carla answered the door wearing a top that immediately recalled Otis Laurel's tirade: her white cotton T-shirt was so thin as to reveal the small circles of her dark nipples.

Alena frequently wore risqué tops, but it was part of her style: a contained, confident fantasy held firmly under control. Carla pretended to be secure, but Harry sensed she was lost, spinning a wild orbit, ready to attract anything that might latch onto her.

If Carla caught his disapproving glance at her breasts, she didn't flaunt the harsh tease claimed by Eddie Laurel's father. To the contrary, she played the innocent niece, smiling happily, throwing her arms out in mock exasperation, announcing, "I'm bored!"

Harry went inside and closed the door.

Carla flipped her hair, gesturing upstairs. "Craig's taking a shower. Sprucing up for his *older* woman. It must be something genetic in this family, huh? Can't hang with people our own age."

Harry didn't want to hear more stories about Tucker with Carla's friends so he started up the carpeted steps.

The house was in surprising order, which he assumed meant Carla and Craig hadn't been home much since Connie's departure for Orlando.

Harry knocked on the hall bathroom door.

"In a goddamned minute!" Craig barked over water and an exhaust fan.

"It's me."

The fan and water shut off. Moments later, Craig, towel wrapped around his waist and smelling of after-shave, opened the door. Steam poured into the hall. "I thought it was Carla again," he apologized. "She's driving me nuts! *I'm bored, I'm bored, I'm bored.*" He mimicked her chirpy tone. "I was always so damned

❖ 239 ❖

glad to be away from Ol' Tuck I forgot what a pain in the ass she is." He passed Harry and headed for his room.

Carla overheard his insult from the bottom of the stairs and shouted, "I'm bored!"

"Shut up!"

What was it, Harry wondered, that made siblings regress in age around one another?

In his room, Craig dropped his towel and started rooting around a suitcase left open on the floor for something to wear. Harry's nephew had grown to be well-endowed as well as muscular.

The kids' sexuality made Harry uncomfortable, for while he'd offered Craig the stereotypical "attaboy" for getting together with Jeanna, the changes in their bodies and attitudes were stark reminders that the clock would not be turned back. Surely, Tucker and Connie had experienced similar, if not stronger, feelings.

Harry pulled closed the door. "I'll be downstairs."

"There in a sec."

Harry stood in the hall a few moments and, once again, felt very much alone.

"There's been a little trouble in Orlando."

Neither Craig nor Carla were so uncool as to show concern, but Harry's pause clearly caused them distress. Carla's eyes widened slightly and she held half a breath. Craig's expression remained indifferent, but the sudden nervous tapping of his foot revealed apprehension.

"Your mother's been arrested."

"What?" Craig was outraged.

Carla was scared. "Why?"

"Apparently, before she left for Florida, she went to a safe-deposit box your dad had and found money inside . . . and that money turned out to be counterfeit."

"Jesus Christ!" Craig swore angrily and stood. "Doesn't that figure!" He paced twice in front of the fireplace and stopped, arms crossed defiantly. "Doesn't that just *goddamned* figure!"

◆ 240 ◆

Carla cried. "What's going to happen to her? Will she go to jail?"

"She's being held now—"

Carla wailed painfully. "Mom's in jail!"

"I've got two very good lawyers down—"

"You have to get her out, Uncle Harry. Whatever happened I'm sure she didn't mean it." She buried her face in her hands and sobbed. "I can't believe Mom's in jail."

"You can believe it," Craig shouted. "And thank Ol' Tuck for this, too, no doubt! That asshole."

Carla lunged off the sofa and charged her brother so fast he didn't have time to fend off her assault. She slapped his face hard and launched a whirlwind of fists. Although stronger and capable of counterattack, Craig only defended himself, covering his head with both arms and turning away until Harry pulled Carla back.

"It's your fault!" she screamed at him. "You're a selfish little prick! You're the reason he's dead!"

"Go to hell!"

"You go to hell!" She tore away from Harry's grasp and ran upstairs.

"Carla!"

She slammed herself in her room.

Harry looked at Craig. "What the hell just happened here?"

Craig rubbed his reddening cheek. "You saw it. She's a nut. All those goddamned drugs she's taken." He dropped onto the sofa. "Yeah, right. *I'm* the reason. Sure—why not? It's *all* my fault. Everything's *my* fault."

"I'm going to talk to her."

"Good luck."

"If I get her back down here, let's try and keep this civil, okay?"

"She's the one attacked me."

"What you said about your father provoked her—and I didn't appreciate it, either."

"It's the way it was."

Upstairs, Harry knocked softly on Carla's door. He didn't hear

◆ 241 ◆

crying or blaring music, either of which he expected. He knocked again. "Come on, let's talk a little more." He tried the door handle, but it was locked. "Come on, Carla."

He didn't know whether to leave her alone or spring the simple lock mechanism and go in. How often did parents face these decisions? And what was the right choice? And what happened if you made the wrong one? Maybe he should leave her be. There had been a few times after his father's death he'd gone off by himself and no one had come looking to hold his hand—he didn't feel any worse off for it. But that was then, this was now. "Carla," he insisted. "Open the door."

In the living room, Craig shouted, "She's got the car," and ran outside.

Harry remembered Carla's confession about sneaking out her window. He sprinted down the stairs and was on the lawn in time to see Craig jump into the street in front of the Taurus. Carla had the station wagon in gear, accelerating head on for her brother, catching him in the high beams, closing in.

Craig screamed, "Get out of the car!"

She didn't slow down.

Harry shouted warning. Craig dodged between parked cars just as Carla swerved to avoid him. In the wrong lane, she sped toward the corner, wheels squealing as she took the turn fast and lost control. The car jumped the curb and bent a street sign.

Harry ran toward her, but Carla stomped the gas and drove off, churning up wet sod beneath rear tires and bouncing back onto the street.

Harry pointed Craig toward the Mustang. They drove in pursuit, but had lost her before they ever started.

Craig smacked the dash. "The stupid little bitch!"

Harry breathed hard. Now what were they supposed to do? Go look for her? Call her friends? The police? In the courtroom, he knew every move. He decided to head back to the house. And when he did, a sedan made the turn after them. The Feds were back on his tail for the first time in days.

* * *

◆ 242 ◆

Maybe it was a coincidence. Harry drove Craig to the house and they went inside. The sedan remained on the street, five houses down.

Harry waited twenty minutes for Craig to finish dressing for his night with Jeanna. Craig stayed mad at his sister, but was glad for a ride into the city.

Harry found it difficult to maintain conversation. What he wanted to talk about, he wasn't sure how to approach, because the sedan followed them all the way to Jeanna's apartment, and when Harry dropped Craig and drove off, the sedan stayed behind.

It wasn't Harry they'd been following after all. It was Craig.

◆ 34 ◆

At Alena's, more lights were on than before. Through tall front windows framed with lace tie-backs, Harry saw her carry two glasses of wine into the living room. She had on a summer nightshirt he didn't like the idea of anyone else seeing her wear, but anyone on the street could.

He walked up the marble steps as Alena handed a glass of wine to someone seated in a corner of the sofa he couldn't see.

Alena saw him then, and turned with some surprise. When she didn't look happy, it was the worst Harry had felt all day. The worst he'd felt in a long while.

She came to the door, opened it, but didn't invite him in.

"You're all right?" It was not what Harry wanted to say, but what he felt safe saying, gauging her expression.

"I don't know how I am." She spoke calmly, but with underlying anger: hard feelings not necessarily aimed at Harry but catching him in their swath.

In the past, rare times their relationship had steered near conflict, they'd plowed gainfully on, leaving minor differences to be washed away in the strong wake of erotic impulses. Tonight, definite barriers were up.

Alena crossed her arms and her wine glass tipped, spilling drops on hardwood, which she wiped with her bare foot.

Inside the expensively decorated townhome, her roommate, Jackie, carried her wine into the other room.

"Are you mad at me? Have I done something?"

"We're very different, Harry." She sounded final. "We see things differently, through different eyes, and different values. It was interesting at first, a little dangerous, and that was exciting. But I don't want to be part of it, Harry. When I walk into a room, I like

◆ 244 ◆

to know I can do what I want when I'm inside and leave whenever I want."

"I don't understand."

"I don't want to be a mob lawyer's girlfriend, Harry, and I sure as hell don't want to work for the mob."

"Alena, we've talked about this. I don't work for the mob."

"Harry, stop. I can't help that I fell in love with you—"

"And I'm in love with you, too. That's why this is crazy."

"Is it? Do you know Daniel Hemingway? A federal agent? I was on I-95 this afternoon coming back from Laurel and he pulled me over. There were two cars, Harry, with serious-looking men in suits inside. Hemingway showed his badge and said, 'Congratulations on getting the AmeriCenter Tower job, Ms. Marlacova. I wonder if we could talk about your meeting with Sam Giardino.' "

Harry swore, "That son of a bitch."

"I knew that meeting was trouble."

"He's trying to intimidate you."

"Well, it's working. I don't like being under investigation. I don't like being watched."

"You keep your curtains open." He bit with that too quickly and regretted it; this wasn't cross-examination.

Alena reacted indignantly. "If my curtains are open, it's because I don't have anything to hide. Not like meeting in back rooms with Sam Giardino. I'm sorry I don't feel for him like you, Harry, but the man is a mobster. You can live with that. I can't."

"He was my father's best friend. He—"

"I know. He paid your way through college and law school. He kept you out of trouble as a kid. And sends you half your clients."

"Alena—" He would have pled with her, but the courtroom had stricken desperation from his voice. As though a jury was always watching his reaction, he couldn't show despair.

"The Feds watch you, Harry, maybe you don't know how close. I don't—I *can't*—be part of that."

"Please let me come in so we can talk about this."

"It won't change anything, Harry."

"Hemingway will do anything to get Giardino. *Anything*."

◆ 245 ◆

"Wonderful, and Giardino is involved with AmeriCenter. We'll be half into the job and the building will get seized by the Feds for something. The firm will end up bankrupt."

"That won't happen."

"I'm telling Cleo to kill the deal." The pain of that decision forced her grip tightly around the wine glass. "The biggest job of my life. The *coup* of my career. And the love of my life. They're all full of lies, Harry."

He braced a hand against the door when she began to shut it. "I've never lied to you."

"Are you a mob lawyer, Harry?"

"No."

She considered him sadly. "That's what you said the other night, and the worst part of it is, I think you believe that." Alena closed the door.

Harry sat in his father's car fantasizing about Alena coming outside, throwing her arms around him, saying she was sorry, and that she had misunderstood. It didn't happen.

He drove around the city and hated every square block. Nothing was as it used to be. A group of addicts were in the alley beside the Court Square Building, shooting heroin and lying against makeshift mattresses of newspapers soaked by the rain. The sick and homeless staggered the streets. The goddamned city had gone to hell. *Gone to hell!*

The homicide rate was skyrocketing. It made for staggering judicial logistics. An average jury murder case took ten days to try. If every defense attorney decided to try every murder case, 3,650 court sessions per year would clog the docket. And you still had to schedule all the aggravated assaults, attempted murders, rapes, thefts, carjackings, and drug cases. There weren't enough courtrooms in the entire country to handle that volume if every defendant exercised jury trial rights. But explain that to folks decrying plea bargains who got their news from reality TV programs designed to incite raw outrage in the hungry quest for ratings.

Harry hated the city, but he kept driving. He couldn't go home.

◆ 246 ◆

The condominium would make him ill if the next time Alena would be there was to move her things out. His apartment would remind him of life *before* Alena: nights in a soulless two-bedroom given minimal life by boxed photographs on the wall and fabric leftovers from days he sought retreat from the bar scene by reupholstering furniture.

Maybe he had missed his calling. Maybe he should have followed more artisan ways. Was it too late? Could he and Alena go into business together? Their own line of clothing was too far-fetched, but they could set up another business. Small, simple, uncomplicated. Unconnected.

Only that wasn't his life any more than these city streets were as when he walked them with his father. A few summers as a young boy ended by gunfire; bullets shot by a man the police never caught, a man Sam Giardino claimed to have "taken care of." Those mere words had never been enough, and they echoed even more emptily tonight.

Near 1:00 A.M., Harry ended up in a smoky club called Silhouettes and told himself it was for business. Jennifer Mulcaney, Little Miss Fellatio, Tierny Wells had called her, danced there when she wasn't being paid for more explicit duties by Sam Giardino.

Silhouettes's liquor license was in constant jeopardy, and only bureaucratic squabbles between city licensing agencies kept violations from coming to a head. Eventually, papers would be served and hearings scheduled.

Harry would represent Silhouettes and he would win because the regulations the city was trying to enforce were so vague and contradictory that any one of a dozen legal arguments, most clear to second-year law students, would prevail. If the legislators were only slightly more inept, they'd be unable to find their way to City Hall, much less waste tax dollars trying to run it.

When Harry's father began representing the club thirty years ago, it had been a tawdry strip joint that always ran a pale second to wherever Blaze Starr's tassels twirled. Eleven corporate shell owners later, Silhouettes was a screendancing club, and Harry represented the son of Jack Walsh's original client.

According to corporate, tax, lease, and liquor board documents, Renni Laslin was Silhouettes's current principal. Laslin was an uneducated and obnoxious man who, luckily for Harry, spent most of the year in Florida. Their primary contact was by phone and, since Laslin's discovery of high-tech, fax. Laslin would fire off hand-scribbled messages for Harry to "grind those city bastards into the crappy dirt they come from." This was a typical response to pointed questions Harry might raise; or, if Laslin was feeling less patient, he'd fax: "You figure it out, counselor."

Harry generally didn't consider Laslin worth the $600 monthly retainer he sent, following an outdated fee practice begun by their fathers, but put up with him for reasons not always clear to himself.

Silhouettes's door was guarded by two behemoth men. They greeted Harry with laughing assurances they hadn't been caught at anything lately. "But when it happens," one said, "we'll call."

Harry went in without paying the ten-dollar cover, and was soon swept into the decadent purple light and thick air of cigarettes and whiskey.

The main room was small and crowded. Hard rock music shook aged walls. Men stood two deep at a long bar facing a stage across which was stretched a thin white curtain. Bright light shining on the curtain from behind caught the provocatively moving shadow of the woman who danced in naked anonymity behind the screen.

Harry had come here once with Alena. He'd needed to drop papers to Laslin who stopped at the club on a drive from New York to Lauderdale. Harry had expected Alena to wait in the car, but she'd wanted to go inside.

They had sat in one of the booths that lined the back wall. One of the bouncers, a man presently serving five years for assault, kept watch to make sure they weren't hassled. Alena had focused on the screendancers as though observing tribal ritual and asked Harry if every guy in the place had an erection. When Harry said he wouldn't know, she asked if he had an erection. Fifteen minutes later, they were having sex in her car.

◆ 248 ◆

There had never been anyone like Alena in his life, and never would be again if she was gone. But he'd made a mistake. She was so outspoken and bold, he had been misled into thinking there wasn't anything he couldn't confess to her, no secret too deep or fantasy too wild. Physically, their relationship knew no extremes, but as liberally as she reacted to him sexually, emotionally there was an unwillingness or possibly a fear to seek out common ground. Mutual pleasure was easy compared to emotional devotion.

"So how's the world's best attorney?" Jennifer Mulcaney spoke over loud music as she slid into the compact booth facing Harry. She wore an outlandish frazzle-hair black wig and see-through body stocking. Frilly white lace barely covered her nipples, which were hard in the cool room. She grasped his hand. "I don't know what you pulled last week, but thanks for beating that case. I should've known that guy was a cop."

Harry tried not to look at her body, but found it impossible.

"You hear," Jennifer asked, "about the snitch who brought the cop to the party?"

Harry's head barely moved, indicating he hadn't.

"He got his face *all* busted up. Serves his ass right." Jennifer stuck her finger in Harry's glass and licked its taste. "Sweet. What is that, soda?"

"Seven-Up."

"You on the wagon?"

"Never much of a drinker."

She found that odd, but not enough to pursue; one of the girls' rules was not to ask the wrong question. Better to stick to the benign. "So what brings you here? You want to collect your fee in trade?"

He smiled polite declination.

"It's okay if you do."

His decision stood.

She sat back. Some of the patrons—mostly French sailors—watched Jennifer instead of the screendancer. She liked being looked at and was completely unconcerned that hers was a politically incorrect way for a woman to act. "All those boys," she said of

◆ 249 ◆

the sailors, "all alone at sea. Makes me want to be a boat sometimes."

Harry drank his 7UP.

"I'm doing all the talking, Harry. You must be here for something. Don't tell me Sam sent you to make sure we got the message to keep quiet about that girl."

"Who's that?"

"The gypsy girl some private dicks've been looking for. It's got something to do with the guy who did your brother."

Harry's insides jumped, but his exterior maintained a half-depressed quiet.

Jennifer shook her head. "Sam doesn't want her found, she's not going to be found."

"She still alive?"

Jennifer let out an odd laugh, and Harry wondered if she'd caught on he wasn't tuned to the word on the street. "Nobody's going to whack her. At least I don't think they are. Girls don't usually get gone." She pitched forward and the length of her wig brushed the table, establishing a privacy screen of synthetic fibers around her face. "But what do you hear, Harry, is she going to get gone?"

Harry shrugged, playing a part.

Jennifer pretended to mope. "Nobody ever tells me the good stuff."

"Me neither."

"Oh, sure." Her body suit stretched across her breasts like opaque snakeskin. "I'll tell you this, though, if she's gonna get gone, whoever does her better not believe in spirits, 'cause I hear she's not just a girl, but tells fortunes, too."

Harry saw leverage to renew his value with Mark Gesser. "Where does she work?"

"You want—?" Jennifer stopped. "Shit, she *is* getting gone, isn't she? That's what you're asking about? Yeah, sure, Sam doesn't want a lot of people talking about her so when she ends up gone it's not such big news."

He looked away as though denying involvement while he burned inside from Giardino's lies.

Barely audible over the music, Jennifer said, "I find where she is, what's it worth, cash?"

Harry left Silhouettes just before closing. He drove fifteen blocks, parked near Jeanna's building, and walked the rest of the way.

The sedan that had followed him—followed *Craig*—remained near the front entrance. Either the two agents seated inside the car knew Jeanna didn't have a car in the garage and would leave by the main doors to get a cab, or they were too lazy to watch more than one exit.

Harry rapped the passenger window so hard both agents jumped. The driver reached inside his suit jacket for a weapon.

Harry kept his hands in plain view and motioned for them to roll down a window.

The man in the passenger seat recognized him.

"Tell Hemingway," Harry said, "I want to cut a deal."

Harry went back to his office and slept on the sofa. He had a recurring dream, but with a twist. Since he first saw newspaper photographs of his father lying dead on the street and read descriptions of the shooting, he'd dreamed of it happening.

His father and Giardino coming out of the restaurant on a day so cold that as they speak, their warm breath turns to mist. Lines of ice litter street gutters. A car starts toward them as the two men shake hands, set to go separate ways. Jack Walsh, Harry's father, sees the car's slow approach, sees the passenger window is down. It takes a second for the warning to register, maybe two seconds. He grabs for Giardino, who pulls away, thinking Jack is sparring with him as they often do. Jack lunges for Giardino to tackle him out of the way but, in midstride, the bullets tear through him. Flesh and blood erupt through jagged tears in his overcoat. In slow motion, Jack Walsh falls; he bounces lifelessly against concrete. Sam Giardino crawls to his fallen friend and screams curses at the gunmen who speed away.

Thursday night, the dream started the same way, only Jack Walsh never made the move to save Giardino. He was already walking away. He watched the car come down the street. Saw the killer's arm extend from the open window, gun in hand, pulling off a series of shots that hit Giardino in the chest, lifting him onto his toes, driving him back into a brick wall where he slid bloodied to the street and died. In the dream, Jack Walsh walked away. He never said a word.

◆ 35 ◆

Harry was back at Jeanna's building Friday morning before eight. He was showered, shaved, and dressed in a blue summer wool suit fresh from the dry cleaner's cellophane.

He entered the tall structure through the garage level and took the elevator to the eleventh floor, thereby avoiding the two ATF agents who had spent a warm night in their car by the front entrance.

Jeanna made a backward exit from her apartment at 8:25, fumbling with her keys, late for work, which according to Cleo Lane started at 8:30 sharp. Jeanna's hair, still slightly damp, smelled soapy with apricot shampoo. She didn't notice Harry as she stuck in a key to lock the deadbolt.

"I need to talk with Craig."

"Jesus!" She jumped and clutched her oversized handbag. "You scared the shit out of me." Her key, left half in the slot, fell to the floor from the weight of a brass key ring. Jeanna bent to pick it up. "You look serious. Is this about his mom?"

Harry nodded.

"Craig's still in bed. He's a sweet boy," she added, opening the door. "Lock it when you leave, okay?"

"Yeah."

The small living room was warm with sunlight streaking through peach miniblinds over a bay window. Jeanna's portfolio and a pair of her underwear were pushed half under the sofa. The sofa cushions were scrambled like cushy mats after a wrestling match.

The single bedroom was dark and cool. Harry turned on a deco standing lamp.

Craig, deep asleep, didn't flinch. Wearing only white boxer

shorts, he was entangled in paisley sheets. His hair stuck up at rakish angles.

Harry jostled his shoulder, but Craig lay as though dead except for his deep breathing. Fraternity living taught sound sleeping.

"Craig." Harry pushed him harder and Craig reacted sharply, coming awake with an abrupt snarl.

"What?"

"Wake up. We've got ten minutes for you to clear your head and another fifteen to talk."

Slowly, Craig rolled face up as though recovering from a vicious tackle. His anger dissolved seeing it was Harry who'd awakened him; now he was merely groggy. "What time is it?"

"Eight-thirty."

"Jesus . . ." He squinted when Harry raised roman shades to let in light. "Where's Jeanna?"

"Left for work."

Craig gathered himself into a waking state, as though collecting files scattered during the night. "You ever find Carla?"

"No. I drove by the house on the way here and she wasn't home."

After a few seconds, Craig said, "Stupid bitch. She doesn't have a license. Car's probably wrecked."

"I figure if she got locked up for something, she'd have called. So she's out doing whatever it is she does." Harry closed the doors to Jeanna's antique armoire: a meaningless act motivated by nervous energy. He was not happy about what he had to ask his nephew. "What do you know about the money?" The question was posed without reproach, an opening volley in the oral examination of someone who might or might not prove to be a hostile witness.

"What?"

Harry stood at the foot of the bed like it was the witness stand. "The money?"

"What money?"

"The counterfeit money."

"What do I know about it?" Craig's surprise seemed genuine.

"The money your mother was arrested with in Florida: had you ever seen a lot of money lying around the house?"

"Money around our house? No way."

"You never saw or heard about any counterfeit money?"

Craig shook his head, still too sluggish to recognize he was under suspicion, if not accused.

"You don't know *anything* about it?"

Craig squinted with confusion. Judging from Harry's tone, it sounded like he was supposed to have a better answer.

"You don't—?"

"No. I don't know about it."

"You're sure?"

"Yeah," he answered definitely.

"Because in . . ." Harry checked his watch. ". . . half an hour I'm meeting with a federal agent about your mother's case. I'm going to try to get her a deal."

Craig again tried to understand why his uncle sounded so negative.

Harry said, "I don't want . . ." He took a breath. "I don't want anyone getting caught in the crossfire, that's all. I want to make sure I know what went down. *How* it went down. Who was involved. Dealing with the Feds is like a race. The first person who cuts the deal wins and everybody else finishes last."

Craig said, "Go for it."

Maybe, Harry reconsidered, he should have been more direct with Craig. The boy was twenty, but that wasn't really that old, not that mature, anyway. Harry had given Craig a chance to confess guilt— guilt obtained by conduct and/or knowledge—and Craig had demurred. Even pulled from sleep into interrogation, he answered without hesitation. But pure denial, Harry knew from his own clients, was the simplest form of defense.

And if Craig was telling the truth, why were the Feds following him?

"Good morning." Special Agent Hemingway's greeting was perfunctory. The tall agent entered the windowless office holding a

Styrofoam cup of steaming black coffee. He sat at the head of the conference table, put down his coffee, then leaned back, hands folded at his waist. He looked expectant of victory, as though its aroma was in the air.

Harry tugged at the cuff of his suit jacket. "I'm caught in a difficult position."

The corners of Hemingway's mouth couldn't help pinching upward with pleasure.

"You're asking me," Harry said, "to divulge information as to your claim that Sam Giardino caused my brother's murder."

"Correct."

"But," Harry interjected, "the information you want isn't related to my brother's killing, but his possession—actually, his *wife's* possession—of counterfeit money."

"One and the same."

"But what does one have to do with the other?"

Hemingway's smile turned mildly sarcastic. "Let's not talk ourselves into a circle. You get me Giardino's end of the counterfeit scheme and I let Connie go. It's a fair shake."

"All you've shown me so far is a videotape of my brother going into Vazinni's restaurant with an athletic bag. That's not a crime."

"Connie's got the money, Walsh. Come on."

"I don't have any knowledge of Giardino's involvement with counterfeit money or my brother."

Hemingway scowled.

"But," Harry added, "I'll try to get that information if—and this is the pivotal point—*if* you show me how you know Giardino had Tucker killed."

"We went through this in Orlando. I'm not telling you my case, Walsh. You walk out of here and have Giardino cover tracks? No way."

Harry stared at the tabletop's imitation wood grain. "You don't have anything, do you? You've got that videotape and that's it."

"I got your sister-in-law looking at—"

"You can't prove her knowledge. I put Connie on the stand, a policeman's widow, and she testifies she thought it was lottery

◆ 256 ◆

money her murdered husband won, and she walks."

Hemingway lurched forward and pointed at Harry. "Your brother was shot in the head six times at close range, Walsh." *Six times*. Close up. It was a hit. Those assholes in Baltimore County homicide think some chubby little mortgage broker did that? Come on. You get a good look at Ronald Showels? You've handled murder cases. Sure, anyone's capable of pulling a trigger in a moment of passion, but how many non-pros get up close and plant *six* shots? Maybe one, maybe two. But six, and all six bullseyes? You think Showels's capable of that?"

"If Giardino did it, I'll do whatever I can to hand him to you, but I'm telling you *I don't know about it*. So the more you give me, the more I give you back."

This wasn't the deal Hemingway expected.

Harry pressed. "You've got nothing to lose. It sounds to me like you've got no case against Giardino. You've got no case against Connie, and even if you did, it's a nothing case. It leads nowhere. Anything I get for you is more than you've got."

Hemingway exhaled sharply.

Harry pinpointed his inquiry. "Why are you following Tucker's son?"

"Screw you, Walsh."

Harry stood.

Hemingway glared at him. "Sit down."

Daniel Hemingway was obsessed with Sam Giardino. Some cops, some federal agents, some prosecutors were like that; they generally didn't last. Either stomach acid ate their digestive tract or they made themselves crazy with a near lover's lust.

"Three fifty-dollar bills," Hemingway began candidly, "ended up in our lab for analysis. They came from a nothing little district court case in Howard County. The State Police had already looked the bills over and sent them back because they thought they were genuine. The State's Attorney, some quirky little bastard, I don't know how he knew, but he sends the paper to us so we run it. It's goddamned good paper. So close to perfect, it's scary—really scary

◆ 257 ◆

if you know anything about global economics.

"Countries that don't like one another counterfeit one another's paper currency. It's economic warfare. The Union did it to the South in the Civil War. If you flood a country with phony currency, it devalues their money. Do it enough, and you've got financial chaos. Now it would take billions to do that to the U.S., but the key is for the counterfeit stuff to be so good, it starts being passed as legitimate. So whenever counterfeit comes around this hot, people get excited."

"How does this fit in with my brother?"

"The case where the money was seized was his daughter's. She got picked up last spring by some yokel park ranger for smoking grass with a boyfriend in the park. It was a minor weed case—a nothing—but when she was arrested, they confiscated these three fifties, and for some reason that assistant state's attorney knew it was phony."

"How'd he know if it fooled the State Police?"

"You tell me."

"Maybe you should have asked him?"

"He doesn't know the lab results. As far as he's concerned, we lost his evidence. He finds out it's counterfeit and charges the girl, we lose our in." Hemingway pushed his coffee cup a few inches across the table, fidgeting with it instead of drinking. "We investigated Carla and, lo and behold, her daddy's a cop with a less than pristine background and family connections to Sam Giardino. When the dope charges against her are dropped, tell me I'm surprised. Her daddy made some phone calls, got a favor or two, and his little girl walked. So we start watching the whole family.

"They're not exactly a Norman Rockwell painting. The girl's a stoner, she spends more time on drugs than a Grateful Dead roadie. The boy, Craig, is a real party boy at Georgetown. Connie looks like she's trying to hold them together, but when your brother starts cheating on her and she finds out, she goes a little berserk." Hemingway derived subtle pleasure recounting details.

Harry hurt inside, but didn't show it.

"To tell you the truth, Harry, I don't know if Connie knows

about the money or not. You're right on that count. Can I prove the knowledge necessary to gain a conviction? Maybe not. But she sure as hell got to that safe-deposit box in a hurry, which makes me think she knew the money was there. But maybe, like your lawyer friend in Orlando told me the other day, she thinks it's lottery winnings. Your brother sure bought enough tickets. He was winning, too. But why not, the odds were stacked in his favor."

"How do you figure that?"

"If you printed lottery tickets, would you print winners or losers?"

Harry couldn't help swallowing.

"This sounding more familiar, Harry? More like Sam Giardino territory? How far of a jump is it given today's technology to get from fake liquor tax stamps to instant lottery tickets and paper currency? That's why the Secret Service has us working the case, along with the rest of what's going on with Giardino." Hemingway pushed his coffee cup some more. "And your brother was in hip deep. He spread a lot of phony money around. He paid off credit card debts, paid off a loan to his father-in-law, paid for a new car. He did it over a few months. He didn't drop a lot of money in any one place, and if we hadn't been watching him, he'd probably still be doing it. And about the same time Tucker's doing this, Craig's spreading a lot of cash around Georgetown. Over a grand a month. Carla drops the occasional phony fifty or passes a lottery ticket— allowance money. Connie still shops mostly with checks or credit cards, but she passed some bogus, too."

Harry didn't suggest explanations that came to mind.

"Once we had a few months of evidence, we paid your brother a visit. This was about three months ago. I give him credit for reacting well under pressure. He didn't sweat, but his excuse was pathetic. He said he was conducting his own investigation of a counterfeiter and any bogus monies he spent must have been mistakenly mixed in with his own money." Hemingway smiled. "Then we told him how much we knew. He stuck by his story at first, but then he knew his ass was had. He said he really had come across the money during an investigation, but that he didn't know why he did it, but

◆ 259 ◆

he spent some of the money he confiscated. And once he did it that first time and got away with it, the second time was easier, the third easier still. He offered to pay the money back. He pled with us.

"I said maybe if he wanted to help our investigation, his indiscretion could be overlooked. I said we were very interested in Sam Giardino. I said we'd seen him go into Giardino's restaurant. I asked if Giardino was his source. He must have figured we had him nailed on that like we had him on the rest. But, we never saw him getting the goddamned money. BUT your brother said, yeah, Giardino was the source. And I said if he gave us Giardino, he was home free."

It was hard for Harry not to react. "So he started working for you?"

"That's right."

"Investigating Giardino."

"Uh-huh. But that's all you get, Walsh. You want more, you give me more."

"What about Connie?"

"I told you, you give me Giardino and she walks."

"How about for the time being?"

"You talking bail?"

Harry nodded.

"Get her parents to put up the house in Orlando. It's paid for. She disappears, her old man'll have heart failure. I'll call the AG down there. We can get her before a magistrate this afternoon— cut her before the weekend."

"I appreciate it." Harry was sincere. The tension in the room had levelled as the judicial process formed yet another strange alliance.

"Talk to her, Walsh. She knows something. *You* know something. Just don't fuck me on this deal or she's going down."

That was a chance Harry was going to have to take.

Harry remembered the times he and Tucker passed silently in the courthouse halls, two brothers acting like strangers. He'd often

◆ 260 ◆

wondered what Tucker was thinking, what his life was really like. Now, to a certain degree, he knew—knew that if Tucker hadn't been a policeman, he wouldn't have been thought of as a "deputized" ATF agent, he'd have been considered a snitch. And lots of snitches died with six shots to the head.

Half an hour later, Harry left the city, heading for Howard County, to talk to the Assistant State's Attorney who had suspected three fifty-dollar bills were counterfeit even though the State Police tested them as genuine.

◆ 36 ◆

Leslie McGinty's prescription lenses were too thick and heavy for the designer wire frames he wore. The pads left deep red imprints along the bridge of his small nose whenever he removed his glasses to wipe his eyes, which was often.

"The damned air in these buildings," he complained prissily to Harry. "They recirculate the same poisons over and over and over. The filters only get changed every six months even though the manufacturer says three weeks."

A portable air cleaner buzzed quietly on a corner shelf. Three small planted terrariums smelled richly of humus and attempted to broadcast desirable humidity into the air.

Assistant State's Attorney McGinty closed his door and cleared a chair of files for Harry to sit. Today was a prep day, which meant no court and a lot of phone calls with witnesses and defense counsel for the thirty cases set on Monday's docket. McGinty assumed that's why Harry had come in, and started looking over his case list. "Who do you have?"

"It's an old matter. From last spring or summer."

"Coming up on VOP?"

"No. You handled a case last summer concerning Carla Walsh. She was arrested with her boyfriend for possession by a State Park ranger."

"If you say so." McGinty squinted even with his glasses on; either bothered by pollens or a bad prescription.

"Carla had some fifty-dollar—"

"Carla Walsh? Is she related to you?"

"My niece. Tucker's daughter."

"Tucker Walsh? The policeman who was killed? He was your

◆ 262 ◆

brother?" When Harry nodded, McGinty offered belated condolences.

Harry thanked him and returned to point: "You thought the fifty-dollar—"

"Counterfeit! Right, I remember." McGinty became enthused. "Really good counterfeit, too. You know those asshole Feds lost them?"

"How did you know they were counterfeit?"

A gleam came over McGinty's watering eyes. "You're talking about my passion. My *real* study."

"You like money?" Harry asked, as though who didn't?

"*Currency.* I'm a collector. My apartment walls are covered with framed foreign currencies. They are the most incredible works of art. Except ours, of course. Boring green. Very plain." McGinty made a face as though tasting something unpleasant. "I can tell a bogus buck from across the room. Currency is very tactile. It has a unique feel to it. You touch it," he quickly rubbed his thumb across two fingers, "and it creates the most wonderful sensation." His expression turned to admiration, then soured again. "I used to have some framed in here, but the cleaning crew was very fond of it. Especially the lire or pesos. All those zeroes. They must have thought they'd stolen thousands, not gum money."

"That's how you knew it was counterfeit? By feel? Not something else with the case?"

"Just feel. How else? I'm going to depend on the State Police lab? They're worse than the people who run blood tests for hospitals. I'll throw darts for you and hit the right answer more often than they do."

"Had you ever seen other cases with counterfeit of that same quality?"

"This is district court. I didn't make law review or have connections to get into a big firm." He gestured with open palms as if to add, *So here I am.* "I'm sorry the Feds lost those bills, though. I'd have loved them for my collection."

Harry had hoped for more. "Was Carla's case dropped?"

◆ 263 ◆

"I don't remember. It might be in my notes. Let's check."

Upon request, a secretary retrieved Carla's closed file. McGinty, fresh from a new eye wiping, replaced his glasses and went through a short stack of papers. "Let's see, we nol prossed in front of Judge Gelfman . . . Oh, that's right, the grass was actually on the co-defendant and we couldn't prove if Carla was smoking grass or a cigarette because whatever they were smoking they tossed into the river. You might want to suggest that to your clients: always smoke dope near a substantial body of water so you can toss it in if the police show." McGinty flipped through pink phone message slips. "I seem to remember getting some calls from a guy with the Balti-more County Police about this case. He asked if I couldn't do something with it."

"Do something?"

"You know, drop it. Which I was going to do anyway." McGinty found his note. "Here he is: Frank Trammell. Runs their homicide division, doesn't he?"

Harry looked at the file to see it with his own eyes. He also saw the codefendant's name: Edward Laurel.

The Taurus wagon wasn't back in front of Tucker's house, and Carla wasn't home, so Harry drove to Fox Chase, where he'd dropped her Tuesday night.

It was a choice by lack of options. He didn't know any of Carla's friends or where she might go, so he tried the only place he knew, and got lucky: the Taurus was on the street in front of the stone rancher.

Not well parked, but Carla had gotten it reasonably close to the curb, although a single tire track dug across the grass showed she'd cut it a little too close on her first swipe. Closer examination re-vealed the rear quarter panel was only marginally dented from im-pact with the street sign. A decent body shop could fix it for a few hundred dollars.

Next door, an older man wearing a John Deere cap piloted his green lawn tractor around a series of mulched dogwoods, trimming more precisely an already manicured lawn. Smelling the air bright with cut grass and hearing the firm roar of the mower's engine told Harry he was deep in the heart of upper-middle-class suburbia.

Harry followed a flagstone path to the front door and pushed the round button, which sounded a deep chime inside. He waited, unable to listen for footsteps inside because of the grass cutter. He rang the bell again.

A man ten years Harry's elder eventually opened the door. "Sorry, I was out back." He was tall, trim, and looked like an old-guard banker or stockbroker getting an early start on his weekend, in pleated Eddie Bauer corduroys and a pressed polo shirt. His downtown haircut was carefully shaved around his ears to minimize coarse grey hairs creeping into the black.

Harry said, "I'm Carla's uncle." The man seemed amenable, so Harry extended his hand, which was received hospitably.

"Nice to meet you. I'm Alan Ford. I'm very sorry about her father."

Harry nodded. "I need to talk to Carla."

"She didn't tell you?" Mr. Ford sounded as though he'd been lied to, and wasn't necessarily surprised. "She and Liza, that's my daughter, went to the ocean for the weekend. They left this morning. I wouldn't have let Carla go, but she said her mother was in Florida, and I thought with everything that had happened . . . If it was bad judgment on my part, I'm sorry."

Harry guessed Alan Ford was good at breaking news to his clients about falling interest rates—if that's what he did. His tone was reassuring and fatherly.

Harry didn't sound like that when he talked to Craig and Carla. Maybe he should work on it. Or maybe it only came after raising kids of your own. "Where are they staying?"

"One of Liza's other friends' parents have a place, but there's no phone. Liza always calls, though. I can make sure she has Carla call you."

"Well, you can tell her, but I'm not sure Carla will call."

Ford nodded. "She's a good kid. She'll call."

◆ 265 ◆

Harry looked inside the house at a marble foyer and rich wood panelling. "It is important I talk with her. When do you expect them home? In case she doesn't call."

"Sunday sometime."

Harry debated a drive to the beach—only three hours. "Do you have the address where they are? I have a couple friends down there who could get word to Carla for me."

"Could I make a suggestion? Let me try getting her to call you— if that's all right." He was being careful not to intrude. "You look as though you're upset about something, maybe something she's done, and sometimes you have to let them make their own mistakes and come back to you. I hope I'm not stepping out of line suggesting that, but there have been times with Liza I thought I'd never survive. But you do survive. She'll call," Ford reiterated. "I'm sure she will."

Harry wasn't making any bets. "Does your daughter know a boy named Eddie Laurel? Or have you heard the name? Maybe a boyfriend of Carla's? Someone she might have come here with?"

"I don't know him, but that doesn't mean Liza might not. Although, I have to admit, Liza is still awkward around boys. She's a little overweight, and not that popular, which is why I'm grateful for her having such a good friend like Carla. They get along so well together."

It sounded to Harry like Alan Ford didn't want to see Carla pulled home from the beach for his daughter's sake. He handed Ford one of his cards. "Any one of those numbers are good to try, but please ask her to use the pager first."

"Okay."

"And I'm going to come back for the car later, so if you see it missing, don't worry. You know she doesn't have a license."

"Liza's done the same thing." He seemed very accepting of that fact.

Out of control, Harry thought. The parents of the world were absolutely out of control.

*   *   *

◆ 266 ◆

Harry stopped for lunch at the Towson Club, which really wasn't a club, but a moderately priced restaurant near the courthouse. The pleasant old stone house was a reminder of past times, positioned between newer, shinier storefronts. Its lunch clientele was primarily the lawyers and judges who were part of, or seeking to be part of, the old-line Baltimore County guard.

When Harry had clerked for Suicide Sheila Parks, she had forbidden him to go to the Towson Club, because the attorneys who ate there were the enemy. Harry had gone anyway and found comfort in the fraternity.

The social setting reminded Harry of what he had learned tagging along with his father: that the adversary process ended with a client's interest, and battles between attorneys—even head-on clashes—weren't to be taken personally.

The stakes had been raised a great deal since Harry's father's time and, today, handshakes and friendships would rarely salvage a legal blunder if the other side could trap you. Generally, though, there was a fraternity among lawyers that often soothed nerves damaged by the only profession where practitioners worked against one another instead of in concert. If lawyers were doctors, there would be no joining forces to save a patient; one lawyer would work to cure, the other to kill.

Hampered by anxiety, Harry's appetite wasn't its norm. Estimating he'd lost five pounds the past week, he forced himself to finish a medium rare cheeseburger. Conversations with other lawyers at the counter provided helpful, if not complete, distraction.

There was minimum discussion about Tucker, only what courtesy required before egocentric attorneys replayed recent victories like baseball fanatics analyzing a manager's moves.

Harry lingered through Bill Messier's lengthy story about a workman's compensation hearing before walking back to the office.

He had hoped submerging himself in familiar surroundings would help clear his mind and provide alternatives to what he believed he had to do. It didn't.

* * *

Marcie followed Harry up the stairs and into his office. She quietly closed the door, turning the knob so George Patterakis, Harry's downstairs cotenant, couldn't overhear. "You forgot these," she said, almost whispering. Marcie handed Harry the sizable stack of phone message slips he'd ignored.

He didn't want to look through them, but couldn't help himself. No Alena. Even figuring she wouldn't have called, he was disheartened.

"It's part good news. Richard Manning called. Connie's going to be released on a hundred-thousand-dollar bond. They're working to get it done today. Her father put up his house."

Harry was relieved at the result, but it reminded him of Special Agent Hemingway, who would soon expect quid pro quo.

"The bad news," Marcie continued confidentially, "is we're starting to get buried."

Files piled in paper-chase mountains on Harry's desk, stuffed with recently received correspondence and pleadings, verified Marcie's concern.

"I'm spending so much time rescheduling, I'm falling behind. I was here until eight last night." She wasn't complaining for herself, but out of concern for the office's efficiency. "And George can't handle most of the new stuff. You know him and criminal cases. If it's not a DWI, he doesn't know what to do. He gets sweaty and nervous."

Harry previewed file labels for case names. "How bad is it?"

"It's not good."

"What haven't you been able to postpone?"

Marcie rattled off the list. "The Jenson deposition Tuesday and Oliva at the suit of State Thursday morning. Rummer answers to interrogatories are already late. And I've got six clients stacked up wanting appointments and Mrs. Givino is calling every hour because her husband didn't bring the kids back on time from last weekend and she doesn't want to let him have them this weekend."

Harry swore under his breath. "All right . . . First of all, Rummer can wait. If they file for sanctions, we'll deal with it. What's the problem with Oliva?"

"The State doesn't want to postpone. They've got four non-police witnesses."

"Prepare a Request For Jury Trial, but hold it until Thursday morning and have a messenger deliver it. Let the asshole witnesses drag their butts to court for nothing. Maybe they'll get fed up enough with the system they won't show next time." Harry rubbed the back of his neck. "Why can't we move Tuesday's depositions?"

"Ron Gillete doesn't like you."

"Screw Ron Gillete. He's an incompetent asshole." Harry looked through the file pile again, wishing it would shrink from its own weight. "Who can we get to cover this thing? Who needs work?" He grabbed the phone with an idea.

Tierny Wells answered on the second ring.

When Harry pulled up in front of Alan Ford's Fox Chase home, Tierny Wells reiterated the comment she'd made upon first visiting Harry's office: "So this is private practice."

Harry stopped the '65 Mustang behind the slightly bruised Taurus.

Tierny asked, "What are we, repo men?"

"Repo men don't have keys." Harry handed them to her. "Follow me back down Joppa. If we get separated, here's the address." Harry handed her his card with Tucker's street number on it.

Tierny paused before getting out of the car. "You haven't asked me if there's anything new on the Showels case."

"I figured you'd tell me if there was."

She nodded, but still didn't get out of the car. "If I'm working at your office, Tommy Birchette is going to get suspicious and stop telling me about Showels. But you must know that."

"It's okay. I appreciate what you've done."

"What's going on, Harry? You're changing course on me."

"Is Tommy going to feel like you tricked him?"

"Tommy and I had a good time. It's nothing serious." She fiddled with the keys. "Why did you change the subject?"

◆ 269 ◆

"Diversion tactic. Did it work?"

"Is everything all right, Harry?"

"Everything's . . . No." He shook his head. "Right now, everything's shit." He smiled grimly. "I appreciate your helping me out at the office. I'll be back in a little while. You have any questions, ask Marcie. She knows more than most lawyers."

It no longer mattered to Harry if the police saw what he was doing. Frank Trammell's homicide group was caught in its own failure chain of hasty attempts to make puzzles fit the pieces. Harry was proceeding on the assumption the police weren't going to be able to mount a strong enough case to prosecute Showels if he was Tucker's killer, or to find the true shooter if Showels wasn't it.

So if Showels was being tailed by the police, as Tierny Wells said, and they saw Harry walking into Showels's office, so be it.

·37·

Resting half his round rear end on his secretary's workstation desk, Ronald Showels ran a fleshy finger along her bare arm and whispered a come-on through his smile.

The secretary, perhaps experienced at dealing with happy-hour drunks at her favorite club, somehow managed to ignore him while editing a document's yellow letters on a dark-blue PC screen.

Apparently East Coast Equities didn't get a lot of walk-in business or Showels didn't care that someone might catch him at his nonsense, because the office door was unlocked and Harry entered in the midst of Showels's sloppy advances.

Seeing Harry, the secretary abruptly grabbed a small stack of mail and announced she was going to the corner box. Whether she was embarrassed or glad for an avenue of escape was unclear.

Showels made a frumpy face and considered Harry an unwelcome intruder. "Whatever you're selling—pass."

The small house/office had an upstairs and basement, both accessed by stairs off the reception area. Showels's office and a conference room split the right half of the first floor. The furnishings were coordinated and moderately expensive, likely leased. The whole operation looked as though it could be packed up and moved in a day.

Besides the computer fan and a radio oldies station, it was quiet. No one else seemed to be home.

"Pass," Showels said again. He waved his hand toward the screen door, which slammed as his secretary walked out. "Whatever you're selling. I don't want it."

Harry said, "I'm Tucker Walsh's brother."

Showels went rigid as though stabbed by a needle. "I've got

◆ 271 ◆

nothing to say to you." His final words quivered as he retreated hastily to his office.

When Harry followed him, Showels panicked. He hurried behind his desk and yanked open a drawer, reaching in. Harry grabbed his arm and the 9mm Beretta slid across an otherwise empty drawer.

Harry shoved Showels into his plush office chair and rolled him back against the wall. He closed the drawer, picked up the phone and dialed. Handing the receiver to Showels, he said, "Tell your lawyer you need to see him right away."

Mark Gesser's Mercedes wheeled into Showels's parking lot fifteen minutes later. He rushed inside, infuriated, but also nervous.

Harry and Showels remained in Showels's office. The only words spoken since Harry had disconnected Showels's urgent conversation with Gesser were Harry's: advising Showels to keep quiet until his lawyer showed up, and telling the secretary she had the rest of the day off when she came back from the mailbox.

"What's going on, Harry?" Gesser remained by the inner-office door, where he had a straight line of evacuation to the parking lot.

"Guy's a fucking nut," Showels yelled, braver now that he had an ally.

"Your client's got a quick trigger finger, Mark. As soon as I said who I was, he went for his gun."

Showels yelped, "What'm I supposed to do? Wait for you to attack *me?* This is my office. I don't have to retreat from imminent bodily harm, right, Mark? It's self-defense."

The issue of justified deadly force had apparently come up before.

"All I said was my name."

Gesser said, "Come on, Harry, given the circumstances he's justified in feeling threatened. The police think he killed your brother."

"Stick to divorce law, Mark, you're better suited for it."

Gesser summoned courage. "Get out, Harry. You've got no right

◆ 272 ◆

being here. As of this moment, you're trespassing."

Harry stayed between Gesser and his client, and between Showels and the desk drawer. "If he didn't kill Tucker, then whoever did set him up. And if that happened, it wasn't Sheila Parks."

"If we knew," Gesser said, "don't you think we'd tell the police?"

"Maybe if *you* knew, but maybe Ron knows and isn't saying. Maybe he's got reason not to." Harry accused him dead on. "Maybe Ron has some overdue gambling debts. Or maybe Ron knows about counterfeit money."

"I want him out of here, Mark." Showels's pink knuckles turned stone-white, gripping his chair arms. He trembled like a firm ball bouncing in a constricting box.

"Harry, this isn't right." Gesser quickly switched from demands to reason since the former hadn't worked.

Harry's stare followed the black holes of Showels's pupils as they danced with alarm. "He knows something, Mark."

"I want him out of here."

"Harry . . . come on."

Harry pressed, "Who'd want to set you up, Ron?"

"Mark, get him out."

"Harry, damnit!" Gesser's pleading came from the doorway; he wasn't moving closer.

"Who are you into so deep who also wanted my brother dead?"

"Harry, please!"

"He knows. He *goddamn* knows something."

Harry wanted Showels to say the name—*say it!* Sam Giardino. Yeah, yeah, I owe money to Giardino and can't pay it. That's why Giardino would want to set me up. He could kill Tucker for ratting on the counterfeit scheme and send me to jail for it. Giardino gets rid of two moles at once, one a snitch, the other a deadbeat who needed to learn a lesson about prompt payment.

This *was* very dangerous ground. Harry felt as though the earth had become unsteady beneath him; long-established territory was shifting like tectonic plates, shaking buildings assumed to be se-

◆ 273 ◆

cure. Showels said nothing, and Harry's desire for revenge swelled as though plunged into his veins like a narcotic.

Quietly, firmly, Harry said, "You know, don't you, Ron? *You know.*" He stood back and turned to leave.

38

Throughout the open foyers and high-ceilinged offices of Interior Visions, creative intensity was pervasive. Designers shuttled between offices and workrooms with upbeat energy.

Palettes of fabrics, wallpaper, and paint chips were spread across spacious tables. Colorful computer screens burst alive with brilliant CAD drawings of AmeriCenter blueprints, which had just arrived on diskettes and were being ravenously attacked like exquisite ingredients presented to five-star chefs.

Cleo Lane strode about with the command of a general and enthusiasm of a teenager. The project's star, however, wasn't in. Alena had called in sick.

Harry went to Alena's office, a cheerful space on the third floor where aged brick walls were washed by overcast light through trapezoid skylights. Twin verde ceiling fans turned overhead. Her desk was a massive old piece, sponge-painted soft hues of green.

Craig came in moments later. He had been having fun playing the role of Jeanna's younger man for the Interior Visions's staff, but now switched his expression to serious for meeting his uncle. Harry told him to close the door. He did.

Harry said, "I want you to see something."

Craig joined Harry by the window.

"See that brown car down the block?"

"Yeah?"

"It's two federal agents. They probably smell ripe by now because it's hot out and they've been in there for God knows how long. At least since last night."

Craig peered intently. "What're they doing?"

"Watching you."

"Me?" His surprise seemed genuine. "For what?"

"They've *been* following you. They've got you spending counterfeit money all over campus and—"

Craig pushed away from the wall and pounded a sofa cushion with his fist. "So now what? They're going to arrest me just like Mom?" He tensed with hyperactivity. "I don't believe this. *I don't fucking believe this!* Goddamn. Goddamn." He ran a hand over bristled hair. "This is great. Just great." He paced side to side. "Christ, I don't believe this!"

"I'm asking you again: What do you know about the money?"

He threw out his hands. "Good ol' Tuck. Yeah, buddy, good old dad sends tuition money and it's phony. *Real* terrific."

"He sent your tuition in cash? Right to you? What happened to checks?"

"Too bad he's dead, we could ask the asshole."

"I told you about talking like that."

"Come on, Uncle Harry, Jesus, you're defending him. For what? We're all a wreck because of him. He hated *you!*"

Harry didn't want to deal with those emotions, he wanted facts. "Why did he send you cash?"

Craig drew back his fist as though to pound the wall, but held short.

"Why did—?"

"Because he was an asshole, okay. Because he was . . ." Craig turned a small circle as though looking for routes of escape. He ended up leaning against warm brick, looking up through the skylights. "I blew a scholarship at school, okay. I had good enough grades and SATs and was decent enough at lacrosse to get a combination deal. It wasn't a ride, but got the tuition and board down to four grand. I got a student loan for half and the asshole paid the rest." Craig slowed down, taking a breath. "The second week of lacrosse season—last spring—I got a wicked check in the Brown game. Some punk middie really nailed me. I got a massive hip pointer that wouldn't heal. I never got back up to speed. At the end of the season, coach told me they were killing the athletic scholarship. I could walk on and take my chances, but he didn't think my odds were good. He had a big recruiting class coming in.

◆ 276 ◆

Really big kids. Six-footers going over two-twenty.

"It took me down. My grades went south. I had a three-five after fall semester that ended up in the low twos. I flunked an English course. And there went the academic half of the scholarship. I went on about a month binge, and then I got my shit together. Last summer, I started working out, doing weights five days a week, taking massive supplements to get thick. I was going to get back that scholarship as a walk-on. No doubt about it. And I was declaring a prelaw major. The trouble was, I needed more money to stay in for fall. I got financial assistance and a student loan for seven grand, got a job painting houses over the summer that made another three, but I still needed almost ten.

"Ol' Tuck came down to school and worked out payments with the administration. Fifteen hundred a month during the school year. He wasn't happy about it, but said he'd work it out somehow. The first payment he sent a check to school. Then he started sending cash to me. A grand or more at a time. He was sticking it in my face."

"Sticking what?"

"I'd always given him a lot of shit about playing the lottery. What a waste of money it was. The cash he sent, he told me, was lottery winnings, and without the lottery my ass wouldn't be in school. I'd be out on the streets working a grunt job like him. He said he didn't want to have to show the cash—I guess he meant not paying taxes on it, whatever—and told me to buy money orders and take them to the business office for the tuition payments. I did, once. But then he got some paper or something from school saying I'd switched my major to prelaw and he went apeshit. He said we weren't having any more lawyers in the family. So I figured, fine, no prelaw, no school. I stopped paying the tuition and started pissing away the money. I had a *good* time. I figured, fuck him. *Fuck him.*" Craig grinned sourly. "And when lacrosse season rolled around, I fucking kicked ass and got a full ticket so I didn't have to worry where the money went. All those big recruits coach's pants were so wet about . . . man, I pictured them as ol' Tuck and drove their sorry butts halfway across the field."

◆ 277 ◆

Harry sat on the edge of Alena's desk.

Craig waited for him to say something. When he didn't, he moved away from the wall and went to the window. He looked down at the sedan. Calmer, he said, "Am I getting busted?"

Harry said, "I don't know." He was running out of comforting lies.

Harry grabbed his messages and headed upstairs.

Tierny Wells was in the spare office next to his. A chunk of files that had obscured the top of Harry's desk were now in front of her. When he looked in, she kicked back and boastfully nodded toward the out pile. "I got you a nol pros in the Brunning case. Jim Adair owed me a favor for saving his big butt in a drug conspiracy case last year. And Jill Sapperstein's giving us probation before judgment for Linton—she says it's my private practice housewarming present."

"Nice job." Harry forced thanks through his distraction.

"I like this so far." On a professional high she apparently hadn't experienced for a while as a prosecutor, Tierny extended her arms and waved them as though dancing. "It feels free."

"Try not to fly out of your chair."

She followed Harry to his office. "I also got a few parting bits of info on the Showels case—figured I'd get what I could before they realize I've defected to the other side. It's not much. The Pimlico tapes netted a big zero. They can put Showels at the track, but not with the bag he supposedly dumped. And still nothing on the alibi witness."

"Which means they're back to square one."

"Back to square nothing. Tommy said Trammell's no longer talking in terms of did Showels kill your brother, but can they *prove* he did it."

"In other words, get a killer for the headlines, then either keep looking for the real shooter or talk yourself into believing Showels is it."

"Something like that."

"Terrific," Harry commented sarcastically.

Tierny gestured to the spare office. "Well, I got work."

Harry sighed. "Me, too." He dove into his backlog of files, trying to catch up and using work as a diversion. But it wasn't long before thoughts of Alena became overpowering.

He resisted as long as he could before opening the desk drawer for the black-and-white photograph he'd taken in his apartment: Alena backlit by sunshine through the sliding glass door, smiling wonderfully.

He couldn't put the picture away or get her out of his mind. He drove downtown.

◆ 39 ◆

He felt foolish and perverse in the dark.

Parked across the street from Alena's townhouse, Harry watched her through the front windows.

She wore a wrinkled T-shirt and broken-in jeans, as if she'd spent the day in them. She looked incredible. Her hair was combed out, but not tended to, fanning across her shoulders. She sat on the sofa, knees bent, bare feet perched on the wrought-iron edge of a glass coffee table. Aiming the remote for the TV, she flipped between channels before settling on one, and the screen's changing colors reflected against the room's white walls.

Harry watched a while before locking the car and crossing the street. When Alena looked up at the window and saw him come up the front steps, he stopped and offered a wave and silent "Hi."

She looked away and her soft lips firmed with conflict.

He tapped lightly on the glass and spoke through it. "We should talk."

Her chest rose with a thoughtful breath. She got up from the sofa and went to the door.

Hearing the deadbolts turn raised Harry's hopes, but she only opened the door partway, just enough to lean against its edge. She stood in the small vestibule that faced sideways to the street.

Harry said, "I missed you today."

"I missed you, too . . . but that doesn't change anything." She spoke slowly and thoughtfully, tranquil after a day of doing nothing.

"Did you talk to Cleo?"

Alena brushed back her hair. "At length. She's not cancelling the contract and told me I was crazy to consider it. She said there'd

◆ 280 ◆

be a mutiny. Everyone's looking to make a lot of money. Not just on AmeriCenter, but other new jobs we get because of it."

"So what are you going to do?"

"I don't know."

He smiled and shook his head.

Alena said, "What?"

He stuffed his hands in his pockets and leaned his back to the wall. "I came down here just to *look* at you. I sat in the car for ten minutes. And the more I saw you, the more I wanted to talk to you. But . . ." he met her eyes ". . . it's still not right. It's not enough."

"We went too far too fast, Harry. The condo was a mistake. We should have taken more time getting to know one another."

"You know all there is to know about me." He pushed away from the wall and reached across the invisible boundary established by the threshold to caress her cheek.

"Harry . . ."

He touched along her jaw . . . traced beside her throat . . . followed the neckline of her rumpled T-shirt down the center of her chest. Her nipples hardened against grey cotton before he touched her breast.

"I watched you from the car and it wasn't enough . . . I talked to you, and it wasn't enough."

As his hand slipped inside her T-shirt and onto her breasts, Alena closed her eyes. "You scare me, Harry."

"Why?"

"Because I don't have any control around you."

"You just think so."

"Thinking so makes it so."

He stepped into the vestibule and lifted her shirt. Cupping her breasts in his hands, he pushed the door closed with his foot. Alena leaned back against the wall and began to slide toward the floor.

Harry caught beneath her arms and held her upright. He pressed his mouth to hers, but withdrew when she didn't kiss him back.

"I can't stop you," she gasped. "If you want to fuck me—do it."

He pressed close, fondling her breasts. "Why are you scared?"

◆ 281 ◆

She turned her face from his. "I don't know."

His hand spread over her breast, then closed two fingers along her nipple. "Why are you scared?"

"It's dangerous."

"What is?"

"How you pretend to be something you're not."

"What?"

"You look composed and calm, but you're not. You look like a nice guy . . . you look safe . . ." she shook her head ". . . but you're not."

He undid her pants and pushed them down her hips along with her panties.

Alena crossed her arms over her breasts. "You look honest," she whispered, "but you're not."

"And that scares you?"

"It scares me that it turns me on."

Kneeling, he maneuvered between her legs until his mouth was against her vagina. His tongue pushed along her seam and made penetration.

Alena raked her fingers through his hair and clutched the back of his head. Her moans filled the vestibule and carried inside the house.

When Jackie, her roommate, came toward the sounds and saw them, Harry didn't stop.

Alena gasped, "Turn out the lights, Jack, okay? Turn them out."

An hour later, they lay naked on the sofa, watching headlights reflect off the ceiling as cars passed on the street. Afraid of what they might say, neither spoke until Alena said she didn't want him to spend the night.

Harry got dressed and she watched.

Before leaving, he said, "I don't want to lose you. Tell me what I have to do to make that happen."

"I need some time."

"I love you."

◆ 282 ◆

Naked, she made no effort to cover herself. "I love you."

"So there's nothing to be scared about."

Harry's pager sounded while he was on I-83 leaving the city. His coat was on the passenger seat and he didn't want to dig into its pocket while driving to check the number; hopefully, Carla was calling from the beach. Maybe Alan Ford's approach with kids would work.

Planning to spend another night at his office, Harry drove there. He checked the pager once he'd parked at his favorite spot under the elm tree out front. The number was local. He unlocked the office, turned on lights, and remote dialed his caller from Marcie's desk.

"Harry, what took you so long?" Tierny Wells sounded to have been pacing the room.

"What's wrong?"

"Ronald Showels is dead."

·40·

Nine-one-one had been contacted anonymously. Howard County police found Showels's silver Infiniti in a far corner of a notorious I-95 rest stop reporters nicknamed Pickle Park. More sex-sting operations went down in the surrounding woods than on Baltimore's famed "Block." Truckers, travelers, and local thrill-seekers came to engage in sordid encounters sometimes arranged in advance, other times at random, taking chances in the dark. So many calls were made to prostitutes from the line of drive-up pay phones, investigators called them Jack-Offs-In-The-Box.

Showels was discovered in the driver's seat of his expensive sedan, leaning against the door, shot once in the head by a slug which entered just forward of his right ear and lodged in his brain.

By the time Harry and Tierny got there, the rest stop entrance was closed and guarded by a trio of Howard County officers. The usually dark lot was brightly lit by portable halogen floods perched on fifteen-foot stands and powered by generators. State and County investigators pored over the scene. An ambulance crew waited for the M.E. to turn over Showels's body or for police scouring the woods to find another one. Overhead, a helicopter swooped low and bore in on thick woods with an intense searchlight.

"Sir," one of the gate officers barked impatiently at Harry, "please get back in your car and move on." He walked hard and fast toward Harry's car.

Tierny flashed the State's Attorney's shield she hadn't turned in with her resignation. "Baltimore County," she advised sharply. "Your body's one of our defendants."

He turned toward his fellow officers. "Let 'em in."

Since defense attorneys were non grata at crime scenes, Harry kept his head low as Tierny led the way. Beyond earshot of the cops, he looked at her and said, "Liar."

"I'm not under oath."

"Impersonating an officer?"

"Minor technicality."

They approached the congestion of bodies swarming Showels's expensive car. Bright orange lines had been strung across the area in a mesh pattern, establishing search zones like an archeological dig.

"Taking this very seriously," Harry noted.

"Hey!" A loud objection sounded from a group of men gathered outside the search zone. Frank Trammell broke ranks with his Howard County counterparts.

"Busted," Harry said.

Trammell made a line for them. "How the fuck did you get in here?"

Tierny pretended to tuck in her preppy-green polo shirt and said, "We were screwing in the woods and came out to see what all the commotion was about."

Harry thought she was taking to private practice well.

Trammell moved closer, zooming in with his intimidating cop stare and expelling sour breath beneath his heavy moustache. "Yeah, well you're going to get the hell out of here right now."

Harry didn't flinch. "Who's Eddie Laurel, Frank? And how come when you got Carla's drug case dropped last summer, you let them put Eddie away for nine months?"

"What are you talking about?"

"When Tucker's daughter got busted in Howard County for possession you made a few calls and got the case dropped."

Trammell was uncharacteristically mum.

Harry said, "While you're working on that one, who whacked Showels?"

No comment emerged from Trammell.

"They finding anything?" Harry asked of the widespread search. "Or is this just another circus lead-in for a case that's going to get screwed up?" Experience had shown Harry that making the impet-

◆ 285 ◆

uous Trammell mad was the way to make him talk.

"You're an asshole, Walsh."

"You're avoiding my questions."

"Tucker was a good friend, all right? He was a good cop." Trammell spoke loud and fast. "His girl got in some trouble and he asked if I could help out. He knew I had some ins. It was no big deal. She was a minor, so she would have gone into the juvenile diversion program anyway. But they didn't even have a case against her. It was the loser she was with—it was his stuff."

"Eddie Laurel . . ."

"Yeah, Eddie Laurel."

"He died this week, Frank. Small world."

"Yeah, I know all about it. Too bad. He had more arrests than the Bullets have losing seasons. And he'd been fucking the girl since she was thirteen if that makes any difference to you. Tucker was a little upset over that."

"Laurel sound like a likely suicide victim to you?"

"Ask me if I care."

"I think that's your job."

Trammell smirked. "Self-righteous mob lawyer . . . Get the fuck out of here, Walsh—and take this little plea-bargain-basement bitch with you."

Driving Tierny home, Harry explained his questions about Eddie Laurel. Tierny asked if he thought Laurel was relevant to Tucker and Showels. Harry said he didn't know.

It was after midnight when Harry pulled up in front of Tierny's apartment building. The distant thump of music at a late-night deck party and droning air-conditioning units interrupted the quiet night.

Tierny opened her door. "It'll be interesting to find out what happened to the tail Trammel supposedly had on Showels."

"And what Showels was doing at Pickle Park."

"You don't suppose parking his pickle."

"Mark Gesser said Showels had rotten luck with women. He

claims he got sued by one secretary he tried to date, and the woman who's supposed to be his alibi vanishes."

Tierny nodded into a quiet stare. "It's odd, though, isn't it? How it feels justified. However Showels died. The retribution . . . It's almost—I don't know, Harry—it's almost peaceful."

Instead of going back to the office, Harry told himself he wasn't tired and went to Tucker's. He had to look harder. Take a deep breath and plunge into a search of Carla's room. Look everywhere. There had to be something else. Harry didn't know what that "something else" might be, but hoped he'd recognize it when he saw it.

And then he went inside the darkened house and smelled smoke.

When he heard the cat thump onto the floor in the dining room, it confirmed he wasn't walking into a blaze, but the scent of recent fire was distinct, as though threads of sulphur still hung in the air.

He turned on the standing lamp and moved into the kitchen, but the odor's strength drew him back to the living room. The fireplace.

He opened glass doors and puffs of grey soot floated out toward his face. He turned on another light and peered beneath the iron log grate. A pile of black ashes and unburned paper had been stamped down by water. Wet trickles ran along singed mortar between fireplace bricks.

The fire had been short-lived and Harry saw why: reaching up inside the chimney, he found the flu was closed. The firestarter had forgotten to raise the damper and, when fire sent smoke billowing into the room, the blaze had to be extinguished with water.

Harry sifted through shredded pages of newspaper charred black from fire and soggy from being doused. His fingers got dirty as though picking through charcoal. Beneath a wet hunk of newsprint, a silver edge caught his eye. He took the object carefully by the corner and pulled it out. An instant lottery ticket: one that immediately reveals whether it's a winner or not once squares covered in inker's print are scratched off. This ticket was a winner.

Alan Ford's phone number was unlisted, so Harry drove to the expensive Fox Chase residence and knocked on the door. It was late, Ford's house was dark, but Harry wasn't concerned about awakening him.

Maybe Carla was at the beach, maybe she wasn't.

The fireplace had been used sometime between 8:00 this morning, when Harry had stopped by Tucker's house on his way into town, and a few hours ago. Craig had been with Jeanna all day and night. Connie was in Orlando. Assuming the cat wasn't a pyromaniac, that left Carla. And there was only one reason Harry could think of to destroy a lottery ticket worth fifty dollars.

When Alan Ford didn't come to the door, Harry circled the large single-level house knocking on windows and calling Ford's name.

A light flicked on, but not inside the house. The neighbor Harry had seen mowing his yard switched on floodlights which brightened his rear yard and a portion of Ford's. The man stood at his back door in a nightshirt, his face stitched with aggravation.

A branch caught on Harry's jeans as he pried himself out from between two waist-high bushes planted against the house. He crossed the lawn, careful to step over a row of pine seedlings that established a flimsy boundary line between the two homes.

"It's two in the morning," the neighbor announced gruffly, talking through the glass door as Harry stepped onto his patio.

"I'm sorry, but I'm looking for my niece. She's a friend of the Ford girl."

"Doesn't give you the right to wake me up. It's two in the morning," he protested again. Short wisps of thin white hair stuck up along his round skull.

"Have you seen a girl next door: sixteen years old, about five-six, dark hair, slender?"

"Seen a couple kids over there from time to time, but not today.

Haven't seen anybody today. So why don't you go home and go to bed like decent people?"

"It's an emergency."

"So call the police." The man turned off his outdoor lights and drew vertical blinds closed across the glass door.

Harry returned to Ford's house and knocked on remaining windows, as though if he knocked harder, he could will the man to be home. It didn't work.

The only other thing he could think to do was awaken someone else. At a 7-Eleven pay phone, he called Orlando.

The phone rang a long time before George Kittle answered. He sounded even more irritated than Alan Ford's neighbor.

"Mr. Kittle, Harry Walsh. I'm sorry to disturb you, but I need to talk to Connie. Carla's missing and I need the names of her friends I can—"

"She's not here."

"Damnit, what happened? Manning's office said—"

"Oh, she's out. Got out at three-thirty this afternoon because I put up my house. She goes right from the goddamn jail to the airport. I risk my house and first thing she does is leave the state. What am I supposed to think about that? I'm up all night taking Pepto."

"Where'd she go?"

As though the word was synonymous with hell, George Kittle said, "Home."

"Connie?" Harry let himself in and called up the stairs.

"Connie!" He turned on lights and started through the quiet house.

The smell of wet smoke lingered.

He checked the kids' rooms and master bedroom. Connie wasn't there, nor were there signs she had been. Bed linens were tucked neatly in place around the standard-size mattress. The bathroom sink and shower were dry, as were the towels. The toilet hadn't been flushed lately, as evidenced by a faint red line around the bowl, a reactive tattoo caused by iron residue in the water supply.

Connie had flown home, but wasn't home.

Harry decided to wait for her. In the meantime, he went into the melee that was Carla's room. Sitting on her bed, he opened a tattered shoe box stuffed with shredded balls of decorative tissue. Beneath the tissue were film canisters containing flakes of high-grade marijuana buds and Polaroid photographs of Carla. She looked a year or two younger, and was naked except for white socks, sprawled seductively across a massive grey boulder in the woods. She looked stoned, smiling at the camera.

In a couple of shots, she wasn't alone, but engaged with an older kid who, if Harry had to guess, was Eddie Laurel. Pictures of them both were tilted, as though the camera had been set on the nearest rock and set on auto-timer. The focus, however, was clear: Eddie was skinny, grimy-looking. His hair was long and tangled. His erection was in Carla's mouth.

Harry felt anger he could barely contain. This was the little girl he had bought stuffed animals for, that he had read stories to, and taken to the park, pretending, at times, she was his daughter, much as Craig had confessed to the fantasy that Harry had been his father.

Those days had meant a lot to Harry; he'd felt a familial closeness lost since his father's death. His contact with Carla and Craig had been broken by his brother's wishes, but now his memories were being smeared by what had happened since. He felt betrayed and cheated, and wondered how powerful his emotions would run upon this discovery if he wasn't a mere uncle, but Carla's father.

It started to rain overnight. Around four in the morning, Harry awakened and heard the drops falling quietly against the bay window. There was no thunder, just soft rain.

Beside the sofa, a tabletop clock ticked seconds toward dawn. Otherwise, Tucker's house was quiet. Somewhere in the darkness, the grey cat lay as silently as Harry, each on their separate vigil.

· 41 ·

"Harry?"

He sat upright quickly.

Connie stood beside the sofa. "Are you all right?"

He didn't feel as if he'd been asleep, but hours had passed. It was daylight, but still raining; water seeping into the chimney intensified the burned-wet odor from the fireplace.

Harry checked his watch: 8:45. "When did you get in?"

"Just now. Are the kids home?"

"No. At least I don't think so."

Connie's stiff shrug reflected disappointment. Her face was drawn and pale. She appeared considerably thinner.

Harry figured between them they'd lost fifteen pounds since Tucker's death. "I called your parents last night. Your father said you'd left."

"I had to get out of there." Connie gazed blankly at the floor. "Have you ever been in jail? Besides seeing clients?"

"No."

"It's horrible. And it's not the hard bed, or the tiny stainless-steel toilet and sink, or terrible food, or other people, it's . . ." As though confession peeled away layers of numbness, she began to cry. "There's no windows. There's nothing to do except sit. You sit with yourself. That's the worst part." Tears streamed along her cheeks and fell onto her blouse. "There aren't any distractions. You're trapped with yourself and there's nothing you can do about it. I would have rather been dead."

Harry brought her to the sofa and held her in his arms. "It's going to be okay." He hoped his reassurance sounded more positive than it felt.

"The only thing that got me through was wanting to be back

◆ 291 ◆

with the kids. As bad as it was, I couldn't imagine what they were going through. Their father gets killed, *I get arrested*. My God! All I wanted was to be back with them, but I come home as soon as I can and they're not here, and then I realize, sure, why should they be home? Why should things be different now?"

Harry's shirt became wet with her tears.

"The house was so empty, I couldn't stand it. I broke down. I saw so many ghosts. Carla and Craig as children . . . and Tucker . . . and you." She held him tighter. "I completely broke down. Rita and Stan took me home to spend the night with them."

"You should have called me."

"I was embarrassed."

"About what?"

She didn't answer at first.

"What?"

"How you looked at me down there—you thought I was a criminal."

"That's not true."

"I don't blame you." Her eyes were red with tears. "I was just doing what my father told me to do. I didn't know, Harry. I found the money in that safe-deposit box and I was scared. I wasn't thinking right. I was half crazy. I *still* feel half crazy."

"It's going to be taken care of."

"I don't know what got into Tucker, or what he was doing." Connie sat back into the soft sofa. "I hardly recognized him this past year. He'd changed. He was so distant and—I don't know— peculiar. Different. He'd always been intense. He had mood swings. But this last time he couldn't seem to get out of it. He kept sinking deeper and deeper . . . It lasted so long."

Harry wiped her eyes. "What was he upset about?"

"I don't know . . . Everything?" she said as though guessing. "I asked him to see a counselor and he finally agreed, but when he got there he was afraid it would get on his record at the department and he'd *never* get promoted then."

"He was trying for lieutenant?"

"All the time. I dreaded those exams. Every year he'd study and

◆ 292 ◆

score well, but not well enough. He usually missed by one or two slots, and then we'd go through it all over again. He'd complain how the department played favorites and about minority hiring practices. That an unqualified woman or black would get the job over him even though his tests were higher and he had more experience. He'd hit bottom for weeks about that, but, eventually he'd come around."

"Was that what happened the last time?"

"We pretty much stopped talking about anything that might start a fight. But I'm sure that had to do with it. That and the wage freeze. Our bills were going up, especially with Craig in college, and the department wasn't even giving cost-of-living increases."

"What about the kids? How did they react to this?"

"Craig hadn't had much to do with Tucker for the last few years. Once he hit sixteen, they became total adversaries. Whatever one said, the other would disagree with on principle. Carla took it better. She called Tucker's mood swings the 'blue funks.' She was always trying to cheer him up." Connie went into the kitchen and returned with a box of Kleenex.

"She'd get him to take her out to the Mall or for yogurt. I think that's when the whole lottery thing started. They came home one night with a whole string of instant tickets and scratched them off. I think they broke even, but you'd have thought Tucker won a million dollars. He was so happy being with her. It was good to see them like that. Carla had always been in line behind Craig with Tucker. Craig was the athlete and Tucker liked seeing Craig's name in the paper and bragging about him at work. I think that's what made it so hard for him when Craig turned against him. And that it happened so suddenly, and so meanly. But Tucker couldn't talk about things like that. He couldn't sit Craig down and find out what was wrong. He just got mad. And the feud began."

"How were the two of you getting along?"

"Tucker and me?" She pulled out a fresh Kleenex and wiped her nose. "I don't know . . . What do you want to know, Harry? Were we still in love? Was the passion fire still going?" She sounded hollow. "I don't know that we were so different from other couples our

◆ 293 ◆

age. Something happens with men when they hit forty. Either forty or a twentieth anniversary. They don't get aroused just by looking at you anymore, or by being with you. Something happens somewhere else, they see a beautiful *young* woman, or a movie, or read something, and get turned on by that, and the wife gets the arousal brought on by some outside source. It's a lousy feeling, Harry. It's like being an alternate—the real thing wasn't available, but you were handy so you'll do."

It hurt to hear her talk like this.

"Two lousy things happen at the same time: your kids grow up and don't need you, and your husband gets bored and doesn't want you. Which leaves you sitting home wondering how you became so worthless so fast." She balled up a tissue and threw it across the corner of the sofa.

"How bad did it get?"

"How bad?" She looked straight ahead, staring at the coffee table. "You mean did he cheat on me? Or . . . did I cheat on him?"

"You don't have to answer."

She grabbed another Kleenex to hold onto. "That I know of, yes, there was at least one other woman."

"I'm sorry."

"Carla took an astronomy course at night at Towson State and made some friends. It was one of those girls." Connie shuddered. "God, that was horrible. Finding out. She called for him one night and I answered the phone. Another woman's voice confused her. She thought I was Carla's sister, and when I said I was her mother, she got even more confused. Tucker had told the girl he was divorced, which was predictable, I guess. But Carla . . . *Goddamn her.* She went along with the story."

"She knew?"

"Yes! I was so mad, I can't tell you. Yes, *she knew!*" Connie's anger raised. "She'd pulled some good ones before, but not just helping her father conceal adultery—she was helping him get laid! We had it out about that. She told me it wasn't hurting anyone. That Tucker needed the release and her friend liked him. I said what about me? How was it I wasn't supposed to be hurt? And she

◆ 294 ◆

says in this condescending know-everything teenage voice, like it's so simple how could I have missed it, 'Mom, you weren't supposed to find out.' "

"I'm sorry he did that to you."

Connie stood tensely. "I'm sorry, too. I'm sorry about a lot of things. I'm sorry he told me not to invite you over anymore. And I'm more sorry I paid attention to him. For what! For what, Harry! What's it gotten me? Loyalty? Servitude! Cooking, cleaning, driving all over hell's acre, and for what! What am I now, Harry! What do I do now!" She picked up a pillow and threw it across the room, scattering knickknacks in the bay window and knocking a dry vase to the floor.

"Connie . . ."

She went upstairs, crying and mad.

The temperature was in the high seventies, but grey skies and steady rain made Harry feel cold. He turned the heat on in the Mustang for a few minutes to knock off the chill, but by the time he was relatively dry and comfortable, he was back in the rain again.

He hustled up the front walk to Alan Ford's house in Fox Chase, hoping the father of Carla's friend was ready to be awakened on a Saturday morning. Harry didn't have any sympathy. Ford's dealing-with-kids strategy had flopped. There had been no call from Carla.

Harry rang the bell and pounded hard on the door when the more civilized announcement didn't work. He waited, shielded from rain by the overhang of the small front landing.

Inside, the house was dark, and it was a dreary enough day to require lights. Assuming Ford was home, he was either a sound sleeper or choosing to ignore early visitors. Then again, maybe he never came home last night. So far, there hadn't been any Mrs. Ford, and Mr. Ford's attitude did lean toward divorced-parent leniency, so possibly he spent the night with a girlfriend. Maybe letting his daughter and a friend go off to the beach for the weekend had been more convenience than liberal parenting.

Harry beat the door again, but in frustration. He looked across the rolling lawns of upscale neighboring homes, their trimmed

◆ 295 ◆

hedges and twenty-year oaks. Over the next few hours, residents would casually come awake to a rainy Saturday, curse the missed chance to tend already neat grass, and go to a mall or the movies.

Harry pulled up his collar and headed back to the car.

· 42 ·

Mark Gesser's new home was a stylish monument to his early success in the legal profession and his qualification for a jumbo mortgage. A long driveway lined with blue atlas cedars curved gracefully through a preserved forest of deciduous trees.

The custom Georgian house sported slate roofs and copper downspouts. An entrance courtyard bordered by miniature roses was a befitting setting for English tea. If the axiom was true that there were never any winners in a divorce case, the theory omitted divorce *lawyers* from the equation.

Yet for all his material wealth, Mark Gesser appeared so tired and depressed, he didn't launch into his usual boastful monologue while showing a visitor into his massive two-story study.

Gesser pulled closed double pocket doors, blocking out the laugh track of a cartoon show his daughter watched in a near wing of the house.

Harry waited for Gesser to decide which of three seating areas they'd use: the antique writing-table desk and leather chairs nestled in a corner, small conference table beneath a crystal chandelier, or sofa and arm chairs by the fireplace and Persian rug.

Gesser opted for the sofa. He leaned into a corner, sitting sideways and crossing his legs. His thick hair was not styled with the usual mousse, but slicked back. His designer suit was replaced by corduroys and a club sweater.

"Reporters," Gesser said with some effort, "were here for an hour last night. All over the goddamned grass. They throw Frisbees while they wait for you to come out and say something. A glow-in-the-dark Frisbee sailing across the lawn. My wife had a fit. She left messages on the lawn service's phone all night. Some poor yutz was

◆ 297 ◆

out here at six A.M., slopping around in the rain to 'estimate the damage.' Christ."

"Mark—something links Showels and my brother."

"And you think I know what that is," Gesser replied in a frustrated tone, making clear that he didn't. "Poor fucking Ron. If it wasn't for bad luck . . ."

"Something somewhere puts them together. In his office, in his house."

"The cops went through Ron's office records last week. The house, too. They got a big fat zero."

"Maybe they didn't know what they were looking for."

"That's the story of their whole case, including who they arrested."

"I want to go through his records, Mark. His files."

Gesser shook his head. "I can't help you. It's all his wife's now. Everything was titled in joint names. Even the business. Ron insisted on his wife having half the shares when they incorporated. I tried to talk him out of it." Gesser made a sour face. "He was in *love*. There was also a buy-sell agreement with the shares: one dies, the other takes in trust for the daughter. So if you want access, talk to Suicide Sheila, maybe she'll give you the grand tour."

Gesser was missing the point. It wasn't necessarily specifics Harry wanted. Harry sat forward in the chair, elbows on his knees. "Showels died for one of two reasons, Mark. Either—"

"Last night, a reporter suggested retaliation." Gesser pushed back a heavy drape and looked outside over a small courtyard and swimming pool washed by rain. "She asked if I thought a cop did it to avenge one of their own. Ron gets pulled over on the pretext of a traffic stop, and bang."

"That's one theory," Harry said. "On the other hand, if Showels didn't kill Tucker—"

"He didn't." Gesser was mad about losing not just his client, but his notoriety.

"All right," Harry conceded for the sake of argument. "So, assume Showels didn't do it, then whoever did had it in for them *both,* right? Kill Tucker and frame Showels. Why? Who knows them both? Who's the link?"

Gesser remained silent.

"Whatever Showels was into," Harry prodded, "you've got no client to protect by keeping it secret."

Gesser let the drape close and looked at Harry. "I don't pry into my clients' souls, Harry. What they tell me I take as gospel unless I see holes the other side can take a poke at. After all, if I know the truth, I can't ethically let them lie on the stand, can I?" Gesser took a breath. "So as far as I know, Ron Showels was an up-and-up businessman." He stopped, but didn't sound as though he'd finished his thought. After a long silence, he continued. "Yesterday," he said in tones of surrender, "you mentioned counterfeit money in Ron's office . . . He went nuts about that after you left. He denied having anything to do with it, but it was how he reacted to the accusation . . . It got me thinking he was scared."

Tierny Wells had been in the office for two hours by the time Harry got there Saturday morning. "Had my fill of unemployment," she explained from behind a desk stacked with files. "I like being in the game." She looked casual but businesslike, wearing a bright orange tennis shirt. "You don't look like you slept."

"Some."

"I got some, too." Her smile bespoke a lack of humility. "Tommy Birchette stopped by late last night."

"Some guys can't stay away."

"Tommy says Showels was on his way to the airport."

"Well that's goddamned interesting—I imagine a condition of his release was not to leave the state."

"You imagine correctly." Tierny unfolded notes written in haste after Tommy's departure many hours after his arrival. "He had a reservation on a Cayman Air flight to Grand Cayman, departing Washington National early this morning."

"This morning? Not last night?"

"A neighbor said Showels put a suitcase in his trunk last *night* around eight—two hours before the estimated time he was killed."

"Why leave so early?"

"Maybe to see if he was still being followed. Gesser threatened to go to the press with the results of Showels's lie detector unless Trammell pulled off the surveillance. He claimed Trammell was interfering with Showels's right to counsel and hampering his ability to prepare his defense."

"Ironic: if cops were following Showels last night, he might still be alive."

Harry parked the Mustang at the curb two houses from Alan Ford's stone rancher and sat inside, listening to rain beat against the old car's canvas top and metal hood.

Family sedans passed by, tires splashing over wet streets. Kids in jeeps roared along, radios blaring, speakers throbbing bass like powerful heartbeats.

Alan Ford would come home and find himself the unfortunate recipient of Harry's frustration. Harry would demand Ford get on the phone and call someone at the beach who could get in touch with Carla. Not when it would suit his daughter to call home, but now. Right now.

Only Alan Ford didn't come home. He *left* home. The dark green Jaguar pulled out of the garage and headed away from Harry. The arrogant bastard had been inside all along, ignoring Harry's hard raps on his front door.

Harry started after him, driving too fast, and had just about caught up when the Jaguar ran a red light onto Dulaney Valley Road. Harry got caught behind a Ford Explorer that didn't seem interested in turning right on red until there was a mile-long gap in traffic. Harry hit the horn. The Explorer ignored him.

Harry strained to look south on Dulaney Valley, but a planted berm and stone wall blocked his view. When the light changed, he swerved around the Explorer and pushed the Mustang to its limits, speeding down the single-lane road.

He caught sight of the Jaguar as it started up the other side of the long valley. An upcoming series of traffic lights would either allow

Harry to catch up or put him too far behind.

The lights proved his friend. He was three cars to the right rear of Alan Ford at the turn into Towsontown Center.

Ford wasn't alone in the car. Someone was in the passenger seat. She leaned over, placed her hand behind his head to pull him close, and kissed him long and flush on the mouth.

Harry pulled closer. It was Carla.

· 43 ·

In the multilevel garage near Nordstrom, Alan Ford wheeled the Jaguar across two parking spaces. He came around to open Carla's door and she smiled at him happily. Holding hands, they walked into the mall. No one stared, some smiled, apparently assuming Ford and Carla were father and daughter.

Suddenly forgetting the respect with which he'd always treated his father's car, Harry slammed the door and followed them.

Inside the upscale department store, Carla and Ford browsed designer dresses, but ended up on the bottom floor, where Nordstrom Rack offered closeout prices with minimum decor under fluorescent lights.

Rows of discounted clothes were crowded with Saturday shoppers, many Carla's age, bargain-hunting with fast-food-earned cash or money squeezed from parents willing to pay to get them out of the house for the day.

Carla picked through a rack of black peasant dresses. Grabbing one by the hanger, she held it to her curving frame and struck mock poses. Ford said something that made her laugh. She replaced the dress and put her arm around him.

Harry watched from across the floor.

Carla led Ford enthusiastically to rows of jackets and tried on a bright blue windbreaker. Ford shook his head; he didn't like it. Carla pouted, but when Ford pointed the jacket back to the rack with a fatherly gesture, she obliged.

Harry circled around long aisles of sportswear and came up on them from behind. He grabbed Carla's arm and said, "Let's go."

She yelped with surprise.

Ford turned to her defense, but stopped on seeing Harry, who bore down on him, muttering, "You're goddamned scum."

"Uncle Harry, let go!"

Harry tightened his grip when she tried to pull away. "I see you with her again, I'm gonna kick your nuts up through your nose."

"Uncle Harry!"

Shoppers stared. A clerk reached for the phone and dialed security, but a guard was already on the way, having seen the encounter from the moment Harry took Carla's arm.

Carla cried, "Let go!"

The guard ran the final steps, feet landing heavily on floor tile. "There a problem here?" he demanded. His tone assumed there was, and that he was going to resolve it.

Standing close enough to smell the richness of Ford's aftershave, Harry glared at him, and Ford's expression replied with unspoken aggression: a sudden change from even-tempered father figure.

"Uncle Harry, let go!"

"You want to let the girl go, sir!" The guard placed a thick hand at Harry's wrist and squeezed hard.

Harry didn't flinch. "She's my niece."

"I don't care, sir." The guard increased his grip, applying pressure while trying to keep the scene under control.

Ford said, "It's all right. I'm leaving." He was mad, not embarrassed.

Carla reached for him. "No. Don't go! Don't go!"

Ford walked off, angered, but composed.

"Alan!" Carla shook her arm, but Harry held on. "Uncle Harry, let go!" When he wouldn't, she slapped him hard across the cheek. "Goddamnit, let go!"

Ford made his exit by pushing through a circle of gawkers.

"Alan!"

"Carla," Harry warned, "shut the hell up."

She cried, "What are you doing to me?"

"Are you sleeping with that guy? He's forty years old."

"I *love* him."

The guard suddenly realized what was happening and released

◆ 303 ◆

Harry's wrist. He looked beyond the spectators for a glimpse of the man walking away, thinking perhaps he'd grabbed the wrong person.

Harry walked Carla toward a side exit by her arm.

A homeboy in a sideways baseball cap hollered, "Yo, man, let the chica go. She can ball whoever she want."

"Yo, man, yo!" his friend chimed in, laughing and grabbing his crotch. "She can ball me, too."

Outside beneath a narrow overhang, shielded mostly from the rain, Harry stood Carla against the formed concrete wall. She kept her head down and her hair fell forward like a rag doll's, covering her eyes.

"I've been looking for you for two days."

"I don't care!"

"You don't care . . . No, why should you care?" He shook her. "Where'd you get those damned lottery tickets?"

"I don't know."

"Well, think."

"I don't know."

"You don't burn tickets that are winners, do you? Not unless you're trying to hide something."

She screamed, "I didn't do anything!"

"You know damned well what I'm talking about."

"I didn't do anything!" she screamed louder.

"The night you wanted me to stop so you could cash a lottery ticket, you wouldn't go in the place that was empty. You had to go somewhere crowded, somewhere a clerk would be too hassled to look close and see your ticket was a phony."

"It was all Dad's stuff," she blurted out. "Dad had all the stuff!"

"Where'd he get it?"

"I don't know!" Her screams scraped raw against her throat.

Shoppers walking into Nordstrom angled toward the far doors.

"You went out with him to buy lottery tickets. So don't give me that shit!"

"I don't know! I don't know!"

"Bullshit!"

"He wouldn't tell me. He said if I knew, it could be dangerous for me, all right! There! Are you happy? And now he's dead! Are you happy about that? Are you happy?" Bent over, she clutched her stomach and sobbed.

Harry leaned against the wall. What had his brother done to his own daughter, to his entire family? He put his arm around Carla. "I'm sorry," he soothed. "God, I am so sorry."

"Don't touch me!" Crouched over, she lunged from the sidewalk into the parking lot. Arms wrapped around her stomach, she staggered a desperate side-to-side course, moving through parked cars as though fishing through a maze. Rain streaked her long-sleeved T-shirt.

Traffic moved slowly through the area: drivers watching Harry walk toward his niece as she ran from him, both of them soaking wet before she finally let him take her in his arms.

"What does this say about us?" Connie asked. She stood against the kitchen door and looked outside.

Rivulets of rain streaked against dark windows; their watery form reflected light of the solitary ceiling fixture hung over the kitchen table.

"She so desperately wants a father figure, the only way she can find that security is to go to bed with an older man. My God . . ." Connie stared sadly through wet windows ". . . my God."

"She doesn't know where Tucker got the lottery tickets or the money. He said it would be dangerous for her to know."

Connie moved slowly, as though the rain had soaked through her. She sat across from Harry.

When his parents bought this table thirty years ago, could they have ever imagined such a conversation taking place across its face? Families were always in motion, ever changing, mostly with the optimistic sense that tomorrow would be better than today. Decisions were made on that basis, and yet the results of such promising intent were often adulterated by outside forces, fate, and poor judgment. Somewhere along the family timeline, events were set in motion that delivered Harry to this day. Maybe it was the day his father had gone to work for Sam Giardino.

Harry left Connie's and drove to his apartment. He was walking toward his door through the rain when a figure emerged through the darkness. Dressed in a long yellow rain slicker with the hood raised, the figure's hands reached out for him. A woman with painted fingernails.

She moved him into the shadows, not to avoid the rain, but to get him out of the light.

· 44 ·

Jennifer Mulcaney, his client, looked at Harry from inside the rain slicker's hood. "I found your alibi girl, Harry. Forget Nicole Matson—it's an alias. Her name's Emily Elay. You want her, you've got about five hours. She's out at the state fairgrounds, but they're taking down tents. She's a gypsy fortune-teller." Streams of rain ran off creases in her hood. "I'm not supposed to tell you this, am I? Sam really doesn't want anyone to find her, does he?"

"No."

She nodded, understanding she could be in trouble. "Then forget about paying me for this. Just don't get us killed." She kissed his wet forehead and turned to run off along the edge of the woods.

Steady rain was bringing the State Fair to a premature end. The fair grounds were sloppy with mud. Even the heartiest of patrons, having hoped to outlast wet weather, were giving up; cars filed through exit gates streaking dirt from the unpaved lot onto macadam roads.

Harry drove in against an impatient line of departing headlights. His tires spun over slick earth as windshield wipers slapped away the rain.

Just ahead, midway lights shone like wet beacons above the striped tops of pitched tents. Amusement thrill rides stood still, colorfully lit mechanical arms jutting into a black sky streaked silver with rain.

Harry parked near the end of an aisle and stepped out into the rain. His Nikes immediately sank into two inches of mud. Water ran cold inside the collar of his windbreaker.

Hunched against the weather, Harry passed through the main gates, careful to step over water-filled ruts.

Rough-looking carny hands stood inside open doors of tractor

◆ 307 ◆

trailers, smoking cigarettes and drinking from flasks, biding the hours until tear-down time.

Along the line of food stalls, exhaust fumes of fried dough and french-fry oil hung low like a sweet cloud. Further to the interior, dark-haired gypsy pitchmen relentlessly hawked games of chance to fleeing customers. Other barkers watched somberly as rain collected in bulging tent tops and ran in sheets off the pop-open tops of truck caps.

A string of white neon lights outlined the teacup symbol of the fortune-teller. The flaps to a harem tent were tied back to stake posts. Three gypsy men argued in rapid Lebanese, standing around a card table draped with white linen.

The tent was provisionally attached to a small moving van. Through a partially opened side door Harry could see the crossed legs of a woman in a white dress.

The men stopped arguing when Harry ducked under their tent.

Harry rubbed his hands together to warm them. He played it very loose. "How you doing?" He gestured to the woman's legs. "That Emily? Friend of mine said Emily was good seeing numbers. Like lottos, pick threes, that kind of thing."

Immediately his friends, two men ushered Harry to a chair at the folding table; the third trotted up the wooden ramp to the woman in the truck.

Seven votive candles were placed on the table and lit with a single match.

The woman descended the ramp wearing a hand-sewn white dress; a series of ruffled necklines laid fancifully across her breasts. Young and very pretty, she smiled the pleasant smile of a con artist. She sat gracefully, swooping her dress beneath her.

"I'll do well for you," she assured, resting her hands lightly on the table. "Since you come out in this weather." Her green eyes were clear and wide with feigned mysticism. Ronald Showels had called them fuck-me-till-I'm-dead eyes. "Even a special price. Twenty-five dollars."

Harry gave her thirty and when he didn't ask for change, she didn't give it.

Settled as comfortably as the hard chair would allow, she placed her upturned palms on the table and indicated Harry should place his hands atop hers.

"You *are* Emily?" The resemblance to Mark Gesser's artist's rendering was striking, but far from exact.

"Yes. I'm Emily."

Harry began to offer his hands, but stopped. He could have asked if her name was Frank and she would have said yes. "What's your last name?"

She closed her eyes as though already slipping into a trance.

"What's your last name, Emily?"

The three gypsy men had retreated inside the truck, renewing their argument behind a now-closed door.

"Emily . . . ?"

"Elay," she said in an ethereal hush.

Harry placed his hands on hers.

"Cold," she commented, and gently stroked her thumbs across the back of his hands. Her eyes remained closed, but pressed together more tightly as though struggling to conjure a vision. "Relax," she urged patiently. "Clear your mind of all thoughts."

Rain beat against the canvas tent and truck roof and splashed into puddles on the midway.

"My friend said you were very good at seeing numbers."

"Yes." Her tone suggested he was distracting her.

"Do you remember him?"

"Shhh."

"Ronald Showels."

Harry gripped her hands just as she attempted to pull them away with alarm. She stared at him fearfully.

"I'm not here to hurt you." He didn't want her calling out to the men in the truck. "I'm not with the police." Harry spoke with quiet urgency. "The policeman who was killed was my brother. Ronald Showels says you were with him when it happened. In a motel."

The stress remained in her hands, wanting to pull free, but Harry held on tightly. She nervously scanned the midway, looking through the rain.

Harry squeezed harder. "Please tell me. Did Ronald Showels kill my brother? Was he with you when it happened?"

"We cannot talk here. It's dangerous."

"It took me this long to find you."

"If my brothers find out what I did . . ." With a certain shame—perhaps contrived for Harry's benefit—she looked as though she might cry. "If they hear us . . ."

"Those are your brothers in the truck?"

She nodded. "Two of them."

"The door's closed. If they—"

"I can't."

"Please. *Please.*"

She shook her head.

"What did you do?"

"No."

"Why didn't you go to the police?"

"I can't."

"Because of your brothers?"

"Yes." She'd started to say no.

"Emily?"

"*He* told me to go there—to the bar. That a man would be there." She answered quickly, to get it over with.

"That Showels would be there?"

"Yes."

"So you did?"

"Yes."

"And what were you supposed to do with Showels?"

"No," she cried shamefully.

"Please."

She kept her head down and whispered unintelligibly.

Harry leaned forward. "What?"

"Go to bed with him."

"Were you with him all night?"

She paused before answering, fearful of the truck door opening. "Yes—I was with him until morning."

"What time?"

"Ten o'clock. The man said stay with him until ten o'clock."

"Showels never left the room?"

"He wasn't a very nice man."

"But he *never* left the room?"

With distaste, she replied, "No." Tears slid over her olive-toned cheeks.

"You said someone told you Showels would be in the bar—who was it?"

"The man with contacts."

"Contacts?"

"For immigration. Everyone in the family uses him."

"What's his name?"

"I don't know."

"Sam Giardino?"

"I *don't* know his name."

"You don't know . . . Someone tells you to—"

"Unless I did what he said, I wasn't going to get the green card."

"Who is he?"

"I *don't know.*"

"Why won't you tell me his name?"

"I tell what you asked about. You wanted to know about a man who killed your brother, and I told you."

"But Showels didn't kill my brother. Someone else did."

"Yes."

"And you know who that is?"

"No."

"You know who told you to meet Showels—someone who wanted Showels's alibi to vanish so he could take the blame."

"Maybe he deserves blame after what he did to me."

"What?"

She shook her head, anger returning to shame.

"Did he rape you? Or hurt you?"

"He made me pretend I was someone else. He said to pretend I was Carla."

◆ 311 ◆

* * *

Harry looked in the living room window. An old musical played on TV. He knocked on the glass.

Connie got up from the sofa and came to the door, belting her robe.

Harry stepped in out of the rain. "Where is she?"

Connie said, "In her room," in a tone that asked what was wrong. When he didn't answer, she started after him up the stairs. "Harry . . . ?

"Stay down here."

"Harry, what's going on?"

"Stay downstairs," he repeated firmly.

Gripping the banister, he took the steps two at a time. Carla's door was closed. He hoped she hadn't gone out the window again. He didn't knock. He went in.

Her lights were off, but she was there: eyes closed, propped up in bed, leaning against a backrest scrunched into the corner. The slender wires of earphone headsets dangled alongside her face, connected to a portable tape player on her lap. The volume was cranked so high, Harry could hear the muffled clamor of hard rock—but Carla didn't hear him.

She jumped when he turned on the light. Their eyes met, and she tried to read him before deciding which personality to shift into: little-girl niece; spacy teenager; martyred daughter of a slain policeman; haughty Lolita.

Harry shut the door. "Turn that damned thing off."

Defiant but obliging, Carla pulled out the earphones. She didn't stop the tape and harsh tin notes squawked from tiny headset pieces.

"How the hell could you keep that secret?" he demanded.

"What?"

Quietly, intending to shock, he said, "Did you ever screw him?"

"I'm in *love* with Alan."

"Not Alan—Ronald Showels."

Connie opened the door. "What's going on?"

"Tell us about Ronald Showels, Carla," Harry demanded.

◆ 312 ◆

Connie backed away as though physically shocked to hear the name.

"Tell us about him, Carla!"

"I don't know him," she shouted.

"A woman Showels had sex with said he fantasized about calling her Carla."

"I-don't-know-him-I-don't-know-him-I-don't-know-him!" Carla curled against the wall and started crying.

Weakly, Connie asked, "What's she done? My God, what has she done now?"

Harry stood in the middle of Carla's room, surrounded by years of teenaged debris.

Carla sobbed. "I didn't *do* anything." She turned slowly toward her mother with pleading eyes. "I *didn't.*"

"Did your father know about you and Ronald Showels?"

"I didn't do *it* with him."

"But you know him."

"No."

"You're lying," Harry accused. "You know he's dead. He was shot, just like your father."

Surprised, Connie said, "What?"

Carla was shaking.

"And Eddie Laurel makes three," Harry directed at Carla. *"Three* people you know killed in one week."

Connie was pained by her daughter's crying. She moved to comfort her until Harry grabbed her arm and shook his head. He had fallen prey to Carla's tears for sympathy a few hours ago—not again. "Wait downstairs."

"Harry . . . I can't."

"With you here she'll keep crying. You leave, she'll try something else on me. Maybe the truth."

"Mom! Don't go. *Please!* I didn't do anything. Eddie had an accident, that's all. He slipped. We were fooling around and he slipped."

"Oh, God." Connie clutched her chest. She drew in a deep breath to steady herself. "Harry, let me stay with her. Ask her

◆ 313 ◆

whatever you want, but I want to be here. I *need* to be here."

Harry warned Carla, "You answer my questions—no bullcrap—and your Mom stays. You start jerking me around, Mom's downstairs and it's you, me, and the police."

"Mom!" Carla held out her arms and Connie went to her, allowing her daughter to bury her face against her chest.

She brushed her hand over Carla's dark hair.

"What happened with Eddie Laurel?"

Carla sniffled.

"What happened—?"

"He slipped," she replied, no longer insolent, but victimized.

"How?"

"We were fooling around—"

"You said that already. Fooling around how?"

"Harry, please, give her a chance."

He was reminded of Alena's admonition about cross-examining family as though they were witnesses. He softened his tone, but not much. "How were you fooling around?"

Carla clutched her mother. "It was something he found out about in boys' camp. That if a boy is close to passing out when he comes, it makes it real powerful."

Connie closed her eyes as though she might cry, but kept stroking Carla's hair.

"I didn't want to do it, but he said he'd done it in camp by himself and it was great—and that he'd been waiting to get out so he could do it with me."

Connie gasped, "Oh, my God," speaking her thought as a reflex.

"I'm sorry, Mom." Carla tightened her hug.

Harry pressed. "So what happened?"

Carla sniffled frequently.

Harry thought it an act.

"We were at the ball field, where we went sometimes. Eddie found some cinder blocks and stacked them end on end. He tried putting them on their sides first, but it wouldn't get him high enough. The rope was too short . . ."

Connie drew her lips inward and bit down.

◆ 314 ◆

". . . Eddie climbed up on the backstop to tie one end and the other end he made into a circle, a you know—like a lasso."

"A noose."

"Uh-huh . . . But it wasn't long enough to reach around his neck until he stood the blocks end on end."

"Then what?"

"He put it around his neck—the noose—and opened his pants and started rubbing himself."

Connie's lips quivered.

"Where were you?"

"In front of him."

"Just standing there?"

Carla hesitated. "I took my clothes off . . ."

Connie stroked her hand more quickly through Carla's hair.

". . . he said he wanted to look at me while he came."

"So how did he slip?"

"The cinder blocks fell."

"How?"

"I didn't see him falling. It happened so fast."

"Weren't you watching him?"

"Harry, please!" Connie couldn't hold back her protests.

"A boy died. The police think he killed himself. His father thinks *she* had something to do with it. Little did I know when he came ranting into my office he was right."

"She didn't *kill* him."

Carla sobbed, "It was an accident."

"Why did the blocks fall?"

"I didn't see."

"Harry, she said it was an accident."

"She was standing right in front of him."

Carla cried, "Because I had his thing in my mouth, okay! And when he started to come it surprised me and when I jerked away he lost his balance and fell! I told him not to come in my mouth! I told him!" She threw herself across her bed and cried.

Connie curled up against her. "It's okay, baby. It's okay. It was an accident."

◆ 315 ◆

"We tried to save him. We got him down and tried, but he was already dead. So we put him back up, otherwise we'd have had to—"

"Who's we?"

Carla cried.

"Who's we!" Harry demanded.

Carla had almost managed not to tell. Now, like Eddie Laurel, she'd slipped. Burying her face in a pillow, whispering as though able to make her confession without implication, she said, "Alan. Alan was with us."

Harry went downstairs and sat in the dark to control his rage.

Harry had no idea how much time passed before Connie came down from Carla's room. She sat silently on the opposite end of the sofa.

"One day," Connie spoke sadly, "she was an innocent little girl. The next day . . ." She started to cry, but almost immediately stopped, biting back tears and wiping her eyes.

Harry rubbed his forehead and fell into a stare at the fireplace. "She knows Ronald Showels."

"She says she doesn't. And I can tell when she's lying."

"It's too much of a coincidence."

"The man killed Tucker." Connie's voice quivered with that horrible belief. "If Carla knew him, she'd say so."

"The other day you said something about Tucker catching Carla downstairs with an older man—that Tucker almost shot them thinking he'd heard a burglar."

"It was this same one: Alan."

"You've known about him?"

Connie nodded. She reached toward the end table for a tissue that wasn't there and ended up wiping her hand under her nose. "She said she'd stopped seeing him. I guess after Tucker was killed . . . I guess she needed someone."

Harry cut off the question he was about to ask. Cross-examination was a difficult habit to break. After a few moments, he kissed Connie's forehead and left without another word.

◆ 316 ◆

· 45 ·

Marion Greenbaum, the attorney Ronald Showels used to handle his mortgage settlements, remained sympathetic, to a point. "I'll do this much, Harry," she advised over the phone. "The back door to my office will be unlocked in two hours. The alarm access code is one-five-seven-three. If you miss a number, hit the pound key and start over. You break in, that's your business. Just keep off the lights and run if the police show up."

"Showels was dirty, wasn't he?"

"Draw your own conclusions."

Two and a half hours later, at quarter past one Sunday morning, Harry parked the Mustang on a street much like his own office address. He walked around the corner to Marion's real-estate title company.

The rain had stopped, though fine drops still slipped off tree leaves and fell like mist to the sidewalk. Four blocks away, the joyous sounds of last call sounded from trendy bars and cafés with outdoor seating.

On the small back porch of Marion's office, Harry looked through window panes inset in the rear door. The alarm keypad blinked a red active light.

Harry opened the unlocked door and a benign pre-siren beep warned the system had been breached. He tapped in the passcode to silence it, then locked the door behind him.

The wood-panelled halls and offices were dark. Harry switched on a penlight and held it below his waist, aiming the narrow light beam along the floor edge.

"Marion?" He called her name as though she was expecting him—just in the odd case any coworkers happened by the office late at night. "Marion?" Proceeding directly to her door, the flesh tingled along the back of his neck.

Though he held contempt for actual crimes, he admired the nerve of those who did this for a living.

Heavy curtains were drawn in Marion's office so he didn't have to be as careful with the penlight. Her wooden file drawers were arranged in a walk-in closet with bifold doors. Harry checked the Ss, but there was no Showels.

A warm sweat broke across his forehead before he remembered Showels was incorporated. East Coast Equities. He shifted to that drawer. There were almost thirty files for ECE. Harry didn't relish going through them all but, like doing case research and finding dozens of cites under an applicable KeyNote, he started with the first.

Luckily, Marion was efficient. She kept a summary page at the front of each file that listed the property address and concerned parties. In Showels's files, the parties generally included Borrower, Lender, Secondary Lender if the mortgage was sold, and, in many cases, Purchaser Under Default, being the person or entity buying foreclosed property at auction.

Almost all of East Coast Equities's loans went to foreclosure; the sale price at auction rarely covered the loan amount and the shortages tended to be substantial. Harry recalled Harrison Tyler saying Showels's appraisals were high and that too much money was being loaned on a given property. There wasn't anything illegal about that, however. It was bad business—terrible business—but nothing on its face to alert an AFT investigation. Nothing Tucker would have been interested in, *unless* the source of funds was tainted. And Harry believed that to be the case. How to prove it, though, how the hell to prove it from benign, legally drafted documents?

Mark Gesser said Showels panicked over accusations of counterfeit money. But that wasn't enough, especially since whatever money passed hands in these loans was long gone. And cash trails didn't hold the heat—unlike negotiable instruments which re-

◆ 318 ◆

quired signatures and clearing-house processing, cash was nearly impossible to trace.

Then again, maybe Harry was wrong. Maybe the loans were all legitimate—testament to Showels's salesmanship that he could broker such lousy deals. Were there that many people willing to take a chance for a 15 percent return?

Harry found the Asian client Harrison Tyler told him about. P'neing Cho. But Cho immediately proved a dead end; he'd sold his mortgages for face value after holding them a few months, so he'd made some money, certainly hadn't lost. It was the party—in this case, corporation—buying from Cho that lost big time.

But the company didn't seem to mind losing. They took hits and kept buying more mortgages. And taking more hits. And buying more mortgages. And taking more hits.

Harry proposed the scenario as a prosecutor's opening statement to a jury: *Ladies and gentlemen, what possible advantage is there to continuously lose money?* Because when he saw the signature on behalf of the corporation, he also saw the beginnings of a case, and maybe even enough evidence to strike a deal with Special Agent Hemingway.

. 46 .

Where's your silver platter?"

Sunday morning, Special Agent Hemingway met Harry at a roadside diner in rural Howard County, well beyond the normal reach of Sam Giardino.

"The silver platter," Hemingway expounded, "with Giardino's head on it."

Harry wrapped his hands around a glass of water. He'd been reading the Sunday paper for fifteen minutes, awaiting Hemingway's arrival. His plate of eggs and sausage sat mostly uneaten; he had little appetite, but had ordered so as not to draw the waitress's wrath for monopolizing a booth. Even though the diner wasn't yet half full, the after-church crowd was due soon.

Hemingway was less concerned for appearances. When the matronly waitress came for his order, he only wanted coffee. His hunger was centered on his case.

Harry said, "Tucker's daughter was the conduit. She brought the money in."

"No way. We followed her. She never had contact with Giardino. Never even close."

"Giardino's not the source."

"Bullshit." Hemingway tightened his fists and pushed down on the table.

"You wanted it to be Giardino so bad you goddamned missed it."

"Giardino killed your brother." Hemingway remained insistent.

Harry shook his head. "And Ronald Showels and Eddie Laurel?"

"Who the hell's Eddie Laurel?"

"Carla's old boyfriend. A link in the chain. A chain that's been chunked apart, and the broken pieces are being buried. You've got one connection to the source and I'm about to hand it to you."

"Name?" the agent asked doubtfully.

"Alan Ford." Harry checked Hemingway's eyes as a litmus test, seeing how the news registered.

Hemingway remained silent, but his expression revealed interest.

"A man I talked to this morning, someone with long-standing bank contacts, tells me Ford's a go-between for foreign companies, mostly Middle Eastern. He peddles influence, exploiting contacts made while he was a low-level diplomat during the Carter years.

"Ronald Showels brokered mortgages to Ford. Mostly, it involved Ford buying the interest of foreign mortgage holders. Bad mortgages. Ford bought them for cash, foreclosed them within months and, in almost every case, took a loss. Ford never bought the properties back in to try covering his losses and never filed suit for deficiencies against the mortgagors.

"He was willing to lose money because, the money wasn't real. Ford was taking counterfeit cash to the settlement table. The foreign mortgage holders—the sellers—ended up, unknowingly, with counterfeit proceeds, but the fake money was so good, it passed like real cash. The mortgage holders were probably a little worried about a cash deal like that, but it's either Ford's cash that breaks them even or someone else's bank check that gives them a loss. Showels had them in desperate enough shape to be willing to take the chance on cash."

"Then, once Ford foreclosed the mortgage, whoever bought the property at auction paid Ford with legitimate currency. He's exchanging phony for real money at seventy-five to eighty cents on the dollar. Not only has Ford found a way to put massive amounts of counterfeit currency into circulation, he gets a far better return than the usual fifteen to twenty cents on the dollar counterfeit sells for on the street. Plus, he's not telling anyone the cash is counterfeit. It's so good, he doesn't have to."

Hemingway considered Harry, then said, "It's a theory, what you're telling me?"

"No. It's fact . . . once you prove it."

Hemingway chuckled sourly, looking as though almost beginning to like Harry. "How much does the girl—your niece—how much does she know?"

"Not much." Painfully, Harry confessed, "She's sleeping with Ford. My brother caught them."

"In the act, huh? Hey, Dad, look what I can do."

"Ford killed Tucker and set up Ronald Showels to take the heat."

"The police don't think so."

"The police didn't find Showels's alibi. I did." Harry manipulated her statement. "She says Ford told her to seduce Showels and keep him in a motel room all night and through the morning Tucker was killed. Ford must have known Showels pretty well. Then again, Showels wasn't much of a secret. He was greedy, horny. Ford probably wasn't even challenged.

"Ford knew Showels was going to be at the bar so he sends the gypsy girl to seduce him. Ford knew the motel where the girl was going to take Showels so he could plant the gun in Showels's car. Ford's even got enough finesse to phone in a false tip about finding Tucker's citation book, saying he found it at the race track, knowing Showels had been there, and that the police would be at least smart enough to check Pimlico security cameras that would have videotaped Showels at the track."

Hemingway shifted positions as though trying to physically fit himself into Harry's hypothesis. "You get all this from your niece?"

"No. I've got other sources, but I can't reveal them."

Hemingway scowled.

"A lot of confidences have been breached. I've got information you'd never get access to."

"How much does Carla know? How close can she get me?"

"She's out. Ford killed her father. He's not getting a shot at her."

"Come on, Harry, you're running me around the barn." Hemingway sat forward. "You're painting a nice picture, but it leaves me with nothing."

"I'm giving you *facts*. Like putting an image on film. I've taken the picture—you develop it."

When the waitress delivered his coffee, Hemingway tossed aside containers of cream and stirred in lots of sugar. Tapping his spoon and setting it on the table, he returned to his personal square one, not wanting to let it go. "So if Ford's the source, how come Tucker made contact with Giardino?"

"My guess is he felt his back was to the wall. You had him for passing counterfeit money, told him you wanted Giardino, so he tried to get you Giardino."

"Why not give up Ford in the first place? Tucker never said anything about him."

"Maybe he was stalling you. He knew there was no way out. If he gave you Ford, it was all over. He was over. He knows about deals made with cops. He knows it's never as good as it sounds. He knew he'd end up going down, maybe not to jail, but surely off the force. It would come out he'd been involved with Ford, not as a cop, but as an accomplice. Or maybe he *was* trying to give you Ford, and that's what got him killed."

Hemingway thought for a while. "So Ford killed Showels, too?"

"And Eddie Laurel." Harry plied supposition to fact like kneading dough into tasty bread. "Laurel was passing money with Carla. He was with her last summer when they were popped for smoking weed—the case that tipped you about the counterfeit fifties she had on her."

"When'd Laurel get it?"

"About a week ago." Harry held eye contact as he grabbed the truth and stretched it. "Ford hung the kid naked to make it look like an accident—masturbation asphyxiation." He purposefully omitted Carla's involvement.

Hemingway emitted another sour laugh. "*Hustler* magazine prints it and the fools do it."

Harry glanced outside. Seated near the window, he kept casual watch over the parking lot.

Hemingway said, "You give this to Baltimore County Homicide?"

"Ford would see them coming and take off unless you've got him under wraps first."

Hemingway took the implied compliment in stride, but said, "I don't know, Harry. If Ford wants Showels dead, why not kill him outright? Why set him up for your brother?"

"Two murders might look suspicious, but frame one target for the other's death and the case is self-closing. The investigation ends."

"Why didn't Showels squawk like a goddamned duck when he was framed?"

"He did. No one listened."

"He never mentioned Ford."

"Showels is in the middle of a cut-throat divorce. He—and his attorney for that matter—thought his wife called in his name anonymously, as an annoyance, never figuring the charges would stick. Besides, why would Showels think of Ford? Things were going well for them."

"So then why does Ford kill him?"

Harry, his glance unwavering, said, "Ford's got a direct line to counterfeit that sweet, he's in with heavy company, people who don't want loose ends. Maybe Ford was finishing this chapter. He wouldn't maintain the same routine for long. Staying in one place increases the odds of getting caught. Maybe it was time to move on and he was cleaning house—with a gun."

Harry was selling it well. An attorney's job was to reconstruct unknowns of the past with facts, inferences, and supposition gleaned from the present and sell it—goddamned sell it—like Ronald Showels peddling mortgages.

"I want to question the girl, Carla. I want her to get me inside with Ford." Hemingway was starting to bite, but not hard enough. He wanted Carla involved.

Harry said, "No way."

"It's not negotiable, Harry. We'll protect her. She'll be safe."

"You've got enough. I've aimed you in the right direction. A hundred-eighty degrees from where you were pointed."

"Don't forget, the deal is for the mother. I've got her dead bang, you want her to walk. I'm asking for an even trade, not just a compass point. You want me to go the extra mile, you've gotta walk the walk, too."

◆ 324 ◆

"I've given you your case." His deal was on the table. There was nothing else he'd offer.

"Not enough. You've been there, Harry. You know how deals get cut. I don't drop a solid arrest just for a name."

Without animosity—strictly business—Harry said, "Your arrest's not that solid."

"Willing to bet years of Connie's life on that?"

"Even if you got a conviction she'd get probation."

"So I'm bluffing—call my bet."

"Ford killed Carla's father. He'll kill her, too if she gets involved in turning him."

Hemingway pushed aside his coffee cup and rapped his knuckles on the table. "Tomorrow afternoon, Harry. Downtown. You bring in the girl and we start putting it into play. I'll coordinate with the U.S. Attorney in Orlando to draft agreements in the mother's case."

Harry stared at his water glass.

"Tomorrow afternoon, Harry." Hemingway repeated. He stood to leave, but stepped back and leaned forward, speaking quietly. "Look at it this way: you've just removed Sam Giardino from the prime suspect list. Can't lose sight of who your clients are, can you, counselor?"

· 47 ·

Alena answered the door wearing one of Harry's old dress shirts. She'd removed most of the buttons so she could sleep in it without getting poked. "I want you back," she whispered, taking him into a loving hug.

"I want to be back." For a brief moment, he felt whole again. All that had been troubling and terrifying seemed cured, but, within moments, anxieties crept in. "I need to talk."

"It's okay, lover. It's all going to be okay."

"I wasn't sure you'd want to see me. You said you needed time."

"I've had enough time. I know what I want." She closed the door and took his hand, leading him inside.

Grey morning light muted the expressive interior palette of the rehabbed townhouse.

"Jackie here?"

"No—at the office."

"Good," Harry replied honestly.

"Cleo's set up a seven-day-a-week schedule until AmeriCenter gets under control. It's going to be hectic for a while." Alena sat Harry on the sofa and curled up against him.

"What about you?" he asked. "Are you quitting?"

"I thought about it, but then what would I do? Set up my own shop? I could raise the money or sign on with one of the other houses, but I don't want to compete with Cleo. She's been good to me. If I left Cleo, I'd have to move to a different city. I thought about D.C., or Charlotte, or back home, but then I wouldn't be with you. And I don't want that—and I know *you* can't leave."

"I've considered it."

"So we could set up our dream business? The Harry/Alena line of fashions?" She stroked her hand across his chest. "It's a nice dream, Harry, but it's not real. We'd end up broke, and broke ruins love every time. It would be nice if it didn't, but it does."

He caressed her hair. "So I guess we're not going to run off to the Outer Banks and rake the shore for clams to steam for dinner?"

"Not until we're old and grey."

"So what about AmeriCenter?"

She exhaled slowly. "I may have landed the contract, but *everyone* is going to be part of it. Not just the profits, but the work. How could I take that away unless I could explain why? A couple nights ago, when you'd gone down to Orlando for Connie, I got together with an old friend—someone not in the business . . ."

Harry worried vaguely it had been an old *male* friend, but didn't ask.

". . . I tried to explain what I was feeling about the project, about . . . well . . . anyway . . ." She didn't want to say Giardino's name. "Janice didn't understand. She thought I was crazy."

An old *girl*friend; Harry couldn't help feeling relieved.

"I don't know, lover . . . maybe my ego got wounded because I didn't really get the job because of talent, but because of contacts. But the more I thought about it . . . who ever gets anything purely on merit?"

Avoiding Giardino's name was like relegating him to the shadowy background from which he'd emerged—like putting the statue of a patron saint back in the closet until the next time it was needed.

Alena continued thoughtfully. "I considered distancing myself from the project. Staying at Interior Visions, but turning over the lead role in AmeriCenter to Cleo. But who would that be fooling? *Maybe* myself, but probably not—not for long, anyway. So I decided to stick with it. And if battles crop up along the way—if I'm not allowed to do my work the way I want to do it . . . well, I'll fight that fight when it comes. It wouldn't be the first time. How many ignorant builders have we had to educate along the way? Tell them sometimes stripes and plaids *do* go together—just not like they

◆ 327 ◆

wear them to their bowling league. This really isn't any different. It's just bigger."

It was different, though. And she knew it.

They spent the day together inside, reading, listening to CDs, catching a few late innings of the Orioles playing an away game against Oakland.

At one point, Harry realized he had not felt a single tinge of outrage over having found his brother's killer. As though he accepted the act, his attention focused more on the prior events that had placed Tucker at risk—and about those matters, he was shocked and he was sad.

Throughout the afternoon and into early evening, Harry never once discussed Tucker, or Carla, or Connie, or Craig, or Ronald Showels, or Alan Ford. He found his silence telling, because it showed he had already made up his mind what he was going to do.

After dinner, Harry and Alena made love—slowly, passionately. Shortly past midnight, Harry dressed. Alena remained naked and walked him to the door. They shared a long goodbye.

Harry waited on the landing until she bolted the door and turned off the light, then he started down the block. He put a quarter in a pay phone and made a call.

48.

During the night, it began to rain again. A steady slow mist fell across the county—a calming mist like that sprayed over deer just before slaughter to prevent fear from toughening their meat.

Harry arrived at Circuit Court shortly after nine. Judge Jacobson was yet to take the bench, waiting for Assistant State's Attorney Markus to clear the logjam of defense attorneys arranging last minute pleas.

Harry stood at the outer ring of lawyers in line to talk with Markus. The courtroom had a surreal aura this morning. Harry felt detached from it, as though if he were to reach out and touch the person beside him, his hand would pass through him. Yet even with this sense of disorientation, he was extraordinarily calm, as though *he* was being sprayed by the mist.

Last night, after Alena's, he'd gone to Connie's . . .

She'd come to the door groggy with sleep, hair pushed flat against one side of her head from lying against the sofa arm.

The TV played an infomercial.

Harry said, "You didn't smell the smoke."

Connie looked at him quizzically.

"The other morning," Harry said, "you came in and I was on the sofa—you didn't say anything about the smoke. That there were ashes in the fireplace and they smelled of smoke. It was very obvious, but you didn't say anything about it."

She blinked and squinted into the bright porch bulb. She shielded her hand over her face to block the light's glare.

"How long have you known what's going on? How *much* do you know?"

Connie remained silent.

"*You* burned those lottery tickets."

When she didn't respond, Harry opened the screen door and went inside. He took her by the arm to the sofa and sat on the coffee table facing her. And waited . . .

"Another day another defendant, huh, Harry?" Arms crossed over the case file held to his body, Matt Ringgold turned toward Harry while the ASA argued probable cause with Ian Murphy. "I hope you're here with a better case than mine. I gotta kid breaks into a stereo shop, steals some portable CD players, and when he can't get a decent price from a fence, tries to take them *back* to the store he stole 'em from for a refund. I swear—goddamned kids weren't so stupid police'd never catch them. Cops only catch three kinds of perps, Harry. The stupid, the ratted out, and the wrong guy."

Connie had said, "We worried about her all the time, Harry. Since she was twelve it's been nonstop. Boys, drugs, shoplifting. She's been wild, but we love her . . . Tucker blamed himself. He thought if we lived in a better neighborhood, Carla would stay out of trouble. We looked for places to move. Around here, out in Hartford County, even up in Pennsylvania . . . something always went wrong. If we could afford the house, the schools were bad. If the schools were good and the area was nice, we couldn't afford the house. And with Tucker's wages frozen, and him not passing the lieutenant's exam, and Craig needing college money, and money we spent on Carla for counseling after the insurance ran out . . ." Connie paused for breath.

"We had to borrow money from my father to keep from losing the house. And Carla kept getting into trouble. The older she got, the more she got into. When she was fourteen, she had an abortion. We didn't know until months after it happened. When Tucker found out, he went crazy. She said she got pregnant by Eddie Laurel, and Tucker went over there.

"I tried to stop him. God . . . I thought he was going to kill the boy. He told Eddie to stay away from her . . . and then, last summer,

◆ 330 ◆

they got arrested together for marijuana. Tucker exploded.

"He got the case set up so Eddie would go to juvenile detention even though the marijuana was Carla's. I knew something was up when Carla didn't object to that. She'd always sworn by Eddie—always said she loved him, but she couldn't have cared less that he was being put away. Then we found out about Alan Ford.

"Tucker caught them in the basement—*our* basement. Tucker said they were doing it right on the floor. He turned on the lights and saw Carla with her clothes off and Ford's pants at his ankles. He almost shot him.

"I think that was the night something really snapped. We got Carla to her therapist the next day and she started going every day, but it was the same act. She said she was addicted to Alan—a convenient lie, as always. It was easier to blame it on an addiction than to stop.

"She kept sneaking out of the house. Alan would pick her up down the block and they'd go to his house. Tucker followed them one night. I stayed home and for hours couldn't stop shaking. Tucker was so close to going over the edge, I was sure that would be the night he did. I was getting scared of him. I'd been spending most nights on the sofa because I couldn't take it. Tucker didn't sleep. He'd pace the bedroom like a caged animal and stare out the window—just waiting for me to ask what was wrong so he could start raving.

"The night he went to get Carla at Alan's, when he didn't come home, I was sure he'd killed him. I started packing a suitcase. I was going to go to Florida to my parents. I couldn't take any more. But then Tucker finally came home. He'd been drinking. He had a small satchel with him. He smiled and plopped it down on the kitchen table.

"He had a look on his face I'd never seen before. He looked evil, but happy. He told me to open the bag. He sounded so aggressive. He didn't say it, but it was like he wanted to say, 'bitch.' Open the bag, *bitch*. I opened it. There was thirty thousand dollars inside."

*   *   *

Dale Markus said, "Harry Walsh," and started going down his list of files, looking for Harry's case. "And how might you be this fine and rainy morning?"

Harry pointed out his client on the docket.

"Yeah, that's right. Du-wayne Jefferson. Three counts B&E, and a record with more hits than the Jackson Five had in the seventies." Markus did a constrained dance and quietly sang the chorus to "Dancing Machine," seguing into, "What's your pleasure?"

"He's in lock-up. I need to see him."

"No sweat." Markus got the bailiff's attention. "Mabelle, you want to play tour guide? Escort Mr. Walsh through the top-notch web of security that is our fine pretrial detainee holding facility." To Harry, he said, "Take your time. Pine Ridge's closed today because of the rain, so I've got nothing to do but litigate."

Facing one another, Connie and Harry had sat forward, holding hands, heads bowed in confession.

On the TV, John Davidson emceed a staged talk show from Hawaii, interviewing a chipper Eurasian man who claimed to have made millions in real estate with no money down. An audience of bright-shirted tourists applauded regularly, eyes gleaming at the prospect of easy, quick wealth, and *no money down*.

"That night," Connie said, "Tucker was so keyed up. He said Alan had given him the money. He said they'd talked all night. That he and Alan had a lot in common, that Alan was more like his brother than you were.

"Alan had gone to Canada to avoid Vietnam, too, only he'd waited until President Carter signed an amnesty plan before coming back. Tucker said Alan was what he could have been. He said he saw that becoming a policeman was an act of protest to spite his father . . . and you. That in his heart, he wasn't a cop, and that's why he couldn't do better on the lieutenant's exam. He said he was like a sinner hiding behind Christ—that it was all a ruse. What he really wanted to be was like his father—and like you.

"He said Alan sold marijuana and LSD in Canada, and had made a lot of money and contacts. When he came back to the

◆ 332 ◆

States under amnesty, he improved his supply lines and ended up selling to high-ups in government. He was a suit-and-tie cocaine dealer.

"A contact got him a job in the State Department, and Alan worked as a diplomat in the Middle East. It was a very active time, with Carter negotiating his peace plan. Shuttling back and forth from the Middle East, Alan was smuggling drugs through the diplomatic pouch.

"I was more scared than ever, Harry. I *was* going to leave him. But then he started talking about the money. How it was printed in the Middle East. It was econo-terrorism, he called it. That flooding the country with its own counterfeit currency would work to destabilize the economy. Tucker called it 'a form of protest.' He said we were going to end up in another Vietnam in the Middle East. That we built up powermongers we could later turn into enemies so the war machine would always have someone to fight. I'd never heard him talk like that. It was ranting—like always—but different. I think he was high.

"He laughed and counted out the money; he gave me half. He said it was ours for the taking. It was free. Alan would give us as much as we wanted. And he guaranteed it wouldn't be spotted as counterfeit." Connie paused.

On TV, the audience applauded a real estate disciple's "confession" of walking away from the settlement table with ten thousand dollars cash in his pocket along with the deed to a rental property he'd just bought with no money down.

"The worst of it," Connie said, "was when I asked Tucker if all this talk meant it was all right for Carla to have sex with someone old enough to be her father. He heaved like he was going to vomit, but then he stared at the money . . . for the longest time he glared at it . . . then he said she was going to be sixteen in a couple months. She could screw whoever she wanted and it was legal."

Harry sat in the small room, awaiting his client.

There were no windows with a view outside, only a half wall of glass imbedded with a crisscross of security wire that sectioned the area in half. A small grille cut through the glass allowed conversation, but no objects, to pass from one side to the other.

Harry's own reflection stared back at him in the thick glass, looking out from behind bars.

"But it did bother him," Connie said last night. "Carla seeing Alan. Tucker wouldn't say so at first, but I heard them talking. Carla would say she loved Alan, and Tucker would say it was wrong. A couple times he went to see Alan, trying to tell him to stay away from Carla, but he'd always come home with more money. It wore on him: taking the money and Carla being with Alan. Tucker knew it was wrong and I think he knew he was going to get caught. He started hiding the money, lots of it, and telling me where it was in case he was arrested. He told me if something happened to him, to run and not look back. To take the money and run. He said he owed me that for all he'd put me through.

"I felt so sad for him then. Even though this was after he'd had his . . . whatever . . . his affair with that college girl. It was a couple months ago. There was so much money. And he'd been holding up okay for a while, but it was like watching him walk up a peak and start sliding off. His nerves got rattled . . . that's when he started taking the Valium. I'm not sure, but I think Carla got it for him. I overheard her telling Tucker something about a forged prescription, but when I asked Tucker, he said he was seeing Carla's old therapist and got it from him. I guess he was lying, but I didn't really want to know the truth. It had gotten to that point between us. The lying and pretending." Connie shook her head.

After she remained quiet for a while, Harry said, "What were you doing all this time?"

"Keeping my head down at first. Pretending, like I said—pretending my family was normal. That nothing was wrong. That Craig and Tucker weren't getting into terrible arguments. That my daughter wasn't spending nights away from home, sleeping with a forty-five-year-old man who was a criminal. And when that stopped working, *I* started taking Valium. There was always plenty of it. I *joined* the crowd. Then Craig came home one day and found me like a zombie. He knew I was stoned. He stormed out. That's when I knew it had to stop."

Dewayne Jefferson was brought into the prisoner's half of the secured meeting room by a sheriff. Contrary to ASA Markus's exaggerated pronunciation of his name, Dewayne was not black, but white.

He was tall and skinny, with a bad complexion and long, black hair tied into a greasy ponytail. Although ten years past his 16th birthday, Dewayne maintained a sulky teenage demeanor, flaunting disobedience. "Heya, Mr. Walsh, you gettin' me outta here today?"

"We've got a couple details to go over."

"Yeah-yeah, shoot man, shoot. I wanna get outta here. Got people to see. Places to make."

Harry didn't look through his notes taken at the detention center four months ago after Dewayne was arrested, because he hadn't asked then what he was about to ask now. Defense attorneys just *didn't* ask; it wasn't part of the game. Through the grille in the glass partition, Harry said, "Did you do it, Dewayne?"

Last night, Connie had said, "After Craig saw me like that, I told Tucker it had to stop and he agreed. He said it was getting out of control. He said he'd stop, but he didn't. He kept getting more money. Then the lottery tickets started showing up. He said it was something new. That counterfeit lottery tickets were like stealing money straight from the state coffers. But he said the tickets weren't as perfect as the bills and had to be passed more carefully. Carla was good at it. They'd go out together and she'd flirt with boys working the lottery machines in convenience stores and they'd cash her tickets. Tucker would brag about how much they'd done in one night, and say it made up for how the state had frozen his wages.

"I knew it wasn't going to stop, so I went to Alan. We'd never met and I expected to hate him, but he was so calm and confident. I told him what was bothering me and he said he understood, but

◆ 335 ◆

that he couldn't make Tucker stop and he was in love with Carla. I pleaded with him, I cried, but he said we all have to live our own lives. We have to do what's best for us. And then he gave me a satchel of money. Almost a quarter-million dollars. He said I should keep it for a rainy day, in case anything ever happened."

Harry asked, "What did you think he meant by that?"

"I guess that Tucker might get caught."

"Or killed?"

"I don't know."

Harry squeezed her hands. "He killed him, you know. He killed Tucker."

"No," Connie cried, shaking her head. "He wouldn't do that. He's not that kind of man."

Harry firmed his grip on her hands. "What happened after he gave you the money?"

She cried.

"Connie?" His voice was very soft.

She shook her head. The short length of her hair fell into her face.

"Connie?"

"Oh, God, Harry," she wailed, looking at him desperately. "He seduced me, Harry. I went to bed with the man who was sleeping with my daughter."

Dewayne Jefferson rapped on the door to the detention conference room and shouted, "I want a new lawyer. Tell the judge I want a new lawyer. This son of a bitch I got's gone crazy on me."

Harry picked up his case file and left the courthouse, not bothering to tell ASA Markus or Judge Jacobson he'd just been fired by his client.

He started walking back to his office, but the length of his steps increased, pace quickening until he broke into a run. Thinking, "What have I done? What have I done?"

Very late the previous night, they had not sat in the private room, but out in the brick-walled garden. Noises of the city were quieted by high walls. The cloudy sky felt low and amber-white, reflecting street lights. Fanciful wrought-iron chairs with soft seat cushions were positioned side by side, facing in opposite directions, so as Harry leaned close to speak, his shoulder touched Giardino's as his words carried to Giardino's ear.

Harry told him everything.

Giardino reflected sadly. "Had I known all this, I would have been more forceful in keeping you from finding out."

Harry was surprised; he would have expected the opposite to be true: that Giardino would have *helped* him.

"Better that Ronald Showels go to jail for a crime he didn't commit than for you to learn about Tucker and his family."

"How can you say that?"

"Ronald Showels placed himself in harm's way, Sonny. Death is not the only penalty for such a choice. And Tucker . . ." He made a dismissing gesture. ". . . very foolish, but he at least deserved a policeman's death—death with honor. Now, his life ends tainted and casts its shadow upon his family. And who will be responsible for them now, Harry?"

"I am."

Giardino nodded. "And I for you. My promise to your papa, to whom I owe my life . . . it now becomes impossible for me to proceed without breaking that promise. However we decide, your life is changed, and will not be safer for it. All your life, you and I, we have walked along the edge of a line, each making slight trespasses across it, but never staying very long. Our connection is a strong one, but not an obvious one—not a provable one. Now, that changes. Unless . . ."

Harry waited.

". . . unless you walk away."

"I can't do that."

Giardino nodded, having known that would be Harry's answer.

Harry was breathless by the time he reached the pay phone. He dialed quickly and, as soon as the line was answered, said, "I need to talk to him. Right now. It's an emergency. I need to talk—"

The line was immediately disconnected, because desperate people said incriminating things, and incriminating things weren't spoken over the phone.

Harry hung up the phone and ran to his car hoping it wasn't too late.

What had he done? Dear God, what *had* he done?

Last night, in the garden, Giardino had said, "Is there another explanation? The gypsy didn't name Alan Ford specifically as the man who told her to stay with Showels."

"It's circumstantial, but it fits. People who know Ford say he has an in with INS. She said the man had those same contacts and was holding them over her."

"Perhaps Ford works with others."

"In the overall conspiracy, I'm sure he does. Locally—his spoke of the wheel—I think he operates solo."

"A wealthy, connected man who murders for the jealousy of a young girl's love?"

"It's one of two motives. The other is that he's tidy. He cleans up his messes before they're noticeable. And wraps them in neat packages. Maybe he found out Tucker was working for ATF. Or maybe Tucker threatened to expose the operation unless Ford stayed away from Carla. Showels and Eddie Laurel happen to be other links in the same chain, so he does them all. He kills Tucker first because that's least obvious. A policeman being killed on a traffic stop doesn't smack of premeditation. Showels wouldn't be alarmed. Then again, maybe it was random, as opportunity allowed. Maybe Showels didn't even know Tucker. Maybe Ford kept them apart."

"What about the boy?"

"Eddie Laurel? I think it's possible those cinder blocks had help tumbling over. Ford was there. Maybe he likes threesomes. Maybe he *wanted* it to look that way so Carla wouldn't doubt him."

"But in a court of law . . . ?" Giardino questioned.

"The case can't be made without Connie and Carla's testimony. And I won't let them incriminate themselves, or tarnish my brother's memory. In his time, he *was* a good cop."

Giardino understood. "So what happens to them?"

"Connie and Carla go to Florida to start over. Craig finishes school up here and makes his own decision."

"And the federal case against Connie?"

"We try it and win it. She thought the money was lottery winnings, not counterfeit."

"That, too, is a risk."

"And the price she pays for putting *herself* in harm's way. If she had come to me in the beginning, I could have helped her."

"And on the stand in this federal case, she can be convincing enough to a jury for them to believe she only thought the money gambling winnings being hidden from the IRS?"

"She fooled me for a while."

"Maybe you wanted to be fooled."

Harry considered that possibility.

"And what if she's convicted?" Giardino proposed.

"If the sentence is more than she thinks she can stand, we arrange bail pending appeal and she spends the rest of her life on the run."

Giardino seemed impressed with Harry's appraisal. It was thought through.

Silence hung long and onerously between them until Giardino said, "Which brings us back to Alan Ford . . ."

Harry felt a chill of fear. He considered Giardino and longed to be connected to the past Giardino represented. "Did you and my father ever talk like this?"

Giardino smiled fondly. "All the time."

Harry took a deep breath that was sweet with roses: Concetta's Innocence. "What was it like for him . . . the first time?"

Giardino placed a hand on Harry's shoulder. "I told your papa the hangman's hand raises heavily to the latch that opens the trap door."

Harry looked up into the white night sky and felt the strong, rapid beat of his heart against his chest. "What did my father do?"

"Your father leaned back in a chair and looked up at the ceiling. He stared at it for a while, considering information we had discussed. I said to him, 'Jack, what do you think?' He didn't answer then, just stared at the ceiling, like he did when he was troubled with a decision. I said again, 'Jack, what do you think? I need your advice.' More time passed—I learned to be patient waiting for your papa's answers. Finally, he looked at me and said, 'Go ahead . . . kill him.' "

Two hours before dawn, the man quietly forced open the sliding glass door and stepped into the kitchen of the stone ranch house. The digital numbers of an automatic coffeepot clock glowed an icy-blue reflection across the counter.

A second man entered behind the first and gently slid closed the glass door.

They walked softly for large men, proceeding directly down the carpeted hall to the bedroom at the far end of the house.

The door was open. They looked in from the hall at the shapes of two bodies beneath the sheet: the middle-aged man and the young girl with the curly dark hair. They had known she'd be there.

Harry sped out Dulaney Valley Road. Perspiration stuck his white shirt to his back. He blinked repeatedly in an effort to focus his vision and his thoughts, both of which seemed hazy.

Although this was much worse, the only other time he had felt anything like this was when trying his first jury case out of law school. His hands had been like ice as he made notes of a witness's testimony. That, as this, seemed a strange illusion, as though he wasn't truly a participant, but had been pulled in by an undefinable magnetism. Something drew him to it.

The two men separated and stood on different sides of the bed.

One man cocked his head to the side, looking at Alan Ford asleep on his stomach, face half buried in a down pillow, breathing through his open mouth. The man glanced across the bed and nodded at his partner.

The second man nodded in reply.

◆ 340 ◆

The first man put the silenced end of the .22 semi-automatic within inches of Alan Ford's temple and pulled the trigger three times. Quiet puffs, like eggs dropped into a nest of cotton, sounded as the shells opened small holes in flesh and breached bone and entered the mass that was Alan Ford's head.

Ford stopped breathing as the blood that initially pulsed from his wounds ran steady, now being spilled, not pumped.

The second man injected the syringe's contents into Carla's vein and said, "You know, I think my son's little girl is going to look like this when she's her age. Real pretty face like this."

"She is pretty," the first man agreed. He went into the bathroom and returned with fluffy bath towels he used to wrap Ford's head before moving the naked corpse to the floor.

The other man came back from taking Carla to the guest-room bed, where the effects of the narcotics would keep her asleep for hours.

Together, they stripped the bedclothes and replaced them with fresh linens. Putting the fitted sheet in place, the man who thought Carla looked like his granddaughter clutched his back and groaned.

"Bend with your knees," his partner reminded. "Bend with your knees."

"Christ, I always forget that."

Harry had expected to find police swarming the house, their yellow CRIME SCENE tape strung around an established perimeter to keep away curious neighbors. He'd thought investigators would be coming and going, uniformed officers questioning prospective witnesses, techs dusting for fingerprints and vacuuming fibers.

But Alan Ford's house was quiet. The sun broke through the clouds and its humid, warm light glowed against green grass. A woodpecker rapidly tapped the bark of a nearby dead tree. The man next door contemplated the effects of recent rains and whether his lawn could use a fresh cutting.

The engine of Harry's father's 1965 Mustang idled easily, stopped on the front street.

After a while, Harry drove away.

His nausea came and passed a dozen times before finally subsiding that evening. When he met Alena for dinner, he waited for her to ask why he was acting strangely, but she didn't. When they went to bed to make love, he expected to be unable to perform, but they had a wonderful time.

It was as though nothing had really happened that morning, nothing at all. Murder trials were so long, so tiring and stressful; it took days, weeks sometimes to clean them from your system.

This turned out to be quite different. Alan Ford had, simply, disappeared. Carla had awakened in his guest bed to find Alan and his car gone. He didn't leave a note, and he never came back.